THE SOUL

The Soul of de Gressier

1960 -1977

Charles Bunker

YOUCAXTON
PUBLICATIONS

ISBN 978-1-914424-22-9
Published by YouCaxton Publications 2021
YCBN: 01

YouCaxton Publications
www.youcaxton.co.uk

Typeset and cover design by Ella Knight Designs

Books in the de Gressier Series

The Soul of de Gressier - Family Tree

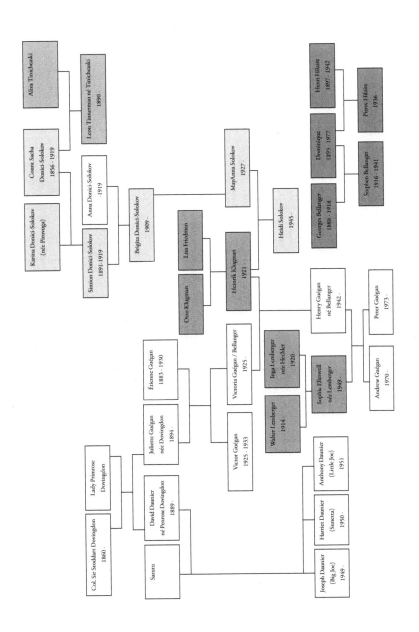

The Soul of de Gressier

This is a story which only the grandchildren can tell for they are not the secret keepers.

Chapter 1

England and France 1960 to 1961

AN "ALSO-RAN" SHOULD have been the way the headmaster signed off Henry Bellanger's final school report but, when parents are paying fees, there is a need for kindness. Instead, it included comforting words about how Henry had made useful contributions to the school during his time there. If questioned, however, neither the headmaster, nor his housemaster, nor Henry, could say exactly what they were.

The fact was that Henry was spoiled; an only child with an inheritance from his great-grandfather which, even after inheritance tax, meant he would never have to work for a living. Col. Sir Stoddart Dovingdon had invested, as a venture capitalist, in the new technologies of the fundamental industries of the 20th Century. These allowed the finest of steels or the best of glass to be cheaply manufactured and it was the shares in these companies, now risen in value beyond anyone's wildest expectation, which made up the investments in Henry's trust fund.

Henry also benefited from a very wealthy grandmother, again on his mother's side. Juliette Guégan had, after the war, rebuilt Château de Gressier into one of the best vineyards and wineries in the Bordeaux region.

Juliette's hope for the future of Château de Gressier remaining safe and sound in her family for the next generation, rested on her grandson's shoulders. Except Juliette, now highly matriarchal, hid any demonstrable fondness she might have felt for Henry. She was beginning to think he deserved none of his benefits for, in her view, he was lazy and narcissistic with an indifference to much of what was around him. A brother or sister would have served Henry well, she often thought, but it was not to be.

As a result of his good fortunes, Henry's bank account was much fuller than any of his peers', and therefore, without merit, he could have the very best in life. Probably Henry's saving grace was that he neither drank alcohol nor smoked. At an early stage, he decided he didn't like their taste or how they made him feel. His resistance was never lowered, and for this reason he didn't touch the drugs that were freely available and used, but not heavily, by his friends. As a result, he kept more money in his bank account than otherwise might have happened, except for his passion for music.

Henry's musical taste was eclectic and across the board. Each week, he studied the New Musical Express magazine and on Sunday night he would religiously tape record the Top Ten show from the radio, swearing every time the DJ spoke over the track being played. He purchased record after record, listening carefully to each one, testing to see if he wanted to hear it again. He rejected about 90% of everything he bought which he sold for a tenth of the original price at a local second-hand shop. With the rest, he catalogued, sorted and wrote comments. Whilst he could naturally analyse a piece of music he could only play the violin and piano indifferently because he never practised. He had the potential to be good but his position in the second row of the violins in the school orchestra was a fair recognition of his talent. However, if enthusiasm for music had been the judge, he would have been the first violinist.

"So what are you going to read at university?" asked Henry's housemaster one day, a question which hadn't dawned on him before.

"Music," Henry offered tentatively.

"Not good enough, sadly," said his housemaster, dismissively. "Better think about it." And so it was that Henry's passion became just a hobby.

Henry was used to being able to have the very best without working for it, and there were only two places he wanted to go to university: Oxford or Cambridge. His school dismissed Henry's chance of ever getting into their hallowed chambers unless he put in the work, and both he and they knew that this was not going to happen. If it was neither of these, then anywhere else would be second best and he was just not interested in that. It was not in his nature. The careers master, whose knowledge of the big, wide world was limited by the fact that he had never held a job outside education, suggested that Henry read chemistry on the basis that this was his best subject at school.

What a ridiculous idea thought Henry, knowing the last thing he wanted to do was work in any industry which needed chemistry skills. He was good at chemistry because he found the subject logical. If he had one frustration it was with the periodic table, where elements were missing. How could it be, he wondered, when mankind could build a nuclear bomb which could destroy all humanity, or put a satellite into space[1], that there were still compounds which had not yet been discovered or could not be made in a laboratory? Nevertheless, he went along with the idea of doing chemistry at university for it followed the line of least resistance.

Henry always wondered whether it was his answer to the question: "why do you want to study chemistry?" which resulted in him being given an unconditional offer at Birmingham University. He resisted his first answer, which was to say that he didn't. Instead, he told the interviewing tutor of his wish to build the elements that were missing from the periodic table. The fact that his offer was unconditional degraded the university in Henry's mind, for following the sentiments of Groucho Marx, 'he hardly wanted to be a member of any club which would want him as a member'. However, since the offer fell into his lap without him having to do an item of extra work, Henry accepted.

---

[1] On 4th October 1957, the Soviet Union launched Sputnik, the world's first satellite. A month later, Sputnik 2 orbited with a dog as its passenger. Unfortunately, the dog died on the fourth orbit due to overheating caused by an air conditioning malfunction.

It was during the long summer holiday of 1961, between finishing school and heading off to university, that Henry picked up a guitar for the first time. With a chord book, he spent sultry summer days and balmy nights strumming away at Château de Gressier. Over the weeks his friends from school visited him there, where they lazed in the fields, swam in the river and watched the grapes in his grandmother's vineyards ripen. It was the idyll of youth; nothing to do between this time and the next. That moment in life when there is not a care in the world, or a chore to be undertaken. The sun is on your back and pretty girls are at your touch. It was a summer which added to Juliette's impression of her grandson as a lothario.

Chapter 2

New Found Estate, South Africa 1953 - September 1961

DAVID DAUNIER READ of his father, Col. Sir Stoddart Dovingdon's death in The Times. He noted with a mixture of delight and interest that he had been survived by his sister Juliette, her daughter Victoria and a great-grandson named Henry. There was no mention of David, as he was known in England as Penrose Dovingdon.

David read the few obituaries which were written of his father. They all stated that it was David's actions in running away, rather than his crimes, which had brought disgrace on the Dovingdon family. He didn't know how this analysis, or his father's death, made him feel. He knew the historical record was wrong, but did it matter anymore? He didn't know. The fact was that he had been estranged from his father for far too long. It was the finality of it all which he found upsetting. It meant that there was nothing more which could be done, even if he had wanted there to be..

That was the past, David thought as he put down the last newspaper with an obituary in it. He and his family's future was undoubtedly here on the New Found Estate just outside of Paarl in the Western Cape of South Africa. Over the years, he had turned a small fruit farm into a successful vineyard and winery, and it had become the centre of a small but thriving community.

Motherhood served David's wife, Satutu, well. She had matured into a stunning woman, keeping her delicate build. She moved quickly, with the grace and serenity of a ballerina. If there had been one change, since she fell pregnant with their first child, it was in the way she spoke. After reading George Bernard Shaw's *Pygmalion,* she took its message to heart, that you are judged by the way you speak. She set about losing her deep African accent. Watching and mimicking the movies of the day, Satutu had learnt to speak perfect BBC English.

When Satutu arrived in David's house, rescued as a girl from a slave market, she found a large but practical abode, of which only a small part was lived in. As a bachelor, David found he needed little else. Following their marriage, and the arrival of children, she had turned the house into a home by furnishing the lounge and dining room and bringing a woman's touch to a place which had been lacking any such influence.

She ran their house, garden and family as efficiently as the movement in a Swiss watch. Every evening, after helping her children with their homework, she would read, write and study. Her motive: self-improvement so she could give her children the best education possible. As in her youth, at no time was Satutu idle.

With the arrival of their children, first Big Joe, then Sunetta and finally Little Joe, came servants, but none of them lived in the house. Both David and Satutu, unsaid to each other, recognised the risk of someone testifying in court that, although married, he, a white European man, and she, a black Xhosa woman, shared a bed.

Apartheid was always horribly present in their everyday lives. It was why Satutu had her own bedroom next to the one she shared with David. She used it only as a dressing room. It was why they also maintained separate living quarters at the back of the house for the non-whites, as the black and coloured people were called.

While there was a clear pecking order, with Satutu in charge of the house, garden and all family affairs, there was a strange equality of treatment with the servants. Unlike other households, their servants would settle down to eat at the same kitchen table and at the same time as the rest of the family. It was just as Satutu had done with David on her first night in his home. Except now, to obey the law, the long table at which they all sat was in fact two separate tables abutted side-by-side. They were together in practice, but by law they were not. This worked unusually well for the discipline of the servants. They had good jobs, were well paid and they knew it. The last thing they wanted was anything which would bring about change. For their part, Big Joe, Sunetta and Little Joe knew that they should never ask a servant to do a job they could do themselves, for to do otherwise would meet with their parents' strongest disapproval.

Satutu and David's children had to work on the farm before and after school, and all day during the school holidays. There were no holidays away from the farm. Every day was a workday. Each morning a list of jobs was pegged to the board setting out their tasks, which each had to complete that day without complaining - as to do so would bring the wrath of their father, so fierce that they would often shake from fear. At harvest time the local school closed so that every child over the age of seven could work in the fields picking the fruit and grapes. "We all work" was one of David's consistent sayings.

Outside their immediate villages and towns, life was difficult for Satutu, Big Joe, Sunetta and Little Joe. Under the apartheid segregation laws, there were many places they were not allowed to go, as they were reserved for whites only. They were constantly subject to the racial abuse which abounded throughout South Africa.

They would each show their French passports which meant that they did not have to carry the much hated 'Passbook' identity card, but more importantly it gave them the position of being 'honorary white'. However, in almost every case, unless David was with them to argue the point, they could not go into 'white' restaurants or sit in the 'white' rows in the cinema. Often, they were forcefully moved to sit in the areas designated for the blacks and coloureds. The two boys found it easier to accept this treatment than face the humiliating inanity of 'the pencil test,' as their kinky hair would stop a pencil from sliding through proving their non-white status. For Sunetta, whose black hair was long, smooth and silky, unlike the wild mane-like locks of her mother, there would be no pencil test. Instead, her fingernails would be examined, upon which, there would be a declaration that they were mauve, not white, which was taken as evidence that she had black blood in her body.

What neither David nor Satutu fully recognised was that, being neither black nor white, Big Joe, Sunetta and Little Joe were never able to fully integrate into either of these communities. There were

7

a few who were colour-blind, and it was from these people that the family found a limited group of friends.

No matter how unfair the treatment, David never gave his views. He preferred not to complain. He took no part in politics, not even voting. His philosophy was simple. All bad men will die one day; hopefully to be replaced by good, enlightened men. Until then, his objective was to keep out of everyone's way, and not draw attention to himself or his family. Instead, he saw his duty as looking after them, his employees and his friends, and allowing others to worry about the wider world.

Big Joe, Sunetta and Little Joe were legally permitted to attend the best white schools because of their honorary white status, but even though David was more than happy to pay, they were refused entry with no official reason given. His children's mixed-race heritage was the real, but unspoken, barrier to entry.

The school for blacks and coloureds had such little government funding that it was impossible for it to hire qualified teachers. David's solution was to open a school in a spare farm shed. At first it was just for Big Joe and the children of his farm workers. Then, when it became time for Sunetta to go to school, a new class was added. Again, when it was Little Joe's time, a third class was added with each class being simply another shed built on the farm. Eventually, each year the school was expanded by opening a new class for pupils coming to school for the first time. The class sizes were always small. Eventually, the local school was forced to close through lack of attendance. At this point, working very quietly behind the scenes, with the village elders doing all the work, David financed the acquisition of the old school and its refurbishment. He then moved his school into it.

Right from the very start of setting up the first class for Big Joe, David was convinced that parents and their children would not value the school if the education was provided free. He insisted parents had to pay the school for each child who attended. He increased his employees' wages by just enough to make sure they could afford to pay the set fee. Nevertheless, the largest subsidy for the school came from him.

He took pride in hiring the best teachers and supervising the curriculum, while Satutu took great care over the pastoral side of the school, making sure the children were fed at lunchtime, drank enough water each day and above all that the classrooms, kitchen and toilets were spotlessly clean. They both insisted that every child learned music and played sport, as neither could imagine school life without them.

Despite the segregation laws making it illegal, the School also admitted white children from those parents who could not afford the fees of the white school. While these children were taught in the same class, they were entered in a register called 'Visitors', differentiating them from those pupils who were enrolled. This way they passed the all too frequent inspections, and by hefty donations to the police's local 'charity', the school and its running was not interfered with.

There was only one blot on the landscape as far as David Daunier was concerned. He hated apartheid as much as the next man. He had every reason to. There was no one who cheered more than David when, in 1961, the 156 members of the African National Congress ('ANC') who had been charged with high treason were acquitted. After serving five years in prison, the judge eventually ruled that these men had no case to answer. "How could there have been?" exclaimed David. "They had only participated in drawing up a Freedom Charter which sought equal rights and the end of racial discrimination. Was this not what the United Nations in its 1948 Declaration of Human Rights required of all nations, including South Africa?" he would ask of anyone who would listen.

Nevertheless, David could see that the ANC was becoming more violent and more extreme. Instinctively, he knew that this made the future bleak for his family. Perhaps it was time for them to sell up and leave South Africa, but where would he go? He couldn't go home. He couldn't go back to England. It was a conundrum which started to play on his mind for there was no immediate answer. Perhaps it was time to return to France, the village of Latoire and Château de Gressier. Perhaps it was time to see his sister again.

Chapter 3

England and France 1961 to 1962

WITH THE EXUBERANCE of youth, Henry went up to Birmingham University; a place which he decided lacked beauty and sounded dreadful, for it was populated with people who shared the most painful accent.

It was in the laboratories where, to his surprise, Henry found there was a chasm between what he knew and what his tutors expected him to know. His lack of knowledge was so vast that, from day one, Henry found himself sinking. His solution was to concentrate on only the subject matters which interested him. He studied in detail the real difference between an alkaline and an acid, and the effects of heat and cold at their extreme level on each of the basic compounds; allowing every other aspect of his course to pass him by.

In response to a distinct lack of women in the chemistry labs, Henry joined the orchestra. His lack of talent consigned him once again to the second row but this time he didn't mind, for even if his bow didn't touch the strings, he could sit there completely absorbed in the beauty of the sound being made by his fellow players.

It was early in the first term, when the students were gathered in the union bar, that a student studying to be a master brewer took to the piano and, with a pint in hand, started to play. It was obvious from this student's frame that many a pint had been sunk long before he was legally able to buy alcohol. Gradually, students disappeared to their rooms to reappear with instruments to join in, as did Henry with his guitar. Slowly, a jamming session started and, after three or four nights, a core group of musicians built around the brewer, had become a band.

Henry used the freedom of university not to shave, grow his hair and generally become fashionably uncouth in his appearance. He followed the brewing course with close interest, played in the band at every opportunity and studied hard, with a new passion, for the things which really interested him; none of which was chemistry. It was a complete shock to him when, not only did he fail his first-year exams, but he failed them badly.

There was a serious gathering of professors and tutors at which Henry was duly chastised and told he had great aptitude for the subject, but his lack of application to study the set course had caused his failure. He would be welcomed back, but he would have to re-do the whole year all over again. Henry thanked them graciously, but the prospect filled him with dread. He had listened patiently, but he didn't say what he wanted to say, which was that their teaching was dreadful. The professors and lecturers were only interested in their own research, and not in their students, who either swam or were left to sink and drown.

Henry spent a miserable summer at Château de Gressier. This time, friends from both university and school came with their girlfriends who, being one year older, were looking even more beautiful. With the added year, there was an increase in confidence which led to many a seduction - but not for him. Sometimes he wished he could drink, so as to remove his inhibitions with the opposite sex, but it was not to be.

At the end of September 1962, when all of Henry's friends had left and the Château was busying itself with the harvest, Henry fell into a deep melancholic mood. His friends had kept his spirits alive during the summer but, as they left, he realised that they, and everyone else around him, had a purpose, whereas he had none. What the hell was he going to do? He had no idea.

Chapter 4

Cape District, South Africa September 1962

IT HAD STARTED as a game. A game which got out of control. Sunetta laughed as she watched her brother Big Joe and his friends forcibly tie her younger brother, Little Joe to a chair in one of the barns on the New Found Estate used to sort and pack the farm's fruit. Mindlessly, they left him and went out to play. There was no reason for it; just the sport of irritating a much younger brother. It was to their fate that they then forgot about him. It was many hours later when their father found Little Joe whimpering in despair. He'd wet himself, so desperate had he been to go to the lavatory. David was incensed.

That evening Big Joe and Sunetta's father was not at the tea table as usual. Satutu, having given them a verbal roasting about their behaviour, oozed sourness in her silence. After tea, Sunetta and Big Joe were summoned to their father's study. His room was unusually tidy. Normally, it was a mess of open books and papers, with crosswords waiting to be finished, as he committed hours to cryptanalysis and the development of mathematical algorithms. It was more than a hobby. It had become an obsession.

David didn't need to say anything. His children already knew they were in deep trouble. His face looked like thunder. Sunetta then had to stand and watch as Big Joe was told to bend over and clasp the edge of a wooden chair, where he was beaten with his father's silver capped officer's cane to the point where he was writhing and screaming with each cut. Sunetta was completely terrified at what was going to happen to her, and what did happen was worse than all her fears. Nothing had prepared either of them for the ferocity which came from their father's uncontrolled anger.

When their mother, Satutu, came to see them, they were both examining the bruising and welts on their naked buttocks. Her first words were not of compassion and sympathy, but of reproach.

"I told your father to double whatever punishment he was considering," she said. "I will not have bullying. I will not have it here. I will not have it anywhere." Her voice got louder and stronger as she spoke.

Satutu then made them turn around again. This time she saw blood was seeping from their wounds. "I've seen worse on a nigger boy's arse for stealing just apples," she said dismissively. For the first time in a long time Satutu spoke with a broad Bantu accent, rather than her usual refined English tone.

That night Big Joe packed a small bag with a change of clothes and his wash things. When the house was quiet, he went around collecting any money he could find. It was with luck he remembered his passport and identity card and then, with the dogs barking, he walked out into the night. He left no note. He was 13 years old.

In the morning, when Big Joe didn't come down to breakfast, a chill went around the kitchen. When Satutu learned his room had not been slept in, she screamed in terror and, with that, time froze on the New Found Estate. It was the last day of September 1962.

Chapter 5

England and France September 1962

"HAVE YOU ASKED yourself what went wrong last year?" asked Juliette speaking in aristocratic French. Thus began a conversation with his grandmother which he would remember all his life.

"It's not that I'm not good enough," replied Henry in French. "They've already offered me a place to do a master's degree to finish the work I did in my first year. It's because I hardly did any of the first-year course work that I have to do it again."

There was a silence.

"So you worked then?" said Juliette.

"Mamie, I worked chuffing hard," replied Henry, deliberately making sure he didn't use a swear word. 'Mamie' was the informal name he used for his maternal grandmother just as 'Bear' had been his name for her father, his great grandfather. "It was just not the work they wanted me to do. Or to be precise, it wasn't the work they wanted me to do for the exams."

Henry leaned back in his chair and cast his view over the valley which was now showing the first signs of autumn.

"It's so unfair because my tutors kept encouraging me to do the work I was doing. I think they found it interesting too. They said they thought they were encouraging me in my out-of-curriculum studies whereas I thought it was the curriculum."

"So what you did in the first year was so important that they want you to do it as a masters when you've graduated?" questioned Juliette.

"Yes," said Henry.

"Well, that can't be bad," said Juliette.

"It is bad Mamie because if I went back, I know I won't do the first year's work. I will only do the work that interests me, and in a year's time I will be in exactly the same position."

"It's a stubbornness which runs in the family," commented Juliette.

"And afterwards, what can I do with it?"

There was a long pause as Juliette waited for her grandson to speak. She was sure he had more to say.

"Oh, it's all fairly pointless knowing how it all began," he said, with a real sense of despair in his voice. "It won't help me find answers to the present and the future."

Juliette shook her head gently, as she wasn't sure she understood what Henry was saying.

"What is it that interests you?" asked Juliette.

Henry stopped speaking French and swapped naturally into native English.

"The very first essay they gave us to write was to provide a critique of the periodic table. I can remember being thrilled, because it was a discussion on the periodic table which I'd had during my interview to go to Birmingham. It was when I was doing the research to write the essay, I discovered that, way back in 1929, Charles Janet had proposed a periodic table of anti-matter. This followed on from work by Paul Dirac who, the year before, had predicted there would be anti-electrons. These were discovered by a guy called Carl Anderson about three or four years later and he called them positrons - for positive electrons. This meant that the work done by Dirac and Janet, suggesting the existence of a parallel universe comprising antimatter, could well be true." Henry was now becoming excited and animated.

"You know all these names and what they did?" asked Juliette impressed.

"Yes, yes," said Henry impatiently. He was frustrated that his flow had been interrupted. "The point being that when matter and anti-matter come into contact, they would annihilate each other."

Only now was Henry happy to pause to make sure Juliette was keeping up. She said nothing.

"Well," he continued, "when you study the periodic table you realise the whole mass of the universe comprises 75% hydrogen and

15

24% helium. It's the high temperature and pressure in the sun which causes its hydrogen nuclei to fuse together to create helium and energy. We get the energy because the mass of helium is less than the mass of the two hydrogen nuclei which are fused to form it. The left-over mass becomes the energy which creates the life we have here on earth. You then start to think about what created the stars, and then how electromagnetic radiation travels from the stars through space to us."

"Electromagnetic radiation?" interjected Juliette, concerned that her grandson was having anything to do with radiation; a substance which she assumed was highly dangerous.

"Sunlight is a form of electromagnetic radiation," he replied, instantly recognising her concern.

Juliette nodded her understanding, although she was finding it hard to keep up.

"Over fifty years ago a guy called Rutherford showed that photons were a form of electromagnetic radiation. Photons have no mass, but they can be absorbed or reflected if they come into contact with something. Then I heard some of the physics professors discussing whether there was something in space which acted like matter. You know, something which is there but can't be seen. I then found in the library that thirty years ago a guy called Fritz Zwicky, don't you just love that name for an Astrophysicist, proposed a thing called dark matter[2]. He was certain the effect of gravity proved it was there. The problem, he said, was that we just can't see it."

"Hang on," said Juliette. "You told me that anti-matter would annihilate matter and now you're saying that it sits alongside it without doing so."

---

[2] Dark matter was later proved by Vera Rubin to exist, but it cannot be seen because it does not react to light. By studying galactic rotations, specifically Andromeda, she found the galaxies in the universe are rotating so fast that their outer stars should be flying apart if gravity in the skies was all that was holding them together. The standard model of cosmology suggests that the total mass–energy of the universe contains 4.9% ordinary matter and energy, 26.8% dark matter and 68.3% of an unknown form of energy known as dark energy.

"Yes, no," said Henry, frustrated. "Dark matter and antimatter are different things. Dark matter is a matter you can't see. Antimatter is exactly the opposite of matter. It's matter's ying to antimatter's yang."

"Ok, so I get it that you can't see Dark Matter, but can you see antimatter?" asked Juliette.

"I don't know, Mamie, probably an antimatter photon might see antimatter. I just don't think we know. It's not something I've thought about. There is so much new work being done on the subject and it's so exciting."

"So, is this what you've been studying instead of chemistry? Why don't you just change courses?"

Henry didn't answer the question.

"So much time has been wasted. Just before the last war so much was being discovered and then it all stopped. It's all starting up again right now; we're on the threshold of discovering what made the universe. I need to be part of it." There was an urgency in his voice.

"Well, why aren't you?" she asked, showing the frustration she felt with his laissez-faire attitude to life.

"There's a new science, theoretical physics. This is where all this work is being done. They use mathematical models to explain and predict natural phenomena. The problem is that the concepts are hard, and my maths is not good enough. Everything in astrophysics is cast in mathematical symbols. I've messed up Mamie. I should have made sure I got into Oxford or Cambridge as that is where the real thinking is being done. It's in physics and cosmology, not in chemistry, that's how we're going to find out how we got here."

Henry paused as something dawned on him.

"Mamie, I've done the whole thing wrong. I can't catch up and I can't be amongst the best."

There was silence as Henry absorbed the truth in his statement. He looked at his grandmother and repeated, "I just can't catch up. Its why I haven't gone back to uni."

"Do you have to catch up?" she asked.

"Yes," he said with exasperation, "but when I've caught up, my maths still won't be good enough. Mass bends light, Einstein proved this. But can I understand or repeat his formulae? Like hell I can!"

"I thought you did chemistry because of Château de Gressier," said Juliette, her voice revealing the disappointment she felt on learning the real reason he had decided to give up his course.

Henry looked at Mamie and said nothing. But the quizzical look on his face prompted her to continue.

"Château de Gressier is the most interesting chemistry set in the world. What happens here is the science of five thousand years. Some people see winemaking as an art, requiring the instinct of an artist, but that is to create a mystique. Everything we do here is science. The ingredients might change very slightly, the amount of sunlight or rainfall, but not so much else. It's the most wonderful blend of nature and science, chemistry and biology, you will find anywhere in the world."

Henry put his hands above his head and leaned back. He paused as he looked into the sky which was darkening with the pink hue of dusk. He felt a chill in his arms.

"Louis Pasteur was originally a chemist," continued Juliette to reinforce her point. "Look at the good he did for wine with his chemistry set. Did you know it was he who proved that it was yeast which was responsible for producing alcohol from sugar during fermentation? Before then everyone thought fermentation was caused by decomposition. Also, he showed that when different micro-organisms contaminated the wine, lactic acid was produced making it taste sour. Before him, everyone knew that less fermentation occurred when the yeast was exposed to air, but they didn't know why."

Henry was listening attentively. "What happens to Château de Gressier after you?" he asked.

"That depends on you," said Juliette. "You are its proper heir. This should be yours one day, if you want to take it over, but you have to want it Henry." Her words were emphatically spoken. "The plan is that, one day, this would come to you, but I'm not doing that if you don't prove to me that you want it, and most importantly, will protect it." Then, in the manner of all great matriarchs, which Juliette was more than capable of being, she got up in silence, collected her shawl and walked inside.

The enormity of what he had just been told struck him. Why had the matter never been discussed before? Why had his mother not mentioned it? Why did his mother never come to Château de Gressier with him?

Chapter 6

Château de Gressier October 1962

HENRY RARELY JOINED his grandmother for breakfast, usually lying in until the middle of the morning, but after a sleepless night, as his mind wrestled with what he had been told, he knew today had to be different.

Juliette hardly acknowledged Henry as he took his place at the dining room table; her attention focused on Le Monde. The coffee was strong and the orange juice sweet as Henry waited for the cooked breakfast he knew would shortly appear.

"I assumed Pierre Hilaire was going to take over Château de Gressier," were Henry's opening words. "I thought he was ..." Henry paused, "family."

"Maybe," acknowledged Juliette, noncommittally.

"But he's in charge, isn't he, Mamie?"

"I'm in charge here," said Juliette firmly. "This is mine and then it's yours, if you want it."

"What about Pierre? There is something extra which makes him important here, isn't there?" said Henry, turning an instinct created in his night-time thinking into a question.

"Your grandfather and great-uncle were responsible for killing Pierre's step father in the Great War," said Juliette, matter-of-factly. Then, looking Henry straight in the face, she added: "And, there's the small matter of his mother being your grandfather's mistress for a long time before he was murdered. Oh, and let us not forget, it was his brother's silence, when tortured by the Gestapo, which stopped the same from happening to me. And, did you know, it was his mother who helped get your mother out of here and to England during the war." Juliette paused for breath, and then said determinedly, "Yes Henry, we owe Pierre's family a lot, one hell of a lot."

"Hang on Mamie," said Henry overwhelmed by flow of new information. "What are you saying? What is all of this? Why's it never been said before?"

"Hasn't your mother told you any of these things?" asked Juliette.

"No Mamie, they're never discussed."

"What has she said of your father?"

"Nothing, she won't talk of him. She just said he worked on the estate, worked with the Resistance, was captured and killed in the war, and because of what you did in the Resistance, she had to leave here."

"What I did, what I did!" said Juliette incredulously, her voice rising in pitch.

"Why has she never been back?" asked Henry, thinking this might give him a clue as to why she suddenly appeared to be affronted by his comment.

Juliette didn't answer.

"When did you two last talk?" asked Henry.

"We write about twice a year. We talk on the phone every time we arrange for you to visit. But the last time we met and talked was when your great-grandfather ... my father, died. The time before that was err ... 1943."

"What, you've only met once in 20 years!" said Henry, incredulously.

"Uhm, I think you should get your mother to tell you about your father. You two need to talk," said Juliette firmly. It wasn't said as a suggestion. It was an order.

"What about, Mamie?" asked Henry, suddenly aware that there was a painful message being delivered in the silence. "What went wrong?" he asked.

"It's for your mother to answer. I will not say another word on this matter."

"Mamie, it's almost as though I've been living two lives; one here in the summer with you, and the other in England. How long have I been coming here? Since I was six," said Henry, answering his own question. "So nearly fifteen years, and yet over that time you two only spoke when Grandpa Bear died."

"These are issues for your mother," said Juliette firmly. "I will say no more than this: de Gressier must be in your soul. If it is not there, then you are not a Guégan, and if you are not a Guégan then it is not yours to have." With that, Juliette wiped her mouth with her napkin, which she discarded onto the dining room table. It was clear that their discussion was over and, as she always did when she didn't like the subject matter, Juliette got up and left.

His mother had left here and hadn't come back. Why? Would he betray her if Château de Gressier was to become his, he wondered? Yet, the thought of it being owned by anyone else was too painful to contemplate. If wondering about his future wasn't bad enough, Henry now found that his past was not as he thought; altogether everything appeared confused. It was all too discombobulating. The only certainty was that he would not be going back to university. He had to find something else to do. But first, there had to be a discussion with his mother.

Chapter 7

Hertford October 1962

"FOR CHRIST'S SAKE, go and have a shower," said Victoria to Henry. They were her first words on entering their home and finding him there. It wasn't just the mess at the front door but her instinctive response to the aroma of an unwashed youth in unwashed clothes.

Henry's journey back from Bordeaux had been arduous and taken him well over twenty-four hours. He was now slumped on the settee. He had raided the fridge, turned on the TV and fallen asleep. He was at home, his place of safety for more years than he could remember. It was where he truly relaxed and was himself.

"And take all your stuff with you," shouted Victoria, as Henry moved to climb the stairs.

"And bring your washing down with you when you're clean."

Ever since they'd moved in, Victoria and Henry spent their days in the kitchen which had been made bigger to incorporate a living and dining-room area.

Even when alone, Victoria ate properly. She laid the table, lit a candle and, in a cathartic regime, took the task of cooking seriously. No ready-made meals or something from a tin, but fresh ingredients chosen, prepared and cooked. It took her mind off the day. Sometimes she would listen to the radio or play some music, but just as often, she would enjoy the silence after the noise of her classroom.

Henry presented himself in the kitchen – shaved, clean, hair washed, and fringe cut. He was wearing a T-shirt, underpants, and a dressing gown, which was once his size, but was now far too small as his frame had moved from being that of a teenager towards manhood.

"How did you get on?" asked Victoria, pleased to have him home after such a long time of being away.

Henry told of stories of his summer, his friends, and his journey home.

"When did term start?" she asked, already knowing the answer. It was nearly two weeks before.

"I didn't go back," said Henry, abruptly. "I stayed on with Mamie."

Victoria, visibly shocked, said nothing. Henry repeated what he had said to Juliette, but this time he succinctly explained why he had not returned to university. His conversation with Mamie had helped him clarify his thinking.

"It's the maths," he concluded. "I can't do the bloody maths. Einstein summed up the whole universe in the equation E equals MC bloody squared. Well, it's got a bit more complicated since then."

Victoria made no protest, even at his swearing, for the arguments Henry had made were cogent. Her instincts had long told her that chemistry would not be his subject.

"What are you going to do instead?" she asked, as they sat at the table ready to eat.

"That depends on you."

"Why me?"

"Mamie said things about Château de Gressier when I was with her; many things which have never been said before."

"Like what?" asked Victoria.

"Like... my father?

Victoria had fended off this question at odd times in the past with a simple answer. This time it sent a shockwave through her body, for the way Henry spoke suggested he might have been told things differently by her mother.

Victoria put down her knife and fork very gently, rested her hands in her lap and stared at her untouched plate. She had been waiting for this moment, but now it had come it was no less difficult. She had rehearsed the words she would say many times, but now she was finding it difficult to speak at all. Her eyes welled up and she closed them. A tear rolled down the edge of her nose.

"Your father is not French. He was a German pilot," she blurted out quickly. "Almost everything you've been told about him has been made up, so we could live here in peace."

There was an obvious silence in the room as Henry absorbed what had been said.

"Is it all lies?" asked Henry, leaning back in his chair, looking carefully at his mother's face as she wiped away her tears.

She nodded. "He was transferred from Bordeaux back to Germany to fly for Hitler, just after I fell pregnant. He was an exceptionally good pilot, all his friends said so, and that was why he was chosen, but I never saw him again."

"So who's Stephen Bellanger?" asked Henry, referring to his alleged father.

"A young Frenchman shot by the Germans for being a communist. He worked on the Estate before he was killed." Victoria paused as the pain of those times returned, hidden away deep in her memory.

"Stephen was very close to your grandmother," she continued. "They worked together getting British pilots back to England. They would take them across the demarcation line in empty wine barrels. It was incredibly dangerous work!"

"Is it Stephen who's buried in the Latoire graveyard, where there's the 'Hero of France' plaque?" he asked.

"I don't know, maybe," replied Victoria. "He was buried in an unknown grave, but Mamie was so determined he would not be forgotten that she reserved a spot for him in the family line and put a plaque with a cross and his name on the wall. I think she thought that if his body were found he would rest there."

Victoria's voice became stultified as she thought back to those frightening times. Like all those who had been through the war she preferred not to talk about it.

"Mamie and I chose Stephen because he was roughly the same age as your father. I could prove I knew him; he was alive when I fell pregnant and was dead shortly afterwards. In fact, at one time, Mamie thought that Stephen and I would marry, so it was highly plausible."

"Did my real father know you were pregnant with me?" asked Henry.

"Not before he was posted, no. He said he would come back to me, but he never did. I wrote to him twice in Berlin, but I never heard back."

"Have you looked for him?" asked Henry, trying to gather as many facts as he could.

"I started to try, but no one wanted to talk about the war, and with Germany divided ... well ... it was too difficult and too ..." Victoria's voice faded as she drifted into her own thoughts.

"What was his name?" asked Henry.

"Heinrik Klugman, Hauptmann Heinrik Klugman," said Victoria, in her best German teaching accent. "His name was spelt with a 'k' not a 'ch', - h. e. i. n. r. i. k. – it was very unusual."

There was silence in the room. Victoria expected Henry to say something more, but he didn't.

"Mamie was furious when she found I was pregnant," continued Victoria, filling the silence. "She thought I was a collaborator and would get punished for being one. Using the name Bellanger when I came to England was simply a subterfuge, to give me respectability, at a time when everything was so dangerous."

"Did Grandpa Bear know?" asked Henry, referring to Col. Dovingdon, his great-grandfather, with whom they had lived from the moment Victoria arrived in England from France.

"Good God, no. He would have been appalled; just Mamie and me."

"Is that why I'm called Henry, after him; Henry from Heinrik?"

"Yes, I thought if he came looking for me, but I was dead then your name would give him a clue that you were his son." She paused. "It was much easier for me to arrive here as a widow, than as an unmarried mother," said Victoria, continuing with her explanation.

Henry got up and started to pace around the kitchen. He walked in and out of the hallway, and then into the sitting room, where he paced up and down before sinking into one of the winged, high-back armchairs. He just wanted to think.

Victoria came into the sitting room bringing Henry a mug of tea, and taking out a coaster from the side drawer, she put it next to him. She said nothing.

"Why?" asked Henry.

"Why did I get pregnant?" said Victoria. "Why did I have to leave?" she continued.

"Yes, all of those," said Henry. It was his surly tone which upset her, and suddenly she felt cross at the way she was being questioned.

"Have you not had the very best?" she said, raising her voice. "Have you not had everything you wanted? Look at you; a darn good education, the best that can be bought. You've had everything. You're darn lucky, do you know that?"

"I didn't have a father," Henry continued, his tone still surly and becoming defiant.

"And neither did thousands, tens of thousands of other children. It's what happens in war. It's tough, but you had Bear," she continued. "He was like a father to you. He was wonderful. You wanted for nothing."

Victoria was now openly angry. Henry had no concept of how hard she had worked to bring him up, and she was not going to be blamed for events which took place well over twenty years before.

"Your great-grandfather made huge efforts for you. Despite being elderly, he played with you as though he was your father. He was quite remarkable."

Victoria's anger drove Henry to silence. He had rarely seen her so agitated. Henry responded by changing his tone, this time speaking softly.

"Mother, I'm not blaming you, and I'm grateful for everything. But ...," Henry paused, as he did not know how to go on. "But there's something between Mamie and Grandpa Bear, and Mamie and you! It's unsaid, but it speaks volumes. What is it?"

"She threw me out, Henry. I was pregnant, and she threw me out!" The bitterness in Victoria's voice was plain to hear.

"She threw you out?" he repeated as a question.

"Yes," said Victoria, emphatically.

"But didn't she arrange for you to go to be with Bear?" he asked.

"Yes, but she didn't know what she was sending me to. She hadn't been in touch with him for years. Not since they fell out over Uncle Penrose."

"The son Grandpa Bear disinherited?"

"Yes, that one."

"He was never mentioned by Bear, was he?" said Henry.

Victoria nodded. "Grandpa Bear thought Uncle Penrose had brought shame on the family so would never allow his name to be said."

"What had he done wrong?"

"I don't know. All I know is that it was incredibly serious, and your grandmother was certain that Penrose was not guilty of whatever it was he was accused of doing. She wanted Bear to help her defend him, but he refused. Because of that, she didn't speak to him ever again, at least not until just before he died.

"What was he like?"

"Who, Penrose?" asked Victoria. "I don't know. I don't think I ever met him. I'm not even sure he's still alive."

"No, my father," said Henry, frustrated that he had not been instantly understood.

"Oh, ... he was young. All the pilots were. He was handsome, tall, kind. He had the kindest of eyes, warm blue eyes. His hair was very blonde and thick. He was always very thoughtful and careful."

"Not so careful with you," interrupted Henry, trying to lighten the moment.

Victoria ignored his flippancy; she was deep in her memories.

"He planned and checked everything. I remember he said his father was a vet who committed suicide. His mother was a surgeon. He wanted to be a doctor too, but the war started and because he could already fly, he joined their air force. He loved flying. I don't know Henry. He was just nice, and I fell in love with him."

"What did he say about the war?" asked Henry, deliberately moving the subject away from love, as he found emotional subjects embarrassing.

"He saw it as a job. I asked him once whether he worried about killing someone. He said that, when he fired his guns or was dropping a bomb, he wasn't killing another person, just shooting down a plane or destroying a boat. He didn't think about the people inside. He always assumed they bailed out or got into a lifeboat or something."

She pondered for a moment. "Somehow it made me feel better about him."

"Do you think he's still alive?"

"I don't know. Sometimes I think he is, and one day he will come and find us. I'm sure if he's alive he'll come back to de Gressier because he loved that place too."

"If he comes back, won't Mamie send him away?" asked Henry.

It was an eventuality which hadn't dawned on Victoria before. The thought suddenly chilled her. Until then she had been sure Heinrik's love for her would ensure his return, and one day they would be together again. The reality that he might have come, not found her, and gone again, had not struck Victoria until that very moment.

The thought knifed Victoria in the gut. It wasn't just about rekindling a love affair. Heinrik had something very precious. Her deceased twin brother's gold hunter pocket watch engraved on the back with the Dovingdon crest and his name - Victor. It was one of an almost identical pair, with her name engraved on the other. This watch had to come home to her. Heinrik had promised it would. The thought of it being permanently lost would be more than she could possibly bear.

Victoria put her head in her hands and stared at the carpet. For so long she'd kept her thoughts on Heinrik repressed, working hard at other things to make sure that her mind was never idle.

"I often wondered what it was that attracted me to him," said Victoria. "Do you know why your second name's Victor?" she asked in an apparent change of subject.

Henry shook his head.

"I had a twin brother. He drowned when I was young. His name was Victor. I named you after him."

"What!" exclaimed Henry loudly. "The Victor in the churchyard; is that Victor your brother? Why's no one said?" There was alarm in Henry's voice.

Victoria nodded weakly, tears welling up in her eyes. "I sometimes think I chose your father because ... well, he made me feel as though Victor was still alive. It might seem odd, but it's true."

"Mother, you've never mentioned a brother, let alone a twin brother. Mamie's never mentioned having a son. What the hell's been going on?" he demanded, ignoring Victoria's obvious distress.

"Oh, how I miss him," said Victoria, and with those words she let out a series of painful sobs, and this time tears poured from her eyes and down her cheeks in the most silent of cries.

"I miss him, Henry. I miss him every single day and it hurts. It hurts each moment of every day. I can't bear him not being around. It's like carrying an ache that never goes. Only a twin knows what it is like when the other is not there. It feels as though your heart beats for only half the time. As though you are only half alive."

Victoria wiped her eyes and nose on her apron, as she tried to gather her composure.

"From the day Victor died to the day I left de Gressier; not once did Mamie and I talk about him. He was there one moment and not there the next, not at our birthdays, not at Christmas. He was just not there. I don't even have a photograph of him. Mamie took them all down. I only see him in my memory." Victoria sobbed again and shook her head. "But that memory fades. I only have his pillowcase and I touch it every day."

Henry got up from his chair and squatted at his mother's side. He took her hand and, in comfort, started to stroke it.

The death of Victor, and the succour offered by Heinrik, would have been given as her reasons for going to Heinrik's bed, but what had been so clear in Victoria's mind at the outset of their discussion, had become confused in the telling of her story..

Victoria rose, left the room, and climbed the stairs. She was gone for several minutes. When she returned, she was carrying her gold and diamond pocket watch which she handed to Henry who hadn't moved.

"This was given to you by Grandpa Bear, wasn't it?" said Henry as he lovingly stroked the glass watch face.

Victoria nodded.

"You said it was one of a pair." He paused. "The other one was Victor's, wasn't it?" asked Henry in an authoritarian tone. "Your brother's!"

"I gave it to your father on the promise that he would bring it back to me."

"And he never did?" said Henry.

Once more Victoria stared at the carpet, but this time she shook her head in a signal of despair. Her silence gave Henry the answer he needed.

"Isn't it strange," said Henry. "I thought Victor's watch had been given to Uncle Penrose."

"No, Uncle Penrose disappeared long before I was born. I doubt if he knows we exist," she said shaking her head slowly.

"Tell me about Grand-père Étienne," said Henry, after a little while. He needed to change the subject. "There's another story there that no one tells, isn't there?"

"I can't, Henry," said Victoria. "It's Mamie's story; at least the bit involving Dominique Hilaire. She has to tell it, not me."

"What, Pierre's mother?"

Victoria nodded.

"Mamie suggested she was Grand-père 's mistress before he died. Is that true?"

"You need to ask Mamie," said Victoria firmly, "but yes, I think so. The thing I can tell you is that Grand-père Étienne was murdered."

"Mamie mentioned he was murdered for the first time a couple of days ago. Why was he murdered? Do you know who murdered him?" asked Henry.

"It's her story to tell too," she repeated. "But yes. I was about five years old when my father was killed. I know he was murdered by a man called ... Coudace, Hugo Coudace! God, I hated that man ... and she stupidly married him!"

"What! Mamie married her husband's killer!" exclaimed Henry in total surprise.

Victoria paused. "Do you know what I remember best about that time?" she said ignoring his question. "I remember the huge bonfire we had on the day he was executed."

"Executed?" interrupted Henry.

"Yes, guillotined," said Victoria, without any emotion. "As soon as we heard he was dead, everyone from the Estate and the village went to his house and we burned everything of his, absolutely everything. God it was fantastic!" Her voice was reliving the excitement of that moment.

Henry's brain suddenly stopped. Surely that barbarism had been left behind in the 18th Century he thought, before reflecting on a severed head falling into a basket. He shivered dramatically as the image filled his mind.

Mother and son sat quietly, staring at the embers as they glowed yellow and red in the fire basket with an occasional flicker of blue. The fact that his grandmother had married her first husband's murderer was a story too far.

"It's as though you're orphaned from your own family," said Henry. "Even though they might be alive, it's as though they're dead."

Victoria nodded, for it was an excellent summary as she thought of her father, whom she couldn't remember, her brother, whom she could hardly remember, and Heinrik. Were these people ever real, she wondered? For over twenty years she had contemplated them. What had happened? The unanswered questions drove her crazy. Her feeling of guilt increased as her memories faded and became confused. It reached a point where her survival was dependent upon suppressing these thoughts, which is exactly what she had been doing year after year, anniversary after anniversary.

"Mamie says she wants me to take over de Gressier, but I'm not sure that's what she really wants."

"Why?"

"I don't know," replied Henry, with slight exasperation. "Perhaps it's because I'm half German? Maybe she thinks you don't want me to have it. Maybe she has other plans."

"Why would she think that?" asked Victoria.

Henry shook his head.

"Do you want to take it over?" she asked.

"I don't want it to go out of the family," he said.

"That's not the same thing."

"Mamie says she will give it to Pierre if I don't have it."

"What, Pierre Hilaire?" asked Victoria in shock.

"Yes, he now manages the place. I get a sense from Mamie that there's a huge burden, almost a debt to him because of what happened in the war. By giving him de Gressier I think she feels she would be settling that debt."

"Did Mamie tell you this?" asked Victoria.

"In a way, yes, but I'd already worked out there was...," he paused, "an obligation but it didn't make sense. Did you know him? Did you know Pierre?" asked Henry.

"Not really, he was only six or seven when I left."

"Do you know, now you've told me about Victor, it makes me think that Pierre is Mamie's replacement for him. It's as though he's her surrogate son, a substitute," said Henry.

"Or a replacement for Stephen ... there was something very close between those two," Victoria added, getting crosser as she did so. The thought that anyone could be a surrogate for her dead brother was deeply upsetting.

"You know Stephen Bellanger and Pierre Hilaire are, were, half-brothers, don't you?" asked Victoria. "Their mother's Dominique. She was a Bellanger and became a Hilaire," said Victoria, trying to fill in all the gaps.

"What, the woman who was Grand-père Étienne's mistress?" said Henry, trying hard to keep up.

"Grand-père Étienne and Mamie's brother, Uncle Penrose, were responsible for killing her first husband, Stephen's father, in World War I. It was an accident, but they killed him all the same."

"Yes, Mamie said something like it a couple of days ago, but it was said almost in passing. How did Stephen's father die? How did Étienne and Penrose kill him?"

"I don't know," replied Victoria. "It had something to do with an accident on a battlefield but I'm sure it's all connected to why Mamie and Grandpa Bear fell out in a big way."

Henry blew out a strange whistle as he shook his head at the complexity of it all.

"It always surprised me that Mamie and Dominique, a wife and mistress, became the best of friends," commented Victoria. "They should've hated each other, but they didn't."

"Perhaps Mamie accepted the affair because she felt guilty at Grand-père Étienne and her brother killing Dominique's husband," proffered Henry. "After all, Mamie said we owed Pierre's family a lot."

"It was Dominique who got me out of France, so perhaps that's part of the debt," added Victoria.

"Yes, I'm sure that's right, but now I know Pierre and Stephen are brothers, well half-brothers, helps make sense of something else. Mamie said Stephen was tortured. She said she owed her life to his bravery. That must add to her sense of obligation to Pierre, mustn't it."

Victoria let out a huge sigh, threw back her head to rest it against the chair back and with her eyes closed she asked: "Did you know Mamie was in the Resistance?"

"Yes, but she'd never said until the other day. It's the others in the village, and on the Estate, who told me," answered Henry. "They quite admire her. Apparently, she got the nickname 'Le Singe Fou[3]' because of the way she treated the Germans."

"Stephen was working on the Estate when he was taken away, later to be shot by the Nazis. I was there on the day he was arrested. I saw it. It was dreadful, truly awful." Victoria paused as she relived those moments. "Do you know, I can still remember the smile on his face when he got into their car. He must have been so scared, and yet he didn't show it. That smile went straight to my mother. It was one of the bravest things I think I've ever seen. I am sure you are right. I'm sure that, in some way, she feels responsible for Stephen's death."

"Is that why Pierre is like a favoured son? Is that why Mamie feels the estate should go to Pierre and not me?" he asked.

Suddenly, it was all so much clearer to Henry. The bloodline to Château de Gressier might be his, but his grandmother's emotional line was to Pierre for many, many reasons. It was why, if he wanted the Estate, he was going to have to fight for it.

Victoria sat quietly absorbing the news of Pierre. As the embers of the fire started to fade, the chill of the night now ate into the room making it cold. Victoria looked at her watch. They had talked for over

---

[3] The mad monkey

34

six hours. She hadn't been able to answer all of Henry's questions, for it happened such a long time ago.

Victoria rose for bed.

"Do you think Mamie will tell me what really happened?" Henry asked.

"I don't know, Henry," said Victoria. "Perhaps, sometimes it takes a separation of generations. Stories in one age must sometimes miss a generation to be told in the next. She might tell you. I just don't know."

Victoria moved around the room turning off the lights ready for bed. Suddenly she stopped and turned towards her son.

"Château de Gressier is a real privilege," said Victoria firmly. "You should want it. You should strive for it. You should earn it. If it's given to you, you should not treat it as a plaything. I don't want you to have it if you don't respect it. Its heritage is far more important than that." Victoria was now extremely firm. "Other than that, my views are entirely irrelevant."

Victoria got up and walked slowly to Henry where she placed one hand gently on top of his head, very lightly touching his hair. "Night-night," she whispered. Henry reached for her hand and held it gently.

"I want it, Mother," he said. "I don't want it to be gone."

"Then make sure you deserve it."

The next morning Victoria and Henry woke to a crisis which would take the world to the brink of nuclear war.

The night they spoke, President Kennedy had announced on American television that Russian ballistic missiles were being deployed in Cuba and thus within 90 miles of the United States shoreline. For thirteen days in that October, Victoria and Henry, along with everyone else, held their breath as Russian ships, with more missiles, sailed towards the edge of a quarantine area set up around Cuba by President Kennedy. No ship would be allowed into the quarantine area without being inspected by the US Navy for weapons. For these few days, the future of Château de Gressier was a long way from both their minds.

Chapter 8

Château de Gressier November 1962

HENRY STOOD AT his bedroom window and looked out over the vineyard of Château de Gressier. Everything had shut up for winter. The leaves on the vines had fallen. They had turned brown and the stems and branches of the vine, misshapen by years of nature, were now clearly on display. The sky was bright blue, with the occasional puff of white cloud rapidly moving across the high sky. Most importantly the world had started to breathe again as the Russian ships had stopped, turned around and were heading for home. Nuclear war had been averted, for just a little while longer.

Henry had arrived late the night before and let himself in. It was therefore a surprise for Mamie when he joined her for breakfast.

"Ceçon! when did you arrive?" asked Juliette, using her nickname for him and speaking, with a lightness which showed that she was pleased to see him. There was no move by her to get up.

"Very late last night," said Henry, as he moved towards her.

"I didn't hear the noise on the gravel. It's the best of alarms you know!"

"I stopped the taxi at the field's edge and walked. I went down and came up through the cellars."

"You mean you can get in past the alarms?"

"Oui Mamie, you know that. It's an open secret. Everyone knows that."

"Mais oui," said Juliette, who shrugged her shoulders in a very Gaelic way, proving that the influence of France, which she had tried for over 20 years to resist, had finally reached into her being. She took

Henry's hand as he leaned forward and kissed her on the forehead. "You've lost weight," she added, critically.

"Mamie, I've only been gone a few days," he protested.

Once seated, Henry remained quite still, although a hot English cooked breakfast had been placed in front of him. It was obvious from his demeanour that he wanted to say something.

"Mamie, I would like to have Château de Gressier one day, please. I couldn't bear being without it. It's been my spiritual home for as long as I have lived," he said, taking her folding of the pages of Le Monde as the moment he should speak.

Juliette said nothing. She sipped her coffee, which was now cold.

"Henry, it's not enough to want it. You have to deserve it too," she said, putting down the paper.

"I know, Mamie, Mother said the same thing. She also said it was my duty and I think that's true too."

"But it's more than that, Henry. It has to be in your soul, deep in your soul, as deep a love affair with our terroir as you have with any living being."

"It is, Mamie, it is," said Henry, with a hint of desperation in his voice.

There was a long pause in their conversation.

"Mamie," said Henry after a long period of silence. "I need to know why I'm named Ceçon? It's an abbreviation of c'est le garçon, isn't it? It's like the boy with no name."

Juliette put down her knife. "Your mother told you?"

"In part," nodded Henry.

"The name Henry hurt too much," said Juliette. "Today, no, but then, yes. I knew Victoria chose the name after your father, but the Germans did terrible, terrible things here. Unspeakable things, and then, when she chose the name Henry Bellanger for you, I knew it was derived from your father's name and that hurt. Also, you have to remember, we all knew the real Stephen Bellanger and the way he was killed, and that doubled the pain."

"I'm a real Henry Bellanger too," protested Henry.

"No, not here, you're not! Here you're Henry Guégan!" responded Juliette, with her voice raised to emphasise her point.

"No one knows me as a Guégan," pleaded Henry.

"Yes, they do! Emphatically, no one knows you as a Bellanger!" said Juliette sternly. "I can't have Pierre and his mother thinking you are Stephen's son. I can't and I won't."

"I thought I was," said Henry shyly. "In the absence of anyone saying anything, well I just assumed. I saw his name on the wall in the churchyard. I saw the date he was shot and, well, it gave me comfort to assume he was my father. I needed to assume. His name, my name on the wall; it gave me a right to be here. It gave me an identity which I feel I have now lost."

Henry played with the hot breakfast plate which he turned nervously around and around in his hands, not yet ready to eat.

Juliette sat back in her chair and looked at her grandson. Unquestionably, he had the look of Étienne about him.

"If you could see yourself and see your grandfather, you would know you have a right to be here," said Juliette, trying to provide Henry with some comfort. It was obvious from his demeanour that Henry was distressed at not knowing who he truly was.

"We could tell them what happened. We could tell Dominique and Pierre the truth. What's wrong with that?" asked Henry.

"Stephen was a little bit older than you when he was shot, such a lovely, handsome man. He would have made an incredibly good husband for ..." She was going to say Victoria, but somehow it was not the right thing to say.

"Henry," said Juliette, using his real name for the first time in a long time, but with the French pronunciation. "The Germans did some terrible things when they were here, so very bad that we cannot talk about them, even today. It was all so very difficult. You went to bed frightened. You woke up frightened. Unless you were here, you will never be able to understand. Not only were they dreadfully cruel to us, but they divided our nation, the nation of France, into Occupied France and Vichy France. It divided its people, and we are still not whole again. Sometimes I think we will never be."

"Yes Mamie, I know that, but it is all such a long time ago."

"But Ceçon, the pain never goes, it fades, but never goes. Please understand that. Look at the big house just as you go in to Latoire. It's on the right, unoccupied now, run-down uncared for. No one from the family dares live there. It was the home of a Vichy collaborator. I will not even say his name. It's proof that the divide still exists."

"Oui Mamie, the pain might not go, but there has to be a time to forgive. Hasn't that time come?"

"When you came here for the first time, at the age of five maybe six, the name Henry just didn't fit - not after a German - I couldn't bear it. I thought of calling you Étienne, after your grandfather but it never seemed right. Please Henry, don't be upset by being called Ceçon. It's a nickname, only a nickname, maybe foolishly chosen, but I didn't know what else to call you. Now, it's who you are to me, and to everyone here, that's the important thing, not some name. It's a name of love and affection. It is honestly."

"We have to tell Pierre and his mother about my name. We will ask them to keep it in confidence, but we will tell them. It's important to me that they know."

"No!" said Juliette fiercely, "never! They do not know your surname and they never will.

Henry was shocked by the force of her rebuke. "Mamie, what happened to Grand-père Étienne?" asked Henry, thinking that his grandfather's affair with Pierre's mother might have something to do with Juliette's protest.

"Your mother didn't say?" asked Juliette.

"No, she said it was your story to tell."

"He was murdered by the estate manager here."

"Why? Did it have anything to do with Grandpa Étienne's affair with Dominique Hilaire?"

"No. No one knew of it except them. Certainly not Hugo. No, he killed for money and greed."

"Mother suggested it was for more than that."

"Yes ... there was jealousy too. At his trial he told how he was obsessed with me and thought that, with Étienne gone, I would become his."

"Did you ... become his?"

"Yes, no, I don't know. We were married for a little while."

"What happened to him?"

"Ah well ... it's not something we talk of, ever," said Juliette strongly.

"What happened to him?" repeated Henry, knowing the answer, but deliberately pressing the point.

"He was executed, guillotined in Bordeaux's jail. Now you see why we never talk about him." Juliette got up and left the breakfast table. As far as she was concerned, the conversation was over.

Henry thought no more about his complicated family past as he poured English-made tomato sauce over his, by now cold, cooked English breakfast, and started to eat. He had staked his claim to Château de Gressier. More importantly, he knew what he was going to do with the rest of his life. He was going to study viticulture and become an oenologist.

Chapter 9

Bordeaux November 1962

"YOU WILL BE joining the world's second oldest profession," said the Dean of the Institute of Wine and Wine Sciences, with a smile as he and Henry settled down to discuss the oenology course at the Université de Bordeaux.

It was a different interview from the one Henry had with the faculty at Birmingham University two years earlier. This time he was a discerning purchaser. It meant that the course content was discussed in detail, with Henry making it clear what he expected his tutors to deliver. He was arrogantly confident that, having worked in the fields and winery of de Gressier for nearly 15 years, his practical knowledge of winemaking would be as good as anyone who taught on the course. What he wanted to learn was the science of wine. In particular, how different grape varieties could be blended for the best results. He noted that the syllabus extended far beyond this remit, as it included courses on marketing, contract and consumer law, and bookkeeping and accounts. Henry wondered whether history was about to repeat itself, as he knew he would not work at any subject which didn't interest him, but nevertheless it didn't put him off.

It was a foregone conclusion, not so much because of his famous grandmother, but the confidence with which he conducted himself in the interview, that Henry would be offered a place starting in September 1963.

It was whilst contemplating what he was going to do with himself until his university course started that Henry discovered the Institute of the Masters of Wine. He was immediately attracted to its qualification and the prestige it held. Henry applied to study and sit the exams, for it was the best, and he only like being involved with the best. To Henry's chagrin, his application was rejected. The Institute was open to only those in the wine trade and not to winemakers, which he considered himself to be. It was a ruling which the institute was not going to change for the next twenty-one years. Determined not to be beaten, Henry sought out their written exam papers. For the rest of his life, he religiously tested himself to make sure he could pass, and if he did not know an answer, he would research it until he did. When the institute's rules changed, and he was both eligible and knowledgeable enough to sit their exams, he never did. It was the fear of failure, which came with growing older, that kept him away.

Henry's thoughts now focused on only one thing: the world of winemaking. A world which went far beyond the shores of France. With the countryside in the northern hemisphere closing for winter, and with a yearning to visit the United States, Henry decided it was time to visit California and find out about the wines of the New World.

Chapter 10

Cape Town, South Africa September 1962 - April 1963

BIG JOE SLEPT rough for a few nights as he hitched into Cape Town. He took a longer, indirect route because he didn't want to be found by his father, who he thought might be searching for him. He was determined not to be discovered and face another whipping.

On the outskirts of Cape Town, close to the airport, Big Joe got a job in a car wash and from there he found digs close by in a shantytown; no more the clean white sheets of his upbringing, but the filth and stink attached to the dispossessed the world over. He was just twelve years old.

Big Joe had his parents' work ethic, and the work in the car wash was no harder than the work he'd been expected to do on the farm. In fact, he cleaned cars faster than his fellow workers and therefore did well from tips, which he could keep. With the extra money, his first task was to clean his digs with disinfectant so that each night he went to sleep with it stinging in his nose instead of the acrid smell of rot and decay which surrounded his new home.

Big Joe missed his mother desperately. He found the loneliness of the night unbearable, so he took a job on the night shift at a nearby American diner. And so, working 15 hours a day, Big Joe found a way to sleep.

Satutu was not sleeping. David was confident that Big Joe would soon return, but as the days went into weeks, and the weeks into months, Satutu's anxiety was badly affecting her health; she wasn't eating, and her body was fading away in front of his eyes. David set about the task of finding Big Joe to bring him home. It was going to be difficult for, as he had found when he first arrived, South Africa was a place in which it was easy to get lost if you did not want to be found. He hired a firm of private investigators and put adverts in all the newspapers throughout the Southern Cape, even the underground ones, with a large photograph of Big Joe, and offering a reward for information leading to his whereabouts.

"Hey, Joe," called out one of his workmates. "There's a picture of you in this paper. What's it all about? Why's yous wanted?" The workmate could not read, but the word *wanted* was widely known by even those who were illiterate.

Big Joe stopped washing the car he was working on, picked up the paper and stared at his picture. The amount of the reward for information leading to his whereabouts was staggering, but what affected Big Joe the most was reading of his mother's grief at his departure. That night, Big Joe telephoned home. The call was answered by his mother.

"I have information on Big Joe," he said, trying to disguise his voice without success for he had forgotten that it was only in the family and amongst the farm and village that he was known as Big Joe.

"Big Joe, Big Joe, is that you?" Satutu asked desperately.

Big Joe said nothing as his mother collapsed on the floor in tears of relief.

Sunetta picked up the phone, "Big Joe?"

"Sunetta is that you?" he asked.

"Yes," she said. "Mummy's crying so much she can't speak. Where are you? I'll get Dad." Sunetta's voice was cracking under emotion strain too.

"No, no," shouted Big Joe. "If you get Dad I'll hang up."

Questions poured from Sunetta's lips. "How are you? Where are you living? Where have you been? When are you coming home?" As always happened to Sunetta when she was anxious or excited, time slowed down, and she started to speak quietly with an emphasis on her diction.

"Not coming home, Hats," he said, using his abbreviation of her proper name Harriet. "It's over between Pa and me."

Satutu had recovered enough to take the phone from Sunetta. "Joe," she said: "I must see you."

"But without Pa," he said.

"Okay, okay," said Satutu desperately. "I must see you. When can we meet? I'm coming now."

"No," said Joe. "We'll meet tomorrow. Come alone and bring the reward money with you. Don't bring Pa," he emphasised once again. "I won't come if you bring Pa. You understand?"

"I understand," she said, her voice trembling with emotion.

The following evening, they met at the American diner where he worked. On seeing Big Joe, Satutu and Sunetta rushed towards him. They both grabbed hold of him and sobbed uncontrollably. Big Joe went quiet, his mouth going dry with emotion. Sunetta broke away first and proceeded to pound her fists on his chest in anger as though she was beating on a drum.

"Don't you dare do that, don't you dare do that again," she yelled. Then she spoke slowly and quietly, "We're mates," she said. "We're mates Joe, you and me, and you don't treat mates like that. Joe, you understand?" she said almost threatening him.

Big Joe said nothing. He simply nodded as he pointed them towards an empty table.

They sat down and Sunetta went to the counter and ordered drinks. She was pleased to be away for just a moment as the emotion was too overwhelming.

At the table Satutu said nothing. She looked at her son carefully and studied his well-being. His hair was longer, but he and his clothes were spotlessly clean. His eyes were bright and when he smiled his white teeth continued to sparkle. With the absence of time, she no longer saw a child, for there was no longer a child to see, but a man. A very young man maybe, but now grown up with a capability and independence which his father would be proud, if they weren't so much the same.

"Where are you living?" she asked.

"Not far from here," he said being deliberately vague.

"Are you working? she asked.

"Yes, not far from here," he replied, again providing no details. "I'm do'in well, making good money," he said boastfully.

"Big Joe, please come home," Satutu begged.

"No," said Big Joe firmly. "I've moved on Ma, and going home would be going backwards."

Sunetta joined them. There was silence as she laid out the drinks. She deliberately sat beside her brother taking hold of his hand, and as she sat close, their arms intertwined.

"What will you do now?" asked Satutu. "Your father will be so disappointed if you don't go to university."

"He only has himself to blame," said Big Joe, with sourness in his voice.

"No Joe," said Satutu. "You're both to blame. We're all to blame. What you did to Little Joe was wrong, and you know it."

"Yes Ma," Big Joe agreed. "I was a kid then. I've grown up a bit since then. What Pa did was wrong too. You have to admit it."

Satutu said nothing.

"And you supported him Ma," Big Joe said defiantly.

"You did wrong Big Joe, but we've all learned a lot since then," said Satutu.

All three held hands on the tabletop and talked. They spoke about their father mostly, trying to understand the complexity of his character. They questioned what it was which drove him to be kinder and more generous outside of his family. As they spoke, both Big Joe and Sunetta quietly wondered about their mother and father's lives before they met. It was clouded in secrets and mystery.

As they chatted there was a slow healing between Big Joe, Satutu and Sunetta, but it was clear to all that a rapprochement between Big Joe and his father was a long way off, and so was not mentioned. They agreed to meet in two days' time in the same place. There was no more to say.

Satutu reached into her handbag and took out 10,000 Rand and handed it to Big Joe.

"I don't expect that Ma," said Big Joe. "I was angry with Pa, and since he buys everyone else with money, well, I thought he could buy this meeting too. But I don't want it Ma, I don't need it, honest, I don't."

"I'm sure you don't," said Satutu. "Whatever you think of your father he's an honourable man, he said he'd pay, and he'd want me to make sure you have it. In fact, I want you to have it Joe. Please take it."

Big Joe stared at the bundle of notes in the white envelope with his name written on it with his father's hand. He looked into his mother's eyes, she nodded gently and smiled. Her face lit up and she radiated a joy not seen since Little Joe was tied to a chair all those months ago. She pushed the envelope towards him, and Big Joe did as she asked. He took the money from the table and stuffed it deep into his inside jacket pocket.

"It's time to go," said Big Joe, taking command. "I'll walk you to the car."

Big Joe didn't want them following him. He had already made plans for his own escape unobserved. At Satutu's car they each hugged and kissed with Satutu holding onto him longer than she might, feeling the muscles in his arms chest and stomach. His strength of character poured into her heart and she knew that, whatever happened, Big Joe would be alright.

When they were in the car Big Joe leaned over Satutu's window and said, "Don't park up and try and follow me," he instructed. "I'll be okay. See you, same time, same place on Wednesday." He stood up, walked back a few paces and watched them go. As he walked back into the restaurant, he opened a slip of paper which he found in his pocket, placed there secretly by Sunetta when they sat next to each other. The paper was smooth white, taken from his father's study, and so he was surprised to find just one sentence written in Sunetta's perfect hand. *It happened to me too, remember xxx.*

"It did Hats," acknowledged Big Joe out loud, and he turned to walk inside.

Chapter 11

California November 1962 – July 1963

HENRY FLEW INTO San Francisco determined to learn about the wines of California. He thought he would be there a few days. As it turned out, he stayed for nearly nine months, returning to be with his mother over the Christmas period. He couldn't bear the thought of her being on her own at this time.

Within the first hour of his visit to the San Francisco City Library, Henry discovered that California had five major wine regions, which were split into more than one hundred smaller American Viticulture Areas. Each area had its own proliferation of wineries from the very largest of producers to some small-volume vintages from highly celebrated micro wineries.

The next day Henry hired a car and headed north out of San Francisco into what were soon to become two of the most prestigious wine growing regions in the world, the Nappa and Sonoma Valleys. Henry popped into winery after winery, visiting as a buyer, but learnt little about what they were doing. The saleswomen who greeted him, for they were nearly always attractive young women, just saw him as a punter to get drunk and sell their wines. Sadly, they had little knowledge of what they were selling. Wine tourism, which was later to become a highly professional business for the area, was nascent in its development.

As Henry sniffed, tasted and then spat out the wine, rinsing his mouth with water, before he moved onto the next variety, he found it all exceptionally frustrating. The fact was that, even remaining sober, his memory of one wine was lost in the memory of another.

It was a dejected man who returned to San Francisco to travel its trams, and wander along the harbour front, for Henry's trip into the winelands had taught him little. It was a chance conversation in a scruffy Italian restaurant, before going to the theatre, which gave him some direction for the next day. After he had explained to a husband-and-wife team that he was touring the winelands of the world, before going to the Université de Bordeaux, they suggested he should go to Stanford University, their old university, instead.

Bereft of alternative things to do, and with the husband's business card in his pocket, Henry drove out of San Francisco to Stanford University's South American style campus with its sandy stone buildings. He wandered around its shop and library. After a little while, he found a young assistant in the Admissions Office who was only too keen to talk to this Englishman about the courses Stanford had on offer.

Henry was to discover that day, although he only became conscious of it much later, how a cut glass British accent was an assured panties remover, for the stronger the accent he laid on, the quicker his seduction of the nubile women of the 'new world'. Henry also discovered something else, a case of Château de Gressier claret was an opener to many a closed establishment.

The young woman in the Admissions Office had family membership at the highly prestigious Menlo Country Club, so it was here that they agreed to meet after she had finished work. A case of wine, the endorsement of his host and the payment of a truly exorbitant membership fee, saw Henry admitted into temporary membership, conditional, it was whispered in his ear, upon him wearing proper attire in future.

It was the requirement to be properly dressed which caused Henry an immediate, and first time, money problem. He was getting very short of cash. He had money in England, plenty of it, but the UK government's exchange control regulations limited the amount of money he could take out of the country to £50 per day. It was this restriction which was now severely hampering what he wanted to do. Luckily, he had a solution in the Banque de Mamie. Although France had similar external exchange control restrictions, by arranging a loan from Juliette he found a way to effectively double his UK Government allowance.

Once the money had been cabled to him Henry went shopping in the enormous Stanford Park's Bloomingdales shopping centre. Thus, adorned in the distinctive style of the Bay Area, he started to make use of the country club and mix with the generation of leaders who would be responsible for the silicon and digital era. It was the start of him creating a network of contacts, some of whom would become the wealthiest men in the world.

It was through the Country Club's membership secretary that Henry was offered an unpaid internship at the Beringer Vineyards in the countryside outside of St. Helena in the Nappa Valley. He accepted with alacrity for, although it was just under ninety years old, it was the oldest continuously operating winery in the region. Out went the red open-top Chevrolet Corvette because it was too expensive to hire, and in came a highly dangerous third or fourth-hand Triumph 350cc motorbike. Three times in the first two days Henry came off this machine, each time badly scraping his skin on the tarmac and bruising himself as he came to a rapid stop.

Henry quickly fell into a double life, enjoying being a playboy with the Menlo Country Club set at the weekend and a farmhand during the week. It was as a farmhand that he started to learn new things about winemaking. In the evenings, being a long way from anywhere, he started to read anything and everything about wine he could find. He read about the plants, the pruning, the fertilisers, the barrels, the presses, the yeasts, the fermentation and the adverse effects of oxygen. He studied the bottles, the corks and the machinery. There was not an element of winemaking he did not study, and as he did so, he wrote down everything, creating his own encyclopaedia of winemaking.

As Henry flew back to England in July 1963, he knew that his biggest learning was cultural. In Bordeaux winemaking was treated as an art and with romance; each winery boasting a special 'je ne sais quoi'. In the nascent wineries of the Nappa Valley, it was a science and a business. If France wasn't careful, Henry concluded, it would lose its cachè of being the world's best producer of wine.

Chapter 12

Cape Town August 1963

DESPITE SATUTU AND Sunetta working hard to bring the two men together, the rapprochement between Big Joe and his father was a slow affair. The two men each agreed that they were wrong but stubbornly blamed the other as being more wrong. The family gene which saw the rift between David, Juliette and their father was operating in the next generation without any dilution.

Big Joe was adamant that he was never coming back to work on the farm, but there was a mild change of heart after Satutu impressed upon Big Joe that all their lives' work would have been worthless if he wasn't around to look after the farm once Pa had died.

"I'm much younger than Pa, but I won't be able to do this on my own," said Satutu. "One day apartheid will end in this country. We must be prepared for when that happens. It could be chaos." Her voice became pleading in nature. "We don't know what will happen, but we will be stronger together, believe me."

It was probably Sunetta's pleading to Big Joe, that he had a responsibility to plan for his whole family's future, which swayed the argument, for there was a love bond between the three siblings which was as strong as it was rare. After much discussion, it was agreed that Big Joe would finish school in the UK and with 'A' levels under his belt he would go on to university to read Land Management.

Big Joe and his father were reunited at the airport for a few minutes just before Big Joe caught the aeroplane to London. They shook hands formally but said little. David handed Big Joe a small box, about 24 inches long and 2 inches wide, wrapped in brown paper.

Satutu and Sunetta said their goodbyes to Big Joe. These were strangely formal, for it was their Bantu birth right which denied them the ability to show their breaking hearts. Was it not the plight of every Bantu mother to see her young child leave the village, never to return? Had she not gone into the unknown from her mother too, just as every animal which roams freely on the range? She'd had Big Joe living with her longer than most she thought, and knowing he was off to a good life in a country which stood firmly against apartheid, gave her the comfort she needed to bear their parting with fortitude. If anything, it was David, with his European sentimentality, who found the parting hard, for he knew that whatever they once had was no longer there.

Once through immigration and seated at the boarding gate Big Joe unwrapped his father's gift. Inside was his grandfather's officer's cane which had been used to thrash him. Big Joe gently stroked the polished wood and then ran his fingers over the silver top, embossed with the Hampshire Regiment's emblem and the steel cap at the bottom. As Big Joe studied how brightly the silver shone, and guessing that his Father had specially cleaned it, his words rang in his ears.

"I no longer need this," said his father, as he handed over his present. He paused, then continued: "But understand this, let your mother down and you won't be coming home again, at least … not during my lifetime."

Big Joe got up and walked to one of the trash bins. There, in disgust, he threw away the military cane and its packaging. His father wasn't going to apologise to him this way. Just as he was walking away from the bin, Big Joe suddenly stopped. It dawned on him that this was not his father apologising, for he would never do such a thing. It was his way of recognising Big Joe's transition into manhood. It was the continuation of a family tradition, from one generation to another, honoured throughout the passage of time. This gift was his father's way of acknowledging him as an adult, a man capable of being an officer. Was this Pa's way of saying how proud he was of him, Big Joe wondered? From the firmness of the handshake and, remembering the warmth in his father's face, he decided it was so. With dampness in his eyes, Big Joe turned and retrieved the cane. When he learnt of its history many years later, it was to become his most prized possession.

Immediately after Big Joe left for England, David's attention turned to Sunetta's education. Like her brother she could not go to one of the better South African universities. Her father insisted that she, too, did land management and that she should go to the Royal Agricultural College in Cirencester, England. Secretly, he thought she would find a good husband there. Sunetta was horrified. She had found a passion for dance and sport, and it was in this area that she wanted to make her career. Why couldn't she go to England and learn to be a ballerina, she would implore. 'It's not serious work' her mother would say, insisting that if she was to study anything then it should be done with French. Were they not a French family, she would argue? The need for culture in the family and the fact that hard work did no one any harm made Satutu determined in her ambition for her daughter.

With her parents' minds made up, the project plan to get Sunetta into university went into the list in David's bulldog clip of torn up papers, from which he managed the running of the whole farm. This early day Filofax™ was now the only physical remnant that David had from his days in the army and the Western Front.

The Daunier household was far mellower after, what had become known as, 'the Big Joe interlude'. The 'menace', with which his children thought their father walked around the house and farm, had gone. There was no doubt that David had been genuinely chastised by the event. He did not want anything like it to happen again. It was not Big Joe's response which had shaken him. He saw that as his son learning to be a man in a man's world; it was something which just had to be done. No, it was the hurt that had been caused, mainly to Satutu but also in some part the pain suffered by Sunetta and Little Joe, which had distressed him. It was a lesson he had well and truly learned. He was also beginning to feel his age, and with it came a vulnerability he had not felt before. He started to wonder what it had all been for if his sons didn't inherit his farm.

Chapter 13

Bordeaux September 1963 - November 1963

HENRY STARTED AT the Université de Bordeaux with enormous enthusiasm. Immediately he found a huge contrast between the Birmingham and Bordeaux campuses. They could not have been more different. Bordeaux was more serious; some might describe it as peremptory in its attitude. As hard as he tried, he could not find the fun which had permeated throughout Birmingham during his first year. The seeds of student resentment, which were to explode with rioting on the streets of Paris five years later, were already starting to appear.

Henry found the science and chemistry of winemaking fascinating. The rest of his course was a huge disappointment. He found the viticulture elements of the course much less interesting than he expected. Studying the exact biological differences between the grape varieties he found tedious, until he appreciated their chemistry. When it came to accounting, he thought the strictures of double entry bookkeeping were incomprehensible. Why, he asked himself, was the debit always nearest the wall, when in any room he sat the damn wall was on all sides? And why, above why, was it that when he paid money into his bank, and they credited his account, it ended up on the debit side of the balance sheet? None of it made sense.

It was in the chemistry department Henry felt back at home. Thanks to his first year at Birmingham Henry had learnt not only how to use the equipment in the lab, but why it worked. Helped by the occasional bottle of Château de Gressier claret, he was given the freedom to use the vast array of equipment which measured and analysed every aspect of a wine's liquid. Using this equipment, he would take samples from two bottles from the same vineyard and of the same vintage and compare and contrast them, making and recording microscopic differences in measurement. He would then take samples from two more bottles from the same vineyard but another year later and then a year after that and do the same thing. He was beginning to teach himself how wine could be classified by its chemistry.

Whenever he thought of a test he might undertake and the equipment he needed was not in the university, he went looking for it. For example, he needed an electronic nose to accurately measure and record smell, likewise a spectrophotometer to record and measure colour. As a result, other chemistry labs in England and France opened their doors to his research, such was the collegiate nature of academics.

Henry's attention to detail, and his recording of data, was as messianic as any man who had suddenly found religion. Once again, he had found one area of the course which had interested him to the exclusion of everything else.

To mark the 100th anniversary of Louis Pasteur's wine research the University's School of Oenology held its First International Symposium of Oenology in the Palais de la Bourse. It was Henry's first year, and it was here he discovered his seventh heaven. For the first time he heard scientists and researchers talk about the work they were doing in chemistry and microbiology, even in the neurosciences, with a complexity way beyond what he was being taught as a first-year student. As he mixed amongst this international group he felt as though he was with his peer group, for there was not a point they were making which he didn't understand or have a view on or wanted to learn far more.

A few weeks later Henry was summoned to the Dean's office for a mid-term review of his progress. He was not worried as he had not missed a day; in fact, he had worked so hard he had been at the laboratory bench most weekends. Surprisingly, his course tutor was there and everything which Henry feared about history repeating itself, should he join Université de Bordeaux, was suddenly proven right. He was told, in no uncertain terms, that if he failed to attend another biology, accounting or marketing lecture without a reasonable excuse, he would be expelled. "The University was not," he was emphatically told, "his personal chemistry set to play with as he wished but a serious place of learning." There was no recognition of the research work Henry had been doing in the chemistry laboratories, albeit that the other scientists in there had admired the painstaking way he went about his work.

Henry had no lectures or tutorials that afternoon. Even if he had it would have made no difference. He got on his motorbike, and with his mind focused only on how unfairly he had been treated, he drove with the same style and speed of his grandfather to Château de Gressier.

Juliette was far more sympathetic to Henry's situation than he could have ever imagined, for she knew, from talking to him over the months, exactly what had been going on.

Henry's voice was close to despair as he told her what had happened. "Those damn people think Bordeaux has some God-given right to produce the best wine in the world, but they don't realise they're competing in a market where stainless steel is replacing oak. Where wine varieties are now being blended precisely to suit the pallet of the buyer. They don't get it. They simply don't get it," he protested.

"Which country should you go to now?" asked Juliette. "Australia?" she said, in a sense making the decision for him that he should leave immediately. "I gather Argentina and Peru produce some good wines too."

"Or South Africa or New Zealand?" suggested Henry. "Where do I go to in Argentina?" Henry asked absentmindedly.

"How do I know?" said Juliette, with exasperation in her voice. "You go to the capital city, Buenos Aires, spend 10 or 12 weeks in a language school learning their funny kind of Spanish, and work out where to go from there."

"Mamie, unless we take care, these new countries are not only going to eat our breakfast they are going to eat our lunch too," said Henry returning earnestly to his theme.

Juliette nodded and then added, "Just make sure you're back by the middle of August for the harvest. I think it's important you are..." Just at that moment came a shout from the kitchen.

"Madame, Madame," shouted her housekeeper in total panic. "President Kennedy's been shot! Quick, quick, turn on the television."

The housekeeper's shouts brought other people from the estate who'd now gathered in total silence around the black-and-white television, as it warmed up. The first sight was of a card which read 'We interrupt this programme for Breaking News.' They then heard the announcement: *"It has been confirmed that President Kennedy has died from gunshot wounds."* There was a pause as the announcer took hold of his emotions before continuing:

"At 12.30 pm Central Standard Time, President Kennedy was travelling in an open top car in a motorcade through Dallas when three shots were fired. Observers saw President Kennedy shot in the head and blood spurt out. ... Mrs Kennedy, who was by the President's side, was heard to shout out 'oh no.' Immediately after the shots were fired a secret service agent ran onto the back of the President's car as it sped off to Portland Hospital where he was pronounced dead." It was 22nd November 1963.

That evening Juliette tried to write to Joe Kennedy, her old friend and former business colleague, to extend her deepest sympathy at the death of his son. She knew he had suffered a bad stroke but wrote in the hope that someone would read him her letter and he would understand. It was her third letter of commiserations to Joseph, and she did not know what else to say. She felt she had said it all before. She had first written when his son Joseph Junior had died in combat during the war. She wrote again following the death of his daughter Kick[4]. She and Joseph had just lunched together in Paris when the dreadful news of his daughter's death in a plane crash was announced.

---

[4] Kathleen Kennedy had been married for only six weeks when her husband was killed by sniper fire during the war. Lord Hartington, a married man, was to die in the same plane crash. It was later reported that they were having an affair and on their way to Paris to ask Joseph's permission to get married. Kick's mother, Rose Kennedy, refused to attend the funeral, attributing her daughter's death to God taking its retribution.

President Kennedy's death reminded Juliette of a story that Jack Morris, a long-standing friend, had told her about Rose Kennedy, very shortly after Joseph Kennedy had started buying de Gressier wine during the prohibition period. Rose was Joe's wife and Joseph, Kick and John Kennedy's mother. The rumour was that, at the age of fourteen, Rose had been sent from Boston, USA on a European educational tour, but it was nothing of the sort. Instead, she was sent to Norwich, England and a Catholic home for unmarried mothers. There she had a baby who was put up for adoption. On leaving the home, and her baby behind, Jack said that the nuns had placed a curse on Rose damning her that she should live to see each of her children die. Was this the curse at work, Juliette pondered. Was this the reason Rose had become so religious – doing the only thing she could do – pray for her adopted child, she wondered.

In difficulty, she wrote as she had done before. She spoke of the kind letter Joseph had written to her when Étienne was killed, and again when Victor had drowned. Once again she reminded him of the happy few days they had spent together at Château de Gressier, when he was Ambassador to the United Kingdom, just before the outbreak of World War II. It was at a time when the weight of the world appeared to lay heavily on his shoulders. She wrote of how steadfastly he bore his burden then, and how she was sure he would be able to bear it now. She offered him and his wife, Rose, her thoughts and prayers. As she blotted the ink dry, Juliette felt another chapter in her life close.

Apart from their evening walks, Juliette and Henry remained inside the Château glued to either the television or the radio. They stayed there until they had watched the President's funeral on the following Monday, 25th November. There was not a dry eye as they watched four-year-old John Kennedy Jnr, affectionately known as John-John, salute the casket of his father. Somehow there were more important things to worry about than Bordeaux University.

The following day, Henry took the bus back to the university. There he gathered his notebooks and things from his university bedroom. He left quietly without saying goodbye. He caught the next train to Paris and returned home to be with his mother in England. He would do what he had done before, teach himself. This time, he was going to become a wine scientist by studying the vineyards of the world. Fuck 'em all, he thought, I'm going to become a leading Oenologist, if it's the last damn thing I do!

Chapter 14

Cape District, South Africa November 1963

IF THERE WAS sadness in Château de Gressier at the death of President Kennedy, there were tears of despair within New Found Estate as David, Satutu, Sunetta and Little Joe mourned the death of a man who was as racially agnostic as any human being is capable.

Like the rest of the western world, the Daunier family hibernated for those four days between Kennedy's death and his funeral. They worried about their future for they knew it was indelibly linked to the fight for racial equality, and that fight had just lost one of its major leaders.

"Who will protect us now against the crime of apartheid and the white supremacists?" asked Satutu, of anyone who was prepared to listen.

Chapter 15

New Found Estate, South Africa January 1964

HANK BELLANGER ARRIVED in Cape Town just after the New Year. During his time in California Henry had decided that his name was too effete and English, so he chose to call himself Hank, thinking it was more modern and in-keeping with the times.

The plane landed in the morning and Hank took the bus into the centre of the city where he got off and wandered around looking for an hotel. He had already discovered that bus and train stations, the world over, were magnets for reasonable quality, cheap hotel rooms. After wandering into three or four, he found one which he thought looked okay and booked a room for just a couple of days as the deal involved him paying up front. There he showered, dumped his rucksack, flight bag and crash helmet.

In the afternoon he went in search of a second-hand motorbike; 250 or 350cc's with around six to eight thousand miles on the clock. Buying the bike was always the easy bit. Getting it taxed and insured was always the challenge, but it was one which could be solved if the shop owner wanted the sale badly enough. Later that afternoon, Hank took the cable car up Table Mountain where he stared out over the Victoria & Albert Waterfront, and across the bay towards Robin Island, not yet the prison of Nelson Mandela, its most famous future inhabitant.

The purchase of the bike was completed the next day, and by lunch time with his panniers full, and his rucksack a much lighter load on his back, Henry headed off to find the winelands of South Africa, with his first stop Stellenbosch. Taking a far from direct route, he travelled first south behind Table Top Mountain through Constantia, where the mega-rich of Cape Town live, and then towards the sea. At the coast, he turned east and rode along the coast road until it naturally turned north again. He found a bed and breakfast close to the Stellenbosch University campus, which he used as his base as each day he travelled out to visit the many wineries and vineyards of the area.

After five days, Henry packed up his motorbike again and drove over the mountains, this time to Franschoek where, from another Bed and Breakfast, he spent another five days visiting the vineyards of the locality. Finally, he headed back over the mountains to Paarl where he stopped for a couple of days and then went on to Wellington where he stayed for a few more days.

At each vineyard he tasted the wines but never drank them. He made copious notes on the colour, clarity, viscosity and smell of their wines, the variety of grapes they grew, the way they looked after their soil, the ingredients they added to keep it fertile, and whether they irrigated their vines during the growing season. Most importantly, if they had a winery and produced their own Estate Wines, he would buy two bottles of wine of each variety from the three most recent years' production, which he paid to have sent back to his mother's house in Hertford, UK.

After Wellington, Hank intended to travel back to Cape Town, sell his bike and go home. As he travelled back towards Paarl he spotted a vineyard he had not seen or visited before. He was attracted to it by the brand-new entrance which he hadn't noticed when he'd travelled past going in the opposite direction. Set in two large brick walls either side of the entrance were two very large blocks of imported limestone into which the words 'New Found Estate' had been carved.

As Hank drove past he felt a familiarity with the name 'Found' for it was the same name as the house he had inherited from his great-grandfather. He thought about it for a moment, turned around and drove up the drive.

He stopped at the white ranch style house at the top of a slight hill and rang the bell. The door was answered by Satutu. There was a standoff as each studied the other, for neither was what they expected. A slim black woman in tight white jeans, a tied white top, long white cotton gloves and wearing a crocheted cap was facing a young faced white boy on a motorbike who looked as though he'd never done a day's work in his life.

They exchanged a few words after which Satutu pointed him in the direction of the office with instructions to look for her husband. At the office Hank was thrown again for he assumed, like everyone before him, that Satutu's husband would be black too.

Given his age, mode of dress and transport, David assumed that Hank had come for a summer picking job, so he sent him straight to the back office where the farm manager signed him up. Henry had his first paid job ever. He was in luck, he was told, as tomorrow they would be picking early season plums.

"Not grapes?" asked Henry surprised.

"Where are you from Ishie Boy? The grapes will be another couple of weeks," said the farm manager and with that he feigned spitting on the ground in disapproval, before pointing Henry in the direction of the dormitory for the transient crop pickers.

Sunetta loved harvest time for the freedom it gave her to run, move, chase and even just breathe, so very different to the claustrophobia of the classroom.

Immediately they got to the first field Sunetta missed Big Joe. For as long as she could remember they had worked side by side at harvest time. In recent years, it had been Big Joe's job to lift the baskets of picked fruit on to the scales and then onto the trailer. It was her job to record the weight collected by each picker so their wages could be calculated, but most importantly to check that no stones had been added into the baskets to increase the weight, and thus their pay.

On first sight Sunetta thought Henry, or Hank as she was invited to call him, skinny; dismissing him as lacking the strength of the other field workers. It was a fact that the loader's job was the hardest. It was solely on racial grounds that the farm manager gave the job to the ishie white boy.

On the very first day of working together Sunetta noticed Hank's legs and calf muscles, the pecks on his chest and the ripples of his stomach muscles. She enjoyed watching as his pale white body reddened and glistened in the sun from the dampness of his perspiration. She was fascinated by his long wavy hair, so very different to the others around. Above all she was enthralled as the boy was not *ishie*. Hank was quietly holding his own, impressing the others as he dealt with the toughest job with a laugh and a string of good-humoured banter, however high he had to lift the heavy baskets.

Whilst Sunetta was observing Hank, he was studying her too. In fact, on occasions he couldn't but help stare, for her face was very round and very pretty. Like her mother's, it sat on a long slender neck. Her hair was black and obviously long, even though it was tied up in a bun to keep out the dust from the trees. Her eyes were large and dark auburn in colour, which mesmerized him as they contrasted brightly against the whites of her eyes. She had the tiniest of noses. Her limbs were long and somewhat gangly, not always acting in co-ordination to her body, like the legs of a new-born lamb just starting to walk.

Whilst she didn't have the grace of her mother, Sunetta stood very tall too. She had inherited Sunetta's perfect skin, albeit a much lighter mahogany in colour. To the observer, Sunetta was in those transformative years; childhood was a long time ago and she had comfortably matured into girlhood. There was no doubt that she would grow into a beautiful woman.

David was always in the fields during harvest, from the lifting of dew until dusk. Although the farm manager was in charge, it was David who stalked the pickers, making sure they did the job properly, encouraging and scolding in equal measure. He had proven to himself that his supervision at harvest time improved the yields and even though he was now aged seventy-three he was not going to give up doing so just yet.

When the loader was full, the farm manager instructed Hank and Sunetta to take it back to the barn where they were to unload and store the baskets in racking until the next day when, before the dew came off the field and they went into another day of back aching work, the pickers would sort the previous day's crop.

There were no other workers in the barn as they were all in the fields, so it was Sunetta's job to hand down the baskets from the trailer for Hank to stack, just as Big Joe had done for years before. After the second or third load had been delivered and safely stacked, they both moved towards the water barrel, as they had done each time before, for a wash down and drink.

Sunetta teasingly flicked Hank with water. He flicked water back. Soon they were in a full water fight just as she had been with her brothers many times before. Then, in one motion, Hank grabbed her, holding her close to him. Squeezing her under the armpits he lifted Sunetta up in one slow movement until she was high in the air with his arms locked. Suddenly, he dropped her, catching her in a horizontal wrap. His left arm was holding her from underneath, and with his right arm, he wrapped her legs around his body. Hank leaned forward and stopped for a moment; both were gazing into each other's eyes. Very gently, almost tentatively, Hank kissed Sunetta on the lips. Sunetta was captivated by the sensation, for his lips were warm and welcoming.

As Hank placed her on the ground, Sunetta abruptly pulled away in embarrassment and shock. After regaining her composure, she responded by gently kissing him back whilst pulling herself tightly into him. Their kissing became stronger and more passionate. The fun which had accompanied all the water games she had played with her brothers, and which had started this one, was gone in an instant; replaced by an unexplained intensity. They both felt overwhelmed by the emotion which caused them to break apart, whilst at the same time not wanting to. Both felt slightly embarrassed by what had gone before.

On the next trip back to the barn, after they had unloaded all the baskets of fruit, it was Sunetta who started another water fight. As before, after they had soaked each other, Hank picked her up, threw her into the air and caught her, again wrapping her around his body. This time Hank carried Sunetta to the back of the barn where he laid her gently on a pile of hay bales. He climbed beside her. She felt excited as his warm breath came close to her face. Soon their lips touched and after a nanosecond of hesitation they were kissing each other passionately on the mouth. His hand gently lifted the edge of Sunetta's t-shirt and he stroked her smooth flat tummy, with one of his fingers playing with her tummy button. Hank's hands moved further on to her young, tender and not fully developed breasts. Her senses

were heightened by his warm soft hands as they gently rubbed her
nipples which became ever more erect as he did so. Hank moved away
from Sunetta's mouth, kissing her ears, neck and then, as her breasts
became exposed, he teased each of her nipples with his tongue, and
for the first time, she sensed them get aroused and start to feel hard.

Sunetta's mind was overwhelmed with emotions she had never felt
before. It was in this confusion that she noticed Hank had stopped
kissing her. She watched as his hands undid the laces of her boots
sliding them both off her feet, which he gently massaged, before
turning his attention to the button on her shorts and unzipping
her fly. Sunetta reached down to stop him, somehow sensing it was
wrong, but in response Hank's mouth moved between her mouth,
her neck, her nipples and the flat of her stomach and, as he kissed
her passionately on the mouth, Hank's fingers gently lifted the edge
of her knickers, and soon they were gently massaging a soft spot
between her legs.

Sunetta found the sensation incredible. This new sensation
consumed her. She didn't want him to stop. On the contrary, she
encouraged him by groaning in delight and kissing him back. Slowly,
he worked her shorts and panties over her buttocks, across her hips
and down to her knees until Sunetta was kicking them off so she
could openly respond to his touch.

Sunetta's eyes, when open, were only focused on Hank's beautiful
face. When closed, her focus was on the ecstasy of the moment. Hank
urgently kicked off his boots and wriggled out of his jeans. Very gently
he moved on top of her and, for the first time, Sunetta felt his erection
press on her pubic bone, as she ran her hands across his muscled back,
his clenched buttocks and tight thighs. Everything about him was so
smooth and so very hard.

Hank moved his hands under her body and then, from underneath,
he held tightly onto her shoulders, sliding down Sunetta's body as
he did so. Holding her so she could not move away, she winced as
she felt him try to push into her in a clumsily misdirected manner.
Sunetta was getting frightened and confused, for whilst she wanted
him to stop hurting her, she didn't want the sensation she was feeling
to stop. Suddenly she threw her head back and screamed involuntarily

several times as he forced himself deeper inside. Hank lifted himself off her chest and in doing so, he streamed into her body and, with his stillness, the discomfort Sunetta was feeling subsided.

Sunetta looked into his eyes and for a lifetime she would remember how his face expressed everything about the moment; at one stage tight and rigid, just as he had felt inside her, and then breaking into a loving satisfied smile as she felt him relax.

As they travelled back to the fields Sunetta thought only of the moment just past; the joy, the pain, the submission. Yet she also felt a huge surge of confidence, for she knew she had something men wanted, and that gave her a sense of power. Hank walked as though he were the cock of the walk, delighted that he'd had sex for the first time with a virgin.

Sunetta and Hank returned from the fields a few more times that day. When the barn was empty, they would make love; with Sunetta not realising that, for Hank, they were just having rampant sex.

Chapter 16

New Found Estate, South Africa January 1964

THAT EVENING, AS Sunetta lay in the bath soaking away the dirt of the day, with feelings of wonderment, contentment, and even some excitement at what might happen next, Hank was walking from the mess house, where he had just eaten, back to the dormitory. It was pitch black with no light from the sky. He was suddenly grabbed, a hand across his throat which slammed his back hard against the wooden fence, his head banged against a jaggered beam. The hand moved higher up his neck, its fingers digging deep into the soft flesh under his jawbone. Hank grabbed the arm in an attempt to release himself, but instead he found he was clinging onto it as the arm went higher, lifting him off the ground by the neck. Then, in an instance, Hank felt himself being grabbed by the crutch, fingers digging deep into his testicles, with the denim material of his trousers offering no protection. From these two points, Hank was lifted into the air until his eyes came directly opposite two white eyes staring at him through the darkness. He was being held there unable to move.

"Has you been messin' with Missy?" came a voice with a deep African accent from just below the eyes. Hank couldn't answer; his windpipe was contracted under the pressure of the man's hand.

"Has you been messin' with Missy?" said the voice again. This time Hank saw flashes of whiteness from his teeth. Still Hank didn't answer, so the man squeezed his balls even tighter, at which point Hank's whole mind was taken over by the excruciating pain in his lower abdomen.

Hank started kicking and wriggling furiously, as he was now fighting for his life, and so the man swung him around and slammed him hard against the wall of the dormitory. The crash of flesh on brick was so furious that all the air was knocked out of him. Hank felt his brain shake violently inside his skull as, after another throw, his head came to a rapid halt against a rock-hard wooden post. Each of the grips was too tight for him to move without causing more pain, and in a state of semi consciousness, he knew he was slowly being strangled to death, and there was nothing he could do about it.

In his confusion Hank heard the voice say. "She was just fifteen last week. Do you get it boy!" Suddenly Hank knew what this was about. The man pulled Hank close so that their faces nearly touched. In a very soft voice, which spoke very slowly, he said, "If you mess with Missy the boss will have me..." Hank didn't recognise the next words, they appeared to be a name, but he heard the rest very clearly, "...skin yers alive and then, when yers dead, we'll feed you to the pigs. You understand?"

Hank nodded vigorously, and just as he feared he was going to lose consciousness, the man released the grip he had around his throat, and still holding him by the crutch, let him pivot to one side and fall. The side of his face hit the ground hard and kicked up dust into his eyes. It was only then that the man released his grasp around Hank's crutch, letting him fall completely. Hank rolled into a ball to try and relieve the pain in his stomach, as his other injuries paled into insignificance against the damage he felt to his testicles.

The man leaned over Hank, grabbed his hair, pulled up his head and said loudly, "shut the fuck up." Then, when he'd got Hank's attention, and speaking in a soft whisper again, he said: "no messing with Missy, got it! The boss will turn this place evil, 'n we's don't want evil, so leave's her alone!"

The man stood up, kicked Hank once - aiming straight into his face, striking his cheek bone just below his eye socket, causing the skin to break and blood to flow. Once more he kicked, this time into Hank's ribs so hard that he thought he heard them crack. He yelled in pain and rolled into a ball to protect himself from more blows, only uncurling when he heard the crunch of departing footsteps.

That night in their own beds both Sunetta and Hank remembered the events of the day. Sunetta lived the romance; his kisses, his touch, his strength and the hopelessness she felt. Half a mile away as Hank nursed his wounds, he relived his taking of Sunetta's virginity from her gasping delights of encouragement to her muffled scream. It was so good he was going to do it all over again. The man in the gloom was not going to put him off. He would need to take more care, far more care, that was all.

Chapter 17

New Found Estate, South Africa January 1964

THE NEXT DAY the routine started all over again with Sunetta and Hank doing the weighing, loading and transporting whilst the others worked the field. Hank puzzled at why they had not been separated. Both came out more prepared. Hank with the results of an early trip to the chemist and Sunetta, now wearing a bra, carried spare knickers, a comb and tissues folded into her pocket. She asked about his injuries and was told that there had been a rag in the dormitory, and it was nothing to worry about, but she knew it was more than that, as she could see the bruises and him wince in pain when he lifted a basket high.

On the third trip to the barn Sunetta flicked water at him, just as she had done before. He lifted her up and carried her over to the hay where, this time, he lay down a tablecloth taken from the dormitory. Rapidly they undressed themselves. After some very heavy petting they were both ready for the coupling when Hank stopped, reached into his pocket, took out a foil wrapper and proceeded to unfurl a condom.

"What are you doing?" she asked.

"Making sure you don't get pregnant," he said, casually. "Yesterday we may have taken too many risks."

Pregnant, the word echoed in her brain getting louder with each recurrence.

"Could I be pregnant?" she asked, in shock.

Sunetta's mouth went dry as her first thoughts were not of her possible child, but of the disappointment of her mother and the anger of her father.

Hank played with Sunetta's body, but she did not respond. Her mind was completely frozen in fear. "You mean that can get me pregnant?" she said in disgust, throwing her hand in the direction of his crutch.

"Of course!" said Hank, surprised at her ignorance.

Sunetta was appalled at her own stupidity and cursed her mother for surely these were things she should have been told.

"And that stops me getting pregnant?" she said.

"Yes," he replied strongly.

"Why didn't you use one yesterday?"

"I didn't have them then" he said, defensively.

"Am I pregnant? Am I pregnant?" she asked him, demanding a reply.

"No, I doubt it. You can't get pregnant the first time," he said, inventing words of comfort.

"We did it more than once," she reminded him.

"Yes, but I didn't come much after the first time. The chances are very small, tiny," he said. "Don't worry about it." But of course, she did. Her worries killed the ardour of that moment and all those which might have throughout the rest of that day.

That evening, after her bath, Sunetta went to the Encyclopaedia Britannica, and read everything about her body and making babies. She was horrified to find that she could get pregnant the first time but became more relaxed as she worked out her dates, and discovered the odds were slight. She felt a strange disappointment as she had already worked out in her own mind that, if she were pregnant, Hank would marry her, Pa would make it so, and they would live together on the farm. There were problems, of course, for in South Africa it was unlawful to have sex with a girl under sixteen unless married. Further, it was illegal for Hank, who was white, to have sex with Sunetta, who was of mixed race. Why was it, she wondered, when she had been educated extensively in the rules of apartheid, she had not been taught how you made babies.

Yesterday Sunetta had felt powerful and confident but now she felt a need to be subservient to the man she knew she was in love with, the man who was the father of her baby. She would do anything and everything Hank asked to make sure he stayed.

Chapter 18

New Found Estate, South Africa January 1964

OVER THE NEXT week, they stopped picking the plums and moved to harvesting the grapes. This meant that Sunetta and Hank's opportunity for lovemaking became sparse. Nevertheless, when they did get those precious moments together Sunetta's actions were about making love; intent on pleasing him, for with each of her orgasm's she found she loved him more and became passionately for ever his. Whereas, if the truth were to be told, Hank's actions were about pleasing her to please himself.

On the Friday afternoon of the second week, when the foreman didn't want a white boy from England taking any more work from the locals, Hank was told to leave. The next day, with his pay in hand, he was sent packing with the first notch of a virgin carved proudly on his imaginary bed post.

Although it was all hands-on deck every day during harvest, Saturday and Sunday were the two days in the week when Sunetta had to help her mother with chores. This meant it wasn't until Monday morning when Sunetta was in the vine fields did she learn that Hank had gone. On hearing the news, she left and walked home, sobbing uncontrollably, where she took to her bed disconsolate in her grief for his leaving.

The fact that Hank had not said goodbye, nor even left a note, and the fear that she might be pregnant and her baby without a father, made her feel totally desolate. It was only when nature came calling and she knew she wasn't pregnant did she emerge from her solitude. She no longer ran, jumped, and skipped like a young lamb or foal in springtime. Instead, she had the poise, confidence, deportment and grace of a young woman, but with a renewed determination. Never, she swore, was any man ever going to use her like that again!

Chapter 19

South Africa April - September 1964

DAVID AND SATUTU watched every news report, listened to every radio broadcast, and read every serious newspaper article which covered the Rivonia Trial[5] which was taking place in Pretoria. Ten members of the African National Congress ('ANC') were on trial, accused of guerrilla warfare, sabotage and treason by conspiring to aid foreign powers against the Republic of South Africa. Amongst the ten defendants in the Pretoria trial was a young black lawyer named Nelson Mandela.

Not one of the Rivonia defendants was prepared to testify as a witness, and in the process submit themselves to cross examination.

---

[5] In July 1963, just eight months before the Rivonia Trial started, South African Special Forces had raided a farmhouse in Rivonia which had been purchased by an underground military wing of the Africa National Congress called 'Umkhonto we Sizwe' or the 'Spear of the Nation,' and sometimes known by just the initials MK. There they found a group of men preparing and studying to commit acts of terrorism. The documentary evidence was overwhelming. Amongst the evidence Nelson Mandela's fingerprints were found, albeit he was already in prison serving a five-year sentence. Umkhonto we Sizwe was formed by the ANC's in response to the Sharpeville massacre when, on 21st March 1960, between 5,000 and 7,000 black protesters, at best armed with rocks, marched on the police station in Sharpeville to protest against the Pass Laws. The South African police opened fire on the crowd, killing 69 people and injuring 189. The massacre was followed very quickly by the government declaring a state of emergency and detaining more than 18,000 people. The Pass Laws were a body of apartheid laws in operation in South Africa which controlled the rights of black people to reside and travel in certain areas. These restrictions were implemented by means of identity documents known as a Pass Book which had to be carried compulsorily at all times.

Instead, each chose to make a speech from the dock putting the Republic of South Africa and its Apartheid laws on trial. Above all, they sought to show to the whole world the injustices of South African society and the unfairness of its legal system if you were black or coloured.

It was Nelson Mandela, named only as the 'First Defendant' throughout the trial, who was to capture the key moment. On 20th April 1964, in a three-hour speech, which had taken him weeks to prepare, he ended it with the words:

"During my lifetime I have dedicated myself to this struggle of the African people. I have fought against white domination, and I have fought against black domination. I have cherished the ideal of a democratic and free society in which all persons live together in harmony and with equal opportunities. It is an ideal which I hope to live for and to achieve. But if needs be, it is an ideal for which I am prepared to die."

Throughout the trial there was silent sympathy in the Daunier household with the ANC, for each member had learnt to keep their opinion secret. It mirrored the strange tension there was throughout the whole of the Southern Cape as the trial continued. It was forcing everyone to face up to the immorality of what the State was doing. But it was the articulate extremists on both sides of the argument who appeared to be doing the most harm. Whilst the silent majority abhorred what was going on they were too cowardly to express the moderate, more balanced view; something which, years later, Satutu would ashamedly accuse herself.

David and Satutu were certain that the court was going to find the ten men guilty for, irrespective of any bias, all the evidence strongly suggested that they were. The public debate was primarily of one thing. Why hadn't Percy Yutar, the prosecutor, demanded the death penalty, when every commentator said that this was what the state wanted?

The Rivonia Trial ended on 12th June 1964 when the Judge sentenced the eight convicted men, including Nelson Mandela, to life imprisonment. With this, it was David and Satutu's hope that the people of Paarl could get back to living their lives as before.

Except this was not to be as, on 24ᵗʰ July 1964, one of the articulate extremists struck. A bomb, made from sticks of dynamite and petrol, exploded on the main concourse of Johannesburg's railway station, killing a grandmother, disfiguring her 17-year-old granddaughter for life, and injuring very many others.

The bomb-maker was a white man called John Harris. He was a member of a small sabotage group known as the African Resistance Movement whose members were supposed to have agreed amongst themselves not to use violence against people, only property. Harris was quickly caught, found guilty of murder and hanged on 1ˢᵗ April 1965[6]. However, it was his actions which crystallised a change of mood by the South African Government, and with it came an unpleasant and radical switch as the police, mainly of Afrikaans background, stopped their soft and silent policing of the apartheid laws within the Cape Winelands and started to enforce them more rigorously and far more viciously.

Some years before, the State had declared the Southern Cape a coloured preferential area. It made life much easier for David, who was white, and Sunetta and Little Joe, who were coloured, than it did for Satutu who, being black, was hit the hardest by the apartheid rules. But, by keeping herself mostly on the New Found Estate, Satutu caused and found little trouble; that was until six o'clock in the morning on 1ˢᵗ September 1964 when the New Found Estate was raided by the police for the very first time.

The only warning the Daunier family had that anything might have been wrong, before their front door was kicked in, was the sound of a fleet of police cars and vans coming up the drive.

Satutu knew immediately what was happening and she put into action the plan she had long prepared. As David rushed downstairs to meet and delay their 'visitors', Satutu stripped their bed of bed sheets in a flash and turned over the mattress so there would not be warmth on both sides. She bundled their sheets into her arms which

---

[6] It was said at the time that, if John Harris's bomb had exploded before Nelson Mandela had been sentenced, it is almost certain he would have been hung, rather than sentenced to life imprisonment, in order to '*décourager les autres.*'

she took to the next bedroom, her dressing room, where she lifted the bottom shelf of the wardrobe and threw the sheets into a hole before putting the lid back. She pulled back the sheets and blankets of the bed, climbed in and moved around rapidly to make it look as though it had been slept in. Only then did she start to dress and put on her daily uniform of crisp clean white jeans, white blouse, white cardigan and crocheted bonnet, which she always wore when she needed to keep her hair under control.

By now Sunetta and Little Joe were awake, and in no time at all, the three of them had David and Satutu's bed remade with clean sheets, while David stood at the bottom of the stairs remonstrating with the police inspector leading the raid.

"I thought we had an understanding," said David firmly, "but it appears not." At that moment Sunetta and Little Joe joined David, almost as reinforcements, on the stairs.

"We did until your lot bombed Johannesburg station," retorted the Inspector.

"My lot," said David. "I don't have a lot," he added testily.

"Bloody liberals," shouted back the inspector, in a strong Afrikaans accent, referring to the fact that John Harris was a member of the Liberal Party.

"I'm not a member of the Liberals. In fact, I've never been a member of any political party – ever!" said David, with rebuke pouring from every syllable.

"Might not be a party member but look at you with your bloody high 'n mighty liberal attitude."

David could tell at once that the conversation was not going well. It was at that moment Satutu appeared from the kitchen with an apron across her front looking as though she might be the maid, except for the value of the diamonds on her fingers, which she secretly turned around, so the stones faced into her palms. She had come down the servant's back stairs.

"Would these gentlemen like coffee, Mr David?" asked Satutu humbly. It was a subservient tone, which her children had never heard her speak in front of their father, or them, before.

"We're shutting down the school," said the Inspector, ignoring the request for coffee.

"You've broken down my door at six in the morning to tell me that?"

"No, we've come to examine your sleeping and domestic arrangements too. We have reports of miscegenation crimes taking place here. You might all be French but when you're in South Africa you have to obey our laws!"

"Missy, will you please show these gentle..." David was going to say gentlemen and then thought this far too pleasant a description for the thugs he saw before him, "...these policemen to your living quarters."

The inspector nodded towards a thick-set Afrikaans policeman with a fat protruding belly who followed a very demur Satutu through the kitchen.

"Why have you shut the school?" asked David. "We have agreed protocols on how the law is to be applied."

"You're teaching whites, blacks and coloureds in the same class and that's criminal. You know it."

"The whites are only visitors. The school's allowed to teach visitors. The blacks and coloured are in the same class but segregated. We have state approval for that. You know we do."

"Not the same white kids day after day. You've got some kids there who've been visitors every school day, some for four years and many more than three."

"But their parents can't afford to send them to school. It's why we have them, and they're getting a better education with us than at the Mission school."

"Precisely, you're over educating the blacks. You are giving them more than the proscribed Bantu Education."

"Of course we are," said David crossly. "Bantu Education will hardly teach a child to read, let alone write."

"It's against the law. Don't you get that?" shouted the Inspector, angrily.

"What! To over educate a child is against the law. Don't be so bloody stupid," shouted David.

"You're under arrest," said the Inspector, determined to shut down dissent, nodding his head to one of the policemen, "and you." He pointed to Satutu who had just returned to the hall, "and you, and you," he continued now pointing to Sunetta and Little Joe in turn.

David was held by the arm by one policeman, but each of Satutu, Sunetta and Little Joe were stormed by the others and viciously forced into handcuffs. David yelled in protest, but the others kept quiet. They said nothing as they had been taught, but also learnt through bitter experience.

David was escorted to sit in the back of the inspector's police car, while Satutu was loaded roughly into one van for blacks and Sunetta and Little Joe were thrown as though they were just baggage into another van for coloureds. Like hundreds of thousands of mixed raced families before, they were being inhumanly forced apart on the altar of apartheid and the very worst kind of racial prejudice!

Chapter 20

South Africa September 1964

THE TWO AFRIKAANS speaking policemen who had arrested Little Joe, together with another thug of a white policeman, gathered around him in a locked and stuffy interview room in the district police station where he had been taken. It was the thick-set policeman with the fat protruding belly who had inspected Satutu's 'living' accommodation who hit Little Joe first; and he hit him hard, breaking his cheekbone and splitting his lip with a round wooden baton.

"Who're your parents, you fucking coon?" shouted the fat bellied policeman, as his baton bounced off Little Joe's body after delivering another blow.

Still Little Joe said nothing. He just yelped in pain.

"Who's your mother?" demanded another of the policemen, yelling violently into Little Joe's ear.

Again, Little Joe said nothing. Determined defiance was streaming from his ever-reducing eyesight. His eyelids had become badly swollen from the fist pummelling he had received earlier from another Afrikaans policeman, who was now standing by the door.

"Who is your father? We know anyway, so why don't you just tell us, you little fucker," the fat bellied policeman continued.

Before he had time to answer, Little Joe was hit hard across the head with a baton which sent him reeling and seeing stars. He instantly knew from the loud crack in his ears that his skull had been broken.

"David Daunier, a white man, is your father and Satutu Ndosi is your black bitch of a mother, isn't she?" shouted the fat bellied policeman.

"Ndosi, Ndosi," said Little Joe out loud. He had never heard his mother's maiden name before. "Sir," he said politely, his voice trembling in fear. "You can see from my passport that I am French. I'm an honorary white. I need to be treated as ..."

Little Joe was trying hard to stick to the coloured man's code when dealing with the police. He had used it time and time before. Always look down, never look them in the eye. Always give your name, age and address; never answer any other questions, just apologise and say you don't know. Never fight back, always say please and thank you.

"Fuck that," said the Afrikaans policeman who was guarding the door. "You think you're going to teach me the fucking law." At which point, he moved forward and struck Little Joe with his baton straight across his face, this time breaking his nose.

There was no yell from Little Joe. He was overtaken by a sudden and blinding headache. He tried to speak but he couldn't. This time the baton came like a rapier, thrust straight into his solar plexus, causing Little Joe to double up in pain. His headache was unbearable, making him vomit into the blood, which was streaming from his nose, before he passed into unconsciousness and collapsed off the chair and onto the floor. With his hands still handcuffed behind his back, and unable to provide any protection, Little Joe's face smashed into the ground.

Little Joe's lifeless body was dragged back to a cell by the three policemen. His time in the interview room had been less than four minutes. Not one question had been asked of their totally groundless suspicions.

As each man left the cell, they planted a heavily booted kick deep into his head or body. It was one of these kicks which forced Little Joe's broken nose back into his skull and hastened his departure from this world into the next. He was just 13 years old and had never done any harm or been a threat to anyone.

David knew nothing about Little Joe's plight. Although there had always been hostility towards white Europeans by Afrikaners, probably arising from their loss of the Boer War, David's interview was nevertheless conducted very differently to his youngest son's. Firstly, mugs of tea had been served all around, and every time David refused to answer a question it was asked again in a different form. For example, when asked whether Satutu and he were married he would simply reply, "It is my constitutional right not to answer such a question," so they would then ask, "Is Satutu Ndosi your wife?" to which he would say exactly the same thing. This contrasted to Little Joe who, each time he did not answer, felt the whack of a wooden baton against his juvenile body.

Throughout David's very extensive interview, most of the focus had been on the school, whereas the focus of Little Joe's interview, or what little there had been of it, concerned the relationship of his parents. They hadn't yet got on to asking him about their understanding of the reason for Little Joe's arrest. They knew he had been arrested because some white kids had been going to a black school. Their wrong, and totally unfounded, assumption was that he had been arrested because he was in a relationship with a white girl. As far as these three policemen were concerned, this wasn't a matter for the courts. It was a matter to be beaten out of him; to make sure he never lifted his eyes to look at a white girl ever again.

In sharp contrast, David was eventually allowed the services of a local criminal lawyer. He couldn't work out whether this was just another, but more rigorous, shakedown for more money, or whether it was the real thing. He feared it was the latter because the mood of his interviewers was getting nastier and more threatening as each minute passed. It was clear from the evidence that the school had been operating in breach of almost every single anti-apartheid law.

David knew he had the thinnest of defence when they showed him photographs of the boys' and girls' toilets. When the school started these were separate cubicles for each of the three races; he had made sure it was so. But, when these came to be re-painted, the signs didn't go back up for the children no longer saw the colour differences their parents saw. It seemed no longer relevant to the children's lives.

Desperate to find Satutu and his children, David was prepared to agree to almost anything to secure his release from police custody. It came only after an extended negotiation between his new lawyer and the Inspector who raided New Found House. It required the payment of a huge bond as surety and, most notably, another large contribution to the non-existent police 'widows and orphans' fund.

Satutu and Sunetta were treated very differently too. Satutu's treatment was far worse for, sadly in apartheid South Africa, conditions in very many police cells were much worse for blacks than coloureds. It was an appalling fact, but the blacker your skin the harsher your treatment.

Immediately on their arrival at the police station they were separated into different cells. Satutu's cell with its tin roof baked like an oven in the midday sun. The air was acrid from the biting smell of stale urine. There was nowhere to sit except on the floor which was covered in dry faeces. By late morning Satutu and Sunetta were both desperately thirsty. Sunetta, of mixed race and fairer skin, was given a drink. Satutu, whose skin was mahogany black, was not. Sunetta was freed of her handcuffs, Satutu was not. After being locked up for six hours Satutu was desperate to go to the lavatory. Her shouts and pleas for help were either ignored or met with the response to "shut the fuck up, bitch." Eventually, sweating in agony from the pain and unable to move her hands to the front to undo her jeans, she squatted with her back against the corner and peed through her trousers onto the floor. As the pools of water gathered around her feet, Satutu cried silent tears of humiliation and despair.

David's first concern on being released was to find Satutu and Sunetta. It was well known that the risk of sexual assault on black and women of colour, when in custody in apartheid South Africa, was very high. Commandeering his new-found lawyer, David was driven to another police station about 30 miles away on the edge of Cape Town where he had been told his wife and daughter had been taken.

The arrival of a white lawyer demanding to see his black and coloured clients was a shock to the system. The desk sergeant and custody officers were expecting to do what they always did with racial cases involving women; hold them until their cells were needed for another more serious matter at which point they would be thrown out on to the streets. Sometimes this could be after a few hours, sometimes after many days.

If you were a white man on a miscegenation charge, there was no simple release. They would, in all probability, be bailed until a trial date was set, often years away. If you were a black man, then your chances of bail were virtually zero. Worse, it was almost certain that you would not come out of a police station unharmed. It was beyond the belief of any white policeman that a white woman would prefer a black man to them. Their ingrained prejudice had convinced them that a white woman 'went with a black man' only out of coercion, even if there was the strongest of evidence to the contrary.

It was very late in the evening by the time David and the lawyer got Satutu and Sunetta back to New Found Estate. They were very distressed, very angry at the situation and very frightened. Their nervousness was made worse as their home had been ransacked by the police. They may have been looking for evidence but, in the most part, it looked as though they had just set out to do wilful damage.

With a sandwich and drink in hand, David and his lawyer set off to secure Little Joe's release. It was just past midnight when they arrived at the police station where Joe was held.

"I'm Nicholas Jackson. I'm a lawyer and I've come to see my client Mr Sidney Daunier," said the lawyer confidently, using Little Joe's Christian name. He had spoken similar words many times before.

"And you are?"

The lawyer repeated his name and showed his identity card.

"I'm sorry you can't see him," said the desk sergeant, well prepared for this moment.

"Why not? I insist."

"He's dead," said the sergeant, in a cold matter of fact way, with no apology or regret.

The lawyer looked away from the policeman straight at David. He showed no reaction to this news. The way it was said made it impossible to believe it was true.

"Are you telling me Mr Sidney Joseph Daunier is dead?"

"Yes," It was a sharp one word reply with no suggestion that the answer would be amplified.

"How? When?" asked Jackson.

"I can't say."

"Can't or won't?"

"I'm not allowed."

"Don't be ridiculous," said Jackson sharply. "My client is entitled to proper representation, and I'm here to provide it."

"You can't represent a dead person," replied the desk sergeant. There was sarcasm in his voice.

"If you're saying he's dead then I demand you tell me how he died, and then you take me to his body."

"He died this afternoon resisting arrest whilst in police custody," said the desk sergeant, as though he were reading a statement in court.

"I have to see him," demanded David, stepping forward to take control. "I'm his father!"

"You can't. He's not here. There has to be a police autopsy before you see him, said the desk sergeant firmly."

"I need to see him now," insisted David, leaning forward to make sure his presence was well felt.

The sergeant, feeling physically threatened, took a pace back at the same time as pressing a panic button calling for help. Immediately there was a rush of reinforcements at his side.

"There will be an autopsy and a coroner's hearing, after which the body will be released to the family for a funeral. That's the order of things, and it's not going to change," said the sergeant, more confident now he had reinforcements at his side.

"Doesn't somebody need to identify the body?" asked the lawyer. "His father is here and ready to do that."

"We don't need that. We have his passport, and we know who we arrested. There is nothing here for you. You should go home. You'll be contacted at the appropriate time."

"I'm his family. I'm his father," shouted out David, now getting visibly distressed. "I must see him, I must. I demand it."

Jackson, sensing the tension and realising that David could be arrested for a second time, took him firmly by the arm, led him out of the police station and settled him in to the passenger seat of his car.

David fought the anger he felt at not being allowed to see his son for, at that moment, he was certain that his boy was still alive.

It was only as he was driven home, and Jackson spoke of what had happened, did it slowly dawn on David that his precious son, Little Joe, was really dead.

Chapter 21

The Cape South Africa September 1964

DAVID RETURNED TO New Found Estate with a feeling of total dread. How was he going to tell Satutu that their baby son was dead?

Satutu heard the car crunch up the gravel drive. She got out of their bed to meet David, expecting Little Joe to be by his side. She was standing on the landing holding the banisters as he entered. Seeing her, he stood still in the hall. He could see the silhouette of her body through the long Victorian linen nightdress which she always wore so perfectly pressed. Her black hair was as wild as the mane on a lion, and as the light behind her head shone through her hair, it gave her an orange and yellow halo. He would remember that sight forever, for she looked so beautiful, and he was about to give her such devastating news; news which would change their lives forever.

They each looked at each other. Not a word was said. Seeing him, Satutu immediately knew Little Joe was dead. She was later to question, many times, how she knew before David had said anything. Perhaps it was Little Joe's absence from David's side. Perhaps it was David's demeanour, for he looked tired and totally defeated. The fact was that Satutu was certain that Little Joe had come to her just before he left this world, but it was only now that she knew that for certain.

"How?" Satutu asked, still standing on the landing holding onto the banisters.

"You know?"

"He's dead, isn't he?"

David nodded and then hung his head as he shook it slowly from side to side.

"How?"

"I don't know," said David, still rigid in the hall.

"Did they murder him?" she asked.

"I suspect so. I'm so sorry," he said, overwhelmed by the guilt of not saving her son.

Satutu just nodded as she drove her back ramrod straight and proudly lifted her chest. David watched as she gracefully descended the stairs. Still David didn't move. Coming to him, Satutu wrapped her arms around him for at this moment she was being determinedly strong, and he was crumbling in defeat. His strength was all used up. David was visibly deflating before Satutu's eyes.

"You must get some sleep," she said, after they'd spent a few moments rocking arm in arm.

"I need a cup of tea and something to eat. I need to write a list," said David, his voice hardly audible. He felt all of his seventy-five years.

Satutu went to the kitchen and put on the kettle. David went into his study, grabbed paper and pen and returned to sit at the kitchen table. He did as his father had taught him: *In a crisis make a cup of tea and write a list.* Not a tear was shed as they talked of Little Joe, laughed at the joy he had brought them and planned his funeral.

It was nearly dawn when David collapsed into a deep sleep on the bed. As David slept, Satutu dressed as she always did in white jeans, white blouse and white jumper. This day she decided not to wear her usual white crocheted cap. The sun was rising as Satutu walked into the village. She was overwhelmed with a feeling of calm. As she walked, she became stronger in her belief in the afterlife. She was certain that her son had gone to a better place. She started to walk taller and with pride as she felt blessed that God had lent her such a wonderful person to be her son, even if it was for such a short time.

As soon as Satutu arrived at the home of the tribal chief, his wife immediately forced her menfolk out to work. Thereafter word spread around the village that the boss-wife had arrived. Very quickly after that they learnt of Little Joe's death, and so the women of the village, all of whom worked on the estate, came to give comfort as was the tribal custom. They sat around and chatted drinking strong black tea sweetened with honey. It reminded Satutu of her own village back in the days of her youth.

"I would like to have my hair permed, to be made just like yours, just like Little Joe's. Will you do that for me, please?" she asked the village hairdresser after they'd been speaking for well over the hour.

There was a protest from the women as they told her that she was lucky to have such beautiful soft hair. They all envied its softness, but none wanted its unruliness and insisted that a perm would be a mistake. For the first time in her life Satutu was determined to make herself look like everyone else, so immediately after her hair was in tight back curls she had it cut very close to her skull.

While her hair was being dried, Satutu spotted a pair of red shoes on a shelf, set aside for Sunday best. She picked them up and tried them on. They fitted perfectly.

"Can I buy these from you?" she asked. "Please, I would be most grateful."

The chief's wife didn't know what to say. She didn't want to lose her shoes and she didn't want to say no.

"I'll pay you as though they were brand-new. Whatever it costs to buy them, I will pay you."

The smile of relief on the face of the chief's wife, and a short nod, indicated that they had a deal.

It was just after lunchtime when Satutu returned to New Found House. David was caught in the whirlwind of a media storm. Already television cameras and journalists from the world's news broadcasters and newspapers had gathered on their drive and lawn. Only those who have been through it truly know what it feels like. Words are not enough to describe the way you are pulled, pushed, and squeezed, all at the same time, in an endless babble of pressurised noise. It kills any ability to think logically, particularly at a time when you are already under emotional distress.

It was into this frenzy that Satutu walked. She immediately saw from the look on David's face that his senses were dangerously past overload.

"We'll have to have our own autopsy," she heard David say over the phone, as she came into his study.

"Who are you talking to?" she mouthed.

"The lawyer," David whispered back.

"Tell him to get here and get here fast." There was urgency in her voice.

"Why?"

"Please David, just ask," she pleaded. "No, please tell him he has to come, and now." The lawyer heard what she said and her emphasis on the word 'has'.

"Ten, fifteen minutes," said David as he put the phone down. For the first time he noticed Satutu's new look. He didn't like it but said nothing. Before her hair had made her look soft and warm, but now, cut short and in tight circles, she looked physically hard, capable of taking anyone on in any fight anywhere.

"David, we're going to make a statement and then they all have to go. I need them to go," she said, referring to the media pack outside.

David nodded his agreement.

"We need to work on it now," she said.

Again, David nodded.

"It needs to be written so there are no mistakes." Satutu started to dictate what to say as David listened.

"Yes, that's good," he said encouragingly. Immediately his time at the UK Treasury, when he had been involved in drafting many a press release, came flooding back. He picked up his pen and started to write what Satutu had been saying. A man, who had been overwhelmed just a few moments ago, suddenly found a renewed confidence and with it a surge of energy.

The first draft was ready in handwritten form by the time Jackson was with them. He ran his pen over their statement using his skills as a wordsmith to sharpen the prose and strengthen some of the meaning. Demanding that all the phones be taken off the hook, so they could no longer be disturbed, Jackson moved David from his desk and pulled over the typewriter. Loaded with several sheets of paper and carbon paper, so there could be copies, he started to type. Jackson read each sentence as he went. As the steel keys of the typewriter clicked when they hit the paper, so deeper into David's memory sank the exact script.

Sunetta came into the room and sat quietly by the side of her mother, resting in comfort under her arms with her head lying on her bosom. She had finished her crying. She told them she had got hold of Big Joe and told him to come home which made David both relieved and pleased.

Jackson read through the script once again.

"You know he was a brother too," added Sunetta. Immediately the words of the script were altered in pen so Little Joe would be referred to as a much-loved son and brother.

With the final script in hand and everyone gathered around ready to go outside, their lawyer suddenly stopped them. "Your house is too full. You need to get all those who do not need to be here outside. It's impossible in here with so many people," he added. Please Sunetta lock every door, apart from the front one, whilst I get everyone outside." David and Satutu acquiesced to the suggestion, and without a word Sunetta left to go about her task.

When the house was quiet, and the press had become very orderly; David, Satutu and Sunetta appeared altogether on the porch. David had put on a clean white shirt, modest tie and his freshly pressed suit. Sunetta had chosen to put on her school uniform in protest at its closure. Satutu went out as she had come back from the village that morning. She carried with her a portrait of her son for all to see.

As David stepped forward to make his statement to the world's press, and the flash bulbs popped, he knew exactly what he was risking. For forty-six years he had lived in anonymity, away from the infamy of the Battle of Célieux Ridge and all that had followed. The British Army would now know where he was. It was time, he decided, to let their wrath fall.

David made his statement. He spoke perfectly, making Satutu and Sunetta very proud of him. He paused at the right moments to give effect, and as he struggled to maintain his emotions every time he said the word 'son', he garnered huge sympathy from those that were there.

"Thank you everyone," said Jackson, "that's the end of the statement. Mr Daunier will not be answering questions. We should be grateful if you would now leave," he said, as he tried to shepherd the trio inside.

"Mrs Daunier," shouted one of the reporters. "Do you have anything to say?"

"Yeah, Mrs Daunier, what you got to say?" shouted another.

The baying chorus from the press animals caught Satutu by surprise.

"There's no statement from Mrs Daunier," said Jackson, trying to bring the press corps under control.

With a nod to the lawyer, Satutu moved forward and took a step down from their porch so she could get closer to the gathered crowd. "I'll answer questions," she said. All that time she had spent learning to perfect her English accent was now about to pay off.

"As is plain for everyone to see my husband is white, I am black, and my children are coloured. It is because we are French that the Republic of South Africa is colour-blind towards us, just as we are colour-blind towards each other in my family and on this Estate. It seems to me that my family should be an example to all of South Africa for, until yesterday, we lived in peace and love and harmony," Satutu paused. "I have a sense that yesterday's arrest and the death of my son is part of the process to get my husband off the land he has farmed for nearly fifty years for otherwise it makes no sense. Ever since we have been here, we have lived peacefully in this community, helped provide schools, created jobs, attended weddings and enjoyed each other's christenings irrespective of race. We have laughed and loved and cried together irrespective of colour. The only time there has been any racial segregation amongst us was when the law required it, for otherwise we are a community which respects all races and all colours equally. This was the way we lived then, and this is the way we will live in the future. There was no hate then and I will not allow the death of Little Joe to bring hate now. Whatever happens we will bring back love into this community for it is the only way forward."

"Miss," shouted one of the reporters. "Are you forgiving those that killed your son?"

"We don't know he was killed," she replied. "All we know is that he died in suspicious circumstances."

"Yeah, but if he was killed, are you saying that you would forgive 'em?" the same voice shouted out.

"If it turned out my son was murdered, and the murderer is genuinely sorry and seeks my forgiveness, then yes, I'll forgive them. I can't go through the rest of my life carrying hate. I thought about it for a long time this morning when, believe me, I hated everybody and everything. But, I knew if I continued like that it would eat me up, just as hate is eating up this nation."

"Miss, why are you wearin' red shoes?" shouted another reporter. "Isn't it odd to be wearin' such bright shoes on such a bad day?"

Satutu looked down at her feet. She then looked up at the audience in front of her. It was the first time she became conscious of their faces, until then they had just been a crowd. They must have numbered over a hundred people, black, white, and people of colour intermingling together as they had always done on New Found Estate.

"The red of these shoes represents the blood of my son," she answered. "The colour is the blood of South Africa shed on the immorality of apartheid which we are all now wading through. I will be wearing red shoes in remembrance of my son until I know exactly how he died and, if he died from foul play, then, until his killer is brought to justice."

There was an instantaneous round of applause.

"Miss," shouted another reporter as the clapping died down. "We're told you always wear long white gloves, why's that?"

Satutu looked the journalist straight in the eye. In that moment she knew from the look on his face that he knew the reason and was imploring her to tell the truth because of the impact it would have.

"You may not have noticed" said Satutu, "but when a white man shakes the hand of a black man or woman for the first time, sometimes even the second, they instinctively look at their own hand afterwards to see if it has become dirty. It is as though they have touched a lump of coal and are checking to see how much black coal dust is left on their hands. It is so culturally ingrained in the white man's mind that black is dirty that they don't even know they are doing it. But, every black man and woman notices, and we say nothing."

Satutu had her audience captivated for, while her voice was playing the softest of melodies, everyone's eyes were on her white gloved hands which moved with the mesmerising grace and precision of a conductor. She continued: "It is one of the many small racially prejudiced things which happen to every black man every single day throughout the world. I discovered that by wearing white gloves I stopped this insult from happening. I do it so I'm not made to feel a lesser person by the person I'm meeting."

There was both a silence and stillness as the truth of her statement resonated and each of them took Satutu into their hearts. She looked around slowly and continued. "After I have met someone once or twice, I no longer have to wear white gloves when we shake hands. They no longer see the colour of my skin first. They see the person I am. They see my disposition; am I happy or sad? They see my mood; am I working or playing? They see the whole of me and not just my colour. It is a crying shame, no ... its worse than that, it's a sin that those who were responsible for my son's life didn't see Little Joe, the person. Instead, they saw his colour and they let him die."

At that moment, there was a click on the phone lines into New Found House. The secret police had tapped into its telephone lines.

Chapter 22

Châteaux de Gressier September 1964

SINCE HE'D LEFT South Africa at the end of January, Henry had travelled extensively throughout Italy, Spain and Portugal. He didn't enjoy Spain or Portugal as both had long been under the suppressive control of vicious dictators. The lack of freedom had suppressed the joie de vivre of what, deep down, he had found to be happy people enjoying their rich culture. In Italy, he found a country rife in corruption with everything appearing to have two prices; the real price and the price which was shown to the government. Henry thought about going into Germany but being a child who grew up in the aftermath of the war, and a son of the country which had caused it, he felt he was not yet ready to go. Although it was twenty years on, emotions still rang deep.

As he had promised his grandmother, Henry came back to de Gressier in the middle of September to help with the harvest. He had been up some time working on his catalogue of wine when his alarm clock rang reminding him it was time for breakfast. He joined Mamie in the dining room of the Cellars for his usual cooked English breakfast. As he sat down to eat he couldn't but help spot the coloured picture of Satutu on the front page of La Monde. "*Shoes soaked in the blood of South Africa*" read the headlines.

"I've met her Mamie," said Henry, matter-of-factly. "I'm sure I met her when I was in South Africa."

Juliette turned to look at the picture on page three. "It caught my eye too because her name's Daunier. It's similar to the surname my brother took just before he left for America," she added. "I thought it might be a clue to where he lives but ..." Juliette didn't finish her sentence. She didn't want to appear to be racially prejudiced by saying the rest ... he wouldn't have married a black woman.'

"Oh," said Henry, not really paying attention as his thoughts were of Sunetta, the young girl whose favours had brightened his day.

"Can I have a look, please?" he asked.

Juliette split the paper and handed Henry the picture on the front page, and the fuller story on page five, which she had not got around to reading.

"I worked there for a couple of weeks. They have a fruit farm. I picked plums," said Henry, as he studied the story.

Juliette grunted for she had no interest in a celebrity story about red shoes.

"She looks different, but I'm sure it's her," said Henry. "She wore white jeans then. It's her hair that's changed. Honestly, I could swear that she had the wildest, softest black hair you'd have ever seen. Can I keep this?" he asked. "I need to write to them."

Juliette grunted her consent.

His breakfast devoured in a few minutes, Henry left, kissing Mamie on the forehead as he always did. "I'm going into the village. I won't be long," he said.

That day Juliette was only interested in one thing in her newspaper. The day before, the Warren Commission had published a summary of its investigation into the assassination of President John F. Kennedy, and she was absorbed by its conclusions. If they had published their findings on any other day, Juliette would have discovered her brother's whereabouts. She would have read that the nephew she never knew had died in a South African police station, but it was an event which passed her by.

Henry returned with every available national paper, both French and English that he could buy. Each one contained a picture of Satutu, for being slim, dressed in white and wearing those vermillion red shoes she was a photo editor's delight. Of all the filming and all the photography, it had been Satutu's words and not David's which had been reported by all media. He was as incognito as he was before.

Henry sat at his desk and for the first time in his life he wrote a note of sympathy.

My Dear Sunetta,

I have thought of you many times since I left New Found Estate as I have very special memories of those days we spent together. I am sorry I was not able to say good-bye, but the farm manager wanted me packed and gone.

I was really saddened to read in the papers today of the death of Little Joe. A picture of your mother, and the story, is in every single French and English newspaper.

I remember Little Joe very well. He was always so bright, cheerful and a real worker. I know from just those few days being with him and you, in the fields, what joy he brought everyone. Because of this I know he will be very sadly missed.

Your mother's words were magnificently spoken. They are reported, I imagine, almost word for word in every paper. Perhaps out of this dreadful tragedy will come some good? I can only pray so.

Please find no time for guilt. I am certain that, in this life, there is no rhyme or reason; bad things just happen to the very best of people.

You are in my thoughts and if there is anything you feel I can do to help, please feel free to ask.

I send you my prayers and my love.

Hank

Chapter 23

New Found Estate, South Africa
October – November 1964

"HIS BRAIN IS missing," said the pathologist on the telephone to Jackson. "I've got him on the slab now. His brain, left kidney and spleen are all missing."

"What? Why?" asked Jackson.

"Probably because they show how badly he was beaten. The bruising around his face is terrible, it's quite appalling."

"Have you taken photographs?" asked Jackson.

"Yes, of course, lots," said the Pathologist.

"From what you've got, can you say how he died?"

"Yes, it's the same reason given in the police pathologist report."

"Ah," said Jackson. "I haven't seen that. Can you send me a copy?"

"Yes, his skull's badly broken. From the blood residue on the inside of his skull you can see he had a huge haemorrhage; that's probably what killed him. Also, his nose is badly broken too; probably pushed up past his eyes into his brain, causing a second haemorrhage."

Jackson winced. "Where's his brain?" he asked.

"I don't know. I phoned the pathology department at the hospital, but they say they'd sent everything to me. I phoned the pathologist who did the work, and he assured me that everything was put back as it should be ready for burial."

"So both pathologists agree on how he died?" asked Jackson, wanting to summarise the situation.

"We do. He died from a brain haemorrhage or haemorrhages."

"Do you agree on the likely events before his death to cause him to have those injuries?" Jackson's style of questioning was as forensic as that which he would use to cross examine a witness in court.

"No, the pathology report says that the broken skull is consistent with his head striking a wall."

"That ties in neatly with the police statements which I've been allowed to see," said Jackson. "They say his head hit the wall several times whilst trying to resist arrest."

"Well, I disagree," said the Pathologist. "Joseph's skull was of normal width. He didn't have what might be called a thin skull. In my view the break in his skull is more consistent with being hit by a wooden truncheon, possibly more than once."

"Why do you say that?" asked Jackson.

"It's not just cracked, but part of his head has been caved in."

Jackson winced again and then grimaced at the news. "What about the broken nose?" he asked.

"The pathologist's report says that the break in the nose is consistent with the boy's head striking a concrete floor."

"Oh, what a coincidence," interjected Jackson, sarcastically. "The police statements report Little Joe suddenly becoming unconscious and falling onto the floor," he added.

"I think the nasal injuries are more consistent with his nose being struck from below, probably with a boot," reported the Pathologist. "It could have been from a punch or a baton, but since he was likely to be sitting down during the interview, the angle of strike is wrong."

"Anything else?" asked Jackson.

"Yeah, you should have seen the kid's wrists. He's clearly been in so much distress that the handcuffs have cut clean through his skin almost to the bone."

"Doesn't that support the argument of resisting arrest?"

"Could do," said the pathologist. "Could also suggest a defensive reflex response to protect yourself when you know you're about to be hit."

"Can I summarise," said Jackson. "The police pathologist's report, which you have been given, supports the police statements that his skull was broken when it hit a wall, while resisting arrest, and his nose was broken when it hit the floor when he collapsed."

"Yes."

"And you are saying?"

"In my opinion the injuries are far too severe for the cause of death to have been as the police pathologist's report suggests."

"I need this in writing," said Jackson. "I need to be able to submit it in evidence to the coroner."

There was a long pause as the pathologist thought through the implications of what was being asked of him.

"I'll be taking one hell of a risk," he said, before pausing again. "I'll think about it. By the way, I don't think Visgoogan wrote this pathology report."

"Who's Visgoogan?"

"The police pathologist. He has a good reputation and to allow a report like that to leave his desk looks highly suspicious. It's not like him. I can't tell you why. It looks as though it has been edited down. There are some normal explanations that are missing."

"Are you saying the police report has been doctored?" asked Jackson.

"I don't know. What I'm saying is it's less thorough than I would expect. Is there a budget?" asked the Pathologist, in a sudden change of direction.

"Why'd you ask?"

"I'd like to get a second opinion."

"If that's what it needs then get it," said Jackson, authoritatively.

Immediately after the two men had hung up, Jackson phoned his contact in the ANC to arrange a meeting. Unknown to the Daunier family, the ANC were about to pay for the second pathologist's opinion, putting the secret police and the Daunier family in direct opposition.

Ten days later the Daunier family were presented with a joint pathologist's report, for alongside their Pathologist's signature was that of Sir John Haith, FRCPath. There was, he concluded, safety in numbers; particularly when one of that number is a Professor of Pathology at one of London's leading medical schools.

Little Joe's inquest was held in late November. Many of the news outlets, particularly those with an anti-apartheid agenda, had spread their cash around the police station where Little Joe had been killed. Very soon the names of the culprits came into the public domain, as did the reason he had been battered to death. It had been mistakenly thought that the coloured boy had been *messin'* with white girls. He had to be taught a lesson; a lesson which had gone tragically wrong.

David didn't go to the inquest. He was a private man before and, for his own sanity, he needed his privacy once again. However, Satutu and Sunetta were determined to be there. David had insisted that Jackson make no mention of the missing body parts at the inquest. It was a fact he had kept hidden from Satutu as he knew how much it would upset her.

Satutu was the obvious choice to be the media spokesman for the family. She had deliberately taken to wearing a white denim jacket, in place of her usual white jumpers, because she felt it accentuated her bust line. Once again, she wore a white crocheted cap, but this time over her tightly permed black hair. With her slim figure in tight white jeans, the vermilion red shoes, her white teeth and bright eyes the camera loved her. She was as telegenic and articulate as the best news presenters. With no discernible accent, those who heard her on the radio always assumed she was white.

David and Jackson spent time briefing Satutu, working through the potentially difficult questions and her answers, but she didn't need either's help. Satutu was a natural, as she deflected any question she didn't like and kept to her own message.

Inquests are normally heard in public, and such was the interest, there were a lot of public waiting outside to attend Little Joe's inquest.

The first time Satutu and Sunetta got an inkling that something was wrong was when Jackson was informed that it was not the usual coroner. Instead, a Judge had been brought in to hear the case. The Judge ordered the inquest to be held in private. Immediately the court was reduced to Jackson, Satutu, Sunetta and their pathologist. Across the court room was Visgoogan and all the police officers who had given witness statements. Satutu and Sunetta quickly identified the three alleged culprits as their pictures had been in many of the papers. They both noticed how, deliberately, none of the men looked at them.

Once the court was clear, the clerk quickly brought the session to order, at which point the judge announced that he had read all the witness statements and had no questions for the witnesses. He then announced his verdict: accidental death. He then released Little Joe's body to the family for burial. By the time Jackson stood up to speak the judge had turned his back and was leaving the court room. The inquest had taken less than two minutes.

Satutu and Sunetta left the court stunned into silence. Where was justice they wondered, as each fought to control their temper.

"There's no point in screaming here," said Satutu to Sunetta, just before they left the building. "Let's go home. We'll start again tomorrow."

In the car park immediately afterwards, there was a private conversation between the two pathologists.

"Did you write this report?" the Dauniers' pathologist asked Visgoogan, as he handed him a copy of the police pathology report which had been filed with the court papers.

Visgoogan took the document and flicked through the pages. Then he studied it far more closely.

"No, er, well yes and no. There are bits missing ... big bits missing." His face frowned as he deliberated at what had happened.

"Do you still have a copy of your original report?"

"Of course I have. It's here."

He opened his briefcase and took out a folder. "Here, have a look," said Visgoogan as he handed over his report.

"But this is the same as the other one you're holding," said Dauniers' pathologist after he had looked at it for a little while.

"No, it can't be," said Visgoogan, in genuine surprise.

"It is. Didn't you look at it before you came to court?"

"Not really, I looked at the first page, but I had been told I wasn't going to be called as a witness, so I didn't bother. Why would I?" asked Visgoogan.

"Will you have another copy back at the hospital?"

"No, I don't think so. Do you know, I thought there was something wrong when you phoned me to ask where the missing body parts were, the brain..."

"Did you see my report?" interrupted Dauniers' pathologist.

"No, why?"

"I sent it to you as a matter of courtesy as it disagreed...," he paused. "Let us just say, it drew different conclusions to yours or, I should say, the two reports we have here," he said, waiving the two documents in the air.

"Everything was back in that body where it should have been," insisted Visgoogan. "I don't make mistakes like that."

"The boy was beaten to death," said Dauniers' pathologist, beginning to get quite angry with Visgoogan.

"I know, I said that in my report," protested Visgoogan.

"Your report doesn't say that."

"That's not my report," Visgoogan insisted, emphasising the words 'not' and 'my' as he waived the report now back in his hand. "The police asked me to comment on whether the injuries were consistent with other known facts from the witness statements, but that's normal." There was panic in Visgoogan's voice as it dawned on him that he was part of a conspiracy. "That's all I did."

"The Daunier family are going to need a statement from you."

"No way," said Visgoogan emphatically. "I won't do that."

"Why not?"

Visgoogan's look said all that needed to be said.

"You could be subpoenaed."

"You really think, given what has happened so far, the court is going to grant a subpoena?"

Dauniers' pathologist knew that Visgoogan was right. "Someone, who's very powerful, has been playing games; destroying vital evidence and doctoring reports," he said.

Visgoogan nodded. "Someone powerful enough to fix it so they could have a security cleared judge to act as coroner," he added. "I think we should both take a lot of care." From the tone with which Visgoogan spoke the implication was very clear. Don't go looking to right a wrong for it will only bring trouble.

The two men shook hands, and each started to head for their cars, then Visgoogan turned back and added: "Just to make it clear, my Daunier file is closed. I will do nothing else. Nothing, is that understood?"

Dauniers' pathologist nodded his understanding, whilst finding these last remarks strangely aggressive. What he didn't know was that Visgoogan was never going to do anything which threatened his lucrative police pathology contract, especially since the secret police had made it quite clear that they knew about his numerous prostitute girlfriends and would use that evidence as the means to destroy him, if they needed to.

The day after the inquest, Satutu, with Sunetta at her side, started a series of media interviews. She virtually ignored whatever question was asked of her. Instead, she made three simple points. Her son had been illegally killed and until the government acknowledged that, then everyone had to accept they were living in a police state where no one was free. Her second message was that apartheid was breeding division; and with division comes fear and hate. The country needs no more hate. The way to end hate was to end apartheid. It was the third point she made which took her family completely by surprise. It was the story which hit the headlines the next day as, for Satutu, it was the single most important issue.

"I am making Little Joe's death about water," she said. "It is the thing which divides the haves from the have-nots. While white South Africa is worrying about filling their swimming pools the rest of the country, particularly the newly created black homelands into which hundreds of thousands of black South Africans have been moved, lack water for sanitation and most importantly clean water for drinking. This is a scandal which is killing hundreds of thousands of people each year." She ended every interview by saying: "If the government won't act to find my son's killer, then they can certainly act to make sure clean water is provided to stop thousands and thousands of other sons being killed."

Satutu had been approached many times since Little Joe's death to join the ANC or simply to speak on its behalf. She refused point blank to be involved. Nevertheless, because of Jackson's connections to the ANC, they assumed she was connected to them too, and so the security services started to harass her at every opportunity. Thankfully, with fame comes a form of protection which is not available to ordinary people.

However, after he had watched the news that evening, there was one man who was convinced that Satutu was deep in the ANC's midst. That man was Dr H. F. Verwoerd, Prime Minister of South Africa. "Deal with her," he ordered. "Keep that bloody woman off the television and out of the papers!"

Verwoerd's instructions resulted in the state showing its overwhelming power. Firstly, Big Joe was detained at Cape Town airport; refused entry because he was French. It was argued that his presence was not conducive to public order. It was only when Jackson got involved that Big Joe was allowed into the country, but only long enough to attend his brother's funeral. Twenty-four hours after that he had to leave to go back to London.

Secondly, two days before Little Joe's funeral, when preparations were in full swing, the security services gave notice to Satutu that she was under house arrest with the condition that she had to be home from sunset to sunrise, and all weekend. She was not allowed visitors and could not use the telephone. Immediately after she got the notice, the telephone to New Found House was disconnected.

Little Joe's funeral was a small, ticket only affair to make sure that it wasn't commandeered for political purposes. It was planned by Satutu and Sunetta with the occasional contribution from Big Joe. Still feeling guilty at not having saved her son, David wanted it to be an event for which she would be proud. He made a few suggestions, but otherwise his main contribution was to walk the estate with Satutu and decide where Little Joe was going to be laid to rest. It was at the spot where they wanted to be buried; directly in the northern shadow of one of the largest trees on the edge of the estate, in the most peaceful of settings.

David got to the church long before everyone else. He wanted to avoid being photographed, and so sat quietly in the pews, content in his own thoughts. Outside the church, the road filled up with people who didn't have an invitation but still wanted to pay their respects.

Sunetta joined Satutu in wearing white with red shoes. It is hard to describe a funeral as a happy affair, but it was. The service comprised the most joyful of singing, with Little Joe's friends bringing laughter in their memories. As the sun started to fall in the sky and with Little Joe at rest in his grave, the Daunier family were able to look back on a day when they felt they had done their son and brother proud.

Chapter 24

New Found Estate, South Africa November 1964

THE EVENING WAS beginning to cool when David sat down in the swinging garden chair on his veranda. He closed his eyes and leaned back against the cushion. There were many days in his life which he never wanted to re-live and today, the day he buried his youngest son was, he was certain, the worst day he had ever lived.

For the umpteenth time David's mind tried to create order and structure over his own philosophy. Had the unnatural act of him burying his son changed his thinking, he pondered, for no child should die before their parent. He was emotionally too exhausted to think properly. He found it all too complicated, for none of it made sense.

Big Joe came and sat by his father's side and in the process changed the pattern of David's swing. David opened his eyes and looked into his son's face and smiled. He was delighted to have Big Joe next to him. They had never really got on. Had he demanded too much of him too soon, David wondered.

"I've really missed you, Joe," said David, looking earnestly at his son. "It's not been the same since you've been gone. It's as though I've lost my right arm. I don't think I realised how much I relied upon you over all those years."

"I've missed you too Pa," said Big Joe.

"Now I've lost Little Joe, it's like I've lost my left arm because I relied on him too."

"It's gonna be tough on all of us, particularly Ma. I don't know how she's been so brave," said Big Joe.

There was a pause in the conversation as they looked out over the vineyards and fruit trees as dusk began to fall, each in their own thoughts.

"What are you going to do when you leave school?" asked David. "Are you still thinking about Cirencester?" he added hopefully.

"I've applied to Sandhurst," replied Big Joe.

"What, the army?" There was shock in David's voice.

"Yes."

"You're capable of getting into Cambridge; you know that don't you? You've had a series of really good school reports."

"The army have got these nine-month commission courses which sound quite good fun. I'd probably get a spell in Hong Kong or Malaysia. If I get accepted, then they'd sponsor me through university provided I signed up for a short service commission afterwards."

"Isn't your allowance enough? We've already said we'll pay any tuition fees which need to be paid. You know that, don't you?" There was a worry in David's voice.

"Yes, thank you, everything is fine."

"Why the army? I don't understand," said David remaining concerned.

"You know Texas Instruments have just produced the first hand-held, battery driven calculator?"

"Yes, made from silicon," said David, for he had maintained his interest in science and technology.

"It's going to change everything, really everything."

"What's that got to do with the army?"

"Who are the earliest and quickest adopters of new technology?"

"Not the army!" said David aghast. "And certainly not the British army - the Americans, well maybe."

"Oh Pa, we're in a huge space race with the Russians. Military spending is going to remain huge for years, and if I do electronics at Cambridge then..."

"What about being South African?" asked David, interrupting his son's flow.

"Interesting point. When I told them at the first interview I was from South Africa there appeared to be no problem, because it's a former British colony, but because I've a French passport, and not South African one, I'm gonna have to go through positive security vetting. After Uni, I'll have been in the UK five years so I could apply for UK citizenship then."

There was a pause as David wondered how thorough the positive vetting would be. Was his secret going to be discovered?

"Any idea on a regiment?" asked David. "The Hampshire Regiment goes back in the family history; I'm sure they'd be interested."

"The infantry, good God, no!" said Big Joe. "Too much brawn, not enough brain. Possibly the Royal Engineers, maybe the signals. If there was a chance for military intelligence, I'd be interested in that."

David's brain was now in a state of confusion. Had his son found out his secret? Was Big Joe testing him or was this the serendipity of life. Was it just a co-incidence that history was about to be repeated?

"Joe," said David earnestly. "Please think twice and then think a third time."

There was a silence between the two men. David was thinking about his war years. He had worked hard to make sure they were buried deep into the recess of his memory. Now, with Little Joe's death, he had a heightened feeling of frailty. He was very conscious that he had a finite number of days left. Suddenly he had an urge to speak about the past.

"You know I fought in the First World War?" asked David.

"Yes," said Big Joe, very gently for he wanted his father to continue.

"I never talk about it because it was so bad. Do you know when I joined up my life expectancy was just six to eight weeks? Eight weeks! You cannot possibly imagine the slaughter. No man should ever see the sights we saw in that war, dying men, with their guts hanging out, screaming for their mothers. Grown men so scared they were physically shaking, some wetting themselves. Men who were convinced that it was the divine intervention of God which meant that they missed the bullets which had killed the friend who had been standing next to him; the same friend who, the Sunday before, had prayed to the same God." There was sarcastic bitterness in David's voice.

Big Joe listened to his father intensely. He'd never heard him talk like this, and he didn't want it to end.

"What did you do exactly?" asked Big Joe softly.

"I commanded men in four balloon sections. Men I had to order into battle knowing they were going to be killed or desperately injured. Not just killed, those that died straight away, they were the lucky ones. When I gave my orders, I knew some were going to die in unbelievably agonising deaths. All because somebody else had given me an order which I had to obey. It was a fuck-up Joe." David pondered his words. "One big fuck-up!" he continued.

Big Joe had heard David swear before, but he'd never used that word. He felt as though he should have been shocked but somehow the f-word suited the moment.

"I stopped believing in God then, or at least stopped believing that prayer did any good. You know, one day I was sitting in my caravan and there was an infestation of ants. They were everywhere. It was when I was pouring boiling water on them that I stopped believing in divine intervention."

Joe waited for an explanation, which was long in coming.

"I thought about the relationship of that ant and how god-like I would appear to it; me, an all-powerful, omnipresent human being. I thought about the ants facing the catastrophe of boiling water. How they would be on their knees praying, asking for divine help and deliverance. There was no way I could hear their prayers, I couldn't speak ant, and even if I could, was it going to stop me from pouring water over them? It was then that I realised life is completely random. There is no divine intervention. There are only the thoughts and actions of millions and millions of people, each of which influences their further thoughts and actions; that's all.

"So you don't believe in a God who made the universe?" asked Big Joe.

"No, well," David paused as he stumbled for his words. "I don't know," he added, not liking the certainty or finality of what he had said.

"Is there an omnipresent God worth praying to?" David asked himself out loud, and then paused again. "No, there isn't. I'm certain of that," he said forcefully, answering his own question. "Is there, out there in the universe, a more powerful, wiser, intelligent force at work? Yes, that's possible. It would be foolish to discount the fact that something much better, vastly superior in knowledge and intellect to human beings exists, but to think that I can talk to it through prayer is as much a fallacy as an ant praying to me in the hope that I might hear it."

"Many people say prayer works," said Big Joe.

"Do you find it works?" asked David.

Joe shook his head, and he shrugged his shoulders in a way to indicate that he didn't really know. "I find meditation helpful, but that's more about me controlling my mind, my feelings, giving me space to relax, and allowing my thoughts to wander."

"Prayer doesn't bring rain in a drought or abate the waves in a storm," said David firmly. "It's ridiculous to think it does. Prayer only works when it inspires people to come together to work towards a common goal, when they decide to act together to achieve something. Sitting on your knees and thinking about a problem might be a start. In fact, it's a damn good start, but it only gets turned into something positive when those thoughts are turned into actions and deeds."

David didn't like the dogmatism in his voice, so he stopped talking. He'd been thinking about these things for years as he picked his crops in the fields. It was the first time he had ever expressed them and now he had done so he felt slightly embarrassed. Until then these had been his private thoughts, his philosophy, not to be used to influence others, but now he felt his own death was not so far away, perhaps it was right that he shared them.

The chair had stopped swinging backwards and forwards.

"I think Pa, you just summed up my philosophy for me," said Big Joe.

"Thinking Joe, it's what makes us the people we are." David spoke more softly. "Those that think and those that don't."

"You know my house master, in a rebuke to a load of us, once said that people fall into three categories; those who talk about people, the also-rans who talk about events, and the wise who talk about ideas," said Big Joe.

"Sounds a very astute observation to me," commented David.

"Do you think it's a good idea that I do electronics?" asked Big Joe clearly seeking his father's blessing.

"Yes," said David positively. "I certainly do. If that's your interest, then I'll encourage you in every way I can. But for God's sake Joe, don't join up to do it. It's just not worth it."

"Why not?"

"I don't think that's the right question. Why would you want to take a totally unnecessary risk if the same goal can be achieved without it?"

"I could be lucky."

"But you increase your chances of being unlucky," said David.

"But you can't go through life not taking risks."

"I agree," said David. "The sound argument is that every risk should be carefully measured, but life doesn't work like that. The longer I live, I realise there is no rhyme or reason to each individual life. The universe and nature has a structure to it. The role each of us plays in this structure. I don't think we'll ever know."

"You're now arguing against yourself, Pa," said Joe, half teasing him. He paused and then asked, "What bad decision did Little Joe make which put him out there?" He nodded his head in the direction of his brother's grave. "There was none. He was far too young. Why was he the unlucky one?"

"Oh Joe, I wish I could answer that," said David, his voice yielding his feeling of total despair. His mouth was suddenly so dry he could no longer talk. Once again, he fought to hold back his tears. He didn't want his son to see him cry. Instead, he patted Big Joe's knee a couple of times and got up. "It's time your mother and I had our evening walk. Soon it will be too dark. Would you like to join us?" With that remark, he was gone.

It was the very next day, after David, Satutu and Sunetta had returned from the airport, having said goodbye to Big Joe, that the South African Government delivered its coup de grâce in its fight to silence Satutu. Her permission, as a French Citizen, to remain in South Africa had been revoked. She had to leave the country within twenty-eight days.

Chapter 25

Cape Town, South Africa November 1964

DAVID KNEW THAT Jackson was not the lawyer he wanted to fight Satutu's deportation order. He was too much of a streetfighter; accustomed to dealing with custody officers in the local police station, and behind the scenes, doing plea bargaining deals with judges in Regional Magistrates' Courts.

David was prepared to fight Satutu's house arrest warrant and her deportation order all the way to the Supreme Court of Appeal if necessary. He was fairly certain that the South African government would not give in at any stage. Hers would be a test case to be taken to the highest court in the land. It would require a lawyer, probably two or three, with the intellect and mental dexterity capable of arguing the finest nuances of immigration law. It would also require a law firm which had an office in both Cape Town and Bloemfontein, where the Supreme Court was based, and most importantly, was not dependant on the Government for a large proportion of its fee income. After numerous phone calls David discovered that there was only one such law firm, Fourie, Chetty and Steyn, and that the man he should be dealing with was a Mr Peter Harrison.

Peter Harrison was as true an academic lawyer as could possibly be found. He was, and looked as though he was, in his early fifties and although he remained slim, trim and very smart he had probably not moved at speed for at least fifty of those years. Exertion was not, he had decided a long time ago, conducive to his well-being.

Harrison had written numerous books on constitutional and immigration law. As a result, the government consulted with him on the drafting of the Constitution Act which created the Republic of

South Africa in 1961, but then ignored his quite considerable advice for political expediency, as Peter Harrison would not be rushed. He was a visiting professor at the Faculty of Law at the University of Cape Town and notorious amongst campus circles for having the least well attended lectures of all the professors. Whilst the minutiae of the historical development of some minor legal point going back as far as Plato and Socrates interested him, it was far from what the students needed to know to pass their exams. There was one other thing about Peter Harrison. It was his incredible politeness and moral fibre. He was unimpeachable and this meant that he was unassailable from the usual tactics of the secret police. Where he found an injustice in an area of law in which he had expertise, then he was determined that the force of law and logic should prevail. He would fight, like a dog protecting its bone, to get justice. If Harrison believed in Satutu's cause then there was no one better in South Africa to fight it, and the security services knew this.

From the description they had, both Satutu and David expected to meet an absent-minded lawyer, with papers strewn everywhere but this was far from the case. His office was large, neat and extremely tidy, with not a thing out of place. There were the minimum of formalities, not even the offer of a drink. Immediately after they had sat down, Harrison returned to sit behind his desk and asked Satutu and David question after question. It was the speed and neatness with which he wrote, often covering exactly what they had said, and almost as they spoke it, which impressed them. He filled up the full line on each page before going on to the next.

During this time Harrison had hardly looked at them. With his questions exhausted Harrison looked up. "Would you like a drink?" he asked. Immediately after drinks were ordered, Harrison returned to study his copious notes which he laid out side by side, probably 12 or 13 pages in all. Then, in total silence, he would pick up a page, underline certain words in green ink and then write a number against it. In this process he was ordering his thoughts.

"Mrs Daunier," Harrison said at last, "this Government has no grounds whatsoever to evict you from this country. For them to do so would be illegal."

David and Satutu looked at each other. They smiled from relief, but said nothing, for the floor had been given to Harrison.

"The first point is that you are a well-established South African citizen. Not only do you have a Pass Book, but almost uniquely you are one of the very few black people to have a South African Passport. Not only that, but the passport was renewed just over eighteen months ago which is a long time after you married Mr Daunier and took French citizenship." Harrison paused. "Please forgive me Mrs Daunier when I refer to you as being black. I mean no offence but the law in South Africa is not colour blind as I wish it were. I use it as it is the legal term for those with your human characteristics."

It was these few words which made David and Satutu putty in his hands. It was clear that Harrison had no interest in the colour of the person, just the legal aspects which surrounded them.

"Yours is an interesting case," he continued, "as you are a citizen of two countries. If South Africa were to try and revoke your South African citizenship, which they can't, then you would not be stateless as you would still be a citizen of France. If you only had South African citizenship then it would be illegal to take away your citizenship of this country, as it would make you stateless."

"Doesn't this make it easier for the Government to revoke Satutu's South African citizenship?" asked David.

"Yes, but there is a thing called domicile which has to be born in mind. I asked Mrs Daunier where she was born, she said here. I asked her where she wanted to be buried, she said here. I asked her if she had ever lived in any other country, she said no. Mrs Daunier can properly establish her domicile as being South Africa. It is another of the reasons why this Government cannot deny or take away her citizenship."

Harrison paused to gather his thoughts.

"The matter of Mrs Daunier's house arrest is quite interesting," he continued. "It's been ordered under the 1960 State of Emergency. As you may know this was brought in after the Sharpeville massacre. It is interesting that, despite the Government having taken these powers four years ago, Parliament has not yet seen fit to revoke them. Now the General Laws Amendment Act, which was one of a number of pieces of security legislation passed in 1960, only permits a maximum of 90 days detention. Accordingly, any detention order which lasts longer than 90 days would be illegal. Mrs Daunier has no end date on her order, so one should be able to assume it would end 90 days after its issue date but, in these circumstances, I think it would be unwise to do so. I am sorry to say that, because of Mrs Daunier's skin colour, this element of the law will be ignored by the police. If she were to venture outside then her arrest and detention in prison is almost guaranteed, albeit unlawfully so. She must, at all costs, give them no reason to arrest her. Mrs Daunier can appeal against her house arrest order now, but I can tell you that she will not win. The best thing to do is to apply to the High Court on the 91st day of the order, asking the court to declare it null and void."

David and Satutu looked at each other, but Harrison didn't notice. He was intent on completing his soliloquy.

"As you may be aware, Mr and Mrs Daunier, South Africa was one of the founding members of the United Nations in 1945. Interestingly though, it has not signed, nor has it taken into its law, the Universal Declaration of Human Rights adopted by the United Nations in 1948 as it is required by the treaty to do. The reasons are obvious. Article 1 states that all human beings are born free and equal in dignity and rights and Article 2 gives everyone all the rights and freedoms set forth in the Declaration, without distinction of any kind, such as race, colour, sex, language, religion, political or other opinion, national or social origin, or property. As you see, the apartheid laws are directly in conflict with the UN's Declaration of Human Rights. Article 9 is of particular interest to you. It says that no one shall be subject to arbitrary arrest, detention or exile. They have given no reason for your house arrest, so it is reasonable to argue that, until they provide a good reason, this is an arbitrary detention and therefore in breach of the declaration.

Harrison got up from his chair. He much preferred to lecture standing up, and it was a lecture he was now giving, albeit that there were only two in this class.

"However, Article 8 is the really interesting article in your case," continued Harrison. "This is because it says: *everyone has the right to an effective remedy by the competent national tribunals for acts violating the fundamental rights granted him by the constitution or by law.* Now, of course, it should have said *for acts violating the fundamental rights granted him by this declaration*, but it didn't thanks to the Russians and in some part the Americans. This was of huge annoyance to the British lawyers on the drafting delegation. They could see how easily a coach and horses could be driven through its intent. The Americans argued that since the objective was that every member of the UN would ratify the declaration and take it into their laws that the objective would be achieved. The UK ambassador wrote at the time that he could not believe how naive the Americans were in believing that Stalin would ever take the Human Rights Declaration into Soviet Law."

"I think you've just told me that if South Africa had ratified the UN's Declaration of Human Rights then we could use it in Mrs Daunier's defence," said David, "but since it hasn't, we can't. Is that right?" David was attempting to prove he had followed what Harrison had said so far.

"Yes, that is exactly what I have told you, but there are complex aspects of jurisprudence and international law which have to be considered and argued. For example, Article 1 of the Declaration also states that all human beings are endowed with reason and conscience and should act towards one another in a spirit of brotherhood. This is a statement of natural justice and this concept is found in most laws in most countries. It is certainly enshrined in South African law, which to a large part is based upon English Common Law."

Harrison had stood still until that moment, now he started to walk around the room. He ignored his clients as he stopped, stared out into the distance at Table Top Mountain, and started walking again, doing this three or four times.

"How did Mrs Daunier get her Pass Book for Paarl?" Harrison asked, suddenly. "She was not born there nor had she laboured there for a continuous period of 10 years when she first applied."

"Mrs Daunier didn't have one when she came to work for me," answered David. "I applied for it on her behalf, as her employer."

"So it's been illegally granted?"

"No, I don't think so."

"Did Mrs Daunier fill in the form truthfully?"

"I filled in the form, and both Mrs Daunier and I signed it; me as her employer. We left a lot of it blank as we were told to do."

"Did you pay any buckshee? No, don't answer that," said Harrison sternly.

Of course we paid buckshee, thought David, remaining silent as he was instructed. The Pass Book permitting her to stay in the Paarl area might never have come if they hadn't.

"Is there a problem?" asked Satutu. It was the only time she had spoken other than to answer a question.

"As a black person you need your Pass Book to be allowed in to certain areas, for example, where you live in Paarl." Harrison was making a statement of the well-known. "Under the law, any government employee of any rank can strike out any permission in any Pass Book," he continued. "With a swipe of their pen they can banish any black or coloured person from any area. This could happen to you. The permission you have in your Pass Book to be in Paarl could be revoked at any moment, in which case you would have to leave your home immediately."

Satutu looked at David. She was suddenly frightened. She had no idea that a low grade, ignorant and unintelligent state worker had such power over her life.

"Moreover, if your Pass Book was illegally obtained ..." continued Harrison.

"It wasn't," interjected David firmly.

"If your Pass Book was illegally obtained," repeated Harrison, "then it would have no locus standi and you would have to leave your home. I stress not South Africa, just your home.

Harrison paused: "Mr Daunier, when I build a case I do so on solid foundations. I do not want to find that Mrs Daunier's Pass Book gives me a foundation of sand. Its issue will have to be investigated by us, of course without arising suspicion, if I am to act on your wife's behalf."

"But in Paarl I've always been treated as an honorary white woman, so they can't do that to me, can they?" she asked. "In any case, they've put me under house arrest there."

"You certainly don't want to be taken into custody. The moment that happens we are ten nil down in the battle," said Harrison sharply.

"But I've lived and worked at New Found Estate for well over 20 years, surely that counts?"

"No, not if your Pass Book is altered in any way to take away your authority to live there," said Harrison, returning to the chair behind his desk.

These exchanges were getting Satutu very angry, just as the Pass Book made every black and coloured South African feel, for it was the instrument which curtailed their freedom.

Harrison watched as, in front of his eyes, Satutu's disposition changed to show her displeasure. Instinctively, he now knew that this lady held some considerable power behind David's throne.

"I think the best thing my firm can do to help is to prepare the arguments to take these issues to court," said Harrison.

David and Satutu looked at each other and nodded.

"It will not be cheap," said Harrison.

"How much?"

"In cases like these we will have two partners, two associates and me working the file."

David winced.

"One team will prepare the attack, and another will prepare the defence. This way we will be able to work out in advance what the other side might throw at us.

"Likely cost?" asked David.

"I am sorry I don't discuss fees," said Harrison. "I leave that to my clerk. The law and money have never been good bedfellows. I am sure he will prepare a budget for you."

It would have been a good moment to close the meeting. Instead, Harrison very neatly piled his papers in front of him where he laid his fountain pen and green biro. He rested his arms on his desk as he leaned forward and clasped his fingers together. For the first time, he studied the woman in front of him. Before that moment, she had been a legal case. Now she was his client he was interested in her. Firstly, he concluded that Satutu had aged incredibly well for he would have put her age between seven and ten years younger than the age of 37 which her papers said she was. Was there, he wondered, something unwholesome about her relationship with David, who looked every bit his age. Harrison didn't normally find black women appealing but there was something about the dark smoothness of Satutu's skin and the whiteness of her eyes and teeth, all set on a long fine neck, which was very beguiling.

"I am not an expert on the security services, but I have been in this job long enough to know how they work," said Harrison. "I do not believe that Mrs Daunier would have been put under house arrest unless they had evidence linking her, or you Mr Daunier, to the ANC."

"I can assure you Mr Harrison," said David firmly, "neither Satutu nor I have had, nor will we have, anything to do with them, or any other political organisation for that matter. Mrs Daunier has been asked many times to speak at ANC meetings, or on their behalf, and she has never done so and will not do so."

"All opinions I express, Mr Harrison, are mine and mine alone. As my husband said, I speak for no one." Satutu spoke softly, for long ago she had learnt that, sometimes, it is the quietest who are heard the loudest.

Harrison was silenced for a moment. Satutu's words were said in such a silky soft voice he found himself being disarmingly enchanted. There was, he had to admit, an aura of grace around her which was totally charming.

"That is good to hear," said Harrison, gathering his composure. "It makes my work much easier, but I say again, I do not believe that Mrs Daunier would have been put under house arrest unless the security services had some evidence linking either or both of you to the ANC. It might be someone who works on your estate, it might be one of your suppliers, it might even be your accountant or former lawyer but, until you find out who it is, you are at considerable risk of being tainted by association."

"And the manifestation of this risk?" asked Satutu.

"You've already seen it; house arrest and deportation. Next will be imprisonment. I urge you to take care, considerable care," said Harrison as he closed the meeting.

It was Satutu who drove them back to New Found House. They had long learned that, when out of their home area, they were less likely to be stopped if Satutu was the chauffeur and David sat as the passenger in the back seat. It was these small curtailments of their freedom which had become so automatic that they no longer noticed.

"Don't turn around and look," said Satutu to David when they were half an hour out of Cape Town, "but we are being followed. We were followed by the same car when we drove in this morning."

"Really," said David for it seemed a strange thing for anyone to do. Then he asked, "Do you have a mirror?"

Satutu passed him her handbag and he went rummaging about for a mirror. How was it that someone who was so well organised on the outside, whose drawers and cupboards were always so neatly stacked, could have such chaos in her handbag? He thought it every time she went delving around in it and, on the rare occasions he mentioned it, her defence was always the needs of motherhood which, as far as she was concerned, trumped any criticism he might make. It was now David's turn to go burrowing and eventually, in despair, he turned everything out onto the back seat.

With a vanity mirror in hand, he used it to study obsessively the car behind and its two occupants, giving a running commentary, albeit Satutu could observe what was happening through the rear-view mirror. Speed up, slow down, take this diversion, take that diversion he ordered, and yet the car behind stuck firmly on their tail.

David and Satutu were both in a heightened state of anxiety as they turned into the drive of New Found Estate. They both had a palpable sense of relief as the car following them slowed, observed where they had gone and then drove straight on.

Without saying anything to Satutu, David went straight to the Estate office, as their home phone remained disconnected. There he called Harrison's clerk. "Do not," he instructed him, "send anything by post to us here at New Found House. We're being watched. Please phone and we will come to you to read it. Oh, and tell Mr Harrison, he is to start work straight away. We will sort out fees," he added. "I'm afraid time is now of the essence!"

"Sunetta has to leave," said Satutu immediately David walked through the front door of the main house. "It's too unsafe for her here. We don't know what will happen to any of us. For some reason it's getting very dangerous."

"It's a cup of tea and list time" said David walking in to his study without acknowledging Satutu's remarks.

"You will need to go too," said David to Satutu immediately she returned to his study five minutes later carrying two mugs of tea."

"No, I can't go. If I go they've won. They can't kill Little Joe and win. They can't, I won't allow it." There was a mix of desperation and determination in Satutu's voice.

David didn't argue. He knew from her steely tone that there was no point, but it was also because he agreed with her. This vile regime should not be allowed to win.

"No, it's you who has to go to look after her," said Satutu.

"That's impossible. I can't leave you here on your own. It wouldn't be safe for you and it wouldn't be safe for the estate either. We already have far too many silly things going wrong."

They both sipped gently at their tea in silence, as each contemplated the problem.

"I wonder if Roedean would take her?" said David out loud.

"Who, what's Roedean?

"It's one of the top girls' public schools in England. It sits alongside Wycombe Abbey as one of the best girls' boarding schools, that's where my sister went to school."

"Your sister," said Satutu, shocked at this news after so long. "You have a sister?" she asked. "Is that her picture on your desk?" It was the first time since Satutu had arrived at New Found House that she asked about the photograph, knowing, as she did so, that she was breaking one of their unspoken rules.

"No, that's not her, that's Drew. She went to Roedean but, my sister and Drew, they're both dead." He knew he was lying about Juliette but to say anything else would raise further complications which he was not prepared for.

"You never said," said Satutu disapprovingly, and "who's Drew? Why do you have a picture of her on your desk?"

"I have never said many things, Satutu, and I have no intention of starting now," rebuked David.

Satutu nodded. In doing so, she acknowledged David's chastise; their relationship was based on not asking questions about their past, and she had just strayed beyond that deepest of understanding.

"Why not Wycombe Abbey?"

"I don't think it will be right for her. A mixed kid in an all-white school like that."

"Eton's just admitted a nigger. A boy called Onyeama," said Satutu, challenging David's perception.

"How do you know that?"

"It was in the papers."

"If we can't get her into Roedean then we will try Wycombe Abbey," he said, and in doing so he stopped the debate.

Roedean was an independent girls-only school set in over 100 acres on the cliff tops of the Sussex Downs, overlooking the sea. David tried to phone the headmistress but, as with all her other calls, his immediate access was blocked. David explained the circumstances to the Bursar and a time was agreed as to when the headmistress and he would speak.

"I am so sorry at the loss of your son, Joe," said the headmistress immediately after David had announced his name on answering the office telephone.

"Thank you."

"May I say how impressed we have all been with Mrs Daunier's handling of the situation."

"You've seen it?" said David, surprised.

"We made her response the subject of debate throughout the school. We constantly look for strong women role models and the way she turned the focus from Joe's death to the need for clean water in the townships gave us a good lesson in anthropology."

"Thank you. I will tell her," said David.

"Are you sure you are not seeking to get your daughter into our sister school in Johannesburg. It seems the obvious place for her?"

"No," said David, perplexed at even the thought of the idea. "Our daughter is of mixed race and we're in a game of political and racial football which we don't understand. Except it is giving us serious problems. Sadly, we need Sunetta out of South Africa for her own safety."

"Oh, Mr Daunier, how clumsy of me, please forgive me. I do apologise. I didn't think. It is just, we are so opposed to apartheid here that, well, we sometimes miss out on the obvious."

"South Africa is going through a dreadful experiment right now, just as the Soviet Union is going through its dreadful experiment of communism," said David. "You have to be here to understand it. Just hope and pray that these lessons are quickly learnt, so that all us who are suffering under the inhumanity of a police state, like we are, are soon free."

"Just so, just so," said the headmistress, conscious that they were getting off topic. In the next few minutes, the headmistress and David agreed the methodology by which Sunetta would be admitted to the school. She would go to their sister school in Johannesburg where she would sit a maths and English written paper. If the marks were good enough then there would be a 45-minute telephone interview between the Headmistress and Sunetta.

"You don't want Harriet in this school to struggle do you Mr Daunier?" said the headmistress, referring to Sunetta's formal Christian name.

"I don't want my daughter to die," responded David. "It's why I have to get her out of the country."

"Indeed, indeed," said the headmistress, feeling suitably humbled. "We will do what we can."

David had said exactly the right thing. However badly Sunetta did in the tests, the headmistress was determined that she was coming to Roedean. Harriet's death was not going to fall on her hands.

As David put down the phone he thought about Drew. If he had not met her he wondered, would he have thought of Roedean? He doubted it.

In January 1965, dressed in her new school uniform, and accompanied by Big Joe, Harriet Daunier arrived as a new girl at Roedean School. She would take her 'O' levels in the summer. This meant she arrived under a certain amount of academic pressure.

Nevertheless, Sunetta was calmed with encouraging words from the headmistress at the end of their first meeting.

"Life is not a race," she said. "No one knows how many days each of us have got, so at your young age don't despair if you are ever behind. There is always time to catch up. I'm sure your Father would agree. Life should be taken like a fine wine, tasted purposely and savoured slowly. For to drink, or live, too fast or too furiously, lessens the senses, and in the process too much of God's glory is lost."

The new 'Harriet' would remember those words forever; whereas her 'Sunetta' character, would forget them, particularly when her body exuded an energy which, sometimes, she felt it impossibly hard to control.

Chapter 26

London November 1965 - September 1966

WHY WAS EVERYONE else having plenty of sex and not him? This question was the focus of Henry's thoughts as he travelled on the slow train from King's Cross to Hertford North. The harvest was in at de Gressier, the grapes sorted, and fermentation was well under way. As things had quietened, he had decided he could leave and come back to England.

He was worrying that, amongst all his friends, he appeared to be the only one sleeping alone. It wasn't, he concluded, that he was particularly disadvantaged in looks. He was sure he was better looking than Mick Jagger, and yet he had the benefits of the stunning Marianne Faithful as his girlfriend. What the hell was he doing wrong, he wondered. When he was abroad he found finding a girlfriend easy and yet, in the UK and France, there was something which repressed his nature. It was, he resolved, a lack of modus operandi. By the time he stepped off the train, to be greeted by his mother, he had a solution. "I'm going to get a London flat," he announced immediately after he had sat down in her car.

Henry's first thoughts were about buying a canal barge. He remembered how friends at university had lived a bohemian student lifestyle on a boat moored within its campus grounds. This took his searches for somewhere to live around the basin at Little Venice. While the idea of slipping from the moorings and travelling the canal network appealed to him, it was the practicalities of living which caused Henry to rent a two bedroomed furnished flat, with a lovely sitting room overlooking the gardens of Little Venice.

It was Henry's fondness for his new flat and a new found social scene which kept him in Europe for the rest of 1965 through to the autumn of 1966. He travelled extensively attending every wine fair, convention, exhibition, almost every gathering of oenologists he could get to. He collected every brochure, book or catalogue he could get hold of, building an extensive library. Again, he always bought two bottles of their last two, or three, year's production. With his Châteaux de Gressier business card and his job description as an oenologist he found he could mix with the top table of the wine industry.

It was the connoisseurs he could not bear. The pretentiousness of the wine snobs and buffs both irritated and bored him in equal measure. He found men standing around comparing wines and guessing at vintages so amateurish as to be laughable when he was able to do so with far more accuracy with the scientific equipment he had been using at university. Why was it, he wondered, that a group of people who would sniff in disdain at those who might attend a Doctor Who convention, would see nothing wrong in debating for hours whether a 1965 wine was better than a 1964 wine? To Henry they were equally as cultist.

Further, being teetotal and with the use of plenty of water and a spittoon, his ability to use his eyes, nose and taste buds to identify and grade wine was becoming finely honed, whilst those who professed to be the experts did not notice their senses decreasing as their alcohol levels increased. Nevertheless, Henry remembered his grandmother's wise words about the romance of wine, and it was his awareness of this point which made him hide his feelings. Thus, he moved easily in the company of wine buffs, introducing himself effortlessly, whilst maintaining a reserved disposition.

Whenever he was asked his opinion on certain wines or vintages, he would always reply, "I don't speak for wine. I allow the wine to speak for itself." He had learnt long ago that, without his chemistry set, it was unwise to comment.

In his flat, and in total solitude, Henry would carefully study every bottle of wine he had purchased on his many journeys, making copious notes as he did so. As he compared and contrasted all the different wines, he was developing a discerning pallet and fine nose. But this was never enough for him for it lacked the precision of the scientist, and his personality demanded precision.

One day, after he had complained bitterly to Juliette for the umpteenth time about the amateur nature of vineyards in Europe as compared to the United States, she told him, quite angrily, to go out and buy the equipment he needed. He did so. He purchased almost all the equipment he had used in the Université de Bordeaux's chemistry department which, to Juliette's chagrin, took all of Château de Gressier's capital expenditure budget for the next three years.

Working almost day and night, Henry went back to every unopened bottle of wine he had in his possession and retested them with the equipment he now had. He kept highly accurate records of the results. He also examined his original notes for that wine to make sure his new notes were not fundamentally at odds with those he made when he opened the first bottle of wine he'd had from the same vineyard and vintage.

It was whilst watching a film on a flight back from a short visit to the winelands of Greece that Henry learnt about the grading of diamonds. How each stone is measured in size, colour, clarity, and inclusions, so it can be uniquely identified. Taking the same principles, but with many more facets, Henry set about producing the Bellanger Chart which mathematically graded and recorded in the minutest of detail every bottle of wine he had ever opened since he started his career as an oenologist.

Alongside the notes for each bottle of wine, David recorded, and graded, every aspect of the vineyard for that year. Not just the simple things like the grapes but the nature and acidity of the soil, the fertilizers and chemicals they used, when and the way they pruned the vines, the methodology of harvest, and then the myriad different ways the wine was made; even down to the different types of wood used in the making of the barrels, the nature of the corks and the manufacturer of their bottles. If any element changed, however small, he wanted it recorded.

As he slaved at his work, Henry began to realise that he had taken on a task bigger than Samuel Johnson's when he wrote the first

English dictionary. Each year there was a new harvest and vintage, which had to be studied and classified, but the perfectionist in him would not allow him to stop and re-assess. He was producing his own encyclopaedia of wine.

Chapter 27

Cape Town December 1966 – January 1967

SATUTU'S APPEALS AGAINST her deportation order and house arrest were going well. She had won in the High Court only to find that the South African Government appealed the deportation decision, and then issued a new house arrest order. Nevertheless, David and Satutu thought that it would be safe for Big Joe and Sunetta to come home for Christmas. Big Joe declined, making a lame excuse, but Sunetta was thrilled to be making the journey. The easter and summer holidays had been hard on her. Although she had spent all the time with her brother, and for most of August they had backpacked throughout Europe on a railcard visiting all the major cities, she didn't like being a nomad. What she found particularly hard was being unable to share the excitement of her 'O' level results with anyone else, for she had done remarkably well in a very short period. University was now a distinct possibility.

It was a stunning young woman who David met off the aeroplane. His daughter had left just under a year ago and in that time Sunetta had developed all the physical advantages of her mother. Gone was the out-of-control energy of youth; in its place, a young woman with grace and calm who, through her deportment, oozed confidence.

It is hot in South Africa in December and January, so Sunetta was disappointed to find that the swimming pool was in a state of disrepair, made worse by the carcass of a young dead baboon which had fallen in and drowned. Following the shutting down of the school, the village children had gone back to swimming in the river as the risks to David and Satutu being arrested, for breaking the apartheid rules, was just too high. For David, now close to approaching his 77th birthday, the appeal of a refreshing swim had started to lose its appeal. He found it was taking too much of his energy.

After Big Joe left and Little Joe died, David and Satutu had become dependent on their senior farm hand, Lereko Naidoo who, from the first day he worked for David, had won the obvious nickname Lucky.

Lucky was the tallest, largest and most powerful man on the farm, with not an ounce of fat on his body. Over the years he had used his strength to make himself indispensable, particularly now David lacked the might of his youth. He confidently expected that one day, in the not-too-distant future, he would be elected as chief of their village. Unknown to him, the village elders had already decided he was not suitable. He carried with him a resentment which they felt, given his exulted position on the farm, was dangerously inappropriate. Further, it was well known amongst the women of the village, and therefore the elders, that Lucky looked down on Satutu. Not only did she come from a different tribe but, in his opinion, she had let her tribe and all black people down by the unforgivable sin of having children with a white man.

Deep down, eating into Lucky's heart was apartheid, and most importantly the fact that his country was being run by white invaders, of which there was just one of them for every three black people to whom God had originally given his country. As far as Lucky was concerned, the white man had stolen South Africa and he wanted it back. The ANC was the force to enable that to happen. He was determined that, one day, not now, not next year, but perhaps in five or ten years, the black man would be in the ascendance, at which point New Found Estate would become his. He just had to wait patiently and, if each day it got a bit harder for the Dauniers, then that would, he thought, hasten the day when they would leave.

It was naturally to Lucky that Sunetta went to ask him to clean out, paint and recommission the swimming pool. He watched her walk towards him. She was wearing the shortest of shift dresses revealing her long legs which only just covered her knickers, as was the fashion of the time. Her long black ponytail swung from side to side, and she wore the biggest of smiles, as she was genuinely pleased to see him.

"I'll make it worth your while," Sunetta said teasingly in encouragement, as she left him after explaining exactly what she wanted.

There was just two days left of her holiday when Lucky invited Sunetta to inspect his completed work on the swimming pool. As she walked through the door into the walled garden, which surrounded the pool, she realised how much she loved this place. Its flowers were raked back to rise high against the wall. With its beautifully watered and mowed lawn, coming just a metre away from the pools edge, it was, in Sunetta's mind, heaven's place on earth.

She immediately saw Lucky who beckoned her forward. She moved to stand by his side examining the clarity of the water and spoke to thank him for his efforts. Lucky sought his reward by beckoning a kiss. She kissed him gently on the cheek. He tapped his lips indicating that was where he wanted to be kissed.

Sunetta ignored his gesture. "It's not just for me you know," she said, trying to offer an excuse for her reluctance to kiss him where he wanted.

"It is!" said Lucky sharply. "Since Little Joe died no one from the village is allowed in here."

"Why?" asked Sunetta innocently.

"It's the white man's rule," he replied with bitterness in his voice. Lucky grasped Sunetta's hand and led her into the summer house which had a smell of fresh paint. Sunetta stopped and examined his work and then, thinking that she was being invited to inspect more, she innocently followed him into the changing room where there appeared to be no difference. The changing cubicles stood as they always had. The benches, shelving and baskets for clothes and towels were as they had been left at the end of last season. There was dampness in the air and wetness all around as Lucky had hosed the room down to clean it up after its period of non-use.

"Time for my present," said Lucky, touching his lips once again. "Time for my kiss," he said, as his body blocked the doorway and Sunetta's way out. It was not a request but an instruction!

Slowly, cautiously, Sunetta moved towards Lucky. This time she stood on the tip of her toes to give him a quick peck on his lips, but, as their lips touched, he grabbed her and kissed her passionately, fully on the mouth.

"No Lucky," she said breathlessly as she broke from his kiss, but he brought her in close to him. He towered above her, and she felt the power in his body as he forced her face into his chest. Sunetta's heart started to thump in her chest as fear began to overwhelm her.

Lucky's hands moved roughly about her clothing. Then, in an instant, she felt him lift up her dress as his large hands started to move inside her panties, around her bare buttocks and back. With each move he squeezed her on to him even tighter.

He ran both his hands lower down behind her legs, then he lifted her up, spreading her legs wide either side of his body, until her face was directly opposite his. He stopped for a moment looking at the delicacy of Sunetta's beautiful face. His excitement was enhanced by the fear starting to yield in her eyes, just as there had been with the other women he had taken. Power, he loved power. Control and power were Lucky's aphrodisiac which made him lethally dangerous.

Using his elbows, Lucky forced Sunetta's legs hard in to his waist so she was being held by his hips. With his free hands he yanked hard at her knickers, tearing the soft cotton material causing the waistband and edging to cut deep into her skin causing deep red marks.

"No Lucky, no!" she said firmly. "Lucky this isn't funny, stop, stop," she now shouted, but Lucky wasn't listening. His mind was focused on undoing his shorts and letting them fall to the ground. With her legs forced wide and with his hands under her bottom, he forced her torn panties to one side as he opened her sex and lowered her onto his erect shaft. Sunetta rose to stop him entering her by clinging around his neck as to let go would mean she would fall back heavily.

"Stop it, stop it now! Put me down!" she commanded, feeling the tip of his weapon starting to move inside her. She wriggled vigorously to try and move off him, but his grip was vice-like. Lucky stepped one leg over the changing bench and leaned forward. Sunetta gripped Lucky tightly around his neck to stop her falling but, as he tipped her backwards, her weight took more of Lucky inside her. Just as she felt the security of the bench slates under her body, he pushed deep and hard, tearing her apart, causing her to scream out in pain; a pain far more intense than she had ever felt before. It was a scream with such intensity that it was music to Lucky's ears taking him to a new peak of arousal.

Sunetta tried to talk. She heard herself yelling in her head; 'no', and 'stop' and 'get off' but no words came out of her mouth as he continued to hurt her with each thrust of his pelvis. She shook her head furiously from side to side and tried to use her hands to push him away, first against his chest and then pushing against his hip, doing anything she could to stop him hurting her.

While deep inside her, Lucky stopped his thrusting and, leaning forward, he kissed her gently on the lips. Sunetta didn't respond. Instead, she stared into his eyes, troubled by the vacancy which she saw there.

"Can't have you having a black baby, can we," he said as he withdrew to relieve himself over her stomach.

"I guess you're no virgin," said Lucky, contempt leaking into his voice.

Sunetta said nothing, she was in too much shock and pain.

"The summer ishie boy was your first I s'pose. Broke you in nicely for me," said Lucky condescendingly, as he took a towel and wiped down her stomach.

Sunetta wriggled away from him, pulled her knees deep into her chest which she tried to cover with her dress, but it was too short to give her the modesty she yearned, so she reached for a towel and wrapped that around her. She was now shaking uncontrollably from fear and the hurt she felt inside.

"But not much of a man about him," continued Lucky, taking his penis into his hand deliberately showing off its length and breadth to Sunetta. "I'll always be better than any white man," he said defiantly.

Lucky picked up his shorts, stepped into them, buckled his belt and looked at her. Under his stare she suddenly realised he was looking at her in total disgust, as though she were just another piece of meat. No words were spoken but Lucky's eyes conveyed everything he intended. Sunetta was to be the latest in his long line of sex slaves.

"If you want a job done, you know where to come and the price." he said. There was no joke his voice.

Sunetta's fear was suddenly replace with a huge sense of foreboding. Something else was about to go wrong. Very, very wrong and she was sure of it!

"Right now, you've just paid the price for our bargain," said Lucky with a smirk on his face. "But one day soon you'll pay with this estate, and then it will be mine."

Those few words struck Sunetta like a dagger through the heart. She knew exactly what he was saying. Lucky had confirmed what her parents had feared; a forced takeover of their farm by the black community immediately apartheid ended, and the land redistribution policies of the ANC were implemented.

"Little Joe was just a casualty in a much bigger fight," said Lucky. "We 'ad to get those white kids out of our school," he added. "We can't go to theirs so they shouldn't come to ours."

"You reported the school to the police?" asked Sunetta. If she was in shock before, this news was devastating for she was certain Lucky was telling her that it was he, on behalf of the blacks, who had set up the whites to kill her brother, a coloured kid.

Lucky picked up his shirt which he scrunched into a ball held in one hand. He stood in the doorway and looked at Sunetta and smiled. It was the smile of a man who knew of secrets. A man who arrogantly believed he was untouchable. It was a frightening smile, for it said, if I want you again, I'll take you. Still carrying that smile Lucky turned and walked out of the door.

Sunetta started to cry and then sob. She felt ashamed, dirty, used. Inside her there was a long lingering pain which hurt every time she moved. She was angry with herself for not fighting or shouting out or screaming. Why had she done none of those things? She hated, even blamed herself for encouraging him.

If Sunetta ever needed any proof, she was now certain she had it. White men considered her black and black men considered her white. She was an outcast to both; to be used by each sect as they pleased. Lucky had brooked no mercy. He had simply taken her without any feeling. She was in no doubt that he would be back to take her again, and again, and then the farm if she didn't find a way to stop him.

Sunetta walked slowly to the shower and in the freezing cold water she washed and scrubbed away the evidence of his attack.

That evening, as Sunetta sat with her parents at their evening meal, she found it impossible to eat as she had knots in her stomach. Every now and again she would shake involuntarily with fear. Satutu, in ignorance of the events, diagnosed sunstroke. Sunetta needed to get away. She thanked God that tomorrow she would be leaving to go back to school. The next day couldn't come soon enough.

Sunetta knew she was running away. She hated the feeling of cowardice which came with knowing that everything, including her safety and that of her family, was at risk unless Lucky was dealt with, and dealt with quickly!

Chapter 28

Argentina September 1966 - Easter 1967

IT WAS AT an Italian wine festival when Henry met the wine buyer from the UK's largest supermarket. It was the buyer's job to select and buy French, Italian and German wines. Interestingly, like Henry, he was no wine junky. Although this man was in his mid-thirties, he looked much younger. He therefore carefully power-dressed to give the impression of a senior executive, which is what he was aspiring to be. He was a man consumed by ambition determined to get to the very top. This drove him to be outstanding in his job. It made the wine buyer stand out from his contemporaries and explained why Henry first noticed him. Henry pumped him for knowledge on the vineyards and wineries of Europe which he should visit. They then had an interesting conversation as Henry shared his knowledge about the wines of California and South Africa, and the threat they posed to European wine producers.

"They will not know what hit them," said Henry confidently.

"Have you been to Argentina?" asked the buyer. "I gather it is the largest wine producing country outside of Europe, but its production is all consumed locally. None goes for export. Apparently, the Argentinians are enormous wine drinkers, several gallons per person per year. I think they may even have the largest consumption of wine per head anywhere in the world."

"It's where I'm going next," lied Henry, for he had made no such plans.

"Then, you must come and see me the moment you are back. I'd be interested to know if you've found some wines that will suit the UK palette."

They swapped business cards and arranged to meet again in London when Henry returned from his trip.

Sometimes the biggest clues are given in the fewest of words and, for Henry, it was the phrase: 'wines that will suit the UK palette'. Was this the case he wondered? Do different nationalities have different taste preferences? If so, was this physiological or cultural? It was a thought which excited and worried Henry in equal measure. It meant he would have to classify a country's taste preferences. Once he had done this, then chemistry would allow him to match the wine to the people. As he left the festival, he knew this analysis was a matter he would have to leave for another day. His next stop would be Argentina.

The wine harvest in Argentina begins sometime in February but some years can be as late as April. Heeding his grandmother's advice of a few years earlier, Henry headed to Buenos Aires in September having had Juliette's permission to miss the harvest. He found a language school in the centre of the city and then found digs. He had heard that the only way to truly learn the language was to live with a family and become totally immersed; only ever hearing Spanish spoken.

It wasn't just for their prowess on the field that Argentina's professional polo players had earned the nickname the 'hired assassins' as, when working on the European summer circuit, they had the reputation of seducing many a willing, but unworldly, maiden. For a third year in a row the brothers Federico and Fabricio Benítez had just returned from playing polo in England, where they had enjoyed the delights of many a polo groupie, not found in the same abundance in their Catholic and sexually oppressed home country.

There was an immediate bon hommie between the two brothers and their new lodger, Henry. Not only did they speak excellent English, but they had a work hard, play hard ethos which Henry found quite inspirational. Each of these three men had family wealth which could see them spend their lives as playboys, but each worked hard at their chosen profession, and in the case of Federico and Fabricio this meant making sure they were properly paid for their polo playing.

It was these two boys who taught Henry the skills and art of polo. He had just a couple of lessons on how to ride, for Henry had never sat on a horse before, but he was quite a natural; possibly the cavalry genes of his great-grandfather passing through the dynasty.

Polo was just the kind of game Henry liked. Firstly, it was played sitting down. It was the legs of the poor horse which ran up and down the field and not his, as was the case in football or rugby. Secondly, there are only eight players on the field at any one time. This means that each player has far more ball time compared to football or rugby where there are either 22 or 30 players. Thirdly, each chukka is only seven minutes long, as compared to the 40 or 45 minutes for half-time in rugby or football. This meant that he got time to rest and have a drink of water as the divots were stamped back into the field. Finally, there was the physicality of it all for, far from releasing tension, he found he built up such aggression on the field that his body was streaming with adrenaline and endorphins at the end of a match. These gave him an enormous sense of good feeling.

Henry's first few games were on wise old polo ponies, who instinctively knew they had a novice on their back. They assiduously kept as far away from the ball as possible, for it was just as likely that their rider would whack them on their shins as the ball. The skill of the horseman is to get even the wiliest of nags into the game, a task which Henry manfully managed. It was through sheer determination that Henry proved to the polo pony who was the boss. His skill on the old nags saw him invited to ride better ponies and play in different matches, in what was obviously Argentina's second national sport.

It was because of polo that Henry stayed in Buenos Aires longer than he originally expected. When he left in early January to travel up to the wine regions, he had already been adjudged a competent player. Federico and Fabricio put this down to the fact that he had a natural eye - ball coordination, but also because he had not once fallen off his horse and hurt himself. It was, they had convinced themselves, a track record which would end sooner rather than later. Would he, after a fall, be just as fearless in the tackle? They suspected not.

Buoyed by his ability to speak Spanish, albeit still poorly, and with a desire to see more of the country, Henry took the bus and travelled to Mendoza City. He had heard that it was in this region, in the eastern foothills of the Andes, where two-thirds of all Argentinian wine was produced, including its Malbec wines which were later to become quite famous, in some part thanks to Henry.

It was a thirteen-hour bus journey, for which Henry was not well equipped. Thus, he was not in the best of moods when he arrived in Mendoza's wide, leafy streets lined with its modern architecture. The poverty which Henry had seen on his bus journey was absent from this city.

Henry did exactly as he had done in Cape Town; settled into a hotel for a couple of days, bought himself a second-hand 350cc Honda motorbike and set out to explore the region. Once again, it might have been said that Henry was one of the first wine tourists, but the wine trails of later years were not, as yet, a figment of anyone's imagination.

At every vineyard Henry introduced himself as a Científico del Vino de France[7] with mixed results. Some thought he was there to steal their secrets and treated him with suspicion. It was these vineyards that refused to sell him their wine. It was utterly ridiculous as he could easily buy their vintages in the local store, which is exactly what he did. Others, and these were the majority, welcomed Henry with open arms. As they showed him around and spoke to him, they began to realise the extent of his knowledge.

For many years, the Argentinian economy had been in the doldrums, driven by the policies of the military dictators who were ruling the country. As a result, the focus of all Argentinian wine producers had been to produce cheap wine for the local economy.

Henry spoke in confident terms about the prices being fetched for the new wines of California or South Africa in the United States and Europe. To the ears of the Argentinian wineries, these were staggering in their amounts. For the first time they heard about micro-bottling and how certain vineyards in Bordeaux were no longer mixing their grapes and producing wine in consortium wineries. They were taking responsibility for their wines from the bud to the bottle. Henry's message was always the same; produce good quality, consistent, well packaged wine and he would be able to sell it for them in Paris and

---

[7] French wine scientist

London. His thesis was so attractive to some of the vineyards that he was invited back several days in a row and, doing what he always did, he paid upfront to get two bottles of the last three years' vintages sent to his mother's house in England.

It was in late March that Henry packed his copious notes into his back-sack and paniers and headed towards La Rioja, as he had heard about its wines. He thought he would make this his last visit before heading home.

It is often sung that 'only mad dogs and English men go out in the midday sun.' Henry suited this adage perfectly. It was with little more preparation than an Englishman sets out for a summer walk, i.e., with just a handkerchief which can be knotted into a cap to protect against sun burn, that Henry left Mendoza City. He had not a single thought as to the problems he might encounter. His only thoughts were on importing Malbec wines into London, and the profit he would make.

Henry started off confidently and drove north towards San Juan, then towards El Fiscal where he headed east, travelling through Parque Probincial Ischigulasto and the southern edge of the Parque Nacional Talampaya. This area is as dry, rocky and barren as anywhere in the world. Nobody in their right mind drives at night, unless they live locally, and certainly not on a motorbike. By the time Henry had passed the fifth or sixth cross on the side of the road, indicating a fatal accident, he knew he must stop.

Night fell very quickly, and with the darkness came the cold. He had no food, no water and no way of lighting a fire, least of all did he know whether it was safe to sleep on the ground. Henry was already very cold when he came to a stop, but now stationery he was beginning to shiver involuntarily. There was a wind building up, and nowhere around could he see any shelter. Many times on this trip Henry had cursed himself for not having purchased a crash helmet, as he had always done before, but now he was very angry at his own stupidity. Taking his clothes from his rucksack he wrapped them around his head and stuffed them around the front and back of his jacket to give him extra warmth.

Using the headlights of his motor bike he found some brush wood, a form of tumbleweed, and using the heat of the engine he managed to start a small fire. However, he couldn't find enough wood to keep it going, fearing to search too far off the track in case he fell into a ravine at the side of the road. It was a long, dark and petrifyingly scary night during which he regularly fired up his motorbike engine. It was only the heat of this which stopped Henry drifting into unconsciousness from hypothermia.

At first light, Henry loaded his rucksack on to his back and set off for the next town which was Patquia. He had no idea how far away it was. It could be 35 or 40 miles away, or it could be around the next bend. Henry travelled at a very modest speed for the next half an hour until his engine started to cough. He instantly knew he had a problem. He was out of petrol. He wriggled his bike from side to side to get what little petrol he had in the tank into the carburettor. It kept him going just a little while longer, but it was not far enough.

For the first time since night fall, a vehicle came into view. In desperation, Henry flagged it down. He sought to siphon some of their petrol and the occupants willingly agreed. It was a plan which had to be abandoned when he realised they had a diesel engine. Henry discussed leaving his bike there and hitching with them into town, only for the occupants to laugh. They knew that, before he had even made it into the next village, it would have been purloined. There was just one piece of good news on the horizon. He only had to push his bike into Patquia, and that was just five miles away. The bad news, as he was to discover later, was that the petrol station was on the other side of the town, and it was a long town.

Patquia was just coming alive as Henry pushed his bike through the town. After filling up his motorbike with petrol and making a hefty payment to the cashier for the key to the men's room, Henry washed away the dirt, grime and sweat of the last twenty-four hours. He rode back into town where he found a café which was just opening.

As Henry sat down to a strange breakfast of toasted bacon and egg empanadas, and a plate of cinnamon churros which he dunked in chocolate, he reflected on the night before and the very precarious position he had put himself in. Little did he realise that the genes of his father, who at a young age had learnt that failing to prepare was preparing to fail, was driving his thinking. Taking his note book and pen, Henry started to write a list of the things which he would always carry to keep him safe. The first item on that list was a space blanket which had just come on the market having been developed by NASA just a couple of years earlier.

The invincibility of youth previously enjoyed by Henry ended in his Talampaya experience. It started an obsession about his basic safety, which had been one of his father's characteristics. From this day onwards, there was not a hotel bedroom which Henry entered where he did not first explore the way to the fire escape, and every aeroplane seat was chosen for its nearness to the exit.

With his motorbike refuelled and his tummy full, and possessed of a new maturity, Henry headed towards the vineyards and wineries of La Rioja. These were similar to those of Mendoza in their culture and method of making wine. It was here that Henry suddenly knew what the supermarket buyer had meant when he talked of a wine suiting the English palette. He was certain he had found it. This time he bought three bottles of wine of the last three years' vintages of every place he visited. The third bottle of Rioja he was taking to the supermarket buyer. He was certain that he had found wines which would challenge the red and white Rioja's from Spain, but at a much lower price.

On returning to his flat in England, Henry set about using his chemistry equipment to accurately analyse each of the wines he had brought back from Argentina. The basic content of the wine, water and ethanol alcohol, was of little interest to him, whereas the colour, taste and aroma which comes from a very small fraction of other chemicals he found fascinating. Henry found the complexity of these other chemicals interesting and studied them very carefully.

The acids, amino acids and volatile acids; the esters including isoamyl acetate; the minerals; the sulphites; the phenols including tannin, acetaldehyde, glycerol, and the higher alcohols and, of course, the sugar; he measured them all to the accuracy of several decimal points. But this was never enough. Henry wanted to know what it was which gave each wine its distinctive flavours; the fruit, floral and spicy features, which every connoisseur used to describe the wine in the bottle. It was the exact amount of pyrazines, terpenes, thiols, botrytis, brettanomyces, geomin and rotundone per millilitre which

Henry set out to measure and record. Although all this activity took place in the chaos of his small second bedroom, Henry was getting results of which any professor in a major university would have been proud.

Chapter 29

Cape Town Easter 1967

SUNETTA RETURNED TO the safety of Roedean far more self-conscious than she had ever been. She told no one of Lucky's attack, but wondered if her friends could tell what had happened to her. Was she a changed person in their eyes? During the day, when she was busy, her life at school was just as it was before the Christmas holiday, but it was at night, when she was alone, that she would see the size of Lucky's chest, his arms, his hands, every part of him. She would curl up in a foetal ball in fear. In each and every one of those moments she knew she had to deal with him; but how? She needed not just revenge, but for him to be gone for good.

It was on a Sunday two weeks into the spring term when Sunetta phoned Big Joe. She did not tell him what Lucky had done to her. If he had been told, then the story would have been different. Instead, she told of how she suspected that Lucky was implicated in Little Joe's murder and explained how Lucky intended to take over their farm by force once apartheid had come to an end.

"Joe," she implored him. "I have to deal with him otherwise the whole family is in danger."

Big Joe was highly sceptical for neither of Sunetta's reasons resonated with him, certainly not enough for him to get involved. Throughout his life he had found it almost impossible to deny Sunetta anything, and so it was again. At her request he put Sunetta in touch with what she described as 'bad men'. As she had suspected, during his absence, Big Joe had met people in his shanty town who would do anything for a fee, and so it proved. She also needed money, which Big Joe also provided. It was with a large amount of South

African Rand, first provided by her father to entice Big Joe home, that Sunetta returned to New Found Estate for the Easter holiday, and its busiest time of year.

At the end of the first week of being home Sunetta went to find Lucky. She made a point of wearing the same dress she had worn when he attacked her in the swimming pool. Shutting down every fear in her body, she asked Lucky if he would be so kind as to attend to the netting on the tennis court, and if he did so, she would see him in the swimming pool at exactly 6.00pm tomorrow, immediately after he had come off the fields.

It was in the early afternoon of the following day that Sunetta smuggled the bad men into the swimming pool's changing room. There they waited with two electric kettles and a primus stove with pan, each containing gently boiling sugary water. Sunetta waited by the edge of the pool. She had purposely worn tight jeans with a buckled belt, chosen deliberately to protect her if anything went wrong.

Lucky walked through the door into the walled garden. He smiled immediately at his prey, for dressed like that he assumed that she could only want one thing. She smiled back encouragingly. He walked around the pool right up to Sunetta, never taking his eyes off her body. Just as he was about to reach out for her, she put her hand up to stop him coming any closer. Still Sunetta smiled, although her heart was pounding out of her body. She played her part perfectly as, still looking directly into his eyes, she reached for his belt and started to undo the buckle. Lucky immediately helped and just as he dropped his shorts to the ground, she reached for the cattle prod stuffed into her belt behind her back. She thrust it into his neck, pulling the lever once, twice, three times. Lucky fell to the floor in agony convulsing as he went down.

At this point, Sunetta's gang of bad men appeared. They stuffed a sock into his mouth so he couldn't scream, grabbed him by the limbs and dragged him inside the changing room where they tied him, spread-eagled, to a bench. Each watched in horror as Sunetta took the boiling sugary water from the kettles and very slowly, deliberately poured it over Lucky's stomach, penis, testicles, and the insides of his legs. He writhed from side to side in pain, but Sunetta wouldn't stop. Instead, she lifted his penis and then his scrotum with the cattle prod and slowly poured the scalding syrup over them to make sure that they were burnt all the way around. The mixture of sugar in the boiling water ensured that it stuck to the skin causing third-degree burns, the most painful kind.

Then, with one man sitting on both Lucky's arms, she took the pan of boiling sugary water off the primus stove and poured it over the front and back of each of his hands and fingers, which he involuntarily moved in pain making the damage far worse.

Lucky was barely conscious when she stuck the cattle prod into his throat, just above his adam's apple. His face showed the pain was unbearable and his eyes were wide-open in terror. Sunetta moved close to him and looked down. "You're leaving here," she said calmly, "and you're not coming back, never. Do you understand?"

Lucky did his best to nod.

Sunetta repeated herself. "You're never coming back, understand? Not to the estate, not to the village, not to Paarl."

Lucky nodded weakly.

"You're to leave Cape Town, got it?"

Lucky was hyperventilating, and in too much pain to do or say anything.

"Understand this," Sunetta said firmly. Her voice was threateningly quiet. "If anything, I repeat anything, happens to me or my family then not only will this happen to you again, but much, much worse. It will happen to your youngest and eldest sons too. Do you get it?"

"Look, we need to get this man to a hospital soon, cause otherwise he'll die and then it will be murder," said one of the gang panicking. They had been involved in some punishment beatings before but none as vicious and calculating as this. In fact, seeing the aftermath of Sunetta's assault on Lucky, they were beginning to feel sympathy for him.

Sunetta ignored the gang member's concerns. "Don't expect your wife or your kids to look after you," she said to Lucky. "To them, you're dead, 'cause you're never coming back. Nod if you understand," she instructed.

His head moved just a fraction. He was in too much pain to do anything else.

"One last thing, when the police ask you who did this, you don't know, understand? To every question you simply say, no comment, nothing more nothing less. Believe me," she said. "Believe me," she repeated, "I can hurt you far more than this, and you'd still be alive."

Sunetta stopped her lecture and stood up, taking the cattle prod away from his throat. Just as she did so, she thought she saw a smile in his eyes, threatening revenge. It signalled a risk that perhaps he hadn't learned his lesson, so she shoved the cattle prod back deep into his neck. "I really don't think you believe me, so just to make sure." She pulled the trigger twice more at which point Lucky convulsed up, falling back and cracking his head on the ground.

"OK gentleman, time to drop 'im off outside of the hospital in Cape Town. Don't do it locally," she instructed as she gave them back their cattle prod. As they bundled Lucky into the car Sunetta paid the gang leader the other half of their agreed fee. It had been money very well spent.

The gang changed cars twice before dropping Lucky outside the hospital in a car whose number plates could not be read. Meanwhile Sunetta picked up the kettle, stove and saucepan and returned them to the kitchen. They had not been missed. She then walked out to Little Joe's grave where she sat down and tried to calm herself. She needed to stop the adrenaline from coursing through her body. She felt truly excited and powerful. She had no care for the consequences of her actions as she was certain she had done the right thing. As she relaxed, there was a renewal in her self-confidence. She had learned how to fight back, and it made her feel good, almost proud. From now on, she would walk a little taller and hold her head a little higher.

The police made some preliminary enquiries, but they weren't very interested. From the nature of the wounds, they assumed it was a black-on-black punishment beating of a rapist. When Satutu told Big Joe about what had happen to Lucky he knew immediately Sunetta was behind it all.

"Did he attack you?" Big Joe asked Sunetta bluntly, when they spoke on the phone at the beginning of the summer term.

"No," she said instantly, before pausing. "He attacked a couple of young girls in the village."

"Oh," said Big Joe, noncommittally. "Did you tell Pa or Ma?"

"No, I was asked not to. I made a promise to the girls' mothers' that I would keep it a secret. Big Joe, it has to remain that way," she said. "Promise me?"

There were some strange co-incidences following Lucky's confinement to hospital. They didn't happen immediately, but things changed. The accidental damage which had plagued the estate for the last three years suddenly stopped. The wiretap on New Found Estate's office telephone ended, and the telephone to the house was re-connected without notice. The Government agreed to drop its appeal against Satutu's deportation order provided both sides agreed to pay their own costs. David readily accepted. The final sign that the government no longer saw Satutu as a threat was when, time after time of doing so, they stopped renewing her house arrest order.

Years later, when apartheid was at an end, the South African Government of National Unity set up The Truth and Reconciliation Commission. Satutu was asked if she would like this commission to examine the case of Little Joe. She thought about it long and hard, studying the papers released by the secret police before she did so. These showed that Mr Lereko Naidoo (Lucky) was a member of Umkhonto we Sizwe, the underground military wing of the ANC. They thought, either with or without David and Satutu's consent, he was using some of the wealth of New Found Estate to finance their terror campaign. The South African secret police concluded that Lucky's burns attack was a punishment, beating by Umkhonto we Sizwe, as part of a dispute about control.

David and Satutu were far more shocked to discover that the ANC had paid for the London Professor's pathology report on Little Joe. No wonder they were suspects. In the end, Satutu decided that it was the two policemen, and not her, who needed to make their peace with what they had done. Her baby son was at rest in her garden, and she was at peace with her behaviour. There was no need to rake up the past on her behalf. It was not going to bring Little Joe back.

Chapter 30

London July 1968

HENRY WALKED INTO the marquee at the Guards Polo Club at Smith's Lawn in Windsor. It was empty except for a few staff busying themselves with final arrangements. He looked at the table plan and identified where he would be sitting. He had been invited with the expectation that he would play a chukka or two, but with Prince Charles confirming, at the last minute, that he would be playing, all the ringers had turned up in the hope of a game. This ruled out any chance Henry had of getting a mount which is really what he wanted. He was therefore committed to spending the day here, being polite to those who he knew were going to drink too much, and inevitably become unattractive.

Years ago, he found these events exciting, for there were always a string of attractive but none too bright young women who offered one advantage; no strings attached sex. In most cases they were all very shallow with their conversation limited to the next event they were going to: Wimbledon, the Grand Prix, Henley, Ascot. It was as though their whole purpose was to be seen and, in the process, find a husband; a trait he found distinctively unappealing.

Henry moved towards his table. It was only then that he noticed a young lady sitting alone. His seat was back-to-back with hers. In fact, the chairs were so close together, it was virtually impossible for him to take his seat without disturbing her. Henry was so deep in his sulk that he didn't pay much attention to her, except to notice that her hair was thick blonde and her white trouser suit fitted tightly over a very slim frame. She looked at him as he took his seat and they both smiled sweetly at each other, saying nothing, for she was also none too happy. She had only agreed to come as a companion for a colleague, but one hour after their appointed rendezvous time, she was still sitting on her own; knowing no one else. Her study of Henry was cursory. In those few seconds she discounted him as another rich, selfish playboy.

Both were deep into their disappointment as they sat back-to-back, not noticing the other, each working out how they might best use the rest of the day.

"Would you like something to drink?" Henry asked the girl in the white suit after a little while. "I'm ordering," he added, feeling it would be wrong to order something for him without asking her.

"Thank you. An orange juice please," she said.

It was with those words that the ice was broken. He had to know where she came from for whilst her English was perfect, she had a distinct accent which made him study her lips when she spoke.

"Where are you from?" he asked, as he now looked into her bright blue eyes.

"Bamberg, Germany," she said matter-of-factly, whilst studying the features of his face as she spoke.

"I know it," he said quietly.

"You've been?" she asked, surprised.

"No," he said, "but," he paused, as he watched her lean back against the seat, already assessing him as a chat-up Jon. "I'm told my father came from there."

"Your father came from Bamberg, Germany?" she said in German.

"I'm sorry, I don't speak German," he said. "Well, only what I learnt in school. I've never been."

Her extensive experience of men and boys lying to impress her had made her cynical of their behaviour. He might be another fantasist she thought. Nevertheless, she smiled sweetly and said nothing.

Henry detected the slight change in body language from interest to indifference, so he added an explanation.

"I grew up believing my father was a member of the French resistance killed by the Germans, only to be told much later that he was a German pilot stationed in France during the war. It was where my mother was then living."

"What was his name?" asked the girl in white.

"I don't know, Heinrik something. It's why I'm called Henry."

"How do you know he comes from Bamberg?"

"It's something my mother remembers."

"Have you ever tried tracing him?"

"No. He was transferred from France to fly as a pilot for Hitler's flight, that's all we know."

"The Germans kept immaculate records during the war. It might be possible to trace him."

Henry was interested in her choice of words: 'the Germans'. It was as though she was speaking of a third person long before she was born. He was sure, in the same circumstances, he would have used the same expression.

"Are you interested in finding him?" she asked.

"It was easier when I thought my father was dead," said Henry. "His non-being was compartmentalised. Suddenly. when you find your father is someone else, who might be dead or alive, it throws you somewhat. I've often thought about it, but if he's alive what do I say?"

"At the moment you have two wonders. Is he dead or alive and what is he like? By tracing him you will at least end one of those wonders and perhaps both," she said.

It was so logical, so obvious, that Henry had to agree it was a good idea.

"Somehow, I think it is something my mother should do first, or at least I ought to agree with her it is something she wouldn't mind me doing."

"I will help you if you like," she said. With that Henry moved seats to be where the girl's companion was to have sat. They started an animated conversation about modern Germany and, as their table filled up with guests, they ignored almost everything and everyone else. After lunch had been served, the table emptied again as their lunch companions left to go and watch the polo without either Henry or the girl noticing.

"What are you doing here?" she asked, changing the subject.

Henry reached across the table and took the menu.

"Wines courtesy of Château de Gressier," he said pointing to the printed card. "We're a minor sponsor. Normally someone doesn't turn up and I get a chukka or two, but whenever Prince Charles plays you can bet everyone will be here, and dammit, he's playing this year."

"Are you any good?" she enquired.

"I played a lot in Argentina and their players know me. I've been picked by them as a ringer a few times in the past."

"Do you keep polo ponies?"

"Good god, no. It costs far too much money. When it comes to polo, I'm a freeloader."

"Except you sponsor this event?"

"It's a darn site cheaper than feeding polo ponies for a year," said Henry, light-heartedly.

"I think I must go and look for my girlfriend," said the girl in white. "She may be here somewhere."

"May I ask your name?" said Henry.

"Sophie."

"I'm Henry," he volunteered.

"I know, you already said, but Henry what?"

"Henry Bellanger, well that's what it says on my birth certificate."

"Good to meet you, Henry Bellanger."

On that, they shook hands. As they touched, her hand felt small, delicate and very gentle to him, whilst to her, his was warm and strong. Each felt a strength of character in the other. It was as though they recognised the other's purpose, although they could not say what that was. They said nothing more. Instead, they looked deeply into each other's eyes as though they were examining their soul. Suddenly both felt uncomfortable at the intimacy of the moment, and their hands parted sharply.

Henry sat back in his chair, for he suddenly felt a surge of adrenalin and his heart started to beat a little faster. As Sophie stood up his eyes cast first on her breasts, followed by her flat tummy, tiny waist, narrow hips and long, so very long, legs. As she turned around and bent down to pick up her bag, it was upon her small, cherry-shaped bottom where his eyes came to rest. She was truly beautiful. She had a perfect body. In fact, she had the looks of the kind of woman he would normally have kept well clear of for, in Henry's view, beautiful women know they're beautiful and this tended to give them an arrogance which he couldn't abide.

Sophie sensed him studying her, but it didn't make her feel uncomfortable as might normally have been the case. It had long been an occupational hazard of hers.

Henry stood up as an auto reflex to his mother's training, who insisted that if a lady was standing, he should stand too. They both noted how tall the other was. Sophie usually towered above most men, making them look foolish, which explained why she rarely wore heels.

"May I accompany you?" he asked.

"Are you sure?" she replied. "You know..." But she broke off her sentence as he interrupted.

"It will be a pleasure."

They made their way towards the entrance of the marquee where they stopped. Sophie looked at him; brushed her fingers through his hair, untucked his jacket pockets, straightened and tightened his tie and brushed down his shoulders with her hands. She smoothed down her trousers, buttoned her jacket and linking her arm through his, she said in a strong, positive manner, "Let's go."

Henry instinctively knew that, in finding this girl, his life was about to change, but he had no idea how much. As they pulled themselves tightly together and walked through the marquee door, Henry was oblivious to the fact that Sophie Elleswell was a supermodel with several multi-million dollar contracts to her name.

They'd only walked about ten paces when they were surrounded by photographers pushing and shoving each other.

"Good God," he said. "Does this happen to you everywhere you go?"

"Yes, pretty much," said Sophie, "particularly at places like this."

"What do you do?" asked Henry.

"You don't know?"

"No, but given this reaction I think I should."

"I'm sorry, that sounds incredibly arrogant," she said. "It's just..." She stopped, turned and looked directly into him. "I'm really very sorry, it's just, well, most people know who I am."

"Well tell me, who are you?"

"I'm the face of La Goviette," said Sophie.

They walked on. The sun had burned off the greyness of the early morning and the warmth of the afternoon soaked into their skin. Henry took some time before he responded by saying, "The makeup people?"

"Yes, I do their hair and makeup adverts."

"That explains it," said Henry. "Being a man, I don't buy those things."

"But haven't you seen me on TV or on a billboard or even in a magazine?"

He stopped and she did too. He looked into her face, took a pace away and looked again.

"Sorry, no, but I can see why they'd choose you. You are very..." Henry paused, trying to find the right words, "beautiful but that word's inadequate because, and I'm not being, er, sycophantic, but you're better than that."

"Thank you," she said gracefully, having been told this a thousand times. On this occasion it was the sincerity of the compliment which Sophie found warmly satisfying, yet also confusing, for Henry was failing badly in the fawning stakes which was atypical of most of the men she met.

They walked the paddock aimlessly looking for Sophie's friend but to no avail. They chatted gently as they wandered. People stared and took pictures of them but neither really noticed as they concentrated, one upon the other. They watched a couple of games and strode the pitch at the end of each chukka putting back the divots with their feet. At tea time they wandered amongst the players as Henry knew them all. The banter was crude and cruel; mainly suggesting he was going to get a better ride in Sophie's saddle, than in the afternoon's games. He took the banter reasonably well, although embarrassed for what Sophie might think. However, the fact that the Prince of Wales knew her escort and addressed him as Clanger, as if they knew each other, was more than enough to impress her.

When they were outside, Sophie immediately pressed him. "Do you think he noticed?" she asked.

"Noticed what?" said Henry.

"I didn't curtsy."

"Good God, no."

"You and everyone else nodded their heads when they first said hello."

"Yes, maybe he noticed, but it doesn't matter." Then Henry changed his mind. "No," he said emphatically. "I can assure you he won't have noticed you didn't curtsy."

"Why?"

"Because, like everyone else, his mind will have been focused on only one thing: the loveliness of the most beautiful woman in the world standing before him ... OK?"

It was from the way Henry said OK, and nodded his head at the same time to confirm his point, that Sophie knew she was being scolded for self-obsession but his smile, which came with it was quietly reassuring.

"In any case," said Henry, "you're German. You don't have to curtsy."

"What's this Clanger name?" asked Sophie.

"We were playing last year, and the end came off his stick and hit my helmet. It was an accident, but it made such a clang that the name stuck."

As a result of an injury, Henry was asked to play in the last match of the day as a ringer for the Argentinians. Although he didn't score, he put up a reasonably good show, at least sufficient for Sophie to be impressed by his skills.

Henry showered and changed quickly, as he didn't want anyone else to be taking his place at Sophie's side. He hadn't yet observed it in himself, but he was already jealously protective of her.

They watched the prize-giving together, with Prince Phillip giving the prizes. Then Sophie asked, "I need to use the phone. Will there be one in the clubhouse I can use?"

"Of course," said Henry. "I'm sure I can find you one."

"I was supposed to be going home with Kathy but she's not here," Sophie said. "I need to phone my booker to arrange a car to get me back to London."

"I'll take you," he volunteered, almost too quickly. "Where do you live?"

She paused, "Central London."

"That works for me too, whereabouts?"

"Marylebone."

"Oh, that works really well because I live in Little Venice."

No sooner were the arrangements fixed than Henry found the excitement of having her to himself for another hour overtaken by his embarrassment at the disgusting state of his 10-year old, left hand drive, Peugeot estate car with nearly 150,000 miles on the clock. It hadn't been cleaned inside or out for at least half its life!

A blanket stolen from the clubhouse was used to cover the front seat and Sophie looked aghast as the junk in the foot well was thrown into the back. She rapidly felt she'd made a terrible mistake, but the fear of being left stranded outweighed the risk of her journey into London in this car, so she climbed in.

They sat in silence for some time as they queued out of the car park and, as they drove past Windsor Castle, she asked, "Have you been in there?" pointing into the distance.

"The Fort?" he questioned.

"Windsor Castle," she replied.

"We call it the Fort," he said seriously. He paused. "It's the name the family uses."

"Oh," she said, impressed by what appeared to be intimate knowledge of the royal family.

"Have you been inside?" she asked again.

Henry paused. "It's terribly bad etiquette for anyone who's close to the royal family to discuss them. It can be guaranteed to get you ostracised so, of course, we all take great care."

"Oh," she said again, then paused and asked her question for a third time. "Have you been inside?"

"No," he laughed, giving up the pretence that he knew the royal family. "I haven't even done the six-shilling tour," and she laughed with him. "I've only ever met Prince Charles at polo."

"Well, I've just done that," said Sophie cheekily.

"So we're equal," he said.

"We're equal," she replied, wondering how true that statement was. Apart from the fact that he appeared to have sponsored the wine, there was nothing which set this guy apart as being anyone special, except he was special, as he made her feel that way.

Henry drove slowly into London. He didn't want to rush when slender thighs and long legs covered in pressed white linen were in view every time he looked down. Although she said nothing, Sophie found it a pleasant change not to be shown off to in a typical boy-racer style. Like the car, Henry's driving was the antitheses of what she was used to. She was getting the sense that Henry was comfortable in himself.

They stopped outside her flat. It was a mews house just off the High Street in a little cul-de-sac. It was prettily dressed with hanging baskets in bloom which brought some freshness to the hundred-year-old cobbles. They sat in the car, taking in the silence after the road noise.

After a few moments and with one bound, Henry was swiftly out of the car and around the other side, opening her door. He watched as her legs stayed together as she swivelled on her bottom to get out elegantly. They stood next to each other, both a little embarrassed.

Invite me inside, invite me inside, wished Henry. Instead she quickly kissed him on the cheek and set off to her front door, where she concentrated on finding her key. He stood there alone and a little bereft.

"May I ask you out sometime?" he asked.

"Yes," she said, "sometime," and with that she turned once again, showing her petit derriere, and left.

Hells bells, I'm going to fuck that! said Henry to himself, and with a hundred percent conquest rate so far, he was pretty confident - although this time he knew he would need to make a change or two.

Back at his flat, Henry yelled into his telephone. "Mother, there's a model called Sophie something, she's the face of something - hair, make-up stuff. She's German. Who is she?"

"Why?" asked Victoria patiently.

"I've been with her this afternoon. I've just driven back to London with her. She was at the polo."

"Do you mean Sophie Elleswell? Very tall, slim, thick blonde hair and petite face but wide, angular shoulders – ugly shoulders."

"Mother, I didn't look at her shoulders," he rebuked.

"Was she nice?" Victoria asked.

"Yes, very. Who is she?" A hint of urgency was now in his voice.

Henry made about a dozen similar phone-calls that evening to his grandmother, and every other woman he felt he could ask. As he lay in bed that night, he knew his motives had changed. She didn't know it yet, but Sophie Elleswell was going to be his wife. He knew he could not bear seeing photos of her everywhere and wondering who else she was with. This one was too precious to be entrusted to anyone's care but his. There was just one snag. She was way out of his league.

He realised he had one piece of information missing. He knew where she lived but he didn't know the address so, at around 3.30 am, knowing he wasn't going to sleep, Henry drove back to Sophie's house and noted the address. He also saw that the lights were on, for unknown to him there was a hive of activity as Sophie was on the 6.30 am plane to Paris.

Likewise, Sophie had not slept well. As she drifted in and out of consciousness she thought about Henry. There were so many conflicts. It was as though he was on the verge of manhood yet unable to give up the free spirit of boyhood. She really hoped that he would phone again. One downside of being one of the world's most photographed women is that you don't get asked out by normal men, only by narcissists and those that have outrageous egos. Yes, Sophie determined, if he smartened himself up a bit, Henry would make a very acceptable boyfriend, until Mr Right came along.

Back at his flat, without thinking over the reason, Henry started to tidy up. He lived in a modest two-bedroom affair but like his car it was both messy and dirty. Girlfriends had commented on its state in the past, but none had been sufficiently repulsed not to get into bed with him. After all its main purpose was as a shag pad.

Slowly, room by room, his flat started to take shape. There were bags of washing for the laundry, bags of clothes and linen to be thrown away, all the washing up gathered and stacked around the sink and a shopping list to bring him into respectability. Only a few pairs of jeans, pressed trousers and shirts, suits and jackets, made it through the sift. Henry was just sitting down with the Yellow Pages to phone for a same day cleaner when it rang.

"You're in William Hickey, this morning," his mother said excitedly.

"Who is William Hickey?" asked Henry.

"He's the Daily Express gossip columnist. There's a picture of you and her."

"Sophie?"

"Yes."

"Says you've been going out together for six months; why did you never say? Says you're a perpetual student. There's a photo of you."

"Mother," said Henry exasperated, "I met her yesterday, first time, okay."

"She's very pretty," said Victoria.

"She comes from the same city as my father," said Henry.

There was a long pause.

"Well, she looks very nice" said Victoria abruptly, completely thrown off-guard by the remark. "Must go, bye," she added shutting down the phone call.

No sooner had Henry put down the phone than it rang again. It was Caroline d'Abo.

"Have you slept with her?" she asked accusingly. There was a hint of jealousy in her voice.

Caroline's great advantage was that she too was very attractive, had a bundle of energy and could be guaranteed to satisfy any man's needs. Her problem was that she was none too bright and very needy.

"No, I haven't," said Henry, then asking, "did you see it in Hickey?"

"No, you're sodding well on page three of the telegraph. Says you've been going out together for six months. You must've been shagging her while still seeing me!" said Caroline affronted.

"I met her yesterday," said Henry emphatically, "so no, I wasn't, and I haven't!"

"Tell me more, tell me more," said Caroline excitedly, ignoring her first charge of infidelity.

Henry looked at his watch. "I'll see you at Piccolo's for a pizza at 2pm and I'll tell you about it then," said Henry, ending the call as abruptly as he could.

With a cleaner booked for tomorrow, Henry set about his job list: flowers for Sophie, putting out the rubbish, dropping off his laundry, getting the car serviced and cleaned, getting a haircut, buying the papers. In fact, his picture was in all the papers which were still wrapped under his arm when he sat down to eat with Caroline.

"Tell me, tell me," she said. And so together, they scoured the pages for stories of Henry and Sophie. He told of their meeting, the day spent together and their journey into London. Henry dwelt on what was an important fact for him; Sophie hadn't invited him into her flat.

The rest of the afternoon was spent in his flat where Caroline was her usual ardent lover, encouraging him to take her time and time again. For while Caroline guessed she was not the only one to share his bed, she was determined that she was not going to lose him to some extra skinny super model. Henry was, as always, enraptured by Caroline's lovemaking, so he thought of little else.

Caroline and Henry were disturbed early next morning with a phone call telling Henry it had not been possible to deliver his flowers, but they would keep trying. Then, as they both wandered his flat in a state of semi undress, an army of cleaners, arranged the previous day, came to transform Henry's flat. As the cleaners cleaned, Henry became, for the first time, very conscious of the numerous poster sized photographs of the Pirelli calendar models which kept him company. It was time for them to go he determined. As they came down it revealed how badly his flat needed redecorating. Another Yellow Pages search, a phone call, and with a decorator appointed, another stage had been taken in the transformation of Henry's life.

It was his second bedroom which provided the insurmountable problem. It was jam-packed with a telex machine and all the chemistry instruments required to scientifically classify wine. Henry had already developed a small trading business importing wines from the countries of his earlier overseas tours. He urgently needed more room than was available.

As Henry contemplated the problem, he was surprised to find that he was suddenly a man with an ambition. He knew exactly how he was going to spend the rest of his life, and with what objective. He was going to make himself the kind of man Sophie would marry. Time was now of the essence.

Chapter 31

London July 1968

A COUPLE OF days later, Henry took the early evening train to Hertford. Once again, he used the journey time to think. As he sat down to supper with his mother, he outlined his plans. He was going to become the largest importer and distributor of wine into the UK and Western Europe. He told her how he had already made £5,000 without risking a penny of his own money. The narcissism and indifference, which Victoria often saw and seriously disliked in her son, seemed to have gone as, for the first time, she saw an ambition in Henry, arising from a passion which she had rarely seen before. Any discussion she tried to have on Sophie received short shrift.

"There's a snag," said Henry, having spoken nonstop for well over an hour about his business plans. "I need Grandpa Bear's Mayfair house. I want the basement and ground floor for offices, the first floor for a showroom and then floors two and three for my flat."

"You know it's yours," said his mother, "but I imagine it's let out. Once it's free I'm sure, if you ask the trustees, they'll agree to you having it."

Henry paused as the thought of asking strangers for his property appalled him. He'd always lived happily within his allowance, often saving money. To go cap in hand to someone else really did not appeal.

Victoria noticed Henry's awkwardness. "Would you like me to phone them and make the appointment?"

"Yes, yes please," said Henry.

"I will do it for you in one month's time" said his mother. "It will enable you to prepare and present your business case."

"Business case!" said Henry aghast. "What are you talking about? I thought you said it was my money."

"It is, but Bear didn't expect you to have it without a fight, or at least demonstrating why you should have it."

That night Henry slept in his old bedroom, as he had done for almost exactly 15 years. Nothing had changed, and he wanted nothing to change. Early the next day, with the same small overnight bag in hand, he caught the boat train from Waterloo as he had to see his grandmother. He arrived late in the evening at Bordeaux's Gare Saint Jean railway station, where he spent the night in the hotel opposite. Early in the morning he took a taxi ride out to Château de Gressier in time to join Juliette for breakfast.

"It's not your normal time of year," said Juliette curtly, as she looked up from her newspaper.

Henry kissed her on the forehead, "I know you're grumpy until after breakfast Mamie," he said, "but I need to talk to you."

"You're getting married?" she asked.

"No. Why do you say that?"

"According to Paris Match you are. The whole village is so excited."

"No Mamie, it's all wrong. We've only met once."

"But it says you've been dating for six months."

"Six hours was the measure of the time we spent together, Mamie. She's really lovely, you know, beautiful and so sexy."

"We don't use that word," said Juliette disapprovingly.

"What word?" asked Henry teasingly.

"That word. By the way, what do you want, money?" asked Juliette.

"Mamie, have I ever asked you for money ... except when I was in San Francisco?" said Henry, duly affronted by her question. "And I paid you straight back when I got home," he added.

Juliette said nothing.

"No Mamie, I want to tell you something and hear what you have to say about it. I want you to tell me if it's a good idea and, if it's not, then why it isn't."

And so Henry started to present his plan just as he would have to do with his trustees.

"Mamie, for the last six maybe seven years, I've travelled the world studying wine. I've been to every country I can get to, and I have notebook on notebook about the stuff. I know more about the wines of the world than anyone else."

"A possible over exaggeration," suggested Juliette,

"No, I do, I promise you," he said with just a little hurt creeping into his voice. "The way wine is judged today is just crap."

Mamie coughed disapprovingly.

"All this sniffing, tasting, spitting and talking, it's just rubbish, complete bullshit."

Juliette coughed again.

"It is nonsense," said Henry correcting himself. "I can do everything scientifically, with chemistry, far more accurately."

"You can't make it," said Juliette tartly.

"No, I can't make it," he acknowledged sarcastically, "but I can very accurately grade its components and compare those to previous years and the ratings they had then. The thing is that I can now buy wine in South Africa, Argentina, Peru, Australia, New Zealand, California etc., at a price I can agree in advance, based upon the chemistry and within agreed bands of tolerance."

"Have you done this to our wines?" Juliette asked.

"Yes of course, and all the vineyards of Bordeaux, Burgundy, Cote du Rhone, Sancerre and the Chardonnays of Chablis. The only ones I haven't done are the champagnes and the sparkling wines."

"What did you discover about ours?"

"Some years you should have won prizes when you didn't, and on other occasions you should have lost when you won. It was all incredibly interesting. It gave me a series of base levels against which our future wine production can be judged. There must have been factors I couldn't take into account, such as politics, even the weather but," he then paused, "what I know is that chemistry has a scientific certainty which makes it easier to trade."

Henry told of his plans for his grandfather's house, the business he would run and his success to date. Juliette listened, while mouthfuls of a huge cooked English breakfast went into his stomach without him even noticing, let alone pausing for breath.

"What do you think?" Henry asked, expectantly.

"I have one observation," said Juliette. "Wine is like ladies' underwear. You pay the most for that which makes you feel the best. The English call it selling the sizzle in the sausage. I think your plan risks taking the lace off the panties or the sizzle out of the sausage. It's like..." she paused. "Take away belief and you've taken God out of religion. Then there's nothing left but a few old buildings. Yes, I am sure the wine industry can be labelled, measured and scientifically accounted for, but that is only a part of it. The biggest part is the romance of wine. It's the romance which adds the premium price, and you destroy that at your peril."

Henry knew she was right. It was advice he would never forget for, although he had no time for wine snobbery, he realised that anybody who broke that illusion would destroy its value and that was not in his best interests.

"Do your scientific work, use it to negotiate your deals, but for heaven's sake keep it private," said Juliette. "The kind of information you now claim to have could destroy any brand, and should you do that, no-one else would ever sell to you again."

Henry nodded again in agreement.

"Henry, I don't think you've got it," Juliette added forcibly. "Anything which challenges the norms of the wine industry, or threatens it, or does it harm, will not survive, and that could well include you! If you don't respect the industry it will destroy you - that is its five-thousand-year promise."

"And my second proposal?" asked Henry.

"That I sell you today 20% of next year's wine production with the price based upon your formula when the wine is bottled?" Juliette popped a piece of bread, butter and jam in her mouth and chewed slowly. "I'll do the same deal you get from anyone else locally," she said.

"Thank you, that's good," said Henry.

"But," Juliette interrupted, "you won't get anyone else to accept your deal."

"Why not Mamie?" said Henry befuddled.

"You've made the fundamental mistake of thinking about your needs and not the needs of your suppliers. Business is a partnership, dear Henry, and you are not being a partner. Every year we sell all the wine we can produce. Our routes to market have remained the same for years. You bring me no advantage, so why would I give up my current customers when I don't know whether you will be in business in two or three years' time? Sorry Henry," said Juliette "but I don't need you, and everyone around here will say the same thing."

Henry instinctively knew that, once again, she was right. She was always right on things like this.

"What deal would you do Mamie?" asked Henry.

"Work it out and put it to me," said Juliette, "then I'll consider it." With that she wiped her lips with her napkin and got up.

"Are you dining with me tonight? If so, please let cook know," she said and, with those few final words, Juliette was gone. Henry stood up, only to find himself alone. Juliette's infuriating habit of bringing any conversation to an abrupt end when it suited her was well known to Henry, but it never quite prepared him for the frustration he felt every time it happened.

Henry spent the morning wandering around, talking to everyone on the estate on what turned out to be the most glorious day. All anyone wanted to talk about was Sophie and when they were getting married. In the afternoon, Henry toured the local villages on his grandfather's old motorbike where he toured the wine shops, supermarkets and cafes talking about the price of wine, finding out how much each bottle was bought and sold for. For all the years he had lived there, he had never had this kind of conversation with them before. Not one of the retailers liked the distributors. Each felt that they took too much margin which was bad for business, but it was precisely in this intermediary role that Henry was making his plans.

That evening Henry dined with Juliette, who this time provided a fount of knowledge on the structure of the wine market. There were already people doing exactly what he wanted to do, and they had been doing it for hundreds of years. Juliette told of Louis Eschenaur, the most prominent of wine merchants and négociants in the war, and his working with the Third Reich to supply them with wine. "The secret, he'd discovered, was to control the consumer," she said.

"Some people are making a fortune selling wines into financial institutions as an investment, making even more money as they store it for them," he told her excitedly.

"Remember the gypsy adage, said Juliette. "You make your money when you buy, not when you sell." It was wise advice which he would do his best to remember.

Henry left early on Saturday morning to take the train into Paris so he could catch a flight to London. He only just made check-in and was allowed on-board because he only had hand luggage. He was the very last to board and as he turned to walk down the aisle, he saw her. He slowed and looked. He was sure it was Sophie. Her hair was tied back tightly and hidden by a scarf, so she looked different. For a few microseconds he was in doubt until she looked up and saw him, and then smiled. Henry smiled back. Sophie waved gently. He just managed to wave back, before he was moved on by an air hostess anxious for him to find his seat.

As Henry sat at the back of the plane, he cursed for Sophie was sitting in business class. Worst of all he had worn the same shirt for three days and he knew he looked a wreck. A visit to the washroom for a shave, teeth clean, hair comb, and a clean but crumpled T-shirt, saw a more presentable Henry leave the plane than had joined it. His heart literally leapt into his mouth when he saw her at the end of the gang plank waiting for him. She was wearing a classic floral dress with a white cardigan and looked quite delightful.

"I was wondering whether you would like a lift into London," she said, her eyes telling him that he should say yes. Henry nodded and mouthed yes please, but no sound came out of his mouth.

Sophie did not travel light. Henry found a trolley, and with three large, heavy cases loaded he made his way through the airport where the Paparazzi photographed them in the same intrusive way as they had done at Windsor.

"I'm so sorry about last week," said Henry shyly, "I don't know where they got the story from."

"It's all made up," said Sophie. "They got your name right and that's all they cared about. It's me who should apologise. I should have warned you. There will be something somewhere in the press tomorrow about our arriving back from Paris together."

"Surely not," said Henry, "nobody can be that interested."

"It's a hazard of knowing me," said Sophie. "Are you all right about that?"

Henry smiled and nodded weakly as he wondered what that really meant. One thing he did know, and that was if Caroline saw a picture of Sophie and him arriving together at Heathrow it would not be well received.

Sophie's driver, suitably attired in a chauffeur's uniform, immediately took over the responsibility for all the baggage as they walked out of the customs hall. Within minutes they were sitting side by side in the back of a black limousine. Henry wanted to reach out and hold her hand, but shyness stopped him. Sophie worked through her emotions as she wanted him to touch her, and yet was glad that he was not being overly forward. They chatted freely as they travelled into town, both telling the other what they had done, until they came to Henry's flat.

"Can I see you again, please?" Henry asked, after a pause.

"That would be nice," she said.

"Can I phone you?" he asked.

"It's not a good idea."

"How do I contact you?"

"You'll work it out," she said grinning, "if you want to."

"I have your home address, but you haven't been there," said Henry.

"True," she replied.

By this time the chauffeur had got Henry's bag from the boot, he was standing at the side of the car with the door open.

"We'll see each other again?" he asked, in a questioning and confirmatory manner.

"If you want to."

She slowly leaned forwards towards him, kissed him on the cheek with genuine tenderness and then quickly sat back into her own seat in an upright position.

"Now go," she said, her voice slightly chiding him, as her hands waived him away.

Henry and Sophie had the same routine when they returned from a trip. They both took long showers and then phoned their mothers to say they were OK.

Sophie wrapped herself in a towelling dressing gown two sizes too big and, for the first time, she mentioned Henry's name. The fact that this boy had appeared in the newspapers with her daughter made Sophie's mother pay particular attention.

"He's so different to everyone else I work with," she said. "The photographers are such arrogant bastards. They think that the right to photograph you gives them the right to sleep with you. Also, they're so damned serious, they never have fun unless they're drunk. The male models are either gay or so in love with themselves that its energy draining."

"Is he good looking?" asked her mother.

"What do you think?" she retorted, knowing that her mother would have studied every picture in every paper.

"His hair's too long," said Sophie's mother.

"He's had it cut since then," Sophie said defensively. "He looks much better with shorter hair."

"He looks as if he has nice eyes," said Sophie's mother, trying to be supportive.

"Mother," said Sophie, "his father is German, a pilot stationed in France during the war." She told the story Henry told her the first time they met. "The thing is he comes from Bamberg."

"What, Henry comes from Bamberg?"

"No, Henry's father," said Sophie crossly. "The thing is, in a lighter moment, I said I would help him find out who his father was. When I said it I didn't really mean it, but now I think I do."

"Is that a problem?" asked Sophie's mother.

"I don't know, what do you think?"

"Has he money?"

"What on earth has that got to do with it?"

"His father probably has a new life, wife, family etc. These things cause big problems, particularly if Henry hasn't any."

"Everything's not about money," said Sophie crossly.

"It is for those of us who lived through the war years, and had nothing," Sophie's mother scolded.

"Leave well alone, child, is my recommendation," said Sophie's mother.

"All right," said Sophie. They chatted a little bit more and then said their goodbyes.

Henry's phone call with his mother was much briefer. He reported, as a matter of fact, his conversation with Juliette and his meeting with Sophie, then bluntly asked: "How do you get the phone number of someone who's ex-directory?"

"Is this for Sophie? Ask one of her friends."

"I don't know any of her friends."

"Do you know who she works for?"

"I don't," said Henry getting exasperated.

"Henry," said Victoria, "she'll have a booker at a modelling agency. Find the agency, find the booker and you'll find her."

"How do I find the agency?"

"Henry," said Victoria getting equally irritated, "she's bound to be in some catalogue. You'll find her through that."

In the meantime, Sophie was equally perplexed. She had found four 'unable to deliver' cards from the local florist, each asking her to contact them, for they had a bouquet of flowers to deliver from a Mr Henry Bellanger. She worried at what he might have thought of her as she had not mentioned them. To add to her agitation, she had no idea how to contact him until Monday morning.

Sunday brought the same flurry of phone calls as there were pictures of Sophie and Henry returning to London having allegedly spent a romantic week together in Paris. All the papers were reporting the same thing; that Henry was Sophie's first serious boyfriend since she had broken up with an actor who, if truth were to be told, she had only met once.

Caroline phoned Henry distraught, accusing him of total betrayal between her sobs. Caroline's best friend telephoned. Henry assured her it was all rubbish. Nevertheless, the best friend insisted on coming around to see him; turning out not to be a best friend at all, for in the boredom of the tirade he decided to change tactics and plied his angry guest with charm, wit, innuendo and alcohol which resulted in them going to bed together for the afternoon.

To be frank, Henry was confused. It appeared to him that after a long period of sexual famine there was now a feast on offer because of his change in status from a nobody to the hypothetical boyfriend of a supermodel. The rich horse-totty of the polo set had always been easy pickings for a quick roll in the hay after a game, but somehow this seemed different.

Monday was a hive of activity, as Sophie phoned the florist only to be told that they would only release Henry's number with his permission. Henry heard the florist's messages to give them a call on his answer phone but chose to ignore them at first, only replying much later. Meanwhile, he was searching for Sophie's agency. It was late Wednesday night when each had the other's phone number. Despite overwhelming anxiety from the fear of rejection, Henry decided to call.

After an initial stumble, they both laid back, Henry on his bed, Sophie on hers, and they gossiped freely. Henry teased her about having been her boyfriend for six months, and his lack of recall of their sex-driven weekend in Paris.

"I'm sorry you broke off with your last boyfriend," he said seriously. "From what I read of him he sounded nice."

"He was nice, he was lovely. But I'm afraid he didn't fancy me. I was not his ... type. He was my date for a premiere fixed up by the agency. I haven't had a serious boyfriend since..." she paused.

"Since when?" asked Henry.

"Since, I suppose, never," she continued.

"What never?" said Henry, astonished. There was a silence.

"It sounds pathetic, but yes. It's the price of modelling. Since I was sixteen, there's no personal life."

"What are you doing this weekend?" asked Henry as a way of changing the subject quickly.

"On Sunday, nothing."

"And next Wednesday evening?"

"Nothing, as far as I know."

"Let's have lunch together on Sunday, get out of London. We'll head out somewhere along the Thames."

"That sounds lovely, will you drive us?" she wondered.

"Yes, if you don't mind dressing down. And next Wednesday," he continued quickly, "we'll go to the Windsor Races. They do a good barbecue, but only if it's nice. It's a magical event. There's normally a boat from Westminster Pier and we'll go down on that."

"Sounds lovely, anything I have to do?" she asked.

"No," he said confidently.

They talked some more and said goodbye, both pleased that they'd made a friend.

Henry punched the air and did a little dance. He was beside himself with joy. He was going to make Sunday special, very special!.

Chapter 32

London July 1968

HENRY CHOSE THE Oakley Court for his lunch date with Sophie. It was an imposing Victorian hotel with rolling lawns down to the banks of the River Thames, where boats gently meandered up and down.

After they had eaten, they wandered the grounds and, at the water's edge, Henry suddenly asked whether Sophie would like to go for a row.

"Can we?" she said.

"I don't see why not. Do you swim?" asked Henry.

"Yes," said Sophie confidently.

Ten minutes later Henry returned with a hotel room key in his pocket, an item so large it was almost impossible to disguise, and the key to the padlock of the hotel's rowing boat.

"Can you row?" she asked anxiously.

"Yes, one dreadful term at school," he replied. "Keep clear of anyone who rows," he added.

"Why?"

"They're masochists. They like self-inflicted pain!" he warned.

Henry rowed and Sophie coxed badly as they meandered down the river with the flow of the current towards Eton and the footsteps of Windsor Castle. They laughed and they giggled as their boating caused chaos with the other craft on the river.

The boater, which Sophie had chosen to wear in accordance with the theme of the river, had been moved from the back of her head to across her brow, making her face a picture of loveliness.

At Eton they moored up and wandered around the village hand-in-hand; looking, browsing in a few shop windows, sharing the things they liked and disliked. They wandered through the grounds of the world-famous school, with its ridiculous tail coated students. Eventually, as the afternoon started to cool, they wandered back to the skiff with ice creams in hand.

At the boat, Henry helped Sophie find her seat. Taking off his jacket he threw it beside her, revealing the huge key fob to the hotel room which he had earlier hidden inside his jacket pocket.

Sophie took the key in her hand, looked down at it and then back at Henry. Her face looked like thunder.

"No, Henry," she said very firmly. "This might be in your plans, but it's not in mine."

Henry climbed in the boat and sat down. Their knees were closely touching as both were leaning forward; Sophie to make her point, Henry because, until that moment, he had been preparing to row.

"If I wanted to hire the boat, I had to have a room," he said in his defence. "They would not do one without the other. Boat hires are for residents only."

"So is this your normal seduction technique?" she asked, sarcastically.

"No," he protested.

"Wine and dine on the river, a row, and then..." She didn't finish her words. "How many times have you done this?" she demanded.

"Never, I haven't, this is my first time here at this bloody hotel!"

"Mind you ..." he continued in a tone trying to make light of the situation.

"How many girlfriends, women, have you had?" she demanded. "No, don't answer that. I don't want to know. You disgust me."

Henry said nothing. There was nothing more to say. So, in a sulk, he rowed up stream, pulling against the current, and with Sophie not steering, his line was straight and true.

Sophie stared at the water, her eyes following the blue paddles as they darted in and out like a cormorant diving for fish. Back at the hotel Sophie broke her silence and said, "I think you should take me home." There was a pause. "Please," she added but the tone made it clear it was an instruction and not a request.

Henry escorted Sophie to his car and then went to the hotel to return the keys. There he collected a business card with the hotel telephone number. They drove back to London, saying nothing, as they listened to a dreadful selection of music from Alan Freeman's Pick of the Pops radio show. It did nothing to lighten the mood.

At Sophie's house, Henry got out of the car and opened the door as Sophie played with her bag in the foot well. Again, he stared at her legs as she climbed out, this time taking less care to be as elegant. At her front door she scrambled in her bag for the keys; her body language indicating that all she wanted to do was get through the door and close it in his face as fast as possible. Just as she found her keys, Henry took her hand firmly.

"Take this, please," he said. "It's the hotel's phone number. Phone them and see if you can hire a rowing boat without being a resident."

Just as she was looking at the business card, Henry leaned forward, kissed her quickly on the cheek. In an instant he was in his car and off. Sophie just stood there. He'd had enough of being chided by a woman who, in this one aspect, had a lot of growing up to do. How dare she sulk like that and spoil a perfect day? There would be no racing on Wednesday.

After a shower, wrapped in her dressing gown, Sophie phoned her mother as she did every Sunday evening. Their conversation was only about Henry and how nice the whole thing had been until she'd discovered his schoolboy plan to seduce her. It was a one-sided discussion as her mother, being a teenager of the war years', forced to the back of her mind her transformation from a teenager into womanhood.

Sophie talked about how handsome he was, but not too handsome. How he had a confidence which could sometimes make him quite arrogant. But, most importantly, he was without angst, unlike anyone else she had met, particularly in the photography and modelling game.

"Sophie," said her mother, "there's an English saying, I heard it being discussed on the radio a couple of days ago, it's that 'a man chases a woman 'till she catches him.' Don't think too badly of him.

He was trying to catch you. It's what men do. Phone the hotel and find out if it's possible to hire a boat without a room. It will tell you if he lied or told the truth, and then you have your answer."

On Tuesday morning Sophie got the phone call from her booker that she both wanted and didn't want. If Henry had lied about the hotel, she would not see him again, but she did not want that. Alternatively, if he hadn't lied then she'd behaved badly, and an apology was due.

"You can't book the boat without having a room," reported the booker. "I've tried. I've said it was for you, but they are quite adamant."

Sophie's heart both sunk and fluttered at the same time. Her stomach felt empty while her face beamed.

"Would you please phone Henry and confirm with him that we are still going to the races on Wednesday evening? If he's in doubt, tell him that it would be nice."

When the booker phoned Henry to confirm Wednesday's outing he first grimaced and, once again, punched the air and jumped for joy. "This is getting better," he said.

Chapter 33

London July 1968

ON THE WEDNESDAY morning, Henry met with his three trustees. The meeting was at the lawyer's office, which was cold and austere, with polished bookcases filled with law books which no one ever read. It was all designed to appear both daunting and highly formidable to those unfamiliar to working in these circles. Henry had never met them before but, in a newly purchased dark pinstripe suit with a white pressed shirt, grey tie, and brightly polished shoes, he was ready to play his part.

From the coffee cups on the table and the papers spread around, it was clear that these men had been meeting before he arrived. They all remarked on how they remembered seeing him at his grandfather's funeral and how long ago that was. As they spoke, Henry realised that the odds of three against one were not that encouraging.

"Henry, what do you know about your trust?" asked the elder of the three trustees.

"I've read the trust deed and the accounts for the last three years, but that's it."

"Has anybody explained what it means?"

"Yes," said Henry, "a long time ago."

"Is it worth a recap?"

"No, thank you," said Henry. "I have some plans for a business I would like to share with you." The confidence in his voice belayed how nervous he truly felt. "I would like to learn how my trust might be able to help." He made a point of emphasising the words 'my trust'.

Henry outlined his plans for the Mayfair house, his business plan for importing and distributing new world wines, his ambition for a bonded warehouse which would store his imported wine and the need for capital to buy a position in the fine wines of France for the investor market. His presentation lasted no more than 20 minutes. His trustees then quizzed him on his presentation for over an hour, each taking it in turn, and with each answer it seemed to Henry that his project moved further away. However, the clarity of his plans and the succinctness of his answers not only impressed the trustees, but it changed their view of him. Until then they had assumed he was a lazy, diffident, rich kid to whom the pleasures of life came far too easily.

"I think this is incredibly easy," said the accountant, who Henry was later to discover only thought in terms of tax and tax law section numbers. Then he poured forth intermingling words like discretionary, maintenance, settlement, trusts, leases and lets, which would take an ordinary person a day with a dictionary to understand. The three wise men all murmured their agreement, with a few comments made as an aside.

"You agree to what I want to do?" asked Henry. He sensed that they were saying yes but was not really sure.

"Yes. Immediately after your mother's telephone call we gave the tenants three months' notice to quit. They are leaving a bit earlier so, in six weeks' time, the house will be yours," said the lawyer in their midst.

Again, the men spoke amongst themselves. The accountant agreed to prepare a draft report setting out all the issues and the next steps. The lawyer would then incorporate all the legal aspects into the report and the senior partner of one of the oldest stockbrokers in the UK, and by far the most influential man in the room, given the fact that, on the raise of his eyebrows, millions could be moved in the buying and selling of shares, agreed to liquidate part of the trust's portfolio to do what was necessary.

There was much talk of buying an off-the-shelf company, offshore structures, non-dom status, capital gains tax, and rollover relief. All subjects which were new to Henry, so he left the meeting with his mind buzzing not really understanding what they were talking about.

Although the three wise men had been inordinately courteous, Henry had not liked the feeling of being hopelessly out of his depth as they had discussed the issues without involving him. The thing about this stuff, thought Henry, is that it's all man-made. If one man could create it then he was certain that he could understand it. With his notebook full of new found phrases, he quietly committed himself to a period of detailed research. It was just as his French grandfather had done forty years before, and as a result had saved Château de Gressier and his grandmother's fortune from the worst recession in modern history.

Henry left the meeting with the three wise men feeling sure he had succeeded but he was not sure at what. It appeared that at some stage the Mayfair house would be his and there would be money coming into his bank account, but when and how much he was not certain. The afternoon was spent buying a new linen suit with blue shirt, dark blue tie and a pair of dark brown brogue shoes. In an effort to impress Sophie, he had his hair cut and paid particular attention to having a close shave before he made his way to Westminster Pier, arriving far too early.

As the clouds surged overhead and the sun darted in and out, Henry waited. In the sunshine it was glorious but in the shade the wind had a biting cold, such that he was getting quite chilly. He looked for a bolthole to hide away in, to get some protection from the weather. The boat, Twin Oasis, was already alongside the jetty with its engine running, but it was not yet open for business. The tide was out and at the turn. Unknown to Henry, Sophie was also early. She was sitting in the back of a large Mercedes, which was going around the block time and time again, for she was not going to get out until Henry was in view and could escort her.

Fifteen minutes before the boat was due to leave Henry appeared at the pier steps. She had never seen him looking so smartly dressed. Yes, she was going to delight in him being her escort for the evening. She was now beginning to see he was much more handsome than she had earlier thought.

Sophie's chauffeur opened her door and Henry watched as a sheer delight unfolded itself from the back seat and came into view. Sophie was wearing a light sky-blue trouser suit with a white blouse and matching blue leather boots. Her hair had been plaited around the front and back of her head and threaded in the plaits were fresh, dainty summer flowers. She looked an absolute picture. Henry was certain that he would be able to close his eyes and picture her face at that moment in his memory until he died. He was completely and utterly smitten. He knew he was in love, and he was never ever going to let this girl go.

It was too chilly in the wind to sit outside and so they paid little attention to anything other than themselves as the boat made its way west and towards the lowering sun. Neither said anything about their strained feelings at the end of the weekend. It was irrelevant, forgotten, as they gloried in the gentle touch, one of the other. They knew no one else in the hospitality tent, where Henry had booked a table. The evening was spent examining the horses in the paddocks, placing bets on those chosen merely for a loose connection with their name, rather than racing form, watching the races, sometimes in hopeful excitement, tearing up their betting slips, and returning to the hospitality tent where the barbeque boys served another round of freshly cooked fayre.

The night was drawing in quickly for, although it was still midsummer, dark clouds had moved across the sky as they boarded the boat to take them down river back to Westminster Pier. Both Sophie's chauffeur and a black cab, which Henry had organised earlier, were waiting for them at the pier. Wishing to avoid a display of one-upmanship, Sophie got into the black cab expecting her car to follow.

Ensconced in the back of the cab, Henry announced that he wanted to show Sophie something, giving the cabbie instructions to the address in Mayfair, which was about to be his new home. When the cab came to a stop, Henry got out and beckoned Sophie to follow.

"I'm moving in here," he announced, pointing to a large Queen Anne terraced house with an imposing doorway.

"When?" she asked.

"Well, it's mine in about six weeks. I think there will be about six months of alterations and renovations, but after that I think I should be able to move in."

"Is the entire house yours?" asked Sophie.

"Yes, it was my grandfathers, and it's been held in trust for me."

Sophie shivered in the cold. Henry took off his jacket which he wrapped around her shoulders.

"Really Henry, who owns it?" she asked. "It's huge."

"Basically, I do...indirectly. It's all incredibly complicated," he professed.

"And for always?" asked Sophie.

"And for always," repeated Henry.

"It's very big, just for you."

"I know but..." Henry stopped. He paid off the cab and walked Sophie around the corner to the Connaught Hotel, where they both ordered non-alcoholic cocktails, and for the second time that day, he outlined his plans.

"Will you help me?" he asked.

"With what?" she replied.

"I have no design sense," he said, both knowing the truth of that statement.

"The architect and I can do all the structural work. I can do all the other project management stuff, but I will get the finishes wrong."

After one drink, they took a cab home. Outside Sophie's front door there was the usual scrabble for the keys. Surely this time he would be invited in. But her guarded, almost secretive behaviour once again indicated that they would be saying goodbye on the doorstep. Then she turned towards him, and Henry took his chance to take her waist into his arms. He pulled her close into his body. He kissed her very lightly and tenderly on the lips, seeking permission to go further. Sophie responded positively. The sensation was making her light-headed, her pulse race, and she felt a glow as his hands moved down over her bottom. For the first time, she felt his manhood against her body as he pulled her into him. Very quickly he turned her around, such that he was now behind her, kissing her neck, with his hands grasping her breasts and tummy. Then, just as quickly as he'd taken hold of her, Henry broke off, giving Sophie a pat on the bottom as he did so.

"Night-night," he said buoyantly. "See you again soon," and with that, he blew her a kiss and climbed into the cab. Sophie felt her body physically deflate as he let her go.

Chapter 34

London July 1968

HENRY AND SOPHIE next met for lunch on Sunday, where they ate outside the restaurant and lapped up the sun before they walked around Regent's Park. They were both carefree and besotted but, because Sophie was flying to Cape Town the next day for a photo shoot, they once again said their goodbyes in the early evening on the street outside Sophie's front door.

"Mother, I'm frigid," Sophie complained to her mother in tears as they spoke on the phone. "I want him to kiss me," she confided "but I can't, I can't," she lamented. "I think I've found a man I love, who I know loves me and wants me, but I can't let him into my life," she wailed. "I so want him, but I can't do it."

It was late when Gertrude, Sophie's eldest sister, rang. "Mummy's told me of Henry," she said. "I gather you've asked her to try and trace his father."

"Yes, I'm inviting him to meet Ma and Pa, during the summer."

"Mummy says you love him but are having a problem er... moving your relationship on."

"I wouldn't put it quite like that," said Sophie, affronted that her conversation with her mother had been repeated.

"Have you slept with him yet?"

"No, of course not," protested Sophie, shocked at the question.

"How many times have you been out with him?"

"Only about a dozen times."

"And you haven't slept with him?" the tone of her voice expressing surprise. "Do you not know the three times rule?"

"What three times rule?" asked Sophie in all innocence.

"Do you fancy him?"

"Yes, he's gorgeous and kind and clever, but..."

"So what's stopping you sleeping with him?"

"Well because ... he's an enigma Gertie. He's both dirty and clean. He's both old and young. He's a real pleb and yet posh. He appears poor and yet he's rich. None of it makes any sense."

"Hell, have you slept with anyone?" asked Gertrude.

"You shouldn't ask that," said Sophie firmly, then she paused, adding, "no, not yet."

"I bet all your friends have."

"Yes, they're in bed with everyone. It's all very free, but I can't be like that."

"Neither could I. It's the way we've been brought up. You need to read a book," said Gertrude. "It's called '*Eine Frau in Berlin*'. It will explain everything. It was first published about ten years ago in New York. You should still be able to get it. Read it on the plane tomorrow. It will explain everything," she repeated. "Phone me when you've read it."

Chapter 35

South Africa July 1968

A PHONE CALL to Sophie's booker first thing in the morning had the agency scouring London libraries looking for the book *Eine Frau in Berlin*. It was waiting for Sophie as she checked in at the first-class desk at Heathrow Airport.

Meanwhile, elsewhere in the airport, Henry was buying a ticket to sit at the back of the same plane. He said nothing to Sophie about going, for fear of being accused of stalking her, but he'd been meaning to go back to South Africa for some time to re-visit some of the major wine producers around the Stellenbosch and Franschhoek areas that he knew from his youth. He wanted to try and persuade them to sell him some of their production. He didn't know where Sophie was staying. It wasn't at the famous Mount Nelson, as he'd checked. He was glad, because he didn't really like that hotel, as the last time he had stayed there, they had been none too friendly to the scruffy youth, travelling on his own. His choice was the Bay Hotel on Camps Bay because the sunset over the beach was one of the most beautiful in the world. In a small sedan car hired at the airport he drove and booked into this small, discrete and very personal hotel.

Other than to relax, he had only one plan for the day. It was to let Sophie know he was here, so he phoned her booker and left her a message. Meanwhile Sophie was in a very bad way emotionally. Her world had been turned upside down by the book she had just read all through the night, unable to put it down for she was certain that her mother had been in Berlin during this time and Gertrude was giving her the most appalling message.

Immediately it was 6pm in Germany, Sophie phoned her sister. There were none of the usual opening pleasantries as she immediately asked, "Was mummy one of the Berlin women?"

"Yes, I think so," replied Gertrude.

"How do you know?"

"You remember Brunhilde?"

"Yes, of course, she was your friend for a long time at school."

"It was her that told me, because her mother... because it happened to her mother too."

"Oh God" said Sophie. "What happened?"

"I was told it was very bad Sophie, very bad. Many men and many times, until they escaped."

Sophie was silent. She didn't know what to say. For her mother was always so strong, and never a victim.

"Sophie," asked Gertrude. Sophie was still silent. "Sophie, are you there?" she asked.

"Yes," said Sophie quietly, not knowing what to think.

"It was thousands of women Sophie, literally tens of thousands."

"Yes, I know."

"The Russians were so damn angry with us for causing the war they killed the men and raped the women without mercy. It was just the way it was."

"Have you ever spoken to Mummy about this?" asked Sophie.

"Good God no," said Gertrude. "I daren't, I daren't."

"What about Daddy?"

"Oh, I think he knows. I'm sure he knows. But I think they've agreed it's something they never talk about."

"Why do you think that?"

"Because whenever a rape case is reported he makes sure the news is never on and we have no newspapers in the house. It's his way of making sure she's not reminded Sophie," said Gertrude.

"Has the holocaust anything to do with this?" asked Sophie.

"No, not really, except it probably added to the hatred the Russians had of us then, and even now. It's easier to do inhuman things to people who have behaved inhumanly," Gertrude offered.

"How do you recover from something like that?" asked Sophie.

"You don't, you try not to think about it, and that way you survive."

"Do the victims never talk about it amongst themselves?"

"No, never. It's their private shame. They can't gang up together and shout 'look, how badly we were treated,' because people will quickly point to the bad things that German women did in the concentration camps. Everyone involved in the war tries to forget. It's the only solution."

"Do we have to forget too?" asked Sophie. She then answered her own question by adding, "but I suppose it is not our memory in the first place, although strangely it is now."

"We bear the scars too Sophie, don't you realise that. It's why you're having difficulty developing a relationship with Henry."

"What?" said Sophie, surprised.

"Other than Pappa, Mamma has trusted no man, and I'm sure her fear of men has come through to us."

"Where did you get that idea from?"

"I read it in a psychology magazine, when I was interested in this kind of stuff."

"Why were you interested?" asked Sophie.

"Isn't it obvious?" said Gertrude.

"What, were you raped too, when?" asked Sophie shocked.

"No, when I started going out, you know, dating."

"Oh, what did you do about it?"

"The obvious," she replied.

"The obvious?" repeated Sophie not sure what she was being told.

"Yes, the obvious, I bedded quite a few men thinking it would help."

"Did it?'

"Yes, in some ways, but in other ways no. It stopped me wondering what it was all about but, on reflection, I think I would have preferred to have been just a bit more selective. There's something very special about the right one. The wrong one makes you feel cheap, sort of a waste of effort; the right one makes you feel fantastic."

They talked girl talk for an hour, as Gertrude gave Sophie an exposé on her past love life, a conversation they'd never had before.

It was much later, when she spoke to her booker, that Sophie learnt Henry was in Cape Town too. She phoned his hotel immediately, where she found him asleep in his room.

"You couldn't keep away," she teased.

"I thought I'd keep you safe from your film crew," Henry retorted.

"When can I see you?" he asked.

"I'm busy all week. I'm flying back on Friday but let me see if I can delay it for a few days."

They discussed what each was doing and where.

"Let me take you up to the area around Stellenbosch and Franschhoek," he asked. "I promise, it's God's own country."

They talked every night from their respective hotel rooms, eventually agreeing that on Friday lunchtime they would drive up through the mountains, past the wild baboons and the wine fields, to a hotel which he knew would be just perfect.

Chapter 36

South Africa July 1968

ON WEDNESDAY HENRY went touring, looking for the vineyard he'd worked at just over four years before. He only had his memory to go on, and a lot can change over that time. He couldn't remember its name or the name of its owners, but he did remember the name of their daughter and he wondered whether he would recognise her or she him.

As Henry drove aimlessly out of Paarl, the road, which occasionally ran alongside and overlooked the Berg River, had a familiarity which made Henry feel he was on the right track. Suddenly, he came across an impressive set of front gates and there he observed them: two very large blocks of imported limestone into which the words 'New Found Estate' had been carved. He recognised them immediately because he remembered how it reminded him of his house in Mayfair which he had inherited from his Grandfather. He stopped, reversed and drove in. As he made his way up the drive to the main house he knew he had been there before for nothing had changed much. It was all as clean, neat and tidy as he had remembered.

As Henry parked his car in the driveway at the front of the house David Daunier came out of the front door, inquisitive as to his visitor. Henry recognised the man, who appeared to have aged more than the four-year gap would have suggested. He was much shorter and beginning to show a distinct stoop from so long bending in the fields. Henry introduced himself and explained that he had worked on the estate as a farm hand a few years before.

Satutu joined them on the driveway and Henry recognised her immediately, for she had not changed at all. Henry offered his condolences at the death of Little Joe, remembering how they worked in the fields together and told of his letter to Sunetta. This put both David and Satutu at ease, albeit that neither of them recognised him.

Henry was invited into the kitchen, where David and Satutu welcomed and entertained all their visitors. As Satutu poured tea Henry outlined his plans to import and distribute South African wines. He explained how he would pay 30% upfront for the wine which would be produced next year with the eventual price being based around a scientific formula which would measure the quality of the wine. As he talked, Satutu studied Henry carefully, for there was something familiar about the man in front of her, but she could not place what it was. Slowly her suspicions as to his bona fides were aroused.

"Where did you learn about the wine business?" Satutu asked in an effort to check him out.

"Château de Gressier, in France, is owned by my Grandmother. I have spent every summer there since ... just after the Second World War."

"What's her name?" demanded David, suddenly, getting very animated as he spoke.

"Juliette."

"And her maiden name?"

"Dovingdon."

"And her husband's name?" David asked, with ever greater urgency.

"Étienne, but he was murdered by the man who was to become Mamie's second husband. Why do you ask?" said Henry.

David sat back and deliberately slowed down, as he tried to hide his shock. Sitting in front of him was his great nephew, and he had just learnt that his sister's first husband had been killed; a man who had been responsible for saving his life. He instinctively knew that, unless he was careful, his secret, well-hidden for over fifty years, was about to be discovered.

Satutu couldn't help but notice David's animation, for she had rarely seen him behave in such a manner. She watched as her husband visibly relaxed again and replied calmly to Henry's question. "Just curious," he replied.

They talked more about Henry's method of classifying wine, which left both David and Satutu intrigued. They agreed to send two bottles of wine from their last three years production for him to classify. Henry insisted that he was to pay for the wine and the shipping costs. There was something about the way Henry was prepared to pay up front which resonated with David; for wasn't this the same way he had dealt with Leon Tinnerman at the start of their foods canning business relationship.

As a throwaway line Henry added, "You will find my office address easy to remember as the house name in Mayfair is very nearly the same name as yours. It's Found House."

"You own Found House?" asked David, far too excitedly for it to be in general conversation.

"Yes, well my great-grandfather did. It was put in trust for me and I'm about to move in. Do you know it?"

David became pensive as he wondered how to answer the question. "It was once quite notorious as a Col. Dovingdon used to live there," he said before qualifying his statement by adding, "I believe he was a highly influential man of his time."

"Did you know Col. Dovingdon?"

"No," David lied, for he had to stop this conversation. "I would like to have done, but we were a generation or two apart."

Satutu knew instantly that David had lied. She did not know why he had done so, but she decided to change the conversation and fast. "Are you not worried that economic sanctions might be introduced against South Africa, because of the political situation here? she asked. "It would stop us doing business with the UK."

Henry was completely taken back by the question. It was something he hadn't thought about as, in front of him, was as multi-racial, multi-cultural a family as could be found anywhere in the world.

"Except those UN resolutions are over six years old, and no one has really bothered to implement them," added David quickly, not wanting Henry to think there would be a problem in buying his New Found Estate wine.

"If they come, then we will find our way around it," said Henry pragmatically, "but under our contract it would be my problem. I will have paid you 30% upfront and I would still be contracted to pay you the rest as soon as the wine had left your vineyard gate."

"So you will make sure that sanctions are specifically excluded as an act of Force Majeure[8] in the contract?" said Satutu.

"If you say so," said Henry, not having a clue as to what Force Majeure meant.

"Thank you," said Satutu. "Let us show you around," she volunteered, "for I am sure things will have changed since you were last here."

David and Satutu walked the estate arm in arm, as they always did, chatting away with Henry until they accompanied him back to his car.

"I was hoping to meet Sunetta when I was here. Will you please tell her I came, and give her my best wishes," he said.

They said they would and waved him good-bye.

"An interesting young man," said David.

"He's been here before, I am certain of that, but I have a feeling he left suddenly, and we never knew why. I'll have to go back through our records and check."

David nodded wisely but, in his discovery of Henry, he had unexpectedly found a solution to a problem which had been bothering him for over 25 years.

---

[8] A "force majeure" clause is a contract provision that relieves the parties from performing their contractual obligations when certain circumstances beyond their control arise, making performance inadvisable, commercially impracticable, illegal, or impossible.

Chapter 37

South Africa July 1968

THE HOTEL HENRY had chosen for his attempted assignation with Sophie's body was delightful. It was built in a remote gap in the wooded hills with breathtaking views down the valley and over the vineyards. It was tastefully furnished and imbued with romance.

There was confusion as, between the two of them, they had three bedrooms booked. It was soon discovered that Henry had booked two rooms, one for him and another for Sophie, whereas Sophie's booker, had booked one room for Sophie too, on her assumption that Henry was not going to be as gallant as it turned out he was. It delighted Sophie that, in booking a separate room for her, Henry had made no presumption that they would be sleeping together. Whereas, on learning that Sophie had booked only one room, it led Henry to assume she expected them to sleep together, and his hopes for an exciting night rose.

They dined inside by a log fire, as it was the middle of winter in South Africa and, as a result of the clear sky, it was cold outside. The dining room was unusually empty, with only three or four tables taken. When the last person was gone, Henry leaned forward and took Sophie's hands.

"I want to ask you something, and I want you to say yes," he said.

His seriousness suddenly worried her.

"What is it?" she said, a bit too curtly.

"I want you..." Henry paused, and Sophie tilted her head prompting him to continue.

"Will you..." he paused again, he was uncertain, whether he should go on? He felt he was about to make a fool of himself, but now he had started he couldn't stop. "Will you marry me?" he said at last, "please."

Sophie couldn't believe the question. It was one for which she was completely unprepared.

Sophie smiled, "You must be..." but she stopped herself from finishing the sentence, which she had intended to end with the word joking, for as she spoke, he had opened a velvet box and was presenting her with a magnificent solitaire diamond ring, sparkling in the candle light.

"The best diamonds in the world come from South Africa," he added inanely, as Sophie processed what was happening.

Henry was suddenly feeling concerned as Sophie said nothing. Then he began to feel foolish, so he took her hand and kissed its back as Sophie examined the ring still in its case. It was a truly magnificent solitaire, set in platinum, a modern style with diamonds pressed down the shank. It was obviously expensive, but without being ostentatious.

"It's beautiful" she said to Henry admiringly, "but..."

"I love you Sophie," said Henry, cutting her off.

"I love you too Henry," said Sophie, but then she paused, "and if I were to get married" she said, "it would definitely be to you, but..."

Her pause was truly hurting him.

"It's too early. We really don't know each other, do we?" she continued.

He always knew she was way out of his class, but he had not planned for this, as a feeling of embarrassment overwhelmed him. Oh, how he wished she would put the ring away, or put it on her finger, or close the lid, or return the box to him; anything but leave it there, as it was, open and stranded by itself on the table. Insecurity was now pounding through his brain. Had he chosen the wrong ring? Was the diamond too small? If only she would study it, he wished silently, as he'd spent a long time choosing both the diamond and the band separately.

"The ring is really beautiful," she said, killing his doubts with her smile. "It's perfect. It's just what I would choose."

"Henry," she said sternly "I just don't know. I do love you. I think you're the perfect man. If I was going to spend the rest of my life with someone, I think it would be you. But I'm not ready. I don't know why, but at this moment I can't commit."

She stopped, for in the moment she realised why she could not yet say yes.

"You've not met my parents or any of my family. I've not met yours. I know none of your friends. You know none of mine. This is crazy as we've known each other less than four weeks. Until..." and she stopped, "Henry, a marriage of two people is a marriage of two families as well."

Sophie passed the ring back across the table. "I'm sorry, I can't take it, not just now, later maybe."

"Sophie, I want you to have the ring, please wear it," pleaded Henry. "Perhaps not on your engagement finger but maybe on the other hand, as a present from me."

"It's far too expensive for that," said Sophie.

"It isn't. It's just..." there was silence. "It's just from me to say I love you."

"I love you too," she said, taking the ring out of the box, which she passed to him. Putting forward her right hand, Henry took it very gently and slid the ring over her ring finger. They said nothing as they held hands and looked into each other's eyes savouring the moment. He was sure she was in love with him; he could feel it, sense it. It was all consuming, for he thought about nothing else when she was with him. Sophie's thoughts were more clinical in nature, for whilst knowing that she loved him, even lusted after him, she was not at all certain that, in the longer term, he would match up.

After a while of saying little nothings, they took the lift to their bedroom floor, where they kissed passionately outside their adjoining bedrooms; each pulling the other's body into theirs. They stopped and held each other tenderly, this time kissing more gently.

"Am I coming into your room, or you into mine?" asked Henry, now confident that they would be sharing a bed together.

Sophie slipped her electronic key from the back pocket of her jeans and swiped it a couple of times until the light on the locking mechanism turned green.

"When we're married Henry," she said, and with that the door opened, she slipped inside and was gone.

Henry moved forward to his own door and, leaning forward, he rested his head against it with his eyes closed. Frustration and anger were building inside him, in equal measure, for he'd never been rejected before. He could have sworn she would have chosen his room for the first time; they always do, simply because it's easier to run away than kick someone out.

Henry went into his room but couldn't stay there. It was all too claustrophobic. He quickly changed into running clothes and made his way outside. The air was damp and cold, biting into his throat as he took gasps of air, but he needed to run, and run fast.

As he moved away from the light pollution created by the hotel, Henry looked at the majesty of the moon and the stars. Perhaps he should have become a theoretical physicist after all, he pondered, for in space everything was certain. There was a logic to the universe, which was absent from his current situation. After about a mile he stopped, lay on the ground with his hands behind his head, and thought of the universe and what it all meant. One day he would go back to university and understand all this. Of one thing he was certain; he did not understand women.

Then it dawned on him, the one thing which was different from all his other seductions; Sophie didn't drink. Was alcohol the aphrodisiac of seduction which was missing in her case? If it was, then there was no solution, for she was as tee total as he was.

Sophie and Henry spent three more days behaving like a honeymoon couple out of their bedrooms, and a priest and nun inside them. The following day they travelled to see the whales at Hermanus and then spent the rest of the time wandering around the tourist areas which were so quiet because it was out of season.

Henry had heard Sophie's message that she was not yet ready to commit to getting married, but he had not taken it to heart. Ever the optimist, he had simply taken their earlier conversation as merely creating a task list to be completed before she said yes. He rushed forward with plans for Sophie meeting his mother, his grandmother, his friends, well some of them, and for Henry to meet her family.

Sophie, for her part, was happy to go along with his agenda. She always knew she wanted to marry and have a family and Henry was proving to be an agreeable companion. But above all, she had a magnetic sexual attraction for him. There was just this inner turmoil which she did not understand, nor could she resolve.

Back from South Africa, Henry and Sophie entered a whirlwind, as he set about refurnishing Found House. Architects and builders filled his day, as walls came down and steels went up to give clear space. The basement was dug down further to make the room larger and the concrete in the back garden dug out to make the lawn. Sophie worked at her modelling contracts before they stopped in the summer. They saw each other only occasionally until the beginning of August, when Sophie flew to stay with her parents for four weeks. In the meantime, Henry had set a date of the end of September to move into his Mayfair home.

Chapter 38

Bamberg, Germany August 1968

SOPHIE'S MOTHER MET her at the airport as she always did. In the arrivals hall they hugged each other, and Sophie offered her right hand to show off the ring, which was admiringly approved.

Sophie's mother was called Inga Lemberger which was Sophie's maiden name. Elleswell was her modelling name created for the French, UK and US markets.

Inga was a petite, very smart woman and it was immediately obvious where Sophie inherited her thick blonde hair and deep blue eyes. Although her blonde hair was made lighter from the white grey, which reflected her age.

"Why on the right hand?" Inga asked.

"Because I told him I wouldn't marry him unless Papa approved."

"Do you want papa to approve?"

"I don't know," said Sophie.

They spoke no more of marriage until they were in the car, out of the airport and cruising gently on the autobahn.

"Do you love Henry?" asked her mother, breaking what had been a long silence.

"Yes I do," she replied, "but I don't know if it's enough to overcome the homesickness I will feel. I've always wanted to come back here and have this as my home. If I marry Henry, it's a lifetime in England, and I don't want that. This is my home," she repeated, reinforcing the point. "I think, if he loves here as much as I do, then the answer 'll be yes."

"Your father says you have enough money, more than enough money, to buy a house around here and settle down. In fact, he's very keen that you do."

"I know Mother, but not until I have someone to share it with.

Chapter 39

Bamberg Germany August 1968

HENRY WAS NERVOUS when he got off the plane. After Bordeaux University he had arrogantly decided that he wouldn't do interviews, but in a space of a few months he was about to do his second, and this one had to go well. As far as he was concerned his future depended on it.

Sophie was there to meet him and immediately she leapt into his arms, unable to keep away. She was nervous too but unlike Henry hers showed by chattering constantly as she'd never done before.

"I've told mother we're not sleeping together," Sophie said almost as an aside as she slipped the ticket into the machine to get the car parking barrier open.

"Oh," said Henry, thinking it a strange statement given Sophie's insistence to date on celibacy.

"Well, she asked where you're going to sleep, sort of checking out with me whether we were sleeping together."

"Oh."

"Even if she...even if we had, I couldn't, not with my Dad in the house."

"Oh."

Sophie's parents lived some distance from the town. As they turned off the road towards the setback house, Henry immediately felt comfortable as, although from its size and appearance it was larger than his own home, it was not so big as to indicate a mismatch. As they approached the house, Sophie described it with great excitement. She clearly loved being here. It was of wooden construction, painted in a mixture of creams and whites causing it to stand out from, rather than blend in with, the landscape.

"Did your father build the house?" Henry asked, getting confused by her description of its development.

"No, before the war it was the weekend home of an elderly rich lady doctor, but it was very run down. She lived only using upstairs because it had once flooded. She hadn't the energy to do the repairs. So, Papa bought the house and extended it over the years. He added the bits where my grandmothers lived, one at one side and the other on the other side, until they died. Do you know, they died a month apart? They lived with us for, I don't know how long, about ten years, and they always addressed each other as Frau Lemberger and Frau Hechler, never by their Christian names."

Sophie's father was a well organised man. He carried in his head a permanent jobs' list. Those which had to be done daily, or weekly, all the gardening and maintenance jobs depending upon the time of year, and the never-ending improvements he wanted to make. All of this meant he never had a moments rest. He was not normally a stern man, but he was well known for his bursts of temper if people didn't do what he wanted; and what he didn't want was this man, Henry, changing their lives. He wanted Sophie home where he could look after her as he had always done. He cursed the day that he had ever agreed to allow her to be photographed by the scout from a Bonn modelling agency.

Immediately after Sophie and her father had shared a long, very natural embrace Sophie formally introduced her father.

"Papa," she said very formally, "please meet Mr Henry Bellanger. Henry, please meet Herr Walter Lemberger."

"Walter," said her father.

"Henry."

Both smiled at Sophie while shaking hands. Sophie didn't smile back for she felt as though it was one gladiator facing another, albeit in the handshake the two alleged protagonists felt nothing like the roles in which Sophie had cast them.

Chapter 40

Germany 1945 - 1950

WALTER LEMBERGER CAME home from the war with just the clothes he wore, the motorbike used for his job as a dispatch rider for the Wehrmacht, and his Luger pistol, which he had never fired in anger. He heard that the war had ended on the radio, which he listened to attentively every night at some remote point in Northern Italy. When the war first started his journeys were typically only of a few miles, but after the Allied forces had taken control of the air, his journeys went for many miles and lasted for many days. Unable to go forward with his mission, or go back to his unit, Walter simply decided to ride home, which he did by stealing petrol as he went, and scavenging anything of value which he could sell a day or two later. Already his mind was on the future.

The depression Walter felt at losing the war was made much worse when he arrived in his home city of Nuremburg to see it flattened from heavy bombing. His morale reached rock bottom when he was told that his father was dead, his home a bomb site, and the fate of his mother unknown. He searched for her for a week and after much agonising he decided, for his own sanity, he couldn't stay. He needed to get away from there as fast as he could and so, with a heavily laden motorbike, he drove out of the city not knowing where he was going. It was dusk when he arrived in Bamberg and it was here that he decided to stop for the night. He was captivated by the beauty of the city, which had at one time been the centre of the Holy Roman Empire, and its rivers, which ran through a town mostly unspoiled by the war. The old historic buildings gave a feeling of permanence about the place. Further, it was devoid of the destruction which surrounded the rest of Germany.

The U.S. Army had been in occupation for over a month and had taken over the Wehrmacht's barracks. At the checkpoint to the city Walter was searched. Amusingly his gun wasn't found in his bag of scavenged goods. He was instructed to go to the US Army barracks commandeered from the Wehrmacht to hand in his motorbike. He reported as ordered and was shown into a hut with a few beds, where he showered in a hot shower for the first time in more days than he could remember. He took time to wash and clean his clothes. His military discharge interview was quick and orderly with a man who perfunctorily went through a list of questions. In answering that his job was a dispatch rider, and in one of those serendipitous moments that happens in most lives, Walter found himself being employed by the U.S. Army as a messenger, simply because he rode a motorbike. His job was to deliver army messages but only to those German officials responsible for the running of the town and the surrounding areas.

He often wondered why they didn't commandeer his bike, but years later he understood. For the Americans, the war was over. All they wanted to do now was go home and the sooner everything was settled the quicker they could do that. As ordered, he removed the German swastika from his motorbike and painstakingly painted on the flag of the United States.

Walter worried about working for the enemy, and if anyone ever challenged him, which they sometimes did, he would spit out in anger that Hitler had been the biggest enemy of Germany. He would then point to the destruction all around saying that he caused this and would then walk away. Walter's job with the U.S. Army was well paid, but he knew it wouldn't last, so he started moonlighting as a courier for the Postal Service, collecting and delivering the post amongst the local villages, towns and cities. It became a very profitable side-line.

It was at Farchlieum that Walter was introduced, by the post-mistress, to Inga Hechler who was trying to get to Bamberg. She had no reason to go there. She was simply determined to get as far away from Berlin, and the Russians, as possible. Walter's motorbike was not designed for a passenger but, seeing the dejection on Inga's face, he agreed to try and help. With Walter sitting forward and Inga putting her arms around his waist, with her thighs pulled tight up against his buttocks, they found they could manage. It was just that, every time he put his arms around her back to pull her into him, to make sure she didn't fall off, she froze in fright as it brought back the nightmare of Berlin.

They arrived in Bamberg too late to find Inga somewhere to eat or sleep, so he fed her in his tiny lodgings and gave her his bed to sleep in while he slept on the floor. From that day forward not one night were they to spend apart as their lives became forever entwined.

Inga sold the things that Walter scavenged. Not least from the former Wehrmacht barracks, where the U.S. Army had so much that they never missed the odd bag of flour or sugar, which Inga would bake into bread and biscuits and offer for sale on a stall by the side of the road close to a crossroads on the way into the city centre. Her stall grew longer as she sold everything Walter could lay his hands on.

Their big break came when Walter learned that the U.S. Army was selling the German staff cars in their possession. There was only one condition to the purchase; all Nazi and Army emblems had to be removed. Walter scavenged a compressor easily enough but finding the paint sprayer was very difficult. However, once this was done, they were in the car business. The two of them worked from the moment they woke at 5 a.m. every day of the week until midnight on weekdays, finishing earlier on Saturdays and Sundays. There was a complete sharing of everything from the start. Every penny they jointly made went into the same safe, each taking out just what they needed. It was only on Saturday and Sunday evenings when, over three rings and a bottled gas cooker, they would prepare a proper dinner and, if they could find it, they would open a rare bottle of wine and feel incredibly selfish.

It would take the two of them to negotiate with the U.S. military, each having just about enough English to share one conversation. Their next breakthrough came when the U.S. Army decided to sell off the German military lorries. It was done under the same condition, that they had to be resprayed to remove all emblems, but instead of paying up front it was agreed that they could pay in stages.

They needed a place to do the work, so they took squatters rights over one of the rare bomb-damaged sites on a corner of the cross roads close to where Inga had her stall. They physically cleared the site by hand to give them the areas they needed. Inga moved her stall onto the bomb site and found that, by stealthily moving the temporary bus stop sign closer to her stall, rather than losing business as she had feared, she was taking more money than before.

Walter decided that, rather than sell the lorries, they would rent them out. So it was that the rental income for the first four weeks lorry hire paid the cost of buying each lorry. From then on everything was virtually profit.

It was from this site that their business took off. Walter did the buying, selling and letting of the cars and lorries and managed the customers. Inga managed the servicing, repair works and all the staff. Even though they were shut to customers on a Sunday, they were both always working, for there were too many opportunities. It was their skill in sourcing spare parts for the car repair business and keeping their lorries on the road which made them particularly successful. When the owners of the land eventually appeared, they agreed not only a rent but offered to pay back-rent, but it was conditional upon them having the right to buy the land if it was ever sold.

Walter and Inga were the only and obvious choice when first Volkswagen, and then Mercedes, wanted to appoint distributors for their cars and they became local celebrities when the first new post war Volkswagen was put on their forecourt for sale.

One Saturday evening, in the warm glow of alcohol and in the arms of the one man who made her feel safe, Inga fell pregnant and so both their lives changed again. Walter knew exactly where he wanted his family home to be. He had ridden past it hundreds of times when making his postal journeys. It was a white painted wooden house about ten kilometres from the centre of Bamberg travelling towards Nuremberg. It had twenty-five magnificent hectares of fertile nursery land with a shallow, fast flowing river dissecting part of the land at the rear, which then rose into another five hectares of pine forest which had been planted on the hillside.

For both Walter and Inga one of the few reminiscences of the war they shared together was the pain and lethargy of starvation. Hunger ate into the very fibre of their being, causing them to think of little else other than food. The inconvenience of being so far away from the city centre and their business was, to them, a small price to pay for the security they would get from being able to grow their own food.

Walter did not know who owned the house so one day he stopped, knocked, and introduced himself to the elderly widowed occupier. He explained what he wanted. For the widow the offer was manna from heaven, as she found the desolation too much. She was lonely, afraid and wanted to move back into the town where she had an apartment and worked as a doctor. But the house was her son's birthplace and home, and his whereabouts was still unknown. Never doubting that he was not alive, she was waiting patiently for him to come home from the war. It meant that the widow refused to sell her sons' birthright.

It was over a picture of her son in his pilot's uniform wearing the Iron Cross 1st Class that a deal was done with Walter. He would rent Dr Lisa Friedman's house, paying the same in rent as they would pay to lease an apartment in the city. He would organise and pay for all the costs associated with her move. There were two other promises. The old First World War aeroplane, in which her son had learnt to fly, had to remain safe and sound in its hanger. Most importantly, when her son turned up, he promised to redirect him to where she would now live.

Walter and Inga moved in to the white painted house just before Christmas in 1948. It was, once again, a very cold winter. The river had frozen solid, so they were able to wade through the snow and cross the river into the forest opposite and collect wood. The makeshift bridge which had once crossed the river had been swept away in one of the many floods. This wood kept the kitchen stove and all the fireplaces in the downstairs rooms burning. It created their own heaven of damp warmth as the water, which had remained in the building since it had last flooded, evaporated into a mist of fog.

The spring saw the building dry with essential repairs made. Pigs and lambs were brought onto the land, fruit trees and vegetables planted and their first baby daughter, Elisa, named after Inga's mother, was born. Gertrude, named after Walter's mother, was born a year later and then on 1st January 1949 Sophie was born, making their family complete.

Walter and Inga both knew that their fathers were dead and where they were buried. They did not have the same information for their mothers and, in a search for their graves, they discovered both were still alive. With no other living relatives, it was easy to persuade them to come and live with them.

The two grandmothers were different. Inga's mother was strong, determined, strict and not at all playful or cuddly, but always had a little treat in hand to reward her grandchildren for good work or behaviour. Walter's mother was warm, soft and entertaining. She sang and danced at every opportunity and was always ready to get on the ground to play. These two provided Walter and Inga with wonderful live-in nannies. It made sure that Elisa, Gertie and Sophie Lemberger had the very best of childhoods.

Inga took such pride in her stall business that she did not want to stop to have her babies; although all the other mothers disapproved of her when she was back at work so soon. She expanded her business first into a small shed and then, over the course of the years, Walter and Inga rented and eventually purchased the other three corners of the crossroads putting alcohol and tobacco into one building, food and household supplies in the second and newspapers and stationery into the third. They made sure that, in the four corners of the crossroads, it was possible to buy almost anything anyone would want to purchase and, with a natural affinity with customer service, they kept their shops open longer than anyone else.

When the widow, who owned the white house, died, Walter and Inga bought their home. The First World War aeroplane was sent to a museum and its hanger, which had been a long-standing feature of the land, was burned. The grass runway was incorporated into the rest of the garden. Nothing was left to show that it was the place where one of Hitler's personal pilots had first learned to fly.

Chapter 41

Bamberg, Germany August 1968

HENRY HAD TAKEN four weeks of nightly one-to-one evening classes, so he could speak some German, mainly to prove to Sophie that he had made the effort. But he was immediately put to shame by Sophie's sisters, both of whom spoke reasonable English. Any English that Walter and Inga had twenty years ago had been lost in the mist of time. Nevertheless, they all got by and the house was full of amusement and laughter as Sophie's sisters, their husbands and her friends all came around to inspect and pass comment on her boyfriend.

For four days, Henry and Sophie did nothing except explore the areas of Sophie's youth. She pointed proudly to the enormous grass banked flood defences built all around the house by her father's dredging of the river and digging of ditches. German engineering at its best she explained; whilst complaining that, with the river so deep he now expected his family to swim in it during the summer, but the water was always far too cold for anything other than a freezing dip on the hottest of days.

They wandered around Bamberg and saw the Lembergers' businesses. Henry was surprised to find that he was unusually relaxed with a feeling of being at home. There was none of the strangeness with which he always identified when he was abroad for, even though it was different, it was one he was comfortable with. Did this prove his father was German he wondered?

It was on the morning of the penultimate day of their holiday with their relationship enriched by being together, holding hands, kissing, cuddling and just laughing that Sophie asked, as they lay on the ground in the garden at the river's edge, "Aren't you going to ask my father whether you can marry me?"

"I'm waiting for you to say yes," replied Henry. "I don't want him to say yes for you to then say no. Will he say yes?" he asked expectantly.

"And I don't want to say yes if he's going to say no."

"Don't you know what he will say?"

"No, of course not."

"And your mother, what does she think your father will say?"

"She's not my father."

"But she must have some clue," said Henry, seeking some comfort as to the answer to his pending question.

"I'm sure she does, but it's my father you must ask."

"Is he waiting for me to ask him?"

"I don't know. It's not something we've talked about," she said quite testily, secretly anxious that Henry might be having second thoughts.

That evening, after Walter had returned from work and he had set about his chores, Henry joined him in the garden for what he knew would be one of the most uncomfortable conversations he was ever going to have. Having prepared and translated into German the question 'could I please have your permission to marry your daughter' there was, to Henry's dismay, a lot of German spoken but not a word of it did he understand. Certainly, there was not a recognisable 'yes' or 'no'. Instead, Walter's hand seized Henry's arm and he led him in a walk around the grounds as he talked as fast as any man had ever spoken. Instinct told Henry that he was to say nothing and just listen.

Sophie sat at the kitchen table as she had done since she was born watching her mother busy herself. She was always active but, except when cooking, baking or sewing, she never seemed to achieve a lot. They both watched as Walter and Henry walked and talked. Whilst Sophie knew the nature of the conversation, and Inga had guessed, not a word was spoken on the subject.

Sophie looked at her mother and tried to envisage her as a young girl. There were no photographs of her which might have acted as a guide; all had been lost in that period of total war. Perhaps it was a time better forgotten but she could not forget what she had been told and so, with the men out of the room and the two of them alone, Sophie suddenly asked: "Have you read Eine Frau in Berlin?"

"That dreadful book? No," she paused. "It brought a slur on all German women. Why would I read such rubbish?"

"Were you not in Berlin in the last days of the war?" Sophie asked, unsure of whether she should continue. "It's just, well, I've read it."

Sophie's Mother stopped what she was doing and stood very still, facing the wall, unable to turn around to talk to her. It was, Sophie observed, as though the shock of the question had turned her into a stone statue. For that was exactly how she had become, frozen in fear. Inga knew this moment might arrive. She had prepared herself for it, but was she ready to deal with it now?

Time stopped. Both of them knew what the silence meant.

"It was terrible Sophie, really dreadful," said Inga softly. Her head fell forward, and she looked, almost in shame, at the floor, for she felt truly embarrassed.

"Nothing I say can describe how bad it was." She was still facing the wall and speaking just above a whisper. "Minute after minute, hour after hour the shells just kept falling. You sat in the basement, with the building above you permanently shaking, as the streets were blown up, waiting to be buried alive. You can't get out because you will be shredded to smithereens from the shrapnel. There's no light, no food, no water. You don't know whether it is day or night. You've gone down there to be safe and you find yourself trapped, for there is only one way in and one way out. There are no men, not even young boys, for they've gone to fight in a defence which was suicidal."

Inga turned very slowly towards Sophie, but her eyes were closed and she was gently shaking her head from side to side in an attempt to wipe away the vision that was now at the forefront of her mind. She pulled back the kitchen chair and sat down directly opposite Sophie, but she didn't look at her. Instead, she placed her hands palms down on the kitchen table, opened her fingers wide and stared at the wooden grain of the scrubbed tabletop.

"Not once have I talked about this, not once."

Sophie sat completely still. Instinctively she knew if she did anything the moment would pass.

"Two million of us Sophie, and no one says anything, just one anonymous book. But who are we? Fifty million killed, twenty-six million Russians dead, seven million Jews killed in a genocide, so who cares about two million German women," she paused. "We women didn't start the war, but we were blamed as if we did."

There was a long silence.

"Every day I manage OK until I see dirty, rotten, broken teeth or hear a Russian voice. That destroys me all over again. I freeze and sweat both at the same time as every moment comes back."

"You've never spoken to anyone?" said Sophie, mirroring the quietness of her mother's voice.

"No."

"To Papa?"

"No, it's my shame. He has his own memories which are not good. It is all best forgotten."

On hearing herself speak those last few words, Inga stopped talking as their poignancy rang home. "Yes, it's all best forgotten," she repeated.

There was another long silence; neither knew what to say to the other.

"It was the woman with the lipstick, that's when the war ended," said her mother reflectively. "I knew then I had to put it all behind me."

"What woman?" asked Sophie very delicately.

"I don't know who she was. She was incredibly thin. I think she was a Jew. Yes, I'm sure she was a Jew. I don't know. We didn't talk. I think she'd been in a concentration camp for she had a number tattooed on her arm. I remember staring at it, but she didn't really notice that. We both arrived at Nüremburg station at the same time. She was looking for her family. Me? I was just running away. We met in the ladies room. I remember it so well. It was a bucket outdoors shielded by a curtain. I don't know how old she was; I think we were about the same age. She was wearing good clothes which were too big for her, mine were filthy and torn."

Sophie's Mother closed her eyes and shook her head. This time she rubbed her forehead as though she was trying to wipe away the memories and then she sobbed.

"She offered me some of her lipstick, Sophie... She offered me some of her lipstick," she repeated. "I started to put it on, but I couldn't. That one act of kindness by someone who should have hated me made me shake so much I couldn't keep still. Do you know she took my face in her warm hands and held it still until I stopped shaking; then she applied the lipstick ever so gently to my lips."

Inga's voice was now hardly audible.

"She should have hated me Sophie, but she didn't...she didn't. Instead, she shared with me something which was so very precious. It was her only possession and she shared it with me. Do you know someone, somewhere, thought that it would help the women of the concentration camps to feel better if they had lipstick? Do you know it was that one kindness, the only kindness, which gave me back my life? It gave me hope."

Inga looked up and saw the tears swelling up in Sophie's eyes. They moved their hands closer together and allowed their fingers to touch. There was silence. It was as though there was no more to be said.

"Coal dust, I can't smell coal dust, coal dust and cement, without it all coming back," said Inga, her voice now much stronger but her gaze still focused on the tabletop. "It's why we live here, in a timber house with wood, not coal, in our ovens." She paused. "The basement was where the coal was stored. When you're being strangled with the pressure on your neck forcing your face into the concrete, you think every breath you take is your last. You remember that breath. You remember it forever. It smelt and tasted of concrete and coal ... concrete and coal. The men, I would never know any of them again but every time ... I swear the smell so frightens me that, even today, I virtually stop breathing."

Sophie said nothing. Instead, she held her mother's hand properly, and with it the warm touch of sympathy flowed from vein to vein, but still they didn't look at each other.

"One time there was a girl next to me, her name was Anneke. She was much younger than me, I guess about fourteen or fifteen. After I don't know how many days, three or four, this soldier had her pinned down. She was lying very still with her top open. The fight had gone from her. He was dribbling onto her stomach and wetting his fingers in his spit. They all did that before they dug their fingers into you." Inga's voice slowed. "I see it now in front of me, all in slow motion. His trousers were already way down, and he leaned forward to kiss her. They always wanted to kiss you as they... Their foul, smelly, dirty mouths, their rough unshaven filthy faces, coming towards you; it was the warning of a pain you can't imagine."

Sophie's mother stopped talking, it was as if the word pain had brought her out of the trance she was in, but still her eyes were focused on the table.

"She punched him straight in the eyes with two fingers, either side of his nose, straight in. I am sure she blinded him, because his eye came clean out of its socket with her fingers. He screamed the same scream as you'd hear from the girls, the women; it was just as high pitched. At that moment, Anneke turned, looked towards me and smiled. It was the first time I'd seen her smile. Do you know she was really beautiful. I can see that smile even now. Sometimes I think I should try and paint it in memory of her."

Inga looked up from the table and Sophie watched as her mother smiled unconsciously as she remembered Anneke's beauty.

"The soldier behind Anneke, waiting his turn, took his rifle butt and smashed it into her head until her skull caved in and she was dead. Despite all their blows, they missed her face and I swear she was still smiling from her victory even when she was dead."

Again the conversation stopped and Sophie heard, for the first time since her childhood, the loud ticking of the kitchen clock, but it was not heard by Inga who was still deep in her memories.

"They really hurt us Sophie. Some say childbirth is the most pain there is, but it's not true. There is nothing worse. How can one man follow another like that? They were like animals, snarling, filthy animals. Some men would take four, five, six women in the night and, oh God, you didn't want to be that woman because they kept coming at you. You wanted to, you tried to, put your mind elsewhere, but you couldn't because they were hurting you so much, taking such a long time until they..." She didn't need to say so she didn't.

"In the morning, when they were gone, you just laid there still, wrapped up in a ball, completely exhausted, in an unbelievable fatigue and too scared to move in case it hurt. I think Anneke knew she would be killed. I think it is why she did it. She was so scared of being pregnant and telling her father. But we all were, just petrified, laying there wondering whether something alien was ... Has anyone told you that in Berlin alone there were just under 1,000 abortion clinics set up to deal with... in a country where abortion was illegal."

As Inga paused, they both noticed that, as the evening sun fell low in the sky, the redness of its rays poured straight through the window. It gave the room a warm glow which brought with it an optimism which wasn't there a few moments before.

"Do you know I was there at the start of the White Rose Revolution?" said Inga. There was a confidence in her statement.

"The White Rose Revolution?" repeated Sophie, never having heard of it before.

"Yes, I was there when Hans and Sophie Scholl were caught scattering anti-Nazi leaflets along the corridors and in the stairways at Munich University. They threw hundreds of them over the balcony into the vast central entrance hall. I remember it so well. It was just after hundreds of thousands had been killed at Stalingrad. Their leaflet was really brave and scandalous because it called Hitler the World War I Corporal and told all German youth that they had to rise up in revolt. The White Rose verses the insignia of the Swastika. It seemed so ideological and romantic."

Inga got up from the table and started to busy herself again in the kitchen by turning on the kettle.

"I knew her reasonably well." Inga continued. "We took the same biology classes. She could have been pretty, but she always had such a serious expression on her face. I don't think she ever had fun. Immediately I saw the leaflet, I wanted to join and be involved and then, when I heard that they'd been arrested and then executed, like everyone else I felt so scared, so ... I did nothing. She's the reason you are called Sophie, did I ever mention that to you?"

"No, you didn't," said Sophie "but it sounds a lovely reason," she answered sympathetically.

"Perhaps it would have been better if I'd been brave and got involved. I'd have been executed like them and it would have been for a purpose. Sometimes I think God punished me in Berlin for being a coward in Munich."

"It doesn't work like that Mama," said Sophie.

There was suddenly a noise outside as Walter and Henry were taking off their shoes having returned from their walk and a serious amount of miscommunication.

"I have never spoken about this before, Sophie, never. Promise me you will never tell anyone. Sophie, promise me," she begged.

Sophie nodded her head.

"You mustn't talk to your father or your sisters."

"Gertie has guessed," said Sophie.

"I know, but I can't talk to her about it. She mustn't know, she must never know. Do you promise me?"

"Yes Mama, I promise."

"Your sisters mustn't know. I have shared with you something I've never shared with them, or anyone else," she said in a panic.

"Mama, I promise."

"You can only say when Papa and I are gone. Until then the shame is mine to bear, to bear alone. It's a closed chapter until then, understood?" Inga was as matriarchal in her instructions as she had ever been.

"Yes Mama, I will say nothing, not even then."

Sophie got up from the table and moved to stand behind her mother who was now at the sink. Slowly Sophie wrapped her arms around her mother and, leaning forward, kissed her on the side of her cheek, tasting the salt of the tears she was silently weeping.

"The chapter's closed Mama, the chapter's closed," Sophie reassured her. But it wasn't, the chapter never closed for any of the women of the Berliner Albtraum[9] until they took their last breath.

---

[9] Berlin Nightmare

Chapter 42

Bamberg, Germany August 1968

ON THEIR RETURN to the kitchen, Henry shook his head immediately he saw Sophie. He had intended to convey the fact that he was none the wiser, but Sophie took the signal to mean that her father had said no. There followed a very irate and agitated discussion between Sophie and her mother and father during which Henry was completely ignored.

It was not, Sophie told her father, his place to say no to any man who might want to marry her. It was her decision, over which he had no veto. The language was so fierce that Henry was seeing a side of Sophie he had never seen before. He didn't know whether he admired her or was frightened by it. Whatever, Sophie gave one hell of a performance.

The discussion ended with Sophie, her face like thunder, taking the diamond ring off her right hand and handing it back to Henry. Henry said nothing. He didn't know what to say. He was in a state of shock. He took the ring and closed his eyes in disappointment. This could not be. As he opened them again, he saw that Sophie now had her left hand outstretched. He was slow in working out what this meant, for her face was still stern. Instead, she wiggled her ring finger up and down impatiently. Henry looked at Walter and Inga for some kind of clue, but their expressions revealed nothing. It was only when Sophie cocked her head to one side in a questioning manner, truly fearful that her father had put him off, that Henry understood what she wanted done.

At that moment Henry, in his stocking feet, bent down on one knee, took her left hand gently and very slowly slid the ring onto the ring finger of her left hand, which he then kissed, to a round of applause from Walter and Igna. At last, they were engaged. Immediately he stood up, Sophie jumped into his arms and cuddled him tight. In doing this the anxiety which was coursing through his body evaporated. Henry's eyes filled up with tears and his mouth went dry. He could not speak.

Sophie's father opened champagne, which Henry and Sophie only sipped in response to Walter's formal toast to their future happiness. After a few excited phone calls the house soon filled up with family and friends and an instant party started in celebration.

That evening they stood on the landing holding each other close as they said their goodnights. Each wanted to delay the moment when they would part to go to their own rooms. Henry wanted to know what it was that made Walter change his mind.

"Oh, he didn't change his mind. He was just telling you that all my money was tied up in a trust and you were not going to get any of it."

"Jesus! Is that what he was saying? I didn't understand a word of it," said Henry.

"The problem was that you wouldn't agree, so he wouldn't say yes."

"But, Sophie, I don't want your money. Your body maybe," he teased as he pulled her closer into him.

"That's what I said, well not the body bit obviously. I said you had your own money, had a good business, and after that he agreed."

They giggled and teased some more, and it was only when Inga appeared on the landing, with looks of disapproval, did they break off from holding each other and go to their own rooms.

Chapter 43

London September 1968

THE JOURNEY HOME the next day was long and tedious. Henry and Sophie were both tired and felt dirty when the taxi arrived at the front door of Sophie's mews house. Henry got out and carried Sophie's numerous cases to the front door.

"Are you coming in?" she asked for the very first time.

"May I?" he asked, unsure.

"I think now it will be all right," she said assuredly.

"Oh," said Henry who returned to collect his bag from the back of the taxi and paid off the driver.

It was the first time since they'd met that he'd been allowed inside Sophie's home. Until that moment they'd always said goodbye at the front door. He quietly cursed as he carried suitcase after suitcase of hers up steep stairs to the first floor, where there was a large oblong room with long windows on either side; one side with a view over the cobbles of the mews courtyard and the other side over a garden before coming face-to-face with the yellow-grey bricks of an unattractive block of flats.

The oblong room was open plan. It was neatly split into three distinct areas by two large oriental rugs covering the old polished wooden floorboards; two large modern floral settees set off the sitting room area nearest the stairs. Then there was the dining area with a solid oak dining table, chairs and sideboard which were obviously German antiques. Then, at the far end, was an open plan kitchen area with all the cupboards and appliances against the back wall. It was separated from the dining room by low matching kitchen cupboards, covered with a work surface. Past the kitchen there was a corridor, off which there were two bedrooms, each with its own bathroom, before coming to another staircase which took you downstairs into the large garage areas below, wide enough for four or five cars.

Henry was immediately impressed because the room had style, for -intermingled with the main pieces of furniture were some small pieces of carefully restored antiques, including two occasional tables, both with an array of photograph frames. On one there were pictures of Sophie's family and on the other there were pictures of Sophie taken at different landmarks in her career. The paintings on the wall were a mixture of modern and classical. Typically, the scenes were of people, but it was not the person that grabbed Henry's attention but the mood of the compositions, each of which told their own story. Henry loved the room for this was just how he envisaged New Found House would look.

"Would you like to shower?" said Sophie. "Then, I'll cook something to eat."

Henry was slow considering the question, for he was still out of breath from carting Sophie's bags up the stairs. She will have to learn to travel lighter, he thought, but it was a wish never to be granted.

"Come with me," she instructed, and taking him by the hand she led him along the corridor where the pattern of long windows continued but this time they were netted with white lace curtains to stop people looking in.

"This is my bedroom," said Sophie, as they walked past a door on the right. "This is the spare bedroom," she continued pushing the door ajar. "I'll get a towel," said Sophie.

"I'll get my bag and wash things," said Henry.

Back in the spare room, Sophie offered Henry a blue cotton dressing gown from the wardrobe, feeling it necessary to explain that it was used by her father when he came to stay.

Henry showered and, under the flow of warm water, he paid attention to having a close shave; with clean teeth he felt a renewed man. He donned a clean tee shirt and underpants and with some reticence wrapped himself in Walter's dressing gown.

In the bathroom next door Sophie was also showering. Whereas Henry was relaxed, Sophie felt she was in a race against time. She removed her make up at top speed and showered with a shower cap to keep her hair dry, which she rapidly brushed into a fringe at the front and ponytail behind. She cleaned her teeth, applied the faintest of lipstick and was just about to start on her eye makeup when she stopped. Perhaps it's time she thought, remembering Rita Hayworth's expression, that 'he stopped seeing Gilda and saw the real me.' With that she wiped off the lipstick with a tissue.

The magic of the moment meant that they both appeared in their dressing gowns in the corridor at the same time. Henry walked up to her, first taking her hand and then holding her tightly around her waist as he pulled her into him. He kissed her gently on the lips. "I do love you, Sophie" he said, "I really do." They then kissed each other as they had never done before, for there was no holding back, no uncertainty.

Lying side by side on Sophie's bed they very slowly and very tenderly started to explore each other's bodies. Sophie was surprised at how relaxed she was in this moment. It had dominated her thoughts whilst on the aeroplane, but now it was exactly how she had imagined. Before, she had been anxious and scared. Would her mother's experiences play through to this moment, she had wondered? But those thoughts were now the furthest from her mind as it was completely overtaken by Henry's touch.

It was Henry who was a bag of jelly; anxious and nervous for he wanted nothing to go wrong. Under her dressing gown there was no bra and just the plainest white cotton knickers; deliberately chosen as they were a far cry from the skimpy panties she had worn at the start of her career. Each of Henry's moves were slow, exploring just half an inch further, each time sweeping his hand over her knickers. He marvelled as her nipples rose and tightened to his touch and was encouraged as her legs moved just that fraction further apart so he could explore the inside of her thighs.

It was the chill of the autumn which prompted Sophie to invite Henry into her bed, and there, under the duvet, he slid his hand into her knickers and took them off for the first time. Quickly stripping off his tee shirt and underpants they lay on their sides and in their nakedness, cuddled as tightly as they could. Henry's hands swept over her back and down over her buttocks. She rocked her body into his, and he into hers. It was just like this, lying on their sides and with the gentlest of movements, that they made love for the first time. For both of them everything was just perfect.

Chapter 44

London September 1968

JUST AS HENRY and Sophie were, out of overwhelming love and deep respect, committing themselves to a life of monogamy, across London, Sunetta was setting out to be a rebel and libertine.

There was disappointment both at Roedean and in the Daunier household that Sunetta had decided to read for an History of Art degree at Birkbeck College rather than apply to Cambridge or Warwick Universities which had both offered her a place; but this was to fail to understand Sunetta's needs, and therefore her motive. She needed to dance.

The fields of New Found Estate had given Sunetta the opportunity to run wild and free, expending the unbound energy trapped in her body. Roedean had helped her focus that energy into dance and with it came a disciplined body that moved with a natural grace to any kind of music which happened to be playing. Sunetta had inherited Satutu's rhythmic genes, and she knew that it was only in London where she would find the quality of dance schools she craved.

The night before Sunetta left New Found Estate to go to university, Satutu came to her room to discuss boys, pregnancy and saving herself until marriage. As she lay in bed, listening to her mother's words of wisdom, she felt a mixture of both upset and anger. Upset that she had let her mother down, for there would be no *white wedding* for her, and anger as she contemplated the injustice of it being wrong for a woman to make love to a man before marriage when the same judgements were not imposed on men.

There was some discussion about Satutu accompanying Sunetta on her first day to university, but David was now quite frail and she did not want to leave him, so it was Big Joe who took Sunetta, helped her find her room and settle her in, just as he had done when she first went to Roedean.

Sunetta found the first day confusing and bewildering, almost overwhelming. After her brother left and immediately the door to her room was closed, she sat on the bed and cried for she was both very scared and lonely. After a few minutes of self-sympathy, Sunetta started to unpack and, as each item found its place in her room, she realised that she had a freedom which she had never had before.

On her third day of university, while drinking coffee in the lounge of her halls of residence, Sunetta said quite casually, "I'm going to the laffenscratch, is there anything anyone wants?"

"The laffenscratch," repeated another student, "what's that?"

"It's the Paki shop around the corner. I need some washing powder and things," explained Sunetta.

"You can't call it a Paki shop," said a girl, who from her head scarf was of obvious Asian descent.

"Why not?"

"Because it's offensive."

"Offensive to whom?"

"Pakistanis."

"Why?" asked Sunetta, genuinely confused.

"Because it is."

"That's not an answer," said Sunetta, in a cautious, questioning tone.

"It's offensive to me."

"Oh, I'm sorry. I didn't mean to cause any offence," said Sunetta, quite bewildered.

"Well you did!" said the Asian girl, with a dogmatism which Sunetta found unattractive.

"Ok, sorry, I'll ask again, does anyone want anything from the laffenscratch?" Sunetta asked.

"You can't say that," howled the Asian woman again. "It's racist!"

"Why? it's a made-up word. It has no racial or offensive connotation. It means a local shop run by one family, nothing more."

Beating a retreat, Sunetta walked to the shops. She felt chastened by the exchange she had just had, but also very upset. Her racially prejudiced ordeals in South Africa were far worse, and yet she had never responded in such a reactionary way. All her experiences had shown that to do so only made matters worse. As she thought more about being called a racist, her hackles started to rise. This woman knows nothing about racism, she thought as Little Joe came into her mind. It was a matter which she was not going to allow to rest.

Back at her halls of residence Sunetta immediately went looking for the Asian woman in the head scarf, who now appeared to be holding court in the common room.

"I think you owe me an apology," challenged Sunetta, "for inferring that I'm a racist."

The Asian woman looked at Sunetta, first confused and then with indignity. "Well you are," she retorted. "You referred to the local shop as the Paki shop, that's an offensive word which mustn't be used."

"Who says? asked Sunetta preparing herself for a fight.

"Decent people," said the Asian woman smugly.

"Who are these decent people and how, and when did they decide?" asked Sunetta. "And, how come they decided that their opinion was more important than my opinion, and more important than my right to free speech?

"Just accept that decent people consider the word Paki as offensive," said the Asian woman, in a tone designed to shut down debate.

"Then sadly you don't understand, or haven't been educated in, the rules of giving and receiving offence," said Sunetta firmly. "They've been well established for a very long time."

The Asian women looked shocked, for no one had ever challenged her on racism before. In an acquiescent middle-class England, ever mindful to be polite to those with a skin of different colour, her word on what was and was not racist had only been hers to opine. For a white person to even begin to challenge her opinion was proof enough of racism.

"The British invented the rule at the time when they had an Empire," said Sunetta, confidently. "It's very simple: offence can only be taken if the giver intended to give offence," said Sunetta assuredly.

"There you have it, a rule invented by imperialists to suit them," said the Asian woman changing tactics with the dexterity that her two years reading law had taught her.

"I'm sorry, but it's a good rule," argued Sunetta. There was now a stridency in her voice which matched that of her opponent. "Look, the maker of a remark cannot possibly know what is in your mind or of your specific sensitivities. Whereas you, the receiver of my comment, could tell by both tone and context whether I meant it to be offensive; and it is obvious, I didn't!"

"There are words which are generally accepted as wrong; nigger, wog, the part of a woman which I won't even say, and Paki are amongst those," argued the Asian woman. "They are defacto banned words,"

"Don't be ridiculous, you can't ban words. You'll be banning free speech next," argued Sunetta.

"Of course you can," said the Asian woman defiantly.

"You can't!" insisted Sunetta. "I've been called nigger and wog all my life, and sometimes those words are used offensively and sometimes they are not. It's my job as the receiver to judge the context in which they are used. It's only when a word is accompanied by an unpleasant adjective that I tend to get upset. For example, I might hear someone ask about me, 'Has the nigger washed the car?' Whilst it's not gracious, and impolite, in its context it is not offensive. Whereas, if someone was to say, 'get out of the way you blank blank wog,' then I do get upset. One conversation is polite, the other is impolite. That's the way this is to be judged; Paki was descriptive, it was NOT offensively used!"

"You sound like Voltaire," said the Asian women. "I disapprove of what you say but I will defend to the death your right to say it."

"Actually, it wasn't Voltaire," said Sunetta, with authority, "those words were written about him by Beatrice Hall," she snorted.

At this point Sunetta felt that, even if she hadn't won the debate, with this last remark she had scored a draw. It was a good time to go. Just when she was at the door, Sunetta turned and looked challengingly at the Asian woman. "Have you heard of Joe Daunier?" she asked. The look on the Asian's woman's face showed she recognised the name but was finding it hard to see the context. Everyone else in the room quickly remembered the newspaper reports telling of the killing of Little Joe.

"Look up his name in the Library if you're in doubt," Sunetta continued. "He was my brother. If you're wondering about the rule of offence given and offence taken, then think about what you intended when you called me a racist, and then think of the extent of the offence you actually gave." With that Sunetta turned, walked through the door and was gone. Little did she know but, at that moment, the Common Room Queen had been dethroned. It was now Sunetta's title for the taking.

Chapter 45

London September 1968 - December 1969

HENRY VIRTUALLY LIVED at Sophie's over the next nine months as the builders had taken far longer to complete the building work on Found House than was expected. It was a chilly June afternoon that they opened the door to a bare, but spotlessly clean, finished building ready for occupation. Everything was just as they wanted. As they walked through the house Henry and Sophie shared their plans for where furniture was to go as they had done many times before. At each point Sophie made a suggestion and Henry was thrilled to accept her ideas. There was just one area which was sacrosanct. The basement and ground floor was to be his domain, fitted to offices with a laboratory filled with testing equipment.

It was at the top of Found House, in what used to be the living quarters for the live-in staff, that Sophie said, "I think we should change our plans for this room. We need to make it into a nursery," she continued with a knowing smile.

"Are you?" asked Henry.

"Yes," said Sophie beaming.

"How?"

"That's a damn stupid question," responded Sophie, with a joke in her voice.

Henry digested the news with surprise. Surely she'd taken precautions since they'd become lovers; but hell, it was the best surprise he'd ever had and his face showed it. As they embraced and cuddled and celebrated their news there were no two people happier, or more in love, anywhere in the world than these two. Their life was perfect.

"We have to get married very quickly, my father would kill me if he knew I was pregnant and not married," said Sophie.

Their life fell into a whirlwind as Sophie honoured her booking commitments. They moved into Found House together, organised a legal marriage in England, then a marriage service in Germany and wedding blessings in England and France.

Sophie's face was singularly the most beautiful sight for, on her wedding day, she wore her hair up, adorned by a classical white veil. So stunning did she look that her photograph was on the front page of virtually every newspaper in the western world. As Henry looked at the picture the following morning, he fell in love with her all over again, and he knew that half the world would be in love with her too.

The blessing at the village church in Latoire, and the reception at Château de Gressier, was organised by Juliette. Although it was not how either Henry or Sophie would have wished it, they both appreciated the matriarchal nature of his grandmother's character so went along with her plans. Again, Sophie wore white, but this time a trouser suit cut to hide her modest baby bump. The veil from her wedding dress was re-tailored so that it could be weaved into her hair, which she wore long, adorned with summer flowers neatly threaded through. The event was saddened by Victoria's refusal to come; arguing one wedding was enough. It was obvious that, even though it would be a happy occasion, it was not one which was going to see a rapprochement between mother and daughter.

There was another momentous decision taken for their wedding day. Henry changed his surname to Guégan, formally dropping the Bellanger name on his birth certificate. It seemed only right to him that his children's names should reflect their lineage. Sophie and he talked about taking the name Klugman, after his father, but since neither knew the man it didn't seem quite right. There was one other reason for choosing the Guégan name above all others; if his father did, one day, come looking for him, he would be looking for a Guégan, and not some name selected from a dead friend.

After a mad summer of weddings and celebrations, it was not until the end of September that Henry and Sophie had their first full day in Found House all alone. In the evening they cuddled up on the sofa as music played quietly in the background, and they talked of the year ahead.

"Rosalind says I need to reposition my brand," said Sophie out of the blue. "Particularly now I'm going to be a mother. Apparently, the market doesn't want mothers!"

Rosalind, Sophie's booker, was anxious at her threatened loss of income by Sophie's pregnancy. It brought forth a lot of management speak, said to persuade Sophie that she had to fill her post catwalk days with something else.

"Your brand?" teased Henry. "Not wanting mothers, ridiculous!"

"Yes, apparently my name face recognition rate is 87% in the 14 to 35 market."

"What, where did you get that from?" asked Henry.

"Voxty did some market research for the agency on all their talent."

"Were you the highest?"

"No."

"Jasmine and Yollanda beat me, but only just. I had a much higher recognition rate with men than with women and I beat them easily in Japan and Asia."

"You mean I'm married to somebody famous, and I didn't know it?" he teased.

"Yes, I don't know, yes," said Sophie flustered, for in her own mind there was a huge difference between the person she thought she was, and the image which was portrayed of her in the newspapers and magazines.

"I hate the way Rosalind speaks of me as a product, but she says it's important I remain in the public eye so that I keep the big contracts. It means I can ... should do other things."

"You don't have to do that," said Henry. "We've enough money, my trading business is doing better than I expected. Take time to be a mummy and then decide."

"I know darling," said Sophie "I agree. But I have worked so hard to get here I don't want to give it all up."

Henry wrapped his arms around her and kissed her neck. They sat in silence as they both contemplated how a baby was going to change their world, and together they gently stroked her tummy, already in love with a human being they did not yet know.

"Rosalind has suggested I might try acting," said Sophie, after a long pause.

"Can you act?" he asked.

"Doubt it, but I could learn. Most of the TV adverts I've done require a lot of acting," said Sophie, defensively.

The idea floated in the air as the music played and the first real fire of the autumn crackled in the grate.

"I think we have to be clever about this," said Henry. "You don't have to be in the public eye. You just need to be in the eye of those who matter. It's their advertising spend that will keep you in the public eye," he added.

"I thought I might do a degree," said Sophie, following her own train of thought and not acknowledging the point Henry had made earlier.

Henry said nothing because his mind was on brand Sophie.

"Let's have some lunches here," she said, changing the subject.

"Who for?" asked Henry.

"The matterers."

"What? Who are they? I don't understand," he said in a tone indicating genuine confusion.

"Those who matter, just as you said."

"Like who?" said Henry, not following Sophie's train of thought.

Sophie listed the names of the chairmen and CEO's of the major retail stores, clothing brand designers, editors of newspapers and magazines as though she was reading from her own list of Who's Who. The music stopped and they both stared at the glow of the fire, the silence only disturbed by the occasional hiss from a splitting log.

"You know these people?" asked Henry, after a little while.

"Well, I've met them, but I don't know them, no."

"So why would they come?"

"Because we've invited them."

"Really?" said Henry, sounding very surprised.

"Please, Henry," she implored, "don't be so thick."

"Why?"

"The men will come because I invited them. It might appear arrogant or boastful, but I promise you, they'll come. The women will come to judge you, our house and talk babies."

Henry smiled and her tummy jerked involuntarily as they felt their baby move under their touch for the very first time. The whole thing amused them, as it did four weeks later, just after the last guests had gone home following the first of the Matterers Lunches. The whole event had been perfect, proven by the fact that most of the guests didn't leave until well into the early evening. It was all thanks to the hostessing flair of Sophie and the organisational ability of Rosalind.

"Debrief, debrief," said Henry, trying to persuade Sophie to talk.

"Only to get into the shower," she said, as she climbed the stairs, pleased at her own wittiness. Perhaps she was learning British humour after all.

They showered together, sharing bits of gossip and then, just wrapped in towels, they threw themselves on to their bed. They held hands and stared at the ceiling.

"Do you know I've sold about £25,000 of wine today?" said Henry excitedly. "I didn't expect that to happen."

"How?" asked Sophie, equally surprised.

"I was asked if I had any of the wine we had at lunch for sale, or if I knew where they could buy it."

"Who asked?" enquired Sophie.

"Piers for one," replied Henry.

"Makes sense, he runs one of the world's largest advertising agencies," added Sophie. "It seems to me they spend half their time getting drunk with their clients."

"Kenneth was the other. Apparently he's on the wine committee of Boodles or Whites, I can't remember which, and he buys for them.

"When did this happen?" she asked.

"When you were upstairs with all the women, I took the men downstairs to see my chemistry set."

"Oh, please don't tell me you bored them showing how you test and grade wine?"

"Er, yes," said Henry, apologetically, "but that wasn't what they were really interested in. It was when I explained the way I insisted on my wines being shipped and stored that they asked me to help."

"And they ordered the wines we served during lunch?"

"Yes."

"I thought it rather nice that we served three different wines with the main course. I know our guests only got a half of a glass to start with, but were you happy with that?" asked Sophie.

"Yes, it worked well because all three glasses were poured at the same time so the person could choose their favourite," said Henry. "What made you come up with the idea?" he asked.

"I don't know who said it, but I was told that wine had to compliment a meal. Then I thought that some people like mustard, others like horseradish, then there are all the gravies and sauces which people then add to compliment it, and I thought I'd treat the wine like that, and give them a choice."

"But you mixed a Bordeaux with a Burgundy with a Côtes du Rhone, so how did you choose?"

"I used your notes. I chose only those which were light but described as being fruity, so they blended rather nicely. It meant that you could move from one wine to the other without jarring the taste buds."

"It seems to have gone extremely well," acknowledged Henry. "Certainly, far better than I'd expected."

"The formula worked; don't you think?" said Sophie.

"What formula, what are you talking about?" asked Henry, a little perplexed.

"The rules I gave Rosalind at the outset," said Sophie.

"Which were?" prompted Henry.

"Only the bosses, no number twos; no one from the same business sector at the same time, so no two retailers or advertising agencies or publishers; no one from the same company at the same time; the same number of men and women; never on a Monday or Friday; never in the season and, most importantly, we stressed it was a private lunch. When Rosalind wrote to everyone to confirm she insisted that it was under the ... er ... 'something rules'."

"Something rules?" asked Henry, teasingly.

"Something house," Sophie said getting quite insistent. "You know, something house rules."

"Cider House?" Henry prompted.

"No," Sophie was frustrated with herself. Her memory was usually reliable but now she was struggling. "Chatham House," she blurted out, "Chatham House Rules."

"What does that mean?" he asked.

"It means that the conversation is in private. It means that anything that is learnt can't be attributed to anyone else. I found it all very quaint."

"Sophie, we've made about £10,000 profit from today," said Henry changing the subject. "Just think how much we would make if we did this thing more often and properly."

"What do you mean properly?" asked Sophie, her voice revealing her disappointment that Henry might have thought it was all less than perfect.

"It's not what you did, no, it's not that," he said, dismissing her hurt feelings just as a misunderstanding. "No, if I did my bit properly and..."

"For God's sake, don't turn it into a wine tasting," said Sophie sharply. "Neither of us could stand that," she continued accurately.

"Oh," said Henry dejectedly. "It's just I don't think any of them knew how complex a product wine is until I started talking."

"For Pete's sake Henry, don't try and sell anything," said Sophie emphatically. "Don't you see, they bought from you because you were genuine, they trusted you."

On Thursday evening, as they said goodbye to their third lot of guests that week, Sophie and Henry were on a high, and then exhaustion took over as their bodies started to wind down after the excitement of the week.

Some of the people they had invited to lunch weren't 'matterers' to Sophie's brand at all, but people that Henry and Sophie thought they would like to meet; two newscasters, two newspaper editors, two magazine editors, three politicians, a sports personality and an actor. All of them came to meet Sophie. Her ice maiden days, when she remained aloof, were gone, as in the security of her marriage and home she had become free and more joyful.

All of the men who came to lunch fell in love with her and all of the women, who wanted to hate her out of jealousy, were thrilled that in future they would be able to call Sophie their friend, for that was how she made each of them feel. For those four or five hours each day Sophie and Henry worked to ensure that their guests didn't have a care in the world. To their guests, Sophie and Henry were beautiful people in whose image they could only aspire.

The thing they could hardly believe, because it had not been planned, was that in those three days Henry had sold just over £80,000 of wine to people with very big cheque books.

The next week Henry and Sophie had the company of the supermarket wine buyer who had prompted Henry to head for Argentina. Like all those who came to a Matterers' Lunch he came primarily to meet Sophie.

"You said something very interesting when we last met," said Henry to the buyer as they moved into Henry's laboratory.

"Gosh, that was a long time ago, I'm surprised you remembered."

"You told me to look out for wines which are suitable for the English palette."

"Sounds like me."

"Well I hadn't realised until then that people's taste buds are very different. Some have more taste receptors than others by a multiple of four; two thousand in some, eight thousand in others. This makes them more sensitive to things like sugar, salt, and bitterness."

The buyer nodded as he wandered around the room admiring Henry's laboratory equipment.

"In some people the receptors are close together, in others they are further apart," continued Henry.

"Are there some nationalities which tend to have more taste buds than others?" asked the wine buyer, playing along with Henry's enthusiasm for his subject.

"Oh yes. It has been proven in ethnic group taste tests that some groups are far more responsive than others as is the case between men and women. For example, Hispanic whites enjoy much higher taste intensity when compared to non-Hispanic. It seems to me that taste is both a physiological and mental thing; how well your taste receptors are connected to your brain."

"So what are you trying to do, classify a customer by taste receptor type and then, based on this, sell them a specific wine?

Henry didn't answer. "You see this machine here. It is the very first machine to smell wine. It will detect the tiniest traces of trichloroanisole and tribromoanisole, the compounds which cork wine and give it a smell or taste."

"Are you trying to work out a way of scientifically grading the aroma of wine?" asked the buyer.

"Of sorts, it's an adaptation of a machine which was developed to detect bad coffee beans. One bad bean in a roast and the whole batch must be destroyed. The original machine sniffs every single bean at enormous speed and if it doesn't smell right then a shot of air punches the bad smelling bean out and into the waste."

There's one hell of a lot of machinery here," said the buyer. "Is this all just a hobby or can you make money with it."

"Oh, I'll make money," said Henry confidently.

"How?"

"I can tell scientifically..." Henry stopped, gathered his thoughts and started again. "If there is a specific wine from a country which is popular here in the UK then I can scientifically match that wine almost exactly, and source it from a far cheaper wine producing country."

"How do you do that?"

"By an analysis of the chemistry; look, I can prove it to you." Henry couldn't resist a smile for he now knew he had the wine buyer exactly where he wanted him.

Upstairs in their kitchen Henry started unpacking bottles of wine from his fridge and from a box on the floor. Each one had its label covered.

"I went to your supermarket this morning and I bought twelve bottles of wine; three French, two Italian and one Spanish, in both red and white. I then matched those wines from estates from four other countries. We're now going to do a blind tasting test to see if we can identify the European wines." Henry made a point of not saying your wine as he didn't want it to be a competition.

Two hours later Henry had made his point. Sometimes they detected the European wine and when they did they both agreed it was difficult to justify their higher price.

"Do you represent each of these vineyards?" asked the buyer.

"No, I'm a wine buyer and wholesaler. I'm not an agent or representative," replied Henry.

"But you can supply these wines?

"Yes, on long term contracts."

"Why, but more importantly how? Who knows what the vintage will be like in three years' time?"

"The best vineyards already sell all of their supply. If I'm to be sold the amount of wine you would like then they are going to have to plant more vines. That takes time, or they have to limit their sales to other customers. They are going to do neither of these things if I offer a one-year contract. It's of no interest to them."

The buyer nodded for it made sense. "How do you fix the price?" he asked. "That must be the hardest thing to do."

"It's where science comes in. I can set the base parameters of their wine using the chemistry for at least the last three years of their production. Using the agreed base, I can then agree with the producer a price per bottle for several years ahead. There is a price adjustment downward if they move outside of the agreed parameters."

"You buy from them on this basis. Would you sell to me on the same basis?" asked the buyer.

"I pay a deposit of 30% a year to secure my order for the next year. This way I guarantee my supply ahead of everyone else. If they have a bad year and their volume goes down the amount of wine I get is not reduced."

"No, I won't do that. I'll pay 100% F.O.B. though," said the buyer as an incentive.

"Free on Board," said Henry to make sure they understood each other.

"Yes, immediately my wine shipment crosses the ships side."

For the next hour they discussed the finer points of how a deal might work but with a handshake and an agreement that the paperwork would follow it was agreed that within the next 21 months wines from Australia, Argentina, California, Chile, New Zealand and South Africa would be on his supermarket shelves courtesy of Found Vintners.

It was only on Christmas Day that Henry and, a heavily pregnant, Sophie settled down for the first time in six months to relax. Sophie played the piano and Henry accompanied her on the guitar as, for the first time, they made their own music. There was a shared guilt as they thought of Henry's mother, on her own for the first time, and Sophie's family, without her, but they were determined that, with their own family growing inside Sophie's belly, their life with each other should come first.

Chapter 46

London October 1969

SUNETTA SAILED THROUGH her first year of university getting just a couple of marks short of a First-Class degree in her year-end exams. Work hard she was told and a first would be hers for the taking at the end of her course. The trouble for Sunetta was that it was too easy. She read the books and wrote the essays, but it was not her passion. In the second week at her first term, she had enrolled as a pupil at the London Contemporary Dance School whose premises were just around the corner from Birkbeck College. Strictly LCDS was a full-time course but because the school was new and needed pupils Sunetta was able to agree a curriculum which mixed and matched with her History of Art degree. She could do without the academic study, but her mind and body needed dance.

As she stretched, pulled, twisted and bent her body with spot on timing to the rhythm of the music, Sunetta was filled with a form of electricity which defined the very person she was. Of all the dance forms it was the Cecchetti Method of ballet Sunetta particularly loved. This was not covered well by the LCDS course so Sunetta took extra classes on Saturday and Sunday, for the classical music to which she danced was her fix against the contemporary music she danced each day.

It was during the second year of university that Sunetta lost control of events. Whilst she was in halls of residence there was a structure about her life. Her meals were provided, her washing was easily done and there was none of the administration involved which comes with running a household. It was in the second year, when she moved into a mixed house shared with six others that the reserve which had preserved her through the first year vanished.

Many years later, when asked what she did at university, she replied drunkenly, "A lot of falatio, God knows why." She took her first man on the second night of freshers' fair at the start of her second year. She then moved on, with almost predatory skill, through the sports clubs of the medical school, law school and engineering faculty of London University. She did not care whether these men were in a relationship or not, for she had discovered that she loved sex. A man only got into her bed if he was tall, lean, muscular and athletic. She only ever invited them back if they had pleased her; many did not make the second trip.

With her degree studies, her dance commitments and now her extra curricula activities, something was going to have to give.

Chapter 47

London January 1970

AFTER A PERIOD of rapid activity which saw doctors and nurses work to a routine they had performed many times before, Henry and Sophie's son was wrapped in a creamy orange blanket and handed her to cuddle. After a few moments' pause, Sophie subconsciously unwrapped the bundle and counted his fingers and then his toes. Satisfied that all was well, she studied his face.

Throughout the whole of his son's birth Henry hadn't taken his eyes off Sophie's face, for even in that most base of human moments he thought she was the most beautiful woman in the world. He ached with the love he had for her and now for their son. They smiled a knowing smile at each other, and then stared at their son whose eyes were gently closed in a deep sleep. Together they watched his breathing and studied his tiny features, his ears, his nose, and his eyebrows. In the quiet of that room, with Sophie wrapped in Henry's arms and their baby lying across Sophie's breasts, there was nowhere in the world, three more contented and happy people.

They had spent many hours discussing names. If it was a boy it was to be named after Sophie's father and Henry's great grandfather, it was just the order that needed deciding. But, with their little baby in front of them, they knew he was neither a Walter nor a Stoddart. He needed his own name. As they looked at him it was as though the boy named himself, Andrew Walter Guégan. Immediately his name was agreed both parents shed tears, not just of joy but from the awe of being responsible for one so very young.

It's hard to tell when you know something's going wrong. The hospital staff probably knew first because they delayed Sophie's discharge. It would not be on the weekend but on the following Monday. On the discharge day Henry arrived in Sophie's room to find her rolled up in a little ball and sobbing. Henry asked what was wrong but there was no response. She was desolate. Henry brushed her hair, washed the salt away from her face and stroked her forehead but there was no reaction. Had something happened to Andrew he wondered? He was not in his cot beside her and so with panic in his heart he rushed out to the nursing station desperate to find his son.

"He's OK," assured the nurse in response to Henry's panic, "Baby's being fed with some water with a bottle."

"But Sophie's very upset," he cried. "What's gone wrong?"

"Mum's having a baby blues day. It always happens, normally a little earlier, but it's to be expected. It's her hormones sorting themselves out. It's nothing to worry about. It's why Baby is with us."

"Oh, thank you," said Henry, reassured.

"It normally takes a day or two," said the nurse nonchalantly, "and she will be as right as rain. Don't worry," she finished confidently.

Henry returned to be with Sophie, who remained detached from everything he did. He cuddled her gently, trying to prompt her to have a shower, but there was no response. Sophie was compliant as the nurse propped her up and supervised Andrew latching onto her nipple; his small, delicate hands resting on her breast. Henry looked lovingly on his son as he suckled, but as he looked into Sophie's face, for the first time, he became frightened as to what was happening. She was showing only one emotion, sadness, and it was this sorrow which was consuming her mind. Henry was overcome in emotion. His brain raced between a mixture of joy, fear, and anger for, in front of his very eyes, the woman he loved was rejecting his son, who needed her for everything that a mother provides.

It was as though, at some moment after Andrew's birth, there had been a death in Sophie's soul. The pain was agonising, for there, lying on her chest, was one so helpless and yet so devoid of help. It was Henry who, after about fifteen minutes, winded Andrew and reconnected him to the other breast. Sophie did nothing to help. It was as though she was completely hopeless, no more than a mechanical feeding machine.

Later that day, Sophie's parents came to see their grandson for the first time. They immediately knew something was wrong. "She's with us but not with us," said Inga, in a very accurate description, after only having been with them for a few minutes. Late in the evening, Henry took Walter down to the hospital canteen to get something to eat, leaving Inga to nurse Sophie. On their return to Sophie's room, Inga ushered them into the corridor where she spoke rapidly in German to Walter, who shook his head as she spoke. Henry had a vague idea as to what was being said but, because it was so important, they consulted a translation dictionary before they spoke. Walter grabbed Henry by the arm and looked sternly into his eyes. "Sophie has asked her mother to help her kill the little one," said Walter gravely, whilst Inga nodded vigorously, approving the translation.

"She said it's the only way to keep him safe," added Inga in a heavy German accent.

Henry didn't speak. Instead, he walked about ten yards down the corridor to where there were a row of chairs and he sat down. Leaning forward, he rubbed his eyes with the palms of his hands. Walter and Inga came and sat beside him. They were silent. They were waiting for Henry to speak.

"We say nothing," commanded Henry. "If we say anything, everything will get out of control." Walter nodded and translated for Inga. She nodded too as Walter spoke in German, for she had already understood what Henry had said.

"I don't understand it," said Henry, perplexed. All of a sudden, the girl who seemed to have everything now had nothing. "How can this be?" he asked the world generally.

Consultant after consultant examined Sophie, including those that Walter had brought over from Germany. The conclusions were always the same. Sophie's symptoms of fatigue, feelings of guilt and worthlessness, of not being able to cope, with constant thoughts of death and suicide, were all diagnosed as psychotic depression. Her brain was hearing or seeing narratives that did not exist, making it impossible for her to distinguish between her own thoughts and ideas and those which were being imposed by a mysterious world.

"It's not unusual, but it's not common," said the consultant. "It's a bad case of the baby blues. We'll prescribe antidepressants, but over time she will come out of it." The consensus was that there was little more that the hospital could do. It would be far better if Sophie were discharged back to Found House and her home.

No one outside the family was told of the problem; all that was said was that there'd been a complication with Andrew's birth which required a small procedure. Rosalind, Sophie's booker, kept prodding for information, as without her top-earning client she was at a loose end, but Henry was well aware of the permanent stigmatism attaching to mental illness of any kind and was determined to protect his family at all costs.

Chapter 48

London April – July 1970

IT TOOK A good few months, and was a very slow process, before Sophie started to engage properly with her son, looking after him as any other mother would.

Sophie's mother and father, who had been living in Found House, returned to Germany, and by late spring everything was back to normal with everyone forgetting how poorly she had been. Sophie resumed her modelling career, limiting her engagements to only her sponsors, working occasionally from Paris but mainly in London; and with this her confidence returned. Henry had his Sophie back.

The Matterers Lunches started again, with politicians and sportsmen added to the cast of those who were wined and dined. The lunches were more professional in their planning as each new guest was fully researched beforehand. Sophie thought it strange to invite devout Muslims, even more so when Henry insisted that Jews would be invited to the same table, saying: "they are both the sons of Abraham," thereby dismissing two thousand years of history in one phrase.

"But the Muslims are from the mistress's line, whereas the Jews are from the wife's line. Does that not give them some precedent?" Sophie argued.

"From the woman's point of view, probably, but not for Abraham, as he would have loved all his children equally," responded Henry. "In any case, the fight is not between the Jews and the Muslims or the Muslims and the Christians. For four hundred years, the main fight has been between the different Muslim sects, for all religions follow the same Golden Rule: love your neighbour as you would love yourself."

Their decision to include people of all races, religions, creeds, castes, ethnicity, and sexuality in their Matterers Lunches was a wise one; particularly when it came to Islam. Sophie and Henry quickly learnt that Sharia law was very flexible and, while earning interest on an investment was contrary to the rules of the Prophet, the holding of an appreciating asset was not, even though that asset might comprise forbidden alcohol. The important thing was that the wine was not actually drunk, but, of course, tasting wine to determine the quality for investment purposes wasn't actually drinking it. Therefore, in the privacy of Henry and Sophie's home, some of the richest men of the Middle East spent many a happy afternoon choosing the wines that they would be laying down as an investment.

This new, very rich, customer base, while being potentially very profitable, gave Henry two immediate problems: buying and storage. He had to go into the market to buy the finest of wines from the main merchants, making only a modest profit, for none of the vineyards would substantially increase their supply to him as quickly as he needed.

It was not just the wine which made the Matterers Lunches special. It was the women Sophie invited too. Each was not only highly attractive but came with world views and experiences which they felt confident enough to express. It gave them a 'je ne sais quois' attractiveness to their male guests.

The first summer after Andrew was born was spent firstly at Château de Gressier, then in Bamberg with Sophie's family where, to Henry's relief, he found that his year of studying German had paid off, as he was now able to join in the family conversations. He started to share his plans for his business, which Walter lapped up, such that towards the end of their visit Henry and Walter were travelling to the vineyards of Germany together, seeking to represent them.

It was during one of the evening walks around the grounds of his garden that Walter asked, "Would you like us to find out about your father?"

Henry stopped for a moment and looked at Walter. It was a strange question coming out of the blue.

"Why?" asked Henry.

Walter never said, but they had already started their research. The reason: Igna's illogical certainty that it was something in Henry's family which had caused Sophie to have her psychotic episode.

"It's just we think there may be a connection between here and Hauptman Klugman," continued Walter. "There used to be an old First World War plane in a barn on this field," he said waiving his hand around, "and there used to be an airstrip across where we now have fruit trees." Walter pointed to a gap in his orchard.

"What connection?" asked Henry, quite fascinated.

"It goes back a long time. When we first moved here the woman who owned it wouldn't sell it to me because she was waiting for her son to come back from the war. She showed me a picture of her son and he was one of Hitler's personal pilots. We think the woman we bought this house from might have been your grandmother."

"You bought this house from my German grandmother?" restated Henry disbelievingly. "You think my father lived here?"

"Yes, at least it's a strong possibility. It needs more research, but Inga and I purchased this house from a Frauline Dr Lisa Friedman.

"But that's nothing like my father's name."

"You're sure Hauptman Henrik Klugman is your father?"

"So my mother says."

"You see, we've been able to trace a Hauptman Heinrik Klugman as being a pilot in Hitler's flight," said Walter cautiously, for he found the word Hitler distasteful to say.

"Mother says he left Bordeaux in October 1941 to go to Berlin as one of Hitler's pilots."

"Then we have the right man because that's what the records we've seen say."

Walter looked at Henry carefully to gauge how he was taking the news. "Would you like to know more?" he asked cautiously.

"What's there to know?" askedHenry tentatively, not sure whether he wanted to hear or not.

"Some of it's not good, or at least, you might not like to hear it."

Henry sighed heavily. "You'd better tell me," he said, reluctantly.

"As you know, your father was stationed in Bordeaux and flew with Aviation Command Atlantic until October 1941. And you're right, he joined Fliegerstaffel de Führer, known as F.d.F in November 1941. It was at Tempelhof Airport in Berlin that he was sworn into the 1st SS Panzer Division Leibstandarte SS Adolf Hitler.

"What?" said Henry perplexed. "He was a member of the SS?"

"The F.d.F was Hitler's personal aviation squadron and Leibstandarte SS his personal bodyguard. It was embarrassing when we asked about it, because everyone wants to forget, but we were told that everyone who joined the F.d.F was sworn in to the SS."

"Oh shit, no!" said Henry. "That puts him deep inside the Nazis, doesn't it?"

Walter didn't answer. He didn't know what to say. Instead, he delivered the facts as he knew them.

"Your father flew out of Rastenburg which was the airfield for the Wolf's Lair, and also Vinnytsia. This was the airfield which served Werewolf. Both of these were Hitler's field headquarters. These were where Hitler based his High Command in the fight against Stalin and Russia."

"Would he have flown Hitler?" asked Henry.

"Unlikely, that was Hans Baur's job. He might have flown the rest of them, Goering, Bormann, Himmler ... We just don't know. We do know he was awarded the Order of the Iron Cross 1st Class in February 1943 at the Wolf's Lair. It would have almost certainly been given to him by Hitler. It means he would have been involved in something heroic."

"Heroic," repeated Henry, stunned.

"His records show he flew many times from Rastenburg to Pitomnik airfield. This was the airfield which supplied Paulus's Sixth Army when they were surrounded at Stalingrad. It's probably why he got the Iron Cross," continued Walter.

"Oh," said Henry finding it hard to process what he was being told.

"You should be proud of him, Henry," said Walter. "He was clearly a brave man."

"Yeh, just fighting for the wrong cause," responded Henry, dismissively, not realising his insult.

"I'm afraid we all were Henry," said Walter, forlornly. It wasn't just one man's mistake but the mistake of a whole nation."

Walter stopped walking and rested his bottom on the edge of an old, very heavy, steel roller, now warm from the sunshine. Henry sat next to him. Unknown to them both, it had been used all those years ago by Henry's father to maintain his landing strip.

"We know your father left Rastenburg in January 1944 to fly to Kropyvnytskyi," said Walter, after a few moments silence.

"Why, where is it?"

"Kropyvnytskyi; it's a city in central Ukraine. He probably went to give orders and take supplies to our retreating army," said Walter.

At the word 'our' Henry was shocked rigid, almost affronted. It was Walter's army not his. Henry's army was the British army, and it always would be. Henry said nothing. He didn't know what to say. Did Walter and Inga see him as German, he wondered?

"From Kropyvnytskyi he was to fly the wounded to Nuremburg, but he never arrived."

"Where, Kropyvnytskyi or Nuremburg?" asked Henry.

"We don't know."

"So I guess he must be dead," said Henry. There was a strange relief at this conclusion, for, if true, his life would be suddenly less complicated.

"We don't know that, Henry," said Walter firmly. "We know that hundreds of thousands of German prisoners of war were released to the GDR[10] in 1953 but we don't know if your father was amongst them. We do know that Baur, Hitler's pilot, was not released to West Germany until October 1955. Do you know it was the same year as the USSR formally declared the end of the war with Germany?"

"But that's 10 years after Germany surrendered. Why was that?" asked Henry.

"I don't know," said Walter after a long pause. "I think it's fair to say that if your father was coming home, he would have made it by now.

[10] German Democratic Republic – East Germany

The only hope is that he was released into East Germany but has been denied an exit visa. Most of them have, you know."

Henry got up and walked aimlessly around the roller.

"There is one more thing," said Walter. "For about eighteen months between ..., Inga and I don't remember exactly, sometime between the middle of 1957 and 1958 we got about a dozen letters here addressed to Frauline Dr Lisa Friedman. They started suddenly and then they stopped just as suddenly. We suspect that they were from her son and came from the GDR.[11] I distinctly remember the last few letters were from Plauen. I went there a lot after the war when I was a messenger for the US Army."

"Then she'll know if Heinrik Klugman is her son, won't she?" said Henry, with an excited urgency in his voice.

"She's dead Henry. I'm sorry. She died before the letter's started arriving. We took the first half a dozen to her lawyer, but we stopped after that as he didn't seem interested. We kept the rest for a long time and then decided to throw them away. There seemed no point in ..." Walter's voice faded. "Her lawyer may still have the ones we gave him, if you want to see if they were written by your father. Do you want me to find out?"

"I don't know," said Henry, his hopes badly deflated. "Do you mind if I write this down," he asked. "It's a lot to absorb and I would like to tell my mother. I think she would like to know."

"Yes of course," said Walter, getting up stiffly. "Let's go inside."

"Would you mind if we do it tomorrow?" asked Henry. With every discussion about his father, he could take it only so far and then no further, but Walter didn't hear. He was ahead of Henry, striding away to get pen and paper.

---

[11] German Democratic Republic – East Germany

Chapter 49

Château de Gressier September 1970

HENRY, SOPHIE, AND Andrew arrived at Château de Gressier just as preparations for the harvest were beginning. They found the place quite different, for Juliette had done to the Cottage, as the east wing of the chateau was known, as she wished her mother-in-law had done for her when she first came to the château in March 1919.

The death of Juliette's mother-in-law in December 1919 had resulted in her husband and her moving from the east wing to the west wing of Chateau de Gressier; from the Cottage, as the east wing was known, into the Cellars from where the estate had always been run. However, over the years, Juliette had spread back from the Cellars into the Cottage; but now she was determined that this should become Henry and Sophie's home. The fact that Henry had an heir, and the family line would continue, meant that Château de Gressier would be secure for another generation. In anticipation, Juliette stripped the Cottage of every one of her personal possessions which she moved into the Cellars, leaving behind only those antique ornaments and paintings which belonged to that part of the house.

The Cottage was given a complete make over. The wiring, heating, and plumbing had been replaced, the kitchen and bathrooms had been completely refurbished, every room had been given a new coat of paint and all the wood was revitalised with several coats of polish. All the soft furnishings had either been cleaned or replaced. Even new towels and bed linen had been purchased, left on the beds to be unwrapped. It was as though the Cottage was a new building in an old shell; the things which kept it the same was that every item of furniture remained exactly where it had been for the last eighty years.

It was not lost on Juliette that, just as in World War II, the Cottage would, once again, be under German occupation. As she thought about Sophie's 100% German lineage, and Henry's German father, she wondered what Étienne would think, but Henry had so many of his French grandfather's characteristics she knew, deep down, she was making the right decision.

Immediately on Henry and Sophie's arrival at Château de Gressier, Juliette made them a present of the Cottage, showing them around as though they had never been there before. Then, she led them up to the Gallery. This was a magnificent room built to connect the first floors of the Cellars and the Cottage. It was set over a richly decorated arch and brought the two buildings together to make a hugely impressive house. The room had large double windows at the front and rear which gave a vista over the whole Estate.

At the top of the stairs, Juliette formally presented Henry with the two keys to this room, one key for entry from the Cottage side and the other from the Cellars side. This was now to be his. Henry unlocked the door and led Sophie and Juliette in.

"Wow," said Sophie.

"I love this room," said Henry. "It's a room which changes every day with the weather but otherwise never changes." It was a true statement as it had not changed from the day of his grandfather's murder. Étienne's desk, table and chairs were still where they had been placed by Henry's grandfather all those years ago, only careful polishing over the last forty years had brought about any change.

"I have preserved this room, not as a shrine to Étienne's memory, but for the next master of Château de Gressier," said Juliette rather grandly. "You, Henry, are now that Master. I will retire at the end of the harvest," she continued. "You, dear Henry, and you, darling Sophie, are to take over Château de Gressier. It will now be your responsibility not mine." It was a noticeably clear statement of intent, not a question or item for debate.

"This will now be your room, your office Henry," said Juliette as she waived her arms around the large room. "We will discuss the arrangements for the hand-over in the morning," and just as she had done all her life, having made her statement, Juliette disappeared into the upstairs of the Cellars wing of the house, firmly closing the door behind her.

Henry and Sophie were completely taken aback by these events. It had not come into their plans whatsoever. Henry looked at Sophie, saying nothing, but his face exuded an expression of apology. Sophie smiled and shook her head in a resigned expression, knowing that she too was defeated.

Henry started the next morning with an early walk around the estate. It was looking in magnificent condition. Some light rain would help, he thought.

"I am retiring," announced Juliette the next morning to a meeting of accountants and lawyers which had gathered in the Gallery. Neither Henry nor Sophie had been given any warning, but they were nevertheless expected to attend. The next generation of Delmas had taken over advising on finance and tax and the next generation of Liards had taken over as the estate's legal advisers. The scene was the same as in February 1919 when Étienne and Juliette had taken over running Château de Gressier; except only Juliette was present at both meetings.

"These are the arrangements I want put in place," declared Juliette, as she set about listing them.

"One," she said. Juliette spoke exactly as Etienne had spoken on the day he took over. "Henry is to be appointed a director of all the companies in my place. I will resign. Monsieur Delmas you are to consult with Monsieur Liard and whatever you agree is appropriate will be Henry's remuneration." Clearly, we don't get a say in this, thought Henry and Sophie at the same time.

"Two, I'm to be paid a pension for the rest of my life; again, Monsieur Delmas and Monsieur Liard are to agree the amount.

Three, in addition to his salary, Monsieur Pierre Hilaire is to be paid fifteen percent of the profits for the Estate for the rest of his life starting from 1st January."

Liard interrupted. "Is he married?" he asked.

"Ah," said Juliette, instantly changing her mind, "for his life or, if succeeded by his wife, for her life for a maximum of five, no, ten years," she said. "This will give them enough to have a good pension."

"Fourthly, I want Pierre Hilaire to have blocking powers over all matters concerning the running of the estate."

"Negative control?" inquired Mr Liard, using trade jargon.

"Yes, I want him to be able to stop Henry doing things. Pierre can't do them, but he has to be able to stop Henry from doing the wrong thing."

"Excuse me, Mamie," said Henry, most politely, "but no." He stressed the word, making it clear he was emphatic upon the point. Juliette was perturbed, for she was rarely stopped in her tracks like this.

"Was there negative control imposed upon you and Grandpa when you took over?" asked Henry.

Juliette didn't answer. To do so would mean conceding defeat.

"I think your grandmother is concerned to stop the possibility of the profits being manipulated to reduce, even stop, the payments to Monsieur Hilaire."

"Monsieur Liard, we do not know each other, but if that is my grandmother's concern then it is one which goes straight to my character and, if that is the case, then surely, I'm not the right person to take over."

"You know of our debt to Pierre and his family?" asked Juliette.

"Both Sophie and I know and understand our moral obligations, Mamie; yours, my mother's, my grandfather's. We are well appraised. They will be honoured. Sophie and I will do our best to make sure it is so."

"I think we can do without the blocking power," said Juliette, after a pause, "but, Monsieur Liard, I want you to write to Henry formally, informing him that he has a direct duty of care towards Pierre Hilaire, and a copy of that letter is to go to Pierre and to both Mesdames Hilaire, his mother and wife."

The meeting closed, as did every meeting, with Juliette getting up and silently walking away when she felt she had made her instructions clear. She had learnt long ago from her father that, if one was not there, any debate would stop. Questions could always be answered later.

Chapter 50

Château de Gressier September 1970

IT WAS MID-AFTERNOON when Henry saw Juliette from the Gallery window. She was walking around the gravel path that surrounded her walled garden. She had worked hard over many years to bring a bit of Englishness to this small corner of France, flooding the place with water to counteract the scorching sun, seeding, feeding, rolling, and mowing the lawn until it was nearly of bowling pitch quality.

Although still slender and upright, Henry noticed that Juliette was walking with a decided stiffness as if her hip joints rasped together. Henry decided to join her. He wanted to be clear as to her relationship with Pierre. He was anxious to make it clear that, if he made a decision that Pierre didn't like then, Juliette was not to interfere.

Immediately he raised the subject, Juliette insisted that, if this was to be a matter for discussion then, it had to include Sophie. Fifteen minutes later, with a large jug of fresh lemon juice on ice poured into glasses, the three of them sat down on canvas tennis chairs surrounding a wooden table.

"Sophie, has Henry explained our obligation to Pierre Hilaire?" asked Juliette firmly.

"Yes, I think so, but I'm not sure I fully understand," said Sophie softly. Why is Pierre so important?" She asked. Sophie was sure she knew but she wanted to hear it from Juliette's lips. "He is not family, is he? His half-brother was not family, was he? Yet it seems there is a bond, a debt, to Pierre's family which arises from a series of extraordinarily complex and interwoven relationships which you would like Henry - us - to honour, but other than in monetary terms we don't know its true nature."

Juliette looked at Sophie carefully appreciating what a smart woman she was. "Yes, there is a debt, a bond as you call it. The relationships are interwoven, but it is not complex. Pierre is family. Not in the biblical sense, but family all the same. Before Stephen, Pierre's half-brother, and I did something stupidly dangerous, I asked him what he thought of me. Do you know what he replied?"

Henry and Sophie stayed silent as they could tell Juliette was not looking for an answer.

"He said I was 'his family.'" Juliette lifted her head and tilted it backwards, looking to the sky as she took a loud breath through her nose. "I asked him the meaning of family. He said it was 'love, trust, loyalty, friendship, support.' Those were his exact words. Unconditional love, trust, ... loyalty, ... friendship, ... support," she said, her words faltering in the emotion from the telling, for she had not spoken his name for years.

We owe Pierre and his family a lot. de Gressier is what it is today because of his efforts and we, you, are never to forget that."

"We won't," said Henry, and the same words were repeated almost immediately by Sophie.

"Your wedding, and marrying with the name Guégan, has created a problem. It has brought out the village gossips. It is now widely rumoured that Henry is Stephen's son. They are saying that Pierre Hilaire is Henry's half-uncle."

Henry snorted, and both Sophie and he shook their heads.

"When they came to our wedding, when Dominique and Stephen were there, was it not clear that Sophie Lemberger was marrying Henry Guégan? Did that not dispel the Bellanger myth?" asked Sophie conscious that their village blessing was at Juliette's insistence.

"I am the only one on the Estate and in the village, who knows Henry's father is a German pilot," announced Juliette in her matriarchal tone, "and it is to stay that way. I don't care about the rumours. They can say what they like. No one else is to know the truth. Do you understand me."

"So we deny that Henry is Stephen's son?" asked Sophie.

"You don't confirm or deny anything. It is none of their business. Just ours," commanded Juliette. "But under no circumstances is it to be know that Henry is half-German. The fact that you are German Sophie, is fine. That creates no problems for us. But Henry, that's different. For nearly thirty years we've lived a lie. It is a lie that cannot be ended, not now, not in my life time and probably not Henry's."

Sophie nodded. Henry showed no reaction.

"The big house ... on the way into the village. The one that's deserted," said Sophie. "Henry told me about it. He said the family there are outcasts for having been German collaborators. Is that your fear for us? If we went public on Henry's father, we'd be outcasts too?" she asked.

"In part, may be a large part," confirmed Juliette.

You had the Luftwaffe here, you served them, you fed them ..." Sophie paused for just a fraction. Why are they outcasts and not you?"

"Like everyone who has lived under an occupation, we lived as best we could," answered Juliette quickly. "But the difference ... we never yielded, Sophie. That's the difference, we never yielded. We never gave in!"

"Henry's mother yielded, didn't she?" replied Sophie, rather tartly.

"Yes, perhaps, ... because she fell in love. It's easy to do at that age, and because of that she paid the price, ... banished to England."

"Banished?" interjected Henry.

"She returned home ...," retorted Juliette snappily.

"Returned home ...?" interjected Henry again.

"When Victoria returned home, she did so with as much intelligence as she could possibly have gathered. After she'd seen Stephen arrested and heard he'd been killed then she knew her duty. Be assured, young lady," said Juliette looking directly into Sophie's eyes. "Everyone in this household, on this estate did their duty."

Sophie was too strong a woman to allow Juliette's matriarchal put down to defeat her. "What has Pierre Hilaire got to do with Henry?" she asked. There was a steeliness in her voice as she set out to understand what she had married into.

"Pierre's mother, Dominique, married Henri Hilaire. She had a son by a previous marriage called Stephen Bellanger. Stephen and Pierre are...were half-brothers," said Juliette speaking with slow clarity.

"Yes, I know. Henry's Christian name is derived from his father's, and his mother took Stephen's surname as her own, pretending they were married," said Sophie. "Henry has told me all of this. But why is it still so secret? I don't understand, the war ended over twenty-five years ago. Isn't it time the lie ended."

"You want to know why?" said Juliette, frustration getting into her voice.

Sophie said nothing.

"Many, many times the Germans in Bordeaux lined up ten, twenty, fifty men and shot them in reprisals for the killing of one of their officers. Some were as young as sixteen. Stephen Bellanger, he was a bit older ..." Juliette paused to gain her composure. "Stephen worked here on the estate. Stephen ... my Stephen was one of those shot." The memories of those times came flooding back and tears filled her eyes.

Henry had heard what had happened from his mother, but he was embarrassed for not having talked about it with his Grandmother before.

"You've been to Oradour?" asked Juliette, looking directly at Henry.

"No, why?" he asked.

"Oradour-sur-Glane, you've heard of it?"

Henry shook his head.

"You must have!" said Juliette crossly. "It's where the German's massacred the whole village; over 640 men, women and children.

Henry shook his head again, as he looked past Juliette to Sophie, to see if she was any the wiser.

"Oh, Henry ... Sophie, you will never understand France until you understand the occupation. It's where the SS shot all the men in their legs, and then set the barn they were in on fire. They were burned alive. Then, with an incendiary bomb they blasted a hole in another barn with all the women and children in it. As they ran out of the barn to escape the flames, the German's machined gunned them to death. They killed over 200 children for no reason, no reason whatsoever."

Juliette had stopped looking at Henry and was now deliberately telling the story to Sophie, who was listening uncomfortably.

"Now we're told it was done by the Gestapo or the Nazis, but it wasn't! It was done by the Germans to us, and this PR disinfectant that the Nazis were then, and today's Germans are now a different people, is used to hide the stink of truth. You Germans were one and the same then, and you are one and the same now."

Henry and Sophie sat silently, for they did not know what to say. Both were equally as uncomfortable at the racial prejudices expressed by Juliette as they were with the guilt they felt for their ancestry.

"Look at Klaus Barbie," said Juliette, switching her look between Henry and Sophie in turn. It was clear from their expression they had no idea who she was talking about. "The Butcher of Lyon?" she continued.

Henry and Sophie said nothing. They were none the wiser.

"He was an ordinary SS officer; nothing special, yet he personally tortured hundreds of French prisoners in the most beastly way possible. It would make you ill if you heard what he did[12]. Despite the fact that he's been sentenced to death, it's an open secret that he's living in Bolivia in the pay of the West German government! Can you believe that, our alleged allies in the EEC[13] prefer one of their proven criminals over us! The war needed to bring about a culture change in Germany, but that hasn't happened, Barbie's the proof! It's always been a country which has put its people ahead of humanity. It's a leopard which can't change it spots and, in some little way, we are reminded about it every day.

Sophie shook her head. "Mamie," she said, using Henry's form of address for his grandmother for the very first time. She spoke very gently: "terrible, terrible things were done in Germany too. My mother ..."

---

[12] The Centre for the History of the Resistance and Deportation in Lyon, France has a cinema which shows throughout the day a film about the trail of Klaus Barbie with numerous witnesses telling of what he did.

[13] European Economic Community later to become the European Union.

"Please, Sophie, please don't raise the issue of the concentration camps," said Juliette, cutting Sophie short as she misinterpreted what she was going to say. "Hundreds of Jews were taken from around here, never to return. Their going has left a hole in this community which cannot be repaired. I can still remember the names, ... many, many names."

"I wasn't thinking of that," said Sophie defensively. "My mother and father suffered terribly too," she said, now determined to make her point. "They were both from big families. They and their mothers were the only ones who survived." Sophie thought about mentioning her mother's story, but remembered the promise she gave, and so said nothing.

"There is one difference, Sophie," said Juliette. "How do you think Pierre would feel if he knew this house, this vineyard was going to the son of a man who was here and whose compatriots killed his brother?" She paused. "No! For unity, for harmony, the previous myths must stay as they are. Henry is not, while I'm alive, ever to be known as the son of a German pilot! Likewise, he is not to be thought of as the son of Stephen Bellanger. When I am dead, then it is for your children to decide what is to be said."

"What are these myths we're being told of?" asked Sophie forcefully.

"That's the point Sophie. Like the Royal Family, we never ever comment on rumours and myths. There are some things only the grandchildren can decide, and this is one of them," said Juliette firmly. "There are facts and myths. The facts will stay our secret until your son is old enough to understand and decide what he wants to say about his grandfather, but for us, this subject matter is closed."

Juliette got up slowly. "I have something to show you," she said pointedly to Sophie. "We need to go inside."

Sophie and Henry looked at each other. They said nothing. There was no need to. They both knew the war years belonged to the generations before them. Theirs were the peace years and best served by forgetting. They held hands as they followed Mamie through to the Cellars and her library.

"These are the diaries of Château de Gressier," said Juliette pointing to a series of leather-bound books, about fifteen or sixteen in number, followed by some file clips holding together many loose pages. "They have been kept by the wives of the owners of this estate since 1860. They are written perhaps, not every day but certainly, two or three times a week. They tell the story of here; everything is in it. It includes some very painful truths. One day, when I am gone, this will be yours to take over, for you to write."

Sophie stroked the leather spines of the diaries very gently.

"I would like to give you some advice. The same my mother-in-law gave me before handing over the diaries for my writing," said Juliette. "Write only your understanding of the truth, your perception of the truth. Be honest and don't lie. Never omit things which you know should be included, for if it is not the truth, every time you re-read it there will be a feeling of emptiness in your soul which will never go away."

Sophie stared piercingly into Juliette's eyes trying to read the woman who seemed to be full of contradiction.

"If it is accurate and honest then, when you read it back, aren't you reminded of the pain and hurt?" asked Sophie. "Should one bring back hurtful memories only for them to hurt you again?" she queried.

Juliette didn't answer. Instead, she asked: "Do you write a diary?" as she handed Sophie one of the oldest books to examine. They were written in the neatest of copperplate hand on plain white paper. Each row was immaculately in line, equidistant one from the other.

"Yes," said Sophie, "I have already adopted your mother-in-law's rules."

"Truth is a perception at a point of time," continued Juliette. "At one time, the truth was that the Sun went around the Earth; now we know it's the other way around. Therefore, never go back in your diary to change something that you've written before. You record the change on the day in which your perception of the truth changes."

Sophie looked up at Juliette and nodded. She knew these were wise words. She looked down at the pages. There was the occasional smudge or crossing out, but it was obvious to see that each sentence had been carefully thought about before it was written.

"There was only one time when I didn't write the truth," Juliette confessed. "It was in the war, when Stephen and I were working as Passers."

"Passers?" enquired Sophie.

"Part of the resistance; we helped get British pilots home again after they had been shot down."

Sophie nodded.

"My truth was to remain silent. It was too dangerous to write anything then. I only put the events into the diary when the war was well and truly over."

After a few moments, Mamie reached for the book to put it back. They had been lent just long enough to make the point Juliette wanted to make.

That evening, with baby Andrew settled in his cot, Henry went to enjoy his Gallery. He tried to understand their earlier conversation with Juliette about his surname. His decision to marry with the Guégan name had apparently re-opened the rumours that Henry was Stephen's son, but hadn't his grandmother always told him that he was known as a Guégan in the village and on the estate, so what had changed to make that happen?

It appeared he could have any name, any father, provided it was not Bellanger or Klugman, and he was not a German pilot's son. She was doubling down on her myth, making sure that nothing else was said which might disprove her version of 'the truth'.

While Henry was in his Gallery, Sophie settled down at the writing desk in the library of the Cottage. She took some sheets of white paper from the drawer, which she tapped into a neat block, and, picking up a cheap biro, she started to write.

Dear Diary, she wrote. Then she added the date. Let me introduce myself. I am Mrs Sophie Guégan, née Lemberger, with a professional modelling name of Elleswell, and if that is confusing then it will be even more so when I tell you that, married to the same person, I was very nearly Mrs Bellanger or Mrs Klugman. I am married to Henry, who today, has been appointed a director of Château de Gressier to succeed his grandmother. We have one son, Andrew Guégan, who has won the nickname of Toddy.

Sophie paused, who am I and how did I come to be here, she asked herself. She thought about how to tell her story, for so much had happened in such a short period of time.

Chapter 51

Château de Gressier 1972

HENRY AND SOPHIE quickly settled into a family routine. The expansion of Henry's business meant that he had to travel to Argentina, California, Chile, New Zealand, Australia, and South Africa to select a bigger range of wines suitable to the UK palate, but from a much wider range of vineyards. He now bought wines for the three largest supermarkets and with the Matterers Lunches bringing more and more wine investors in as customers he was finding it hard to cope. He'd also introduced into his contract with his supplier vineyards minimum production standards which they were happy to comply with, as he was paying more per litre than anyone else and paying one third up front. It also meant that the number of people he employed increased, as he appointed one person as the account manager for each supermarket. He had further staff to deal with other customers, and the massive amount of paperwork it all produced.

Henry was constantly investing in new more powerful analytical equipment, always delighting in the detail of the analysis of any wine, particularly the different vintages from the same vineyard. He had always thought that his school friends, who spotted trains or collected stamps, had a strange kind of addiction, without recognising his own affliction. However, with so much going on there was a large backlog of wine samples which weren't being tested and this had to happen as payment under contract was dependant on the results.

Henry's biggest disappointment came when he hired his first chemist straight from University, quickly followed by a second, to do the wine testing which he so enjoyed; for it was under the chemistry lens that he instinctively knew what was going on in the wine industry around the world.

However, there was one bright light on the horizon as the UK would be entering the European Economic Community on 1st January 1973. This would mean that the border between the UK and Europe would end, and with it would come a huge reduction in the amount of administration and red tape.

"Of course, you don't have any money," said Martin Sheds, their accountant and tax advisor to Henry and Sophie as they examined the accounts of the previous year. He had just broken the news of how much tax they had to pay in both France and England. "You've got yourself into paying for wine up front and you don't collect the money you are owed. There is a small fortune outstanding from your customers. You need to hire a finance director," they were told, "someone who will focus on collecting the money from your customers."

After months of interviewing, Henry and Sophie found Vincent Ainsworth. He was not only a man they liked but he had just the right amount of obsessive-compulsive disorder to bring financial order to their lives. With him on-board the cash flow of the business was transformed, and the profits improved. Ainsworth had an efficiency of working about him which Henry could only admire. It made him far more than an accountant. He was a genuine business manager too, with an ability to make the complex seem easy. He moved amongst people with an easy charm, as he was very relaxed with himself, until it came to the matter of film; a subject on which he was such an obsessive that, once started, a conversation would almost never end. If he was not working, Ainsworth was at the cinema, sometimes seeing the same film many times over. He wasn't married and although the UK had legalised homosexuality three years before, it would be a very long time before he would be ready to share with anyone his fifteen-year relationship with his boyfriend.

It was Ainsworth who quickly and easily bullied Henry into changing his terms of trade with both his suppliers and customers. It was a simple conversation," You either change your terms of trade or you will go bankrupt," said Ainsworth to both Henry and Sophie "and I won't be here to see that," he added for good measure.

It was therefore with a certain amount of financial contentment that, in July 1972, Henry and Sophie packed up Found House and moved into Château de Gressier, planning to stay there until the harvest was over. A few very big buyers were invited to stay with them for a couple of days, but the invitation came with a strict rule; no wine business would ever be spoken.

The first few days of every visit was spent with Pierre discussing the running of estate, and the precise plans for the harvest, as had always been done by Juliette long before Henry took over. Henry wisely deferred to Pierre in every respect, trusting him implicitly.

On the very first evening Henry and Sophie went out for a walk. They took the same route that Étienne and Juliette had taken all those years before. They walked down the hill by the edge of the rows of vines towards the river. They walked past the tobacco crop, which was almost too small to make it worthwhile, but still got planted each year. Past a small crop of maize for the animals which were still on the farm. It was hard to give up the self-sufficiency culture which survival had demanded 25 years before. They walked across the mowed lawn, which Juliette never came to but insisted was immaculately maintained in memory of Victor, and then they sat on the benches under the trees; Henry on the one engraved Victor, Sophie on the one marked Victoria.

Sophie was wearing a loose-flowing, bright, floral halter-neck dress with a thin white cardigan to keep off the chill. For the first time in her life she was wearing no underwear. The day had been particularly hot and humid and after an early evening shower she had simply slipped the dress on over her head, missing out on dressing properly, intending to do so later, but as the evening went on, she enjoyed the coolness and freedom it gave her.

Henry and Sophie moved to the water's edge. They sat side-by-side on the grass as they listened to the crickets, scratching their legs in the distance, making endless clicking sounds as they tried to attract a mate. They lay on their backs, waggling their legs in the air, laughing as they pretended to be crickets attempting to attract one to the other.

While lying there, Henry ran his hand over Sophie's smooth legs. As he unconsciously noticed how cold they were. His hand travelled to the warmth of her naked bottom, which she wriggled delightfully under his touch. They kissed gently and, with the sun travelling into another new morning, they made love as though they were newfound lovers, never wanting to let the other go.

The next night, and many nights after that, they made it their routine. They would walk to the same spot in anticipation of their lovemaking, which was always adventurous and pleasing, and afterwards they would lie on their backs, stare at the stars, and marvel at their place in the universe. Two people could not have been happier or more contented.

On their last night at the estate, before heading back to London, they sat on the riverbank and watched the river flow. There was a change of mood in both of them. It was not just that an idyllic summer was coming to an end, or the pressures which would be facing them both in the next few months. It was a shared thought which sobered them.

"I guess I must be pregnant," said Sophie.

"I've been guessing that too," said Henry. They paused.

"I might ..." said Sophie forcefully.

"We'll deal with it," said Henry, cutting her off quickly, knowing exactly what she was going to say. "We did last time."

Sophie paused. "You don't think I should have an abortion?" she asked.

"Good God, no," protested Henry.

"It's just that when I'm ill, you have to look after me," she said.

"Just as when I'm ill you look after me," said Henry, trying to close down the debate.

"But this is different, and, in any case, you're never ill."

"Sophie," said Henry, looking directly into her eyes which were welling up with tears. "It's not an option," he said firmly, then added, "God decided that every child should have two parents. It's so that if something happens to one, the other would be there."

"Henry ..." Sophie paused. She always started a statement with his name, particularly when she wanted something badly. "Please bring me straight home after the baby is born. Please don't leave me in hospital. I just couldn't bear being in that place. I know I will get better quicker if I am at home."

"Of course," said Henry.

"Promise?"

"Yes."

"What if I don't get well again?" mithered Sophie.

"You will," said Henry. "It was only for a little time last time. It might not happen again," he added encouragingly.

They both lay on the ground for a long while. Henry reached across and kissed her on her forehead and then her shoulders. As he did so she felt the strength in his body and instinctively she felt better. She knew that his strength would protect her.

Henry lay back and looked into the sky, thinking about the baby they were about to have. Small clouds were racing across it, changing the night into different layers of darkness as they hid a bright moon. If he had been a soothsayer, he would have told fortunes on the signs that the sky gave that night; light moving into darkness.

Chapter 52

London April 1973

PETER GUÉGAN WAS born in London. Just as before, Sophie had a very normal pregnancy and birth, and for a couple of days Henry and Sophie celebrated in the joy of their second son. Four days later, Sophie fell into a deep depression and with it her family descended on Found House en-mass. Henry kept his promise and brought Sophie and their son home from hospital as soon as possible. Victoria looked after Andrew and Peter, and Inga focused on Sophie in a routine which saw Henry reduced to the rank of errand boy.

As before, Inga was insistent that Sophie did not take any anti-depressant pills. Instead, she put her on a strict routine of exercise, including jogging up to Hampstead Heath and a cold outdoor swim in the lake, both morning and evening. Inga's demand was simple; if she could do it at her age then Sophie could do it at hers. The paparazzi had a field day with pictures of Sophie sold to every paper. Each commented on how good she looked and how hard she was working to get her figure back after the birth of her second baby. It was the very least of Sophie's cares.

Meanwhile, Henry was thrilled. He had a solution to a problem he had been facing. He was consistently told that it was important to warehouse his wine either as close to the vineyard or the end customer as possible, for reputedly vibrations from transportation were thought to have an adverse effect on some wines. Provided a wine could stand for a few days after being transported, Henry's scientific tests could not detect any difference, so he was very jaundiced as to the point. However, he was not going to risk damaging his reputation with clients, and so it was one of those few myths which he allowed on himself; after all, the correct storage place would mean that more could be charged and therefore he could make more money. The thing he insisted on was that his supermarket customers avoided storing his wines in their large sheds, for in this environment the wines baked in the summer and froze in the winter, which affected its quality. If his wines were to get to the supermarket in the best state possible there had to be a coordinated just-in-time delivery system between his warehouses and their distribution centres, so that his wine spent the shortest time in their oven and fridge warehouses.

Storage, originally a spin off from his business, grew larger and larger by accident, as all over France and the UK, Henry found every bit of underground storage he could, often purchasing wines from the vineyard on the understanding that the seller had to store the wine for free. Sophie and Henry amused themselves at the thought of them charging for storage which somebody else provided for nothing.

Henry's permanent solution was a large, abandoned inland chalk pit equidistant from Folkestone and Dover harbours. It was wide and long enough for 1 million square feet of storage on a single floor with the ability to have four floors of storage each 20-foot high. His plan was to build a huge concrete block which would then be buried deep underground. This would allow nature to keep an ambient temperature inside.

Sophie and Henry discussed the plans for the Vaults, as they called it, in detail. Her interest in the project was the first sign that she was getting better. The concept was easy, but the engineering was complex. They had to plan for the forces of nature to be extreme and, as anyone who has a simple basement knows, keeping them dry is a challenge in itself. After hours of discussion with architects, planners and engineers, Sophie and Henry agreed that they would build the Vaults as three separate projects. Each project would be a building of three stories high comprising 900,000 square feet. They would backfill on two sides and only partially cover the roof of each building. It was not what Henry wanted, but Sophie and Ainsworth convinced him that, although in the long run it would be far more expensive, it would be the least risky option.

For the second and last time Henry went to see the Trustees of his trust. They agreed to liquidate every last penny to enable him to buy the chalk pit land and start the building. There would be nothing left. He would need a bank loan to complete the project but with more than one bank director attending a Matterers' Lunch, and with Ainsworth confident in the economics, the money was easily raised. It was in the resultant banking paperwork that the complexities arose. It seemed to Henry that the bank insisted on taking a charge on almost everything he owned and even things he didn't!

Chapter 53

South Africa 1973

SUNETTA LEFT BIRKBECK College in June 1971 with a very shaky lower second-class degree to the immense disappointment of her tutors, all of whom saw her as a wasted talent. This was not the view of Robin Howard of the London Contemporary Dance School, who took Sunetta into his company for his autumn season. However, it was a yearning for South Africa and home which led Sunetta to refuse a role in his Company's spring tour. Instead, she headed back to New Found Estate for Christmas. Above all, she wanted to be there for her father's eightieth birthday.

Once back in New Found Estate there was more than enough to keep Sunetta occupied as the jobs never seemed to end. It was at Christmas in 1972 that Sunetta spoke to her mother and father about applying for a South African passport. She thought it odd that she was a citizen of France when she had visited the country only once. She told her parents that South Africa, for all its ills, was her home and she wanted to be recognised as belonging to that country.

As far as David was concerned, the solution to all citizen and immigration matters lay at the feet of Mr Peter Harrison of Fourie, Chetty and Steyn, and so it was that Sunetta came to be sitting in the offices of Mr John Harrison, Peter's son.

Father and son could not have been more different. Both were slim, trim and very smart to look at but John was not only more flamboyant than his father but took pride in being physically fit and keeping permanently active. He was as articulate as his father but, whilst legally competent, he lacked his father's intellectual rigour. His colleagues saw him as far more of a front man, which is where he excelled. Playing for safety, they put around him the technical support required for, as they argued, anyone can be a lawyer, but it takes a special kind of man to win new clients.

John Harrison was everything that Sunetta sought in a man. He was tall, lean, clean shaven, muscular and had such an overwhelming confidence in himself, and his attraction to women, that it was past being called arrogant. Over a long alcoholic lunch Sunetta was completely captivated as he hardly spoke. Instead, he encouraged her to share her views on everything from the politics of South Africa, the reasons for the success of the Springboks to her time as a student at boarding school and in London. If Sunetta had her way he could have taken her there and then on the dining room table for not once since her first love affair with Hank had she felt such lust for a man.

There was no need for them to meet again but Sunetta insisted that they meet the following week. Their meeting was perfunctory, just a few minutes. In his room Sunetta saw pictures of John's wife and their three children but these were quickly dismissed from her mind as they headed out to lunch.

They dined at a table which overlooked the city and out towards the sea. They chatted as animatedly as they had done before until John left the table for 10 minutes. She assumed he had gone to the bathroom or to make a phone call. Instead, on his return, he placed a bedroom key on the tabletop. It sat there, like a phallus, causing not a word to be said about it. Sunetta knew exactly what it meant and, so graciously and in silence, she gathered her things and slipped the key into her bag.

That afternoon she fell in love with a married man; a man who was both interesting and interested in her, a man who was the most energetic and considerate of lovers.

They met many times after that; once, sometimes twice a week. The hotels changed but the arrangements never did and with each moment they spent together Sunetta wanted him more; to marry her, have his babies and become an all-consuming part of his life. This was her dream up to and including the day she discovered she was pregnant.

Sunetta waited until after they had made love, and were enjoying a post-coital glow, before she told him. On hearing the news of his pending fatherhood, John kissed her gently and held her tightly in his arms; everything about the moment said, 'don't worry, I'll keep you safe'.

"What do we do?" Sunetta asked after an eternity.

"What would you like to do?" John replied.

"I want you to marry me," said Sunetta. "I know you'll have to…"

"Impossible," said John interrupting her. This one word was said with a firmness that would brook no debate. "I can't even admit the baby is mine," he said. "I would lose my job, my income and my family. God damn it, we're in bloody South Africa," he added desperately.

"Will you provide for us, your child and me?" she enquired, in the politest of tones.

"I assumed you were on the pill," he said, "otherwise…" He didn't need to end the sentence as the rest was obvious.

Sunetta got the sense he was avoiding the question. "Will you provide for us?" she asked, this time far more firmly.

"How can I do that when what we've done is illegal," he answered.

Sunetta rapidly got off the bed and moved away from him fast. "Do not give me that lawyer crap," she responded angrily. "We aren't discussing some fine point of law," she added sarcastically, "we're talking about your child. Will you provide for him … her?"

Sunetta knew what he was going to say next, even before he said it. Her mouth went dry in anticipation.

"I think it's best for you to go to London for an abortion," he said matter-of-factly. "I will pay for it. In fact, I will come with you."

Sunetta exploded angrily. "You're a fucking shit. You're a lump of fucking shit," she yelled, retreating naked into the bathroom. Although her eyes were welling up, she was far too angry to cry. She slammed the bathroom door closed, leaned against the back of the door and sunk to the floor. There she hugged her knees tight into her chest in an attempt to control her breathing which was now in a panic.

Very slowly Sunetta calmed down. Sluggishly she unwound herself and spread her legs wide across the floor. She felt her tummy, thinking how strange it was that something was growing inside her which she couldn't yet feel. It was then Sunetta realised that her worry was not about having a baby, or being a single mother, or even being responsible for another person, but it was telling her mother which frightened her. She knew that Satutu would feel let down, and this was the last thing she wanted to happen. Then she remembered the dignity of her mother; that beacon of calm and grace in the worst of calamities, and at that moment, Sunetta knew what she had to do.

Sunetta returned to the bedroom this time with a towel wrapped around her body and collected her clothes and handbag from the chair. In the bathroom she showered, got dressed, applied her make-up and prepared to leave. John had put on his trousers and shirt and little else as he waited anxiously for her to materialise. Sunetta appeared from the bathroom and marched to the bedroom door which she opened forcefully. John stood close by trying to find some words to say but there was just a fiery silence between them. In the doorway, she turned around and looked him straight in the eye. Then, totally unexpected to both of them, she slapped him as hard as she could across his face, knocking it ferociously to one side. John did not raise a finger to defend himself.

"Goodbye," she said, "we," she continued, emphasising the word we, "will never see each other again!"

Chapter 54

London October 1973

"I THINK WE have been buying and selling counterfeit wine," said Henry to Sophie as they packed up after one of their Matterers Lunches.

"What?" said Sophie, not sure what she was being told.

"Counterfeit wine, cheap wine, packaged and sold under a more expensive label."

"How do you know?"

"Because we have two wines under the same label and the chemistry is not the same, not even close, but the year's the same. The problem is we've sold over three hundred and fifty thousand pounds of this wine, which we will have to buy back if I am right."

"We don't have that kind of money."

"I know - sometimes I think I should ignore it, but it's a time bomb waiting to hit us."

"Where's the wine from?"

"Château Rabôut."

"No, that's not possible."

"I know - I don't understand it."

"You can hardly accuse them of producing counterfeit wine, can you?"

"I know."

"What does your Grandmother say?"

"I haven't told her. I need more evidence before she'll believe me. We've always bought Rabôut wine directly from their Estate. However, in the last couple of years we've very quickly sold our allocation from them, so we bought the extra we needed from their Paris shop."

Sophie said nothing as she waited for Henry to finish his explanation.

"The wine we have direct from the Estate, I'm convinced is theirs. It's the wine we get from their Paris shop that's counterfeit."

"Can you prove it?"

"I think so. You put the two wines in a glass next to each other and you can see the difference straightaway."

"Surely the shop has to give you your money back?" said Sophie.

"I think so. I hope so."

"So we won't be out of pocket?"

"I hope not."

Over lunch Henry casually asked the editor of one of the UK's leading tabloid newspapers whether he had ever hired a private detective.

"Good God, yes," he replied. "Our business is entirely dependent upon them, especially when we are being sued for defamation."

"It's just I need to check out one of our competitors," said Henry. "We can make the usual checks but I'd like to know far more about the people behind the business."

"I'll introduce you to a couple of good agencies. If they come from us they won't fleece you. The rest of them are a bunch of spivs."

"Why's that?" asked Henry naively.

"Typically they find out about ninety percent of what's relevant in the first week. They then give you ten to fifteen percent of what they've got, promising you'll get more if you pay more. You might have agreed a £1,000 fee upfront but the way they keep providing what they've got ends up costing you five or ten times what you agreed."

"Are they all like that?"

"Not those acting for the blue chips. Their reputation won't allow it. But the rest you can't rely on," said the editor. "There's many a wise man whose been suckered out of a small fortune by this set of charlatans," he went on. "If you think our journalists are animals just wait until you meet those that really do go through your dustbins!"

After months of hard detective work into the affairs of Château Rabôut, and in particular their shop in Paris, Henry had a file fit for prosecution. Rarely had such a comprehensive report into organised criminal behaviour been better prepared outside of a police force.

Henry wondered long and hard what to do. He contemplated going straight to the police but the damage to the French wine industry would be huge as confidence fell out of the market and he would be no better off than anyone else for his pains. He decided he was only interested in one thing: protecting his name, his reputation and his investors' money. It was up to others to protect themselves.

It was an easy thing for Henry to invite Maurice Rabôut to join him for lunch. The pretext was his wine orders for the years ahead. It was a balmy Thursday lunch time when Henry and Maurice sat outside on the pavement of the restaurant on the Rue de Bearn in the heart of Paris. After a few pleasantries Henry produced two bottles of wine the labels both hidden by plastic covering.

"I want to show you something," said Henry as he proceeded to remove the foil cap and withdraw the corks of both bottles. He half-filled two glasses of wine. "It's a blind testing," he continued.

"Is this one of your new world wines you're trying to sell?" asked Maurice.

"Something like that," said Henry as he started to pour the wine from the second bottle.

It was obvious from just looking that one was lighter in colour with less body than the other, although both of them had a clarity which was supported by their smooth taste.

"What do you think?" asked Henry, not touching his glass.

The maître d' came rushing over demanding that they only drink wine bought in the premises. Henry was upset by the distraction and quickly assured the maître d' that he would pay any corkage charge that he liked to levy.

"What do you think?" Henry asked again.

"This one will retail for between FFr25 to FFr35," said Maurice pointing to the genuine wine. "Whereas," he continued, pointing to the lighter counterfeit, "this is an ordinary table wine and will retail for between FFr 8 and FFr 10. Where are they from?"

"I don't know," said Henry. "Let's have a look," and with that he removed the plastic covering the label. "This one," he said, pointing to the genuine wine, came directly from Château Rabôut's vineyard. "This one," said Henry, removing the covering from the label of the counterfeit wine, "came from your shop in Paris."

"Ridiculous," said Maurice, taking immediate offence. "It's not possible!"

"You will see that the labels are identical, but the wines are not." Henry turned the bottles so the labels faced Maurice. He pretended to study them but in practice he was trying to think of something to say.

"Before you say anything more you might like to read this," said Henry, as he handed over a dossier. "It's for you to keep. It sets out precisely what's been happening, and when and where but most importantly it documents your involvement."

Maurice picked up the report and flicked through its pages.

"I have in stock £296,400 of wine which I bought from you and Château Rabôut Estate. I need you to buy it all back, not just the counterfeit wine, but all of it, because you've made the rest of the stock worthless."

Maurice looked at Henry as though he was quite insane. "There's a saying which applies in these circumstances. It is caveat emptor," he said.

"Maurice that is nonsense and you know it," said Henry. "It's all I ask. I want you to buy back all the wine you've sold me, every bottle. No more no less!"

"And then what?" asked Maurice.

"I don't know," said Henry confused. "I just want to protect my reputation, the reputation of my customers and, of course, their money."

"And if I don't, then what?"

"Then a dossier just like that one, along with a bottle of your counterfeit wine, will go to the police."

"I'll discuss this with my family," said Maurice, as he shot from the table like an animal sprung from a trap."

"One week," said Henry who wasn't sure that Maurice had heard him, so he shouted after him. "I expect to hear from you within one week!"

Chapter 55

London October 1973

SUNETTA TRAVELLED TO London on her newly acquired South African passport and a visitor's visa. She lied to her parents telling them that she had been invited to dance with London Contemporary Dance School for a season. With her savings from having worked on New Found Estate for the last eighteen months, together with a large cheque from John Harrison in her bank account, Sunetta rented a flat with the intention of having her baby there. But she soon realised that she couldn't work and look after a baby and herself at the same time. It was an impossible task. She thought long and hard about adoption but knew that the pain of parting with her baby would be more than she could bear.

One cold, late, autumn day, very scared and with terrible foreboding, Sunetta climbed the steps of the clinic for an abortion. It was a day she would remember for the rest of her life. It would never go away. Sometimes she thought about it on a Wednesday because that was the day of the week; sometimes she thought about it on the 14th day of the month because that was the date in the month; sometimes she thought about it when she saw another child of the right age; but she always, without fail, thought about it on the anniversary. She had asked whether it was a boy or a girl but was advised that it would be best if she didn't know. She imagined it was a little girl, for that is just what she wanted, and so on each anniversary she would know her age, imagine what she would look like and wonder what she would be doing. The discomfort of the abortion was nothing like the guilt which Sunetta suffered and, for the rest of her life, nothing would make that pain go away.

Chapter 56

London November 1973

THE JOURNEY FROM Bordeaux to London by car was always hard and arduous, particularly with a new baby and small child. Sophie often cursed the fact that they drove around in a battered second-hand estate car when everyone else they knew drove, if not a new car, at least one which didn't make them look like paupers. She could never understand why her husband, who was so fastidious about his chemistry set and his wine records, could not care less when it came to his car. It made him look poverty stricken. Pierre Hilaire, de Gressier's manager, always got the new car and Henry had the pass-me-downs. Sophie put it down to some kind of perverse reverse snobbery, but as she sat there surrounded by her children's filth, she had answered her own complaint.

It was nearing the end of the day, and both were tired. All they wanted to do was to get the children in the bath and into bed. There was a sigh of relief as they arrived in Chesterfield Street but as they tried to turn right to park outside Found House they found the road blocked by a police car with flashing lights. They slowed down to look up the road to see what was happening. Flames were leaping up the outside of one of the buildings.

"That's our house," screamed Sophie in alarm.

"That's our house," shouted Henry, almost in parallel time, driving around the police car, mounting the pavement and stopping about 100 yards away from their house as they saw flames leap from the basement.

There was no fire engine but about six men were all tackling the blaze with fire extinguishers.

"What the hell are you doing?" shouted the policeman.

"That's my house," shouted Henry.

"Is there anyone inside?" the policeman shouted back.

"No, I don't think so. It's Sunday evening and no one should be working."

Receiving the answer he wanted to hear, the policeman went off to move his panda car to let the first fire engine through.

The flames had taken hold of the wooden window frames and the front door and were climbing high on the outside of the building.

Sophie stayed rooted in the car, leaning forward with her hand over her mouth, paralysed by the thought that they might have been inside.

Found House, as with all houses built at that time, had a coal cellar which ran from the bottom of the basement steps to deep underneath the near side pavement. The doors to the coal cellar had been burned through and the contents were now firmly alight creating a new hazard. It was becoming unbearably hot, driving back the men with now empty fire extinguishers. The heat of the flames was now breaking the glass in the windows, which were being blown out, causing the curtains inside to catch fire.

Henry ran back to Sophie, "There's no one inside?" he asked desperately.

"No, I don't think so, but what's happening?" she shouted back.

"I don't know," shouted Henry in return.

Very quickly and efficiently, the first set of firemen had their hoses out and were pouring water onto the blaze. As other tenders arrived, including a huge turntable ladder, the new arrivals followed the instructions of the first lead fireman. Ambulances and more police cars arrived, dominated by the red police cars of the special branch.

It wasn't until the flames had stopped leaping from the basement that the firemen were free to break down the double front doors and, wearing breathing apparatus, drag their hoses into the house. Within minutes of their fine spray of water hitting the flames around the windows, the front door and the coal bunker, the blaze was put out. Only the basement and the first two floors had been badly damaged.

Henry joined the group of men standing around with empty fire extinguishers who had first tackled the blaze. They had a camaraderie about them which was more than a group of men who had just joined in a fire fight.

"Where have all the fire extinguishers come from?" said Henry, as he approached them. "Do you know what happened?" he asked the group generally.

"Arson," said one of their number.

"We're just wondering which one it was intended for," said another.

"Did you see it happen?" asked Henry.

"No, but there was a smell of petrol, so it's bleeding obvious."

"Where are you from?" asked Henry.

"The Ambassador's house over there," said one of their number, as he pointed directly opposite.

"I'm down there," pointed another.

"I'm over there," pointed a third.

"We need to get back. We need to make sure this wasn't some kind of distraction event," said one of the group, and with that they started to disperse.

"Do you know who did it?" Henry called to the departing men.

"Why?"

"I live here," said Henry.

"Hell's bells, you're a lucky bastard," said one.

"Unlucky," said another.

"We know it was a French car and the fire was started by the driver, he was seen driving away. We'll get the rest from the videos. We'll each have a look now." With that the group departed, each to their own task.

Henry went back to his car. The fire was virtually out, although steam was still rising as the cold water hit the retained heat of the concrete. He slammed the car door shut, threw himself back against the seat and closed his eyes. The smell of the fire was impregnated into his clothing.

"It was arson. Maurice Rabôut has just tried to set fire to our house," he exclaimed.

"What?" shouted, Sophie looking completely aghast.

"The fire was started deliberately by a person in a French car. I'm sure it was Rabôut who was behind it."

"Why?"

"Destroying evidence, I suspect."

"No, Henry, no," yelled Sophie. "No, no, no, no. I told you to go to the police," she shouted furiously.

There was a tap on the window and the policeman from the panda car was summoning him.

"Excuse me, sir; the commissioner would like a word."

"I'm going home, Henry," said Sophie. "I'm not staying here."

"Home?" asked Henry, puzzled by the thought, as this was her home.

"Well, we can't stay here, I'm going to..."

She got out of the car and Henry did too.

"Give me the key," she commanded.

Henry took his car key from his chain. He knew better than to argue when Sophie was fired up like this. He handed the key over thinking it best that she looked after the children and he looked after the situation here. "Why don't you go to my Mother's," he suggested. "I'll touch base with you there."

Henry's attention was drawn by the policeman reminding him that the commissioner wanted to see him as Sophie climbed in to the car. She adjusted the driver's seat and mirror and, with a look of contempt, drove off through the maze of haphazardly parked emergency vehicles.

"How dare he risk his family in some stupid detective work," she said out loud, angrily. Not once did she look back at Found House for she was determined never to return. Her last look at Henry was of sheer disdain. He was standing there alone and completely forlorn.

Thanks to the quick work of the special branch team of police officers, guarding the diplomatic premises which made up Henry's neighbours, the house had been saved. The structural damage was minimal. It was badly damaged outside with the doors, windows, carpets and curtains having to be replaced. The antique furniture, pictures, and photographs were all safe. It was the smoke and water damage which were going to take its toll. The worst hit was the

---

basement where all Henry's staff worked. His precious laboratory was unharmed.

As Henry wandered through the house, he was hugely surprised to find Vincent Ainsworth in the garden, sitting quietly with a beer and a large ladder propped up against the rear wall ready should he need to make a rapid exit. He looked as though he was a man at a summer barbecue.

"What are you doing here?" asked Henry amazed.

"I was working and about to go home when the fire started," answered Ainsworth. "I'm here per our fire procedures," he said, mockingly as well as matter-of-factly. The commissioner joined Henry in the garden at which point Ainsworth left saying something about dealing with the insurance claim.

The commissioner was dressed in his formal uniform which he always wore when he was on duty. This was so he was properly attired should he, at any time, be summoned by Her Majesty the Queen. This evening, his formal dress would be used to put at ease the ambassadors living all around Found House who were convinced that the attack had been intended for them.

"Stay there," said Henry to the commissioner immediately he started questioning him on what had happened, "I'll be back." He disappeared inside only to return a few minutes later with the Rabôut dossier and five open bottles of beer. For the first time since he had decided he didn't like the stuff, Henry was going to drink alcohol for he was desperate to take away the acrid taste of smoke from his mouth.

"We weren't a mistaken identity," said Henry handing over the dossier and passing around the beer bottles.

"I believe we were deliberately firebombed because of what's in there." He pointed to the document. "It's evidence of a huge wine counterfeiting operation by Maurice Rabôut. You know the car had French number plates, well, he's French." Henry told the story up to and including his meeting in Paris.

The commissioner said nothing as he turned the pages on the folder. "You gave this to him?" he asked.

"Yes," said Henry.

"And you didn't tell the police?"

"No," said Henry sheepishly.

"Why?"

"Because the damage to the French wine industry would have been devastating if it got out," replied Henry, certain in his actions.

"You were therefore complicit in the cover up of a crime?" said the commissioner; his comment made more as a statement rather than a question.

"No, I was simply trying to make sure that the damage done was undone."

"Excuse me, sir," said a man in plain clothes. "We have the car on CCTV, together with a fairly good image of the two men." His manner and mode of speech immediately identified him as a policeman.

"Two men?" repeated Henry shocked.

"Yes," said the policeman. "Both aged between twenty-five and thirty-five. They each dropped four petrol bombs, about milk bottle size, into the basement either side of the front door. It's all very clear. We have the car, a Renault, and the number plate. The fire brigade has told us that petrol was also squirted through the letter box into the hall."

Two hours later Henry was sitting in Paddington Police Station carefully studying the videos. He was pretty sure Rabôut was one of the arsonists, but he felt unable to confirm that with 100% certainty. He didn't know the other man. Later that night in the Connaught Hotel, after he'd showered and whilst waiting for room service, Henry phoned his mother, grandmother and Sophie's parents to tell them what had happened. No one knew where Sophie was.

"Say nothing other than it was a terrorist attack and a case of mistaken identity," he instructed. "It's what we've agreed with the police. Sophie's PR agents will be dealing with it on that basis, so please keep to the same line." His final request was that they get Sophie to phone him as soon as they could. "She's bolted with the children," he said. "She saw the flames, instinctively knew what had happened and drove the children away to safety." With each further phone call, he was embarrassed to admit that he didn't know where she was or where she was going.

Sophie was cursing. She was bitterly regretting letting out her former mews home as that would have been the ideal bolthole to take the children. Plan B would have been to go to Victoria's house as Henry had suggested, but she was so cross with him that the idea didn't appeal. She would have preferred to drive to her parents, where she would have felt best, but she feared that they were getting too old to deal with her children. She decided to return to Château de Gressier and that was where she was heading. She drove through the evening to Portsmouth hoping to catch the last ferry to Ouistreham. Although she managed to get tickets and a cabin and it was not allowed, the deck-crew, thrilled at having a beautiful celebrity in their midst, allowed her and her children to sleep soundly in her car on the car deck. They woke them up just as they were reaching the shores of France. It would take Sophie two days to get back to the estate, as she was in no mind to be rushed. On this journey there would be plenty of time for her children to play.

During the night, Juliette phoned back three or four times checking on information. She was plotting. Meanwhile, there was real concern mounting as to Sophie's whereabouts.

Juliette's phone call with Henry was succinct. "Next Thursday night," she demanded, "you have to be at George Cinq Hotel in Paris. I've booked you a room and you are to be there. We're going to sort this out once and for all," she said.

"How?" asked Henry.

"Don't ask," she said, "just be there."

Chapter 57

Paris November 1973

JULIETTE BOOKED INTO the George Cinq Hotel on Wednesday night with two of the largest de Gressier farmhands. The rumours of her going to Paris on 'a mission' and taking two bodyguards with her spread throughout Latoire village with excitement. She was, once again, their 'Singe Fou' - mad monkey. She instructed her two bodyguards that they had to buy navy suits, white shirts, black shoes, black socks and black ties the very next day. She too spent Thursday shopping; not for power clothes but for an expensive item of jewellery to wear on her jacket as a statement of wealth. She had the game plan clear in her mind and this gave her an energy and excitement which she had not felt since smuggling allied pilots in wine barrels during the war.

Henry arrived on Thursday evening as instructed and, on Friday morning, he found Juliette taking centre stage, sitting at a highly polished antique table in the largest of the hotel's private meeting rooms.

"Have you the evidence?" she asked, as he leaned over and kissed her on her forehead in his normal greeting.

"Yes," said Henry.

"And you'll present it as we agreed?" she asked.

"Yes."

"After that, please do and say nothing," she instructed.

Henry noticed that they were speaking in English, which was unusual, for they traditionally spoke to each other in French. They then sat in silence. Juliette sat bolt upright, her hands on her lap as she focussed on the meeting ahead. Henry felt the slow passage of time, trying the occasional attempt at conversation without success. As the moments passed, Henry noticed how Juliette became more and more tense. The clock on the sideboard gently struck eleven o'clock. Juliette checked the time against her diamond encrusted wristwatch. It was therefore with some relief that the door opened and in walked Monsieur Gaston Rabôut, the door held open for him by his son, Robert.

Monsieur Gaston walked slowly, bending over and leaning heavily on two walking sticks. He was smartly dressed in the best of clothes, which had seen better days. Robert followed, tall and elegant with a light tan setting off his silver hair. Henry stood up to greet them but Juliette stayed seated. He started to make his way around the table to greet her two guests, as one normally would, when she instructed Henry to take his seat. She pointed to two carefully placed chairs, indicating where her guests were to sit, in the process making it clear that there would be no welcome from her.

"Is Maurice Rabôut not coming?" Juliette asked. "The invitation was to all three of you."

"Sadly, no," said Robert. "He is in London and we have not been able to contact him."

"Ah," said Juliette, immediately recognising that there was now no need for the two navy suited heavies outside the door.

The two men sat quietly. Gaston and Robert had come, not because Juliette had told them they must, but out of respect for her. The fact that she had travelled all the way to Paris to meet them indicated the importance of the meeting.

"Monsieurs," she said, immediately the two men had settled down, "thank you for coming. Please excuse the lack of warmth in my greeting, but we have very grave issues before us."

Gaston fiddled with his hearing aid so he could hear better.

"Henry has something to show you," she added, nodding at him to start his demonstration.

Henry did exactly as he had done with Maurice, pouring wine from one bottle into two glasses and passing them across the table. He did the same with the second bottle, this time passing the glasses over with the solemnity of a priest passing bread at Communion. It was immediately obvious to the two men that the wines were different, but each said nothing. Gaston was certain that the first wine was from his estate. He always swore he would recognise his wine anywhere in the world, and so it proved. His certainty was suddenly put in doubt as Henry unveiled two identical Domaine de Rabôut labels. He pushed the two bottles across the table towards them for their examination. Not a word had been spoken throughout the whole of Henry's presentation.

"May I examine the corks?" asked Robert.

Henry passed them across. "You will find that they are from the exact same supplier," he said.

"But how?" exclaimed Gaston, immediately feeling both anxious and defenceless at the same time.

"I'm afraid there is worse news," said Juliette, now feeling slightly sorry for them. She knew from the detectives' reports that they were not involved in the counterfeit wine, but their reactions had satisfied her of their innocence.

"Monsieur Gaston, your grandson; Monsieur Robert, your son, Maurice is wanted by the British police for arson and attempted murder. That is why he is not here with you. I am sorry but in case you are in any doubt of the veracity of what I'm telling you, here is a copy of his international arrest warrant. I suspect the police visited Château Rabôut this morning, whilst you were on your way here, as they are looking for him."

Juliette paused, allowing the two men time to study the form which, while in English with French in smaller type below, had Maurice Rabôut's name typed at the top in the centre.

"Regretfully, Maurice firebombed my grandson's home last Sunday, setting it alight with eight Molotov cocktail petrol bombs. He can be clearly seen on the video deliberately setting fire to Henry's house. There is no doubt that it's him."

The colour drained from their faces, as they looked at Henry, whose expression confirmed everything Juliette was saying, albeit that her video evidence claim was highly exaggerated.

"I'm really sorry, Monsieur," said Gaston, addressing Henry. "Please accept my sincere apologies. What can we do?" Juliette held up her hand, instructing him not to say anything further.

"Here are two folders," she said, and then stopped as she indicated to Henry that he should pass out copies of his detective's dossier.

In Juliette's original plan she had intended to set out her demands straight away but, seeing the look on the faces of the two men in front of her, it was obvious that anything she said would not be heard. Their brains were being drowned out in their own thoughts. Instead, she announced, "Henry and I will leave you alone for thirty minutes. I will arrange for coffee and water to be delivered. You need time to read the report and consider the implications, particularly for Maurice, and also for you two financially. There is a financial section in the report. Please read it carefully." And then, as she always did, Juliette stood up to show the meeting was at an end. As she rose, Monsieur Gaston and Monsieur Robert stood up too.

"May I suggest you ask your lawyers and financial advisers to be here no later than 3 pm today. I fear we are going to need them." Then, with great dignity and poise, Juliette left the room. Henry followed, wondering if he could admire a woman more, for his grandmother had proved, once again, to be seriously formidable.

Juliette led Henry into the next-door meeting room which she had reserved earlier. Already sitting in there were both Monsieur Delmas and Monsieur Liard, waiting as they had been duly instructed. Both stood up.

"I thought you had retired, Madame?" said Liard, as they shook hands.

"Well, I'm about to have the best fun I've had for a long time, and it's only for one day," said Juliette.

She briefed the two men as to the circumstances of their meeting and to say that they were both shocked and surprised was an understatement. Above all, they knew the implications for France and its wine industry if this news should break.

The meeting resumed exactly 30 minutes later. This time, as Juliette entered the room, she made the point of shaking Gaston and Robert's hands, holding them longer than necessary as she smiled and looked warmly into their eyes. A woman, even at 78, knows how to use her wiles to get her way with men, and with these simple actions, the antagonism which they had earlier felt towards her was disarmed. Henry followed Juliette's lead and shook their hands too. He resumed his place next to his grandmother. Monsieurs Delmas and Liard were introduced and instructed to sit next to each other at the head of the table. There was a strange silence as Juliette prepared to speak.

"I think we all appreciate the implications for France and the French wine industry if Maurice's counterfeiting of Rabôut wine were to become public; so this is what is going to happen. If, Monsieurs, at any stage you leave this table, the negotiations are at an end and the chips will fall where they will. Do you understand?" Both men nodded.

"Firstly, Maurice will have to plead guilty at his trial. I have spoken to English criminal lawyers. You have to accept that he is going to get a sentence of life imprisonment. That is the law in England for arson. It is likely the judge will set a minimum tariff of fifteen years, and he is likely to be eligible for parole after about eight years. If he pleads not guilty and goes to trial he will still be found guilty because the evidence against him is overwhelming. If he goes to trial, the counterfeiting of Rabôut wine will come out as the motive and then there will be nothing any of us can do. In all probability, he will get a much longer time in jail because the crime of counterfeiting will be added to his indictment. There will be no reduction on tariff which would happen if he had pleaded guilty. Further, in jail he will have a dreadful time. He might even be killed. He will almost certainly be badly injured because of the hate which will be held against him. Lots and lots of people are going to lose their livelihoods if the reputation of French wine is destroyed courtesy of Maurice. Please understand, this is a condition precedent to all negotiations."

Juliette paused to make sure they understood.

"Let me understand you, Madame," said Gaston. "It is a condition that Maurice pleads guilty at his trial."

"Yes, that is correct," said Juliette. "If this term fails, then all terms fail. Do I make myself clear?"

"And what if we can't persuade him?"

"I'm afraid it's your responsibility to make sure you do. It would be best if you took him to the police with a lawyer and a pre-prepared statement of admission and guilt. This way, he will be able to answer all the police questions by simply saying no comment."

The two men said nothing as they anticipated there was worse to come.

"Monsieurs, your Paris wine shop's trading business is now worth nothing."

"Why are they worth nothing?" enquired Robert.

"No one will buy any wine from you if they know you have sold false wine in the past. You will have no customers."

Robert looked at Gaston; whose expression told him that Juliette was right.

"The Paris premises are worth approximately 1.25 million francs," Juliette continued. "This is what's going to happen. I'm going to buy the wine shop for its premises value. Henry will be the sole director but you, Monsieur Robert," said Juliette pointing to him, "will remain as its general manager at a salary which my advisors will negotiate and agree with you as appropriate."

Robert said or did nothing. He knew there was more to come.

"The Rabôut estate is sadly worth very little now, no more than agricultural value. If I add in the value of the Château, all the equipment and buildings then it is worth just over 2.5 million francs. Monsieur Gaston, I'm going to buy 51% of Château Rabôut for 1.25 million francs. This time you remain a director, again at a salary my advisors will agree. Henry will also be appointed as the only other director alongside you, but he will have the casting vote on any matters regarding the running of the estate."

Juliette paused as, for just that moment, she was reminded of her father and the way he would dictate terms to those who came seeking investment. There was a power about it which was immensely stimulating.

"Gaston, you will still live at Château Rabôut," she continued. "It will remain your home until the death of the latter of you or of your wife."

The look on Gaston's face suggested that she had crossed a line which would be unacceptable to him, so she deviated from her planned script and explained.

"Monsieur Gaston," she said. "If this comes out, you are going to be sued by every customer you have ever had. The legal bills alone will bankrupt you. This way your home and reputation are protected."

Gaston looked down at the table.

"The two purchase prices, totalling 2.5 million francs, will go into an escrow account," said Juliette. "It is this money which will fund the buyback of all Château Rabôut wines throughout the world and not just the counterfeit. I estimate that it will cost about that amount of money."

"It can't cost that much to buy-back the wine," protested Robert. "Maurice cannot have sold that much into the market."

"It's true," said Juliette "but Bordeaux wines have increased a lot in price over the last three years and we will have to buy it back at its investment value."

"But he cannot have spent that kind of money," said Robert, making the same point in a different way.

"According to the detectives' report, the money has gone into high living, drugs and very expensive girlfriends, so don't be surprised at the amount of the debt," added Henry much to Juliette's annoyance as it interrupted her train of thought.

"From London, Henry will lead the buy-back campaign using Maurice's records. A bottle from each case will be tested and the counterfeit wine destroyed. We might be able to re-sell the genuine wine which will offset some of the losses. When we know the last of the counterfeit wine has been purchased Henry will purchase the remaining 49% of Château Rabôut for its then market value less the amount that the compensation we have to pay out exceeds 2.5 million francs."

Juliette paused and stared hard at the table. She tried to think whether there was anything else she wanted covered.

"During this process you two gentlemen will have your reputations and jobs. At the end of it, if all goes well, you will both have enough capital to make you financially secure."

"And what if the buy-back costs less than 2.5 million francs? Do we get the excess money held in escrow?" asked Gaston, showing himself to be the better businessman of the two.

It was not a question Juliette had expected, nor did she have a prepared answer.

"If, at the end of the buy-back period, the counterfeiting remains completely private, then yes. If not, then no, it will come back to Château de Gressier."

"Then it is in your best interest to allow the scandal to become public," accused Robert.

"And in the process destroy the value of French wine, the value of my vineyard and the one I'm suggesting I buy from you. You're being ridiculous," Juliette added, spitting out the last word. "I'm risking everything to be involved with you."

Deciding this was a good moment; Juliette placed the fingers of both hands on the edge of the table and stood up to address them.

"Gentlemen, the fact is that, thanks to Maurice, you have lost your wealth. There is nothing I can do about that. I believe this proposal keeps your dignity, preserves the reputation of Rabôut wine and, most importantly, saves the wine industry for France. I am sorry for the circumstances you find yourselves in, but I commend my proposals to you. If you want to accept them then Henry, Monsieur Delmas and Monsieur Liard will agree the details and finalise the arrangements within the parameters I set out earlier. There is no need for me to be consulted on anything else."

All five men stood up as Juliette walked slowly around the table. Monsieur Gaston noticed, for the first time, that she was wearing the medal awarded to her for gallantry during the war. "La Croix de Guerre," he said approvingly. "Is this another of your battles, Madame?" he said with a hint of irony.

Juliette smiled but said nothing. She shook each man gently by the hand and left, for she had no more to say.

Juliette's framework of a deal was, after much discussion and negotiation, agreed by Gaston and Robert. Throughout the rest of the day, and into the night, secretaries with typewriters came and went as contracts were drafted and re-drafted.

At each break in the meeting Henry tried to phoned Sophie. He knew from her booker and Juliette that she and the children had arrived safely at Château de Gressier but the phone to the Cottage was never answered. He was anxious to speak to her to tell her what was going on and why he wasn't there. This led to him becoming immensely frustrated when Gaston and Robert argued about the small things; the cars they could drive, the length of their holidays and the size of their expense accounts. There was an emotional discussion with Gaston's wife as a schedule of personal effects in Château Rabôut were listed and it was made clear that everything else would belong to the Rabôut estate.

At 12 noon the next day, all the contracts were ready for signature in front of a notary public who would, on reading the documents, explain the deal as it was drafted. Henry went to look for Juliette. He knocked on her door and phoned her room every five or ten minutes over the next hour. Eventually, now very concerned, the hotel manager let him into the room. Juliette was sitting upright on the bed, lying against a stack of white pillows, still in the suit from yesterday's meeting with just her shoes kicked off. She looked peacefully asleep, but a touch of her cold hand told him that she was dead.

In her hand were Étienne's medals. At the very last moment of her life, she was thinking of him. The manager agreed to call a doctor and readily accepted that she should stay where she was until late that evening. The last thing any hotel wants is a hearse at its door.

Henry went downstairs and said nothing of the events upstairs. Instead, he sat and signed papers with Gaston and Robert for about an hour until the Notary Public, who had trebled his fee for working on a Saturday, declared the transaction was complete.

Shortly afterwards Henry was handed a note by a receptionist to tell him that the doctor had arrived. This was Henry's cue to take Monsieur Delmas and Monsieur Liard to one side and report Juliette's death.

"When did she die?" asked Liard.

"Last night, possibly yesterday afternoon," said Henry.

"Has the doctor certified death?"

"Why?"

"Taxes," said Liard quickly, at which point, the Delmas brain was immediately on the same track.

"If she died after the deal was signed, then the estate is worth about 2.5 million francs less, saving about a million francs in taxes."

"No, he hasn't certified her death yet. It's why he's here now."

"Good, delay it. Get the certificate dated and timed as late as possible. It might be important. In fact, get it dated and timed now because the notary will have recorded the time the deal was completed."

Henry accompanied the doctor to the hotel suite, who did as he was asked: certified the date and time of death when he saw the body, recorded the cause as an aneurism, although there was no evidence of this, and collected his fee from the hotel - disappearing with another duty unquestionably completed.

Downstairs, there was a continuing discussion between Monsieurs Delmas and Liard, wondering how Juliette expected Châteaux de Gressier to pay for her acquisitions. It was not a matter that they had dared ask her while she was alive. It would have been impertinent to have questioned her authority.

Henry returned to the meeting room and told Gaston and Robert Raboût that Juliette had died. There was the routine expression of shock, driven mainly by the fear that their work of the last day might have been wasted. Only then, when they had absorbed the news, did they extend their sympathies and use it as an excuse to leave.

"Cesçon," said Liard, using Henry's long known local nickname very shortly after Gaston and Robert had left, "we have been discussing and neither of us know how Madame expected to pay for all of this. I do not believe there is money in her account in France. We assume either you have this money in England or Madame has savings somewhere.

"Are you sure?" said Henry shocked. "She wouldn't have done this without having the money at hand, would she? I certainly don't have that kind of money!"

Monsieurs Liard and Dumas looked at each other and said nothing.

"Gentlemen, will you please speak to Vincent Ainsworth and brief him," said Henry. "He has to be involved in every aspect of this."

With that, Henry left the room without saying goodbye. Monsieurs Liard and Dumas looked at each other. From the way Henry departed, it was obvious that Juliette's genes had been passed from one generation to another.

Chapter 58

Paris November 1973

BEFORE HENRY LEFT the hotel, he went to his room where he phoned Victoria and very shakily broke the news of her mother's death. He didn't like her silence at the end of the phone, so he did all the talking. He reported her magnificence in the meeting, but how she appeared to have left him with a huge problem. He urged, and then instructed his mother that she had to come home immediately. Juliette's funeral would be in Latoire village church. She would be buried alongside Étienne and Victor and she had to be there.

On Henry's part it was a sad, tearful conversation, whereas Victoria was far more detached, less emotional, even sanguine throughout. Later, as she contemplated the news, and wondered at her lack of mourning, she realized her relationship with her Mother had been killed on the banks of the River Garonne just over thirty years before.

"Mother," asked Henry, "would you be so kind as to phone Sophie and tell her the news? We've hardly spoken since Found House was firebombed. I really don't think I could speak to her right now."

Henry took the train from Paris to Bordeaux and then a taxi to Château de Gressier. He did no work; he simply stared out of the window, lost in his memories of the past and his anxieties for the future.

Juliette's death somehow made the reconciliation between Sophie and Henry easier, for it was obvious to Sophie, from Henry's demeanor, that the death of Juliette had affected him deeply. He was, for those few moments, a man without fight.

That night Henry and Sophie wandered through all the rooms of the Cellars. It badly needed the same kind of update and refurbishment which Juliette had organised for the Cottage the year before.

"It's the tradition that we now move in here," said Henry to Sophie.

"What happens to the Cottage?"

"That's for the next Generation......when they are old enough," he replied.

They stopped their tour of the Cellars in Juliette's library. The room, as always was cold despite there being a well stacked fire in the grate.

Sophie took out a couple of the leather-bound diaries and sat down to glance through them. "So seamlessly Château de Gressier moves from one generation to the next," she observed out loud. "Is that always the plan? Do Andrew and Peter take over one day?" Sophie asked.

Henry didn't answer. He was still contemplating her earlier question about the Cottage. Sometimes decisions are easy. It made sense if Château de Gressier became their family home. London would now be just an office and a place for Henry to stay when he was working there.

Chapter 59

Château de Gressier November 1973

VICTORIA FELT NERVOUS throughout the whole of her journey. This turned into a deep anxiety as the taxi turned the corner and onto the drive which led up to Château de Gressier. At first appearance, it looked as though nothing had changed since she left thirty-one years ago. In that time, Victoria had seen her mother just once and only for a few days, when Juliette's father had died. There was little reconciliation between mother and daughter then, and there could be none now.

Sophie, on hearing the taxi tyres crunch on the drive, came out to meet Victoria. The two women hugged as though they were mother and daughter. There was a genuine fondness between them.

"I have a bedroom for you with us," said Sophie, as she carried Victoria's luggage in to the Cottage. Victoria last remembered it as a boarding house full of German airmen and now, looking around, she could see it was a home again. There was then the thrill of Victoria being joined by her grandchildren and, for the next hour, nothing was more important to her than being with Andrew and Peter.

Victoria bathed her grandchildren and with the excitement of having their grandmother present, it was much later than normal when Andrew and Peter went to bed.

"Listen out for the kids," commanded Sophie to Henry as she led Victoria from the upstairs of the Cottage, through the Gallery into the upstairs of the Cellars. As Victoria walked through the Gallery, she looked at her son sitting at her father's desk, his head bowed deep in concentration. From her first glance, she would have sworn it was Étienne sitting there, and with it she was transported back to being aged five and how it was such a special treat to be in this room with only him.

Sophie was aware of the sensitivities between mother and daughter, for Victoria had spoken in depth about her treatment at Juliette's hands. It was in recognition of this that Sophie had taken great pains to depersonalise the Cellars before showing Victoria around, even removing from the kitchen anything which might carry a memory. So, all the little personal things like mugs and spoons were packed and put into the loft for storage.

With Sophie in tow, Victoria wandered around the Cellars staring out of the windows, remembering the views and touching the wooden panels and furniture. She lingered in Victor's bedroom and then in her own. Nothing seemed to have changed. Even the earthly, dusty smell of the land remained the same.

Victoria walked into Juliette's bedroom. It was the one room which had been thoroughly modernised. It held no memories for her. No sooner had she walked in than she turned and walked out again. Sophie led Victoria down the stairs and into the kitchen, which was old, battered and well used, then through to each of the living rooms

"Henry's going to ask you something," said Sophie, as Victoria wandered into the Cellar's library, touching things randomly, almost to prove to herself that they were real. "He's going to ask you to come and live with us. He would like you to have the Cottage and we will move in here; into the Cellars." Sophie paused. "Please don't say I said anything, but I wanted to warn you. I also want you to know it is something I would like too."

It was late when Sophie, Henry and Victoria sat down to eat in the kitchen of the Cottage. Everything had been prepared by Juliette's cook. It only needed to be heated through before it could be served. Although it was a solemn occasion, Henry bounced with joy to see his mother at Château de Gressier. He was genuinely happy that Victoria was now back in, what he saw as, her home.

"Come, sit," said Henry in French, tapping the kitchen table. "I have something to say." The chairs were scraped back on the flagstones and Victoria and Sophie did as they were told.

"Mother," said Henry firmly. "You are to have the Cottage as your home. Whether you like it or not, it's yours to live in. We are moving into the Cellars. Don't protest; it will make no difference. If you are not here, it will just stay empty. For our part, we would love you to live here."

Sophie was shocked at the forcefulness of Henry's remarks, for they were not made kindly, as an invitation should. Instead, they were given as though they were an order from a son to his mother.

"Given everything that has happened," Henry continued, "this is where Sophie and I will be making our home. It's where your grandchildren will be, it's where you should be too."

"There's a lot of work to be done to the Cellars before you can move in," observed Victoria.

Henry took no notice, to his mind the refurbishment of the Cellars was just a detail. Instead, he was on to his next subject. "I have two gifts," said Henry. "Mamie bought this for you," he said to Sophie, handing over the box which contained the diamond brooch which Juliette had bought the day before she died, and had worn at the Raboût meeting. "She bought it for you as a home warming present," he lied. "She was so pleased you had decided to live here."

Sophie took the box and opened it and, on seeing the dazzling display of diamonds, she gasped. She had worn some very expensive jewelry in her time, all of it lent, but this piece surpassed almost all of those, for it was perfect in both taste and design. Something told her that this was not the right moment to put it on so she closed the box, but couldn't resist opening it, again and again. It was an item she would treasure forever for she owned no jewelry as valuable or as beautiful.

"Mamie wanted you to have these," Henry said to his mother, handing over Juliette's Croix du Guerre and Étienne's war medals. "She was holding them when she died," he added. Victoria took them but showed no emotion on receiving them.

"They will mean far more to you when you read Mamie's diary of those days," said Henry. "Here, I've marked it for you. He handed over one of Juliette's bound leather books. "It was written in March

1946, after the war when one of the airmen she saved wrote to her. His letter is in there too."

"When did you read all of this?" asked Victoria.

"For the first time? Last night," answered Henry. I'd seen them bound, but never looked inside before. It was as though they were Mamie's private papers. When did you leave here?" asked Henry.

"March 1942," replied Victoria, matter-of-factly.

"Then you should also read what she says in her diary about the death of Henri Hilaire," for it explains a lot about those times.

"Have you invited Dominique to her funeral?" asked Victoria, in a panic.

"I'm sure Pierre will have told her."

"No, no, that's not good enough. She must sit in the front row with us, as though she is first family. It's very important. She needs to be invited!"

"Why?"

"Because it's what she would have wanted. Ever since my father's funeral, Dominique and Mamie have sat together on occasions like this."

"But wasn't Dominique your father's mistress?" asked Sophie thinking she knew the Guégan family history. "Surely, she shouldn't have been there at all, let alone in such a prominent position," she queried.

"If you go back further in the diaries you will find the reason, for I'm sure it will all be explained," replied Victoria. "If it isn't then come and ask me."

That night in their bedrooms, while Henry and the two children slept, Sophie and Victoria studied Juliette's diaries, each wanting answers to the issues raised by Henry.

Juliette was a brilliant diary writer. She did not just describe the events, but the mood and scenery within which those events took place. As Victoria read, she could see in her head exactly what was happening. It was as though an old silent cine film was being re-played in her imagination and, with its reading, so much was put into context.

As her mother wrote of the day of Stephen's arrest, Victoria could remember being there, watching from the window. She remembered Stephen's confident smile as he looked at Juliette before he was driven off. She read on:

"He was always like a son to me. The son I never had. I loved him like a son, but he was also a man; a very brave man; a dependable man; the kindest and very best of men. He had a magnetic attraction which was impossible to resist at the best of times. Add danger, an experience so powerful that only the two people involved can understand, and you have your answer as to why our relationship was as full as it could be between any man and any woman. If you were there, then you would understand. If you were not, then it will be a mystery which will defy you."

"It's betrayal," said Victoria under her breath, as she realised those coded words told her what she had always suspected. Now, in these pages, she had it confirmed; her mother had taken Stephen, the man she always thought she would marry, as her lover.

Victoria put down the diary and stared out over the room seeing nothing. Did Dominique know that her son had been seduced by her best friend? she wondered, and then immediately doubted it. It was something which should be too private to be shared, and yet it was there, in black and white, in her diary.

Victoria turned the pages in the diary forward to March 1942 and started to skim read the pages. What had she written about her own parting she wondered? Then she read:

"I cannot sleep. I will never sleep again for I have said goodbye to my very best friend today. My heart has been ripped out. Someone I have known all her life and with her going I have no need to live. She didn't have to go and yet I made her. If I was deciding for just me, then she would have stayed and we would have risked everything together, but there were now two of them and it was too dangerous for her to stay. I am sure my best friend will hate me forever, but that is a small price to pay to give them a chance of safety and freedom."

Victoria checked the pages. It had not been added later. It was there, written as it happened. Had she made me hate her, Victoria wondered. It was more complex than that she thought. It all started to go wrong when Victor died. She had to read Juliette's diary of that time. Why had her mother loved her brother more than her? Would she find the answer in these pages she wondered?

In her emotional tiredness Victoria flicked through a few more pages. There was something embarrassingly intrusive and yet compulsive about reading someone else's diary. A few pages on she read:

"*I heard today that my best friend arrived home. I can now start to breathe again knowing she is safe, but I will not sleep. I will never sleep until she is home. I don't pray. I can't pray. I can only hope, and I hope upon hope that one day she will come back to me and then the pain will be gone.*"

As her eyes wandered through the pages Victoria's eyes fell on Juliette's writing on the day of Henrie Hilaire's funeral. She wrote eloquently describing the reading of Hilaire's last letter. Then she read:

"*Dominique said it was the image of babies being ripped from their mothers before they were sent to the death camps in Germany which killed him. He could never get it out of his mind. It helps my pain to know that I helped my best friend avoid such agonies, for imagine what would have happened if her condition had been discovered and by whom.*"

"Bitch, you sanctimonious bitch," was Victoria's response to reading those words. "You're justifying the unjustifiable," she thought. How could she post-rationalise sending her pregnant daughter away like that?"

No one else was up when Victoria left the Cottage to walk to the village church the next morning. The air was damp, and the night sky was giving way to a red morning hue as she arrived at the river's edge. It was just as she had remembered it, but somehow it was much better. Everything was immaculately manicured. The plane trees, which had grown to full size, had been stripped of their leaves. She spotted the wooden bench seats placed in the middle of the lawn and walked towards them. They were in the same spot they were when she left all those years ago, only newer.

Victoria sat on the first seat and choked at what she read: 'In memory of Victor and Victoria who so loved this place'. Before each had their own seat, why did they now share them, she wondered? She moved to the second bench to read what had been engraved there. It was the same. Instantly, from those few words, Victoria realised that, in her mother's eyes, she was already dead.

Victoria turned to look at all that was around her, but she couldn't see. Overwhelmed by those few words, her eyes were full of tears. "In memory of Victoria," she said to herself. "In memory of Victoria," she repeated, as she sat down on the second bench in shock.

As Victoria's eyes cleared, she started to admire all that was around her. In her mind's eye, she remembered the summer of 1940 and the beauty of the naked airman running around the riverbank. She thought of Heinrik and wondered if he was alive and if so where he was. Had he come to find her and been sent away? She was sure they were in love with each other then, but now, she was not sure. It was all such a long time ago.

Victoria sighed a deep sigh as she got up and walked towards the road. It was then that she noticed it had gone – La Bête Blanche. The huge white ranch house on the hilltop opposite was no longer there. Instead, the view went from the fields into the sky and with the realisation of how natural it made everything look, Victoria was suddenly overcome by the beauty of the place. It was nearly winter and yet it was still heaven on earth, she thought.

Using the path which ran by the side of the road, Victoria climbed the hill until she came to the steps which took her on to the path towards the church. She walked past the church door and towards the churchyard, and with each step, she reverted to being that little girl again; remembering how she held on to her mother's hand as they walked behind the coffin to bury her father, and then her brother.

Victoria found her father's grave and stood staring at it. It was such a long time ago that she could no longer remember him or what he was like. She then moved next to Victor's grave where she felt the deep emptiness which his loss had given to her life. She started to cry, not for Victor but for the loneliness which had been throughout her life; no brother, no father, no mother, and no husband. Victoria sat down between Étienne and Victor's graves and she did exactly as she had done the day after her brother had been buried. Ignoring the cold, she started cuddling the damp ground where his body lay beneath.

"Shall I come home?" she asked her twin brother quietly. She listened hard into the ground for his reply, but she heard only the sound of her temple pulsing. Sitting up again, she spotted the memorial to Stephen fixed against the graveyard wall and read the inscription: 'A Hero of France'. At that moment a Robin came and perched tamely on Victor's head stone. Its head flicked rapidly from side to side until its bulbous eyes settled to stare at Victoria, who, not daring to move, stared back. Each was entranced with the other. "Is this you Victor?" she asked herself silently. "Is this you telling me to come home? No sooner had she asked herself the question than the Robin flew off as fast as it had come.

Victoria walked back to Château de Gressier via the roadway; up to the T junction where she turned right. She stopped where Étienne, her father, had been murdered. There was now a stone memorial cross to mark the spot. It had not been there when she left. As she walked, she kept hearing the young childish voice of Victor talking to her, by the time Victoria arrived at the side door of the Cottage she had made up her mind. She had decided she was going to retire and move back to Château de Gressier. She was coming home.

Chapter 60

Château de Gressier December 1973

THE VILLAGE CHURCH was so packed for Juliette's funeral that they were standing three and four deep in the aisle. It had not been like that since Etienne's funeral. Juliette's coffin was followed into the church by Victoria with Henry at her side and Sophie behind. It was on Sophie that everyone's eyes fell as, forever the supermodel, and albeit demurely dressed, she looked stunning. The three of them took their seats in the front row which had been reserved. Dominique and Pierre were already sitting there.

"It's good to see you again," whispered Dominique to Victoria with a warm smile across her face. Victoria recognised her immediately and smiled back. The woman who had helped her into a canoe was older, perhaps a little thinner and her hair a little greyer, but she had not aged. She was just as beautiful as she ever was. Victoria was certain that the same could not be said about her.

Just after Victoria had sat down, Dominique did something which was quite natural for her, but which took Victoria quite by surprise for, as they sat shoulder to shoulder, she made sure that they held hands.

It was the village mayor who gave the eulogy for he knew Juliette's story as well as the myths which surrounded her. He spoke eloquently of how she saved Château de Gressier after the First World War and dealt gracefully with the deaths of Étienne and Victor. He told of her work for the resistance in the Second World War and how she rebuilt the estate once again. He revealed the open secret of her nickname, 'Le Singe Fou' which caused everyone to laugh in embarrassment. After that, he went into some of the very many acts of generosity in which

Juliette had been involved but for which she had demanded total secrecy; explaining that he only knew because he was her emissary in many of these matters. "If there was ever an example needed of a beneficial dictator," said the mayor affectionately, "then one need look no further than Juliette."

At that moment, Victoria had the same thoughts about her mother as had plagued those of her unknown cousins in South Africa many times. They consistently worried why their father, David Daunier, could be such a strict person inside their family and yet so generous outside of it? It was a conundrum which both sides of the family found hard to understand.

As she was contemplating this issue Victoria recognised that the Colonel and Juliette had been driven by the same ethos. They saw it as their duty to lead and serve. It was what the Colonel did, and it was what Juliette had done. Nothing was going to take them from that path. How well was Henry doing she wondered. He was leading, she was certain of that, but was he serving? Victoria wasn't sure.

Dominique continued to hold Victoria's hands as Juliette's coffin was laid to rest above that of her husband. They sprinkled some soil on the coffin lid and after a few minutes silence they walked away so that others could do the same thing. Dominique turned and, still holding Victoria's hand they stood facing Stephen's memorial stone.

"He's not there," said Dominique, as they stared at the place which Victoria thought was Stephen's grave. "It looked so peaceful where he was, I couldn't bear to move him. Perhaps, when I'm buried with Henri then that would be the time he came here too. We could all be together then."

Victoria said nothing. She didn't know what to say.

"I believe you took his name," said Dominique, after a little while,

"Henry's not his," said Victoria, defensively.

"I know. I'm certain Juliette would have said otherwise."

Victoria had prepared for this moment. She had practised the line in her head so many times and in so many ways that she was ready to deliver it at any moment: *I know my father was sleeping wtih you but, did you know my mother was sleeping wtih your son?* Except she didn't.

Instead, she kept silent; what would be the benefit of her knowing? None.

"Does Henry know who his father really is?" asked Dominique, after a little while.

"Yes, but ... it's a long time ago. Circumstances then and circumstances now ... I used to think we would be married," continued Victoria, before pausing and then adding for certainty, "Stephen and me."

"Henri and I thought so too," said Dominique. "So did your mother. You would have made a lovely couple."

"He was so brave. I watched him run towards her. It was as though he was rushing to save her. I watched him being taken away from de Gressier. Do you know he gave her, ... he gave Juliette, the happiest, handsomest of smiles from the back of the Gestapo car? Honestly, if you hadn't seen it you wouldn't have believed it."

"Your mother said the same thing," replied Dominique, choking with emotion.

Victoria closed her eyes. "I can see his face and that smile, even now."

"It took us a long time to find him after he was shot," said Dominique, her composure re-established.

"Why was that?"

"He was buried in an unmarked grave, as were all of the others. Their bodies were spread around different churchyards. You see that plaque on the wall. Your mother put that up determined he would never be forgotten."

"I was here," said Victoria. "Although it was wooden then." She paused. "Hero of France," she read out loud from the stone plaque which had now replaced it.

Dominique turned and, still holding Victoria's hand, walked a couple of paces to face her husband's headstone. "A committed Catholic in a protestant churchyard," she commented. "How his church could let him down in his hour of need I will never know."

"Henry told me that he killed himself in a protest, like a Tibetan monk setting himself on fire. Is that true?" asked Victoria.

"Far too romantic I'm afraid. It's true he died and protested about the behaviour of the Gendarmerie Nationale à Bordeaux through a letter he'd written to be read at his funeral, but it was nothing as dramatic as Henry described. Like every priest who sets himself on fire, it has a short-term effect, but the reality is that it makes little difference in the long run." Dominique was circumspect, almost sanguine as she spoke.

"He was a very good man," said Victoria seeking to find some words of encouragement.

"I know. When we buried him here your mother agreed that I could be buried here too."

"What, close to my father?" said Victoria with a shrill in her voice which she had not intended.

"Yes. She said it was her way of thanking me for helping to get you out .... save your life."

"Save my life?" questioned Victoria, alarmed.

"Your mother was scared, petrified. She was certain you and she would be arrested at any moment. She wasn't just a Passer. After Stephen's death she stored and hid arms for the communists and other resistance groups all over the estate. You heard what the mayor said."

Victoria shook her head, for she couldn't believe what Dominique was telling her.

"I truly loved your father" said Dominique, misreading Victoria's head shaking. "He needed me. In the end I think your mother realised that."

Victoria had nothing to say.

"Do you know, the burden of leadership in a war never goes away; even after it has all ended? Your father's burden was one of the heaviest. If, after the war, I helped lighten his load a little then I have no shame in that." These words were spoken so calmly, so confidently by Dominique that they had the desired effect of completely disarming Victoria.

Was your son helping my mother's burden when they were in bed together? was what Victoria wanted to say, but with Dominique's change of tone, she changed her mind.

"We did no harm," Dominique continued. Whilst our affair was secret, we hurt no one. She then paused. "Did you know your mother kept a diary?"

"Yes, I started to read it last night. Have you read it?" Victoria asked.

"No, but on quite a few occasions she told me what she had written."

"Do you really think my mother sent me away for my own safety?" asked Victoria, returning to the previous subject.

"Yes, I'm certain of it."

"She could be so damn stubborn," said Victoria, reflectively.

"So, according to your mother, could you."

"Do you know she never forgave her father for not supporting her brother in the First World War? She held that grudge against him until just a couple of days before he died," said Victoria.

"Yes, just like you," said Dominique bluntly, grazing Victoria's sensitivities. "She told me that you never forgave her for sending you away."

"You don't know what it was like, being pregnant and in a strange country at war."

"True," said Dominique, "but I know better than most the price that your mother had to pay in pain to make sure that you were safe." The two women faced each other but said nothing as they chose to stare at their feet instead.

"It's back to the burden of leadership, isn't it? The responsibility for your decision never leaves. You just have to live with the consequences, don't you?" said Victoria.

"You do," said Dominique sharply, "but what makes it worse for those that lead is that their judgement, their decisions, get questioned in the future, but with the benefit of hindsight. No doubt, if your mother had the benefit of foresight, she might have made a different decision, but she didn't have that luxury."

Dominique paused, and Victoria didn't know what else to say. She felt that she had just been chastised. "Come on," said Dominique after a small pause, "while you and Henry are still here no one else can leave."

Sophie, Henry, Victoria, Dominique and Pierre found each other and, all holding hands, they walked united back to Château de Gressier, where both the Cottage and the Cellar were prepared for their guests. Far more people attended the reception than had been catered for so, it was with phone calls to arms, that more delicacies arrived including the dreaded English sandwiches, which Sophie and Henry had insisted on serving. The advantage of a wake in a vineyard is that there is always lots of good wine to drink.

It was late afternoon, and almost everyone else had gone home, when Victoria led Dominique into the library of the Cellars and sat her by the fire in Juliette's armchair. It was a room Dominique had been in many times. It was one place where, in those rare moments, the two women could sit together and find comfort in each other's company.

"I thought you might like to read one of Juliette's diaries," said Victoria, as she deliberately chose one of the leather-bound volumes from the shelf and handed it to Dominique to read. "This covers the war years. Some of it was written after the war, particularly those bits which she couldn't write about then for safety reasons."

Victoria wanted to stay to watch Dominique's reaction, but it was her grandmother duties which reluctantly called her away.

Victoria got back together with Dominique just as she and her son Pierre were leaving. They were the last to go.

"Thank you for sharing your mother's diary," said Dominique, as she kissed Victoria on the cheek. "She wrote so nicely, so affectionately, about Stephen and Henri. I found it both interesting and quite a comfort. The thing is," she added poignantly. "I was there too ... so perhaps I am one of the few who really, really understand! "

Chapter 61

Château de Gressier December 1973

IT IS SAID that a combination of wind, tide, and low air pressure creates the perfect storm and that is the situation which faced Henry and Sophie when they sat down with Ainsworth and their lawyers and accountants in the Gallery at Château de Gressier to review the financial situation which was now before them. Unlike Étienne and Juliette, who had sat opposite each other at the same table for such meetings, Henry and Sophie sat side by side in the middle.

The first item noted that, as planned, Maurice Rabôut had reported to a police station in London, accompanied by his lawyer, with a statement in which he admitted fire-bombing Henry and Sophie's London home by mistake. There was the hint of a political motive, but it made no sense. The first condition in the contract between Gaston, Robert and the company which owned the de Gressier Estate, was satisfied. They were now on the hook. The next stage would be when Maurice appeared in court to plead guilty, with the final stage when he was sentenced. At each stage, the de Gressier business would become more and more committed to implementing the agreed cover up plan.

The British police wanted to contact every one of Rabôut's customers to warn them of their possible purchase of counterfeit wine, but representations by the French embassy in London to the UK Foreign Office resulted in the acceptance that this was a civil, and not a criminal matter which France would sort out.

The first weak link in the secrecy chain came when, despite Henry's strong objections, the Ministry of the Interior insisted that a former President of the Syndicate des Vins de Bordeaux et Bordeaux

Supérieur oversaw the buy-back process. If Juliette had been alive she might have been able to persuade him otherwise, but Henry held no political clout in France. It was an issue he would have to deal with later, but not now.

Since it was money and finance which was the big issue before them, Henry asked Vincent Ainsworth to lead the meeting. To say that Ainsworth was un-amused would be an understatement. If he had been consulted at the start of the Rabôut negotiations he would have told Henry to run away, but he hadn't been given the opportunity because, at that stage Château de Gressier, was still owned by Madame Guégan. The transfer of her shares to Henry, although planned, had not yet taken place.

It was as a result of Juliette's death that Château de Gressier had become Henry's and, because the contract with Gaston and Robert Rabôut had been with Château de Gressier, so did 51% of Château Rabôut and the shop in Paris become his. Conversely, so did the liability of purchasing them which amounted to a further FFr 2,500.000.

"Let us start with Château Rabôut," has anyone visited it?" asked Ainsworth. There was silence.

"Well, I have examined the accounts of Château Rabôut for the last three years and they have lost money every year, sometimes quite a lot."

"What?" said Henry. "They must make money."

"I'm sorry, Henry. They don't," said Ainsworth firmly.

"I'm afraid Monsieur Ainsworth is right," said Mon. Delmas, Juliette's long-standing accountant. "The Rabôut estate loses money every year."

"How?" asked Henry, visibly distressed at the news.

"We don't really know, but from the information I have been able to get so far it appears they sell seventy percent of their wine to local customers. They have hundreds of them buying half a dozen cases at table wine prices," reported Delmas.

"But they almost started the investment market," said Henry, in a mix of annoyance and disbelief.

"Monsieur Rabôut considers these are long-term commitments to his community," added Liard, having gleaned the same information during his negotiation with Gaston and Robert's lawyer.

"What happens in the local retail market?" asked Henry.

"I imagine the wine price is ramped up to just below London and Paris prices," added Delmas.

"So the Château Rabôut estate makes a loss while the local traders make an exceptional profit. Am I right?" asked Henry, the incredulity in his voice demonstrating how he felt.

"That appears to be about right," said Ainsworth.

"Christ, no wonder Maurice produced counterfeit wine," commented Henry despairingly.

"I don't understand," said Sophie, looking puzzled. "Maurice had more demand than he could meet and yet his grandfather was selling too much at ridiculously low prices. Am I right?"

There were nods and murmurs of agreement around the table.

"Well that seems a pretty easy fix," said Sophie confidently. "If we up the prices to their proper market price, which we should, then we'll stop the losses."

"You'll have to up them dramatically, Henry," said Ainsworth, "because we need to factor in about one million French francs of remedial maintenance work, and about a third of that has to be done before the next harvest, otherwise there's a risk of no wine at all. The rest of the work can be spread over a couple of years after that."

"How do you know that?" asked Henry, ever more aghast. "Are you telling me that I've got to find about a third of a million in cash so the wretched place can produce any wine at all next year?"

"I had a long conversation with their book-keeper," said Ainsworth. Monsieur Delmas joined in and helped in the translation, "but that's not the worst of it. There are bank borrowings of around FFr 600,000 which, following the purchase of Rabôut estate, has become immediately repayable on demand.

"But they don't have any bank borrowings," insisted Henry.

"They do Henry," confirmed Liard who looked to Delmas for support. "It was in their disclosure letter."

Sophie stopped the meeting again. "Can I please understand this? We've bought a business knowing, but not knowing, it owes FFr 600,000 to the bank. Is that right?"

No one would answer her question for her summary was right, and they all felt too embarrassed for Henry to say anything.

"What about the Paris shop?" asked Sophie, seeking to break the embarrassed silence.

"I called in there on the way here," said Ainsworth. "It's Robert's hobby and he operates it as such. It trades at about break-even. The ground floor of the shop has potential but at the moment it's very inefficient retail space. There's a good basement for storage but the floors above are just not used. They're full of junk."

"We went in there too," said Liard, referring to himself and Delmas. "We think it's been a good buy, but it needs modernising. I don't think any money has been spent on the place since ... well before the war."

"There is enough upstairs space to make it work just like London," said Ainsworth. "Have a retail shop downstairs and in the basement, then a board room and entertaining space and above that residential accommodation."

"What? Are you suggesting we start running a series of Matterers Lunches from there, just as we do from London?" asked Sophie.

"It's how you got your London business started," replied Ainsworth. "It seems to me that there is the same potential in Paris. Also, it will make a good place for the Rabôut wine buy-back to be organised. From a brand protection point of view, it would be better if it was done from there, than say here or Found House."

There was a general murmur of agreement to the points Ainsworth was making.

"The thing is," Ainsworth continued, "it's going to take about a third of a million francs to do the place up, as well as time."

"I don't think my French is good enough," said Sophie, anxiously referring back to the discussion on organising Matterers Lunches.

Henry slipped his hand over hers, and said warmly, "It's improving all the time, and you have such a sexy accent. You'll do fine."

Sophie bristled, for it was rare that Henry spoke to her in such a condescending tone.

"We need to talk about Madame Guégan's Estate," said Liard.

"Indeed," agreed Delmas. "We've ascertained that she had just over FFr 1.25 million in cash and realiseable investments and her English trust has about another £1 million which can easily be liquidated. This will yield about £600,000 after English taxes.

"I thought she had some cash somewhere which she was going to put into the deal. I didn't believe she would have entered into this transaction without it," said Henry, almost in self-justification, and then added. "It helps explain why she insisted that the payments into the escrow account were phased."

"The problem is that you can't use her cash to do the deal because all her money is now frozen until we get probate, and that is going to take us months to get," said Liard. "Also, there's going to be a large death taxes bill to pay, and her cash is going to have to be used to pay that," he added.

"Do we have an estimate?" asked Henry.

The lawyer and accountant looked at each other wondering who should impart the bad news. Delmas spoke up assuming, because it was numbers, it should be him. "It could be between FFr 1.8 million and up to FFr 3.8 million depending upon negotiations."

"You mean out of all of this chaos I've got to find another two to four million francs. You've got to be joking." Henry paused. "Why is there such a huge variation?" he asked, completely bemused by the range.

"It all depends upon agreeing the value of the de Gressier and the Louis Estates," replied Delmas. "Of course, we will argue the lowest possible values for both estates and bring in the liabilities in respect of Château Raboût, but we thought we should give you what could be an outside estimate."

Henry rested his elbows on the table and put his hands on his face, as he stared at the wood in front of him.

"When do the taxes have to be paid?" asked Sophie.

"Some will have to be paid now and the rest at the end of next year, but there is a program which enables some of it to be paid by instalments."

"Let me get this right," said Sophie firmly. "Château de Gressier has an obligation to find FFr2.5 million to finance someone else's product recall. The cash which was to finance this is no longer available because Madame Guégan died, and because she died, we now have an additional tax bill of up to FFr4 million.

"It's a good summary," admitted Henry. "We're just going to have to borrow the money from the bank."

"That's not going to be that easy, Henry," said Ainsworth. "When we do the accounts for Château Rabôut we're going to have to book a product recall liability of FFr2.5 million, and that liability will also come into the consolidated accounts of de Gressier, because it is now a subsidiary company."

Henry looked at Delmas in hope that this would be wrong advice. Instead, Delmas nodded to agree with what Ainsworth had just said.

"So I can't borrow the money we need."

Ainsworth nodded.

"Is that all the bad news on the table?" Henry asked, despairingly. "Please don't anyone tell me there is more."

"We have to talk about the Folkestone project," said Ainsworth.

"We should explain for the benefit of Monsieur Delmas and Monsieur Liard about the Folkestone vault," said Sophie, "I'm not sure they have the full picture."

Henry nodded.

"Henry bought an old chalk pit close to Folkestone where he is building the first of three very large three-story underground cellars," said Sophie. "Each one is just under sixteen football pitches."

"Ideal conditions for the storage of investment wines," added Henry, defensively.

"Except, we're not; the contract is now for just under 2.7 million square feet at a build price of £27m," corrected Ainsworth.

No, we agreed we were not doing it all in one go," said Sophie, immediately concerned. "We agreed," continued Sophie, looking at Henry disbelievingly.

"It became so much cheaper to do it in one go," replied Henry sheepishly. When we got into the engineering issues it was just the way it had to be.

"What issues," asked Sophie, angrily

The amount of concrete shutter and steels needed to deal with the back-compression once we infilled. If we had the other side of the quarry wall to put pressure against then the costs came down quite dramatically. Didn't they Vincent?" said Henry, seeking an ally.

"There was also the absorption of the costs for the installation of the services. The site was two miles from mains electricity and three miles from mains water. It meant there was no development gain until the third unit was built and the whole site finished," he added, in an attempt to strengthen his argument.

"But you signed the bank loan papers for just the first warehouse, didn't you?"

Henry didn't answer.

"The bank agreed to lend him more when he went to them and asked for it as a single project," said Ainsworth.

"How much more?"

"75%" replied Ainsworth.

"More or in total" asked Sophie sharply.

"In total."

"That still means we've got to find 25% .... that's nearly £7m. We don't have that kind of money."

"It doesn't quite work like that, because they are lending against the land value as well, which has gone up in value now we have planning permission," explained Ainsworth.

"We need an extra £2m," said Henry "and when I told Mamie, she agreed to provide it," he added. "She said I could take out a loan against Château de Gressier to finance it."

"Well that's now not going to happen, is it?" The sarcasm in Sophie's voice was noted all around the table. "In any case, why didn't you say?"

Henry didn't answer. How could he say in front of all these people that the changes in her mental health following the birth of Peter had made him nervous about sharing his change of plans with her.

"Well, we've got to find our commitment of £250,000 in fourteen days' time if we are to get the permission to drawn down the next

£750,000 from the bank to pay the next instalment to the contractor," said Ainsworth, bringing the matter back into focus.

If Henry had started out chairing the meeting, it was now Sophie who was leading the agenda. "Is there anything else," she asked, controlling the anger in her voice.

The room was silent.

"In that case, I suggest we adjourn and meet again at two o'clock. I have organised food in the dining room of the Cottage," said Sophie, and with that she got up and went.

Chapter 62

Château de Gressier December 1973

AS FRENCH ONION soup was served with baguettes, chacuterie, cut tomatoes and cheese in the dining room, the conversation was dominated by the professionals debating various tax treatments and alternative strategies. Henry adjourned to the library, came back with pen and paper and started to write furiously, making notes and tearing up sheets as he reordered his thoughts.

Sophie hadn't joined them. She checked on their children and then disappeared. She also needed to get her own thoughts clear. Halfway through lunch Henry thought he should find Sophie which he did. She was sitting in her anorak on a bench in Juliette's walled garden.

"It's a fuck up Henry, a complete fuck up," said Sophie, as he sat down. It was a word she very rarely used but it seemed appropriate for the occasion.

"I agree. It's not good," said Henry, but there'll be a way through. We just have to find it."

"Well we have to recognise we're homeless for a start."

"No, don't be daft. He then thought further and asked, "how come?"

"Found House is pledged to the bank to do the Folkestone project, but that's now so big its unfundable by us. It means that one day the banks will foreclose, and we will lose our London home. You heard Vincent call it a vanity project which will never make money because it is. It's too big, far too big for our needs - not just now, but forever."

"He's wrong. It's half our current storage capacity," argued Henry, "for which we are currently paying rent."

"More like a quarter," countered Sophie. "It started at half, but you forgot you've trebled the footprint."

"Then there's here, de Gressier. We've just made this our home only to discover we must find FFr 2.5 million to settle a liability, which was not ours, if we are to stay here. To make things worse it appears that no bank will help us. How long do you think it will be before someone forecloses and we are thrown out of here too?"

"It's not as bad as all that. We'll have to juggle some balls for a few months, may be a couple of years but it will all be okay. I know it will," said Henry confidently.

"Says the man who bankrupted himself in two simple moves and got his wife and children homeless," rejoined Sophie sarcastically.

"It looks bad now, but it will be getter. We just need to work through each of the problems, one by one."

"Without money Henry, without money! Please don't be so damn naïve." It was then that Sophie lost her temper. "Just go away," she shouted in anger. "Please just go away!"

Chapter 63

Château de Gressier November 1973

THE MEETING WITH Ainsworth, Delmas and Liard did not resume after lunch. The accountant and lawyer went back to their offices in Bordeaux. Ainsworth went into the offices of de Gressier to meet with Pierre Hilaire and understand the finances of Château de Gressier.

Upstairs in the Gallery, Henry summarised the issues discussed in the morning, slicing and dicing the problems each way, for Sophie's analysis had truly worried him. Before his Grandmother's death he had received nothing from her, but a job at de Gressier. The ownership of the de Gressier Estate had still not been gifted to him as she had promised. After her death, thanks to the liabilities of Rabôut estate, he still had nothing. It was this conclusion which made him focus on funding the Folkestone Project for if that was secure then Found House and his home would be secure too, as would his income. It was a good project. He would have to find an equity partner, that was all, and he would start tomorrow.

Sophie spent the afternoon playing with her children and it was early evening, while Victoria was bathing the children, when she went to look for Henry in his Gallery. "I think we should go for a walk," she said, "even though it's getting dark." The temper which Sophie had earlier displayed, had died as she had come to her own conclusions.

Once outside, Henry felt he could breathe again. Inside, he had been hot, sweaty and bothered as his problems crowded in around him. Sophie took his hands and led Henry towards the river on their usual walk. The moon was bright in the sky lighting their path.

"When did you change your mind on the Folkestone project," asked Sophie, as they started to walk.

"When you were ... poorly ... with the baby blues," Henry replied cautiously.

"I think we need to take the Folkestone Vault out of the equation," said Sophie. "I think it's crowding out everyone's thinking."

"But it made economic sense," said Henry, even wondering whether it did as he spoke those words. "We were saving significantly on engineering and backfill costs and if we don't make it underground and secure like every other cellar, then all I've got is a huge warehouse which cooks and freezes like everyone else's."

"But Henry, how are we going to fill it?" asked Sophie.

"It will take time," said Henry, "but once investors know that we have the best storage in the UK, I think we'll attract a brand-new clientele."

They walked on further.

"If we get the Paris Matterers Lunches going, then that's going to help fill that storage space isn't it?" said Sophie.

"I agree," said Henry.

"I haven't told you this," said, Sophie, "because I thought I might turn it down, but La Goviette and Circum have each offered me three-year contracts at a million pounds a year. If I accept these contracts then that would help fund our share of the Folkestone build costs, wouldn't it?"

Henry paused before answering. He needed to digest what he had just been told.

"Yes," said Henry, "and given what Ainsworth was saying, it would appear, if we did it properly, you could convert all that income into an investment in the building tax free."

I'm also sure there's enough money in my Trust account to meet our share of the build costs, at least for the next six months, maybe a year to keep the bank lending. I need to talk to my father."

"If you take those contracts where are we going to live?" asked Henry.

They'd reached the two Victor and Victoria benches and sat down on one of them.

"I'm not going back to London," said Sophie emphatically. "They tried to kill me there. We'll live here, until we are turfed-out, and then we'll decide."

"And the kids?" asked Henry.

"Let's hope your mother wants to stay here. If she does then they'll stay here. We'll just have to do a lot of commuting."

"Will you find time to do a new set of Matterers Lunches in Paris?" asked Henry.

"Everything I do for Goviette and Circum will be Paris based," she said. "So, yes, we'll be able to do the Matterers Lunches again. It will help improve my French."

"We could stop the Folkestone Vault project and do it a bit later," suggested Henry.

"No," Sophie said firmly. "It means putting our lives on hold as we wait for other people. No," she reaffirmed. "We don't do that."

Chapter 64

Château de Gressier November 1973

THAT EVENING, VICTORIA knocked on the door of the library in the Cottage and walked in to join Henry and Sophie who were gathered around the fire. The children were asleep but there was a mood of weariness in the house. "May I join you?" she asked.

Sophie stood up and offered Victoria a chair.

"I would like to accept your offer and move here permanently," she announced as she sat down.

"That's lovely," said Sophie, her face beaming. Henry nodded his approval.

"I will move in at Christmas, at the end of this term, it will be a good time. I will give instructions for my share of grandpa's trust to be wound up. It will provide about half a million pounds and my house will provide another £200,000. We can use this to help you with your current problems," she added having heard about them over supper.

"No, mother," said Henry firmly. "We can get through this without ..."

"I'm sure you can, but our house has never been really my home. It's just been somewhere for us to live. My home, my heart, my soul is here, and if I can help keep it, then that's what I want to do."

"Mum," said Henry, "it might not have been your home, but it's where my childhood was. It was my home. The last thing I want you to do is to sell your house. Let's keep it for a little while. Who knows what will happen here. It's all too risky."

"Okay, I'll keep the house," said Victoria. "But the trust, it's far too complicated. I'd still like to shut that down, pay the tax and then we can have the cash ready should you need it."

"Thanks, mum," said Henry.

"Yes, thank you," added Sophie, "but there is one thing."

Sophie explained to Victoria their strategy of her going back to work so they could fund their Vaults Project in Folkestone, but this was dependent upon Victoria being at de Gressier to help and supervise. When she heard what each of Sophie's contracts were worth, Victoria could only agree it was the sensible thing to do. Sophie was going to earn in one year what it would take Victoria two lifetimes of working as a teacher to earn.

Just as she was leaving to go to bed Victoria stopped. "Could I ask one thing," she said.

Henry and Sophie nodded.

"We need to have all the lights on."

"Why?" Sophie asked puzzled.

"The de Gressier lights light up the valley. It's the homing star for everyone in the village. It says all's right with the world. It's how it's always been, and it's how it should be again. It allows de Gressier to stand for something; it stands for hope!"

"Yes," said Henry enthusiastically, "it always used to be like that. We'll make it so again. Right now, we need some hope!"

That night, Sophie and Henry made love and, for the first time in their relationship, their lovemaking was mechanical and without thought for the other. Both were exhausted from the efforts of the day and ready for sleep, but it was their minds, troubled by the day, which stopped them giving as they had always done in the past. It had been an unhappy coupling, both wondering whether it had been worth the effort.

Chapter 65

Rabôut Estate, Bordeaux November 1973

THE NEXT DAY at 7.30 am Henry arrived at the Rabôut estate unannounced. It was after a 60-minute drive from Château de Gressier. He was sure that his appearance at such an early hour would be a shock.

Henry's first problem was how he should behave. As an owner he could and should go anywhere and do anything. As a guest, he should ask first. His conundrum was resolved when he decided that the house was private, and the rest of the vineyard was open to his inspection. For the next hour, Henry wandered everywhere, first just observing and then, when his list became too long to remember, he started to write his points down. All the vineyard hands noticed Henry poking about and so it was left to the vineyard's foreman to approach him.

"Can I help you?" he asked.

"No, thank you," said Henry.

"If I may ask, then what are you doing?"

"Waiting to see Monsieur Rabôut," replied Henry.

"May I ask why? asked the foreman.

"No, thank you," said Henry politely, keeping his identity close to his chest.

"May I ask who you are?"

"Monsieur Rabôut will know my name. It's just a little too early to disturb him," said Henry, enjoying his game and at the same time being impressed with the firm, but polite way which the foreman had been handling him.

"I think it's best that I take you to see Monsieur Rabôut," said the foreman. "Please follow me."

Henry was led to the house, which was open, where he was taken by the foreman immediately into the dining room. Henry was surprised because Château Rabôut was jam-packed, from wall to ceiling, with dusty stuffed dead animals staring down from on high, as though it were a Scottish hunting lodge in the most appalling clash of architectural styles.

Henry stood and waited, watched by the anxious foreman. Eventually, Gaston Rabôut arrived, and he and Henry shook hands, at which point Monsieur Rabôut introduced Henry to the foreman with the words, "Thomas Cannen meet Henry Guégan. He owns Château de Gressier and is the new owner of Rabôut estate."

"Fifty-one per cent owner," corrected Henry.

"Pleased to meet you," said the foreman totally shocked, for he had been told nothing of the deal that Gaston and Henry had done. The two men shook hands for the first time.

"Thank you, Thomas," said Monsieur Rabôut. "I'm sure we will be able to manage."

"Has this got something to do with Maurice?" asked Thomas.

Gaston didn't answer. Instead, he just pulled a face and nodded.

"I will come and say hello before I leave," said Henry at which point, Thomas smiled an anxious smile.

"Cesçon" said Rabôut, "excuse me, may I call you Cesçon? It's the name that everybody knows you by."

"It will be an honour," said Henry as they shook hands again. Henry immediately noticed a difference now he had accepted that he could be called by his nickname. It was gentler, less formal.

"I'm sorry to say my wife and I cannot live with the deal your grandmother negotiated," said Gaston.

"Monsieur," said Henry, "I cannot live with the deal my grandmother negotiated either."

"The books, the papers, the photograph albums, they're not on the list of my personal effects in the agreement, but they are mine, they mean nothing to anyone else. These can't be owned 50-50, what am I supposed to read, to look at every other page?" argued Gaston.

"Monsieur, your vineyard has not made money for the last five years. Each year, the losses get bigger. You know this. You have a huge maintenance problem and if it's not solved, by next harvest Rabôut estate will produce no wine, and it's going to take about 300,000 French francs to fix it."

"There has to be a change in our agreement," said Rabôut emphatically.

"Indeed there does," said Henry. "We should be investing what's needed into the estate on a 51-49 ratio but you haven't got the money to meet your share and I'm not prepared to put in 100% to make the business more valuable for you, and more expensive for me to buy the rest of your shares further down the line."

"I've lost hard," said Gaston. "I am not a man for partnerships. I expect to take counsel and make my own decisions. There has to be a change."

The two men were so busy making their point that they weren't hearing the message that the other was giving. However, it was in the way that Rabôut spoke that Henry could see what it was that made him capable of building such a wine estate. He liked him. He could see it clearly. He was used to doing business using the rules created 30 years ago, since when such rules had dramatically changed.

"You go first," said Rabôut.

"I have to buy all your remaining 49% in Rabôut estate for one franc. That's it. It's the most I will pay. In return, Rabôut estate, will pay both you and Madame Rabôut a pension."

"My wife and I have a pension under the deal with your grandmother," said Rabôut. "You are offering me nothing more."

"The deal that you have from my grandmother is worthless. Unless I put money into Château Rabôut, it's bankrupt. In those circumstances, it won't be around to pay you any pension."

"I could sell my 49% and I'm sure I would get more for it than that."

"There's no other buyer for your 49%," said Henry sharply. Honestly, one candlestick from a pair is always worth much less than half the value of the complete set and, in this case, given the financial state of the estate, your candlestick is worthless."

"How do I know Château Rabôut will be around to pay my pension?"

"You don't," said Henry sharply. "Your choice is a certainty of nothing, or a gamble of something."

"We might be able to deal Cesçon," said Rabôut. "On the estate, there's a little cottage. It's semi derelict. My wife and I want to move in there and make it our home. We want to take our possessions from here and go there, and what we take will be ours absolutely."

Henry and Gaston walked the 10 minutes to the cottage Gaston had spoken of. It was much larger than the term cottage would have suggested, but even so Henry knew that they would have to make some hard choices in moving out of the Château and downsizing into this place.

"I want to show you the cottage my son did up," said Gaston, walking another three or four minutes. Hidden in a wooded area, surrounded by a manicured garden, was a true French cottage, beautifully restored to picture post card quality on the outside and tastefully redecorated within.

"Is this cottage owned by the Estate?" asked Henry after they had wandered around.

"Yes, but it's occupied by my son. He did it up"

"I have a proposal" said Henry, after some moment's contemplation. "We'll do up the cottage as you ask and we will lease that one to you, and the other one to Robert, rent free for the rest of your and his life."

"And there will be no rent?" asked Gaston, not having heard properly as he had come out without his hearing aid.

"No rent, no service charge, nothing. You just pay for property taxes, water and electricity. The things you use. Mrs Rabôut and you can stay here until the end of your days. This means you could leave here, and it could be rented out, with you getting the rental income until the last day either of you or Madam Rabôut lives," said Henry.

"And I can take the family papers and heirlooms," confirmed Gaston.

"Yes, everything and anything from the inside of the château. You can take each and every one of the stags heads, if you want!" said Henry pointedly.

Both men had got exactly what they wanted out of the negotiations. Each now felt able to move forward with their lives.

Let's start getting this place fixed up," said Henry confidently. "The deadline is Easter."

Chapter 66

Rabôut Estate, Bordeaux November 1973

HENRY WENT TO see Thomas Cannen while Gaston Rabôut went to see his wife to tell her the news about them moving into the Cottage.

"It's pretty damn desperate here," said Henry, as his opening remarks.

"You can say that again," replied Cannen. "I have several questions, but my first one is do I report to you or Monsieur Rabôut?" he asked.

"Monsieur Rabôut and I have just agreed that I am acquiring 100% of Château Rabôut, so you now report to me."

Cannen nodded as he absorbed the news

"Do you live on the Estate?" asked Henry, more by way of conversation than fact finding.

"No, we have our own house in the village," said Cannen.

"Are you married?" Henry asked.

"Yes, with three children, and we're all from these fields" he said pointing in the direction of the vines. "I've made the wine here for the last 25 years. No one else has done it but me," said Cannen proudly. "You need me," he proclaimed.

"I am sure that's the case," replied Henry. "Certainly, I hope it's the case." Then he added cautiously, "but we'll see."

They discussed the jobs list which Henry had jotted down during his early morning inspection. Cannen added extensively, proving his knowledge of the estate. The two men got on well together. There was a comfortable repartee of a partnership, with one just slightly the senior partner.

"Do you have a pension from the estate?" asked Henry.

"No, it's been a contention with Monsieur Rabôut for some time. In fact, he doesn't pay me particularly well."

"That's because the estate doesn't make money," said Henry.

"And that's because he sells his wine to the locals too cheaply," said Cannen, the annoyance biting into his tone.

"Precisely," said Henry. "We're going to increase the price, and immediately. I can sell all the wine which goes into the local market at full price. And that's what we're going to do." The locals can have a discount but not at the current 70% rate and not at the volumes they are getting now. They have been making fools out of you.

"Monsieur," said Cannen. "I need some security from you if I'm to do all this work that you ask. I don't think it is fair that I spend another ten years working doubly hard for no gain. I think if I cannot look to my financial future here, I will have to look elsewhere."

Henry stopped and looked Cannen straight in the eye. This was not a man who bluffed, and Henry knew he needed him.

"Here's my proposal. In one year's time, if what's on that jobs list has been substantially completed, then you will get an annuity from Château du Rabôut equal to 10% of the profits for as long as you or your wife shall live. It's exactly the same deal as my grandmother has with the de Gressier general manager. If we don't get on, or the estate doesn't improve as I expect, then we will be parting company. It's a binary decision: in with pension or out without one. Is that fair? asked Henry.

"If you confirm it in writing I will meet my part of the bargain," said Cannen.

"Then I will meet mine," said Henry.

Both men stood up and shook hands.

As he drove back to Château de Gressier, Henry wondered how he was going to explain to Sophie and Ainsworth that he had agreed to spend more money doing up a cottage at the Rabôut estate when they were so hard up. But, with all the shares of Château Rabôut under his control, he was sure that he would be able to buy the necessary equipment that the estate needed on hire purchase, saving his own cash resources. He thought that his mother's money from her grandfather's trust fund would help pay to do up the cottage, and perhaps even the Château, after Gaston and his wife had moved out. It would allow the best wine buyers to stay at the Château Rabôut. This had worked well to encourage investors in Château de Gressier wine, and Henry was sure it would be the same for Rabôut wines too.

Henry knew that someday soon, Cannen would need to know about the counterfeiting, but not yet. They had to get to know each other much better before he was let into the secret. At least, thought Henry, a plan was beginning to come together.

Chapter 67

London December 1973 - Easter 1974

SUNETTA WAS WELCOMED warmly by the London Contemporary Dance School but there was no going back. It was now in the grip of a new generation of students excited with trying new things. She took a couple of dance classes, but it was obvious to all that this once top scholar was, at the age of 24, no longer dance fit. With that, she was discarded by the new clique as a 'has been.'

Sunetta cast around for work. Courtesy of Roedean, which had given her Pitman's shorthand and typing skills, albeit now very rusty, she found temporary employment through one of the London staff agencies. The fact that she could add a London University degree to her CV meant that she was able to get the better jobs away from the typing pool, but there was nothing inspiring about typing from someone's terrible dictation or their scrawled handwriting.

Christmas Day was Sunetta's worse day of the year. She spent it completely on her own, not seeing anyone at all. She thought she might go to the local pub but, outside the door, she felt it was a sign of desperation to go in, so she returned to her flat where, in a haze of unappealing television, she thought about all the men she felt she had truly loved, from Hank Bellanger through to John Harrison, and wondered where they were now.

Boxing Day was a very much better day for Sunetta, as she spent it with her brother, Big Joe. She was so proud of him. He had not joined the army as he once thought. Instead, after University in Manchester and doing a master's degree at Warwick, he had been accepted to do a doctorate at Imperial College, researching into the electrical storage properties of a highly focused set of materials. As he had predicted, digital technologies were now changing the world and he was meeting his ambition to be a part of it. His only problem was that his research grant was minimal, so he was supporting himself with extra money working at waiting tables - and the one day no waiter is allowed off is Christmas Day.

Sunetta cooked their Christmas dinner in Big Joe's tiny studio apartment after which they walked the streets and parks of London. As they walked, it was a throwaway line from Big Joe which was to set the direction for the next stage in Sunetta's life. "You should join a gym," he suggested.

Neither Rick Bussell nor Sunetta Daunier stood a chance. Immediately they saw each other there was an immediate animal attraction. Bussell's appetite for women was as voluminous as Sunetta's was for men. Apart from being the opposite sex, there was one other thing different between the two of them and that was Bussell laughed. He joked and laughed at everything as though he had no care in the world, whereas Sunetta's default position was to be serious. As is often said, an ugly man can laugh a woman into bed but, when you have the chiselled good looks of Bussell, with the toned body of an athlete, it doesn't even need a bed, as Sunetta found via a rapid but very energetic coupling in the gym's towel store cupboard. He passed her test and was invited back for seconds and thirds.

Bussell was the manager of the gym Sunetta had joined, first as a customer and then, a few days later, without any qualifications, as a member of the gym staff. She led dance and aerobic workout classes. Immediately after Christmas these grew in popularity as customers put into effect their New Year's resolutions. Bussell's area manager noted that there wasn't the usual sudden drop off in the number of attendances, which normally take place after the post-Christmas surge, in Sunetta's classes. She was proving her worth to the business.

Bussell had one other attraction for Sunetta. He was always where 'it' was happening. If there was an event in London, which there was every day, Bussell was invited and Sunetta too. From film premiers to fashion show parties, to the opening of the latest club; Sunetta found she was living in the fast lane - a fast lane supported by a growing and endless supply of cocaine. It was Bussell's fuel which made him alert and gave him confidence to be the life and soul of every party. Sunetta found cocaine made each one of her pleasure receptors aroused and far more sensitive. She found a feeling of freedom and invincibility. Life was tremendous fun.

It was after working in the gym for about eight weeks when a head office audit revealed that Sunetta had no right to work in the UK as she had arrived on a South African passport and a visitors' visa. She pleaded she was also a French citizen but her out of date French passport left behind in Cape Town was of no help. She had to leave.

There are some problems which are easily solved after fifteen minutes of drug fuelled love making, and so it was with Sunetta's work permit problem. Rick Bussell and she would get married. Then, as the wife of a British Citizen, she would get full residential status and be allowed both to stay and to work.

It was on Easter Saturday when Sunetta walked into Westminster Council Chambers on the arm of her brother for the simplest of marriage services. Half an hour later she left as Mrs Rick Bussell and with her new British Passport in her full name of Mrs Harriet Harmony Bussell.

The wedding reception was small, lively and alcoholic, made up of people none of whom Big Joe liked. He thought they were all transient friends. Meanwhile at New Found Estate both David and Satutu were in a deep depression. They had been invited but David knew he could not go and Satutu was not prepared to travel without him. They were finding it hard to comfort each other. It was a long way from the wedding in the local church, surrounded by all those who had seen and enjoyed Sunetta growing up, which they had both secretly envisioned.

Chapter 68

Paris January to Easter 1974

SOPHIE AND HENRY were working themselves into a frenzy.

When you're being paid a million dollars a year by La Goviette, the cosmetics company, the photographic and filming schedule is cruel. When you are paid the same amount to be the face of Circum, a mid-price international clothing chain, you must wear what they are selling, unless it is top designer wear. Then, when a watch range, jewellery designer, hotel group and other product endorsements are added to the mix, which nearly doubled Sophie's income, it put her under constant pressure to pay attention, not only to her look but her every move.

Just as it was before she had children, it became impossible for Sophie to nip down to the shops. Even a simple shopping expedition has to be planned, and this doesn't just happen if you have to make sure that you do nothing to damage the brands which are paying you. It requires hard work.

Sophie's booker was delighted that she was back in the game, and she drove Sophie's schedule hard to the point that, when Sophie got back to Château de Gressier on Saturday evenings, all she wanted to do on Sunday was to sleep. There was one advantage, there were no catwalks or fashion weeks in her schedule.

Henry was driving everyone, including himself, hard. He was in a panic to get Maison Gelina, the shop purchased in the centre of Paris from the Rabôut's, refurbished and opened.

Maison Gelina was opposite the Church of Madeleine, near the Place de la Concorde. It had been an excellent buy. Henry's grandmother had negotiated a deal at well below its market price.

There were two things which stopped him selling and taking the profit on Maison Gelina. Firstly, Rabôuts' lawyer had insisted on an 'embarrassment' clause in the contract which meant that if the house was sold in the three years after the purchase, then the majority of the profits would go to Gaston and Robert. But most importantly, with Sophie spending so much time in Paris, he thought he would fashion it into 'Found House number two', and make it a second family home. It was this which created the biggest of challenges.

Maison Gelina was old in every aspect from its dusty velvet curtains to its polished oak floors. It was in the style of a Paris bordello of the Edwardian era. The only area for customers was fifteen feet between the shop front and its big, imposing counter. There was a huge stock room both behind and in the basement which no one ever saw. Keeping as much of the original as possible, Henry wanted the whole area opened up, with the bottles stacked on display so the customers could touch and feel the bottles. The counter had to be made smaller and moved to the side, so that customers could wander the whole store.

Henry took French architects and designers to Found House and explained in great detail its operations, even to the point of the chemistry lab, which, even though he knew it would hardly ever be used, he felt gave confidence to his investors. He carefully articulated the style he wanted to achieve but, as the refurbishment work progressed, he found he was fighting every point with the architect, who seemed to think that everything could be replicated in stained pine rather than using the existing polished mahogany which is what Henry wanted. "It has to look authentic because it is authentic," he demanded.

It was when Henry found the shops prized antique brass lamps strewn on a skip, that he lost his temper. He sacked the architect and project manager and took charge of the work. His problem was that he could not start the product recall until he had contacted the big investors, and he didn't want to contact the big investors until he could invite them to a Matterers Lunch at Maison Gelina, and he couldn't invite them to one of those until the refurbishment was complete because, at that moment, the shop was a shell, and the rest of the house uninhabitable.

It was into this depressing situation that Robert Rabôut appeared at Maison Gelina just a few days before Easter. Henry had agreed with him that he need not come to the shop during the refurbishment. It was important to them both that Robert should look after his son until after his trial, and ensure he pleaded guilty. It was with news of Maurice's sentence that Robert returned to his shop to see progress, or more precisely a distinct lack of it. It was obvious for everyone to see that Henry was in trouble with the project.

"He's got 16 years," said Robert to Henry, immediately they met, referring to Maurice's prison sentence. He tried hard to make it sound as though he wasn't blaming Henry, but he found it almost impossible for, in part, he was.

"I am sorry," said Henry. "It's been a bad experience."

"He's got life, of course, but his tariff has been set at 16 years," said Robert. "It means he'll be eligible for parole in about 8 years."

"He'll still be a young man," said Henry, trying to find something consoling to say.

"I think Gaston has forgiven him. At least he was in court to see him sentenced, and then he visited him in prison as soon as he could."

"That's good," said Henry.

"My sister and her daughters aren't going to forgive him though. They depended on their annual dividend from the vineyard to make their life comfortable. Now they have nothing," continued Robert. "It's made things very difficult between us."

Henry just pulled a face, for what else could he say.

Over a mug of tea, Henry outlined to Robert what he was trying to achieve with Maison Gelina: "old authenticity and quality in a modern setting. It was Sophie who put the style into Found House," he explained. "She gave it class by taking the very best of the antiques, those that had been in the family for generations, and re-setting them for the modern times." As he said these words, he realised how desperately he missed her.

"Did you see the cottage which is close to where my father is going to live," asked Robert.

"Yes, I really loved it. It's just how I want Maison Gelina to be refurbished."

"I did that," said Robert. "Did you know?"

"Yes," said Henry. "Your father was very proud of your achievements there."

"Have you ten minutes?" asked Robert.

Henry nodded, and with that they were off, in a quick walk across Paris to a beautiful house with a walled garden.

"This is my last project. I bought the house and converted it into four apartments. There's one left," said Robert.

Henry was given a tour of the house. The style was just as he wanted for Maison Gelina. The stone flagon floors, the preserved original wood, even to the strength of the new brass fittings on the heavy doors, showed everything had been done with quality and care.

"I would like the job of refurbishing my father's cottage," said Robert, after the tour was over. "He was supposed to be in by Easter, but nothing has been started. Its why I've come to see you."

"I know. I scream at architects and builders every day and still nothing gets done."

"Then you should appoint me to project manage it for you."

"What, for a fee?" asked Henry.

"Of course, you're paying others and getting nowhere. You should pay me instead and I'll get the job done. It's what I do."

They walked back the way they came.

"How long did it take you to do the place we've just seen?" asked Henry.

"Sixteen weeks from the day I got vacant possession of the place."

"How long would it take you to finish Maison Gelina if you started it now?" enquired Henry.

"To put it just like the place I've done?" asked Robert.

Henry nodded, and then added, "but obviously, to the architect's design and drawings."

They walked on for some little way, both in contemplation.

"The bulk of the heavy reconstruction work has been done. The first fixings all appear to be in. It's just plastering, second fitting and decorating. That's say twelve to sixteen weeks. The big problem will be the shop fitting, keeping the counter the same while making it smaller. Overall, I would say 20 weeks."

"Would you take over running the refurbishment of Maison Gelina as project manager?" asked Henry, realising Robert's skills were the obvious solution to his problem.

"Depends," said Robert.

"On?"

"I want the same deal on my cottage at Rabôut Estate in the new deal agreed with my father," said Robert.

Henry was confused for in his offer to Gaston he had made it clear that Robert would have a lifetime tenancy on his cottage too. Hadn't his father told him he wondered. Why was he raising it now, some three and a half months later?

The pause in conversation allowed Robert to add, "and, as I said, I want to project manage the doing up of my father's cottage."

"And payment?" asked Henry adding for clarity, "your fee?"

"My job is for only two and a half days a week, it's all I've ever worked in the shop," said Robert.

The word shop interested Henry, for it showed exactly how he saw the business.

"Do you have any other building projects on?" asked Henry.

"No," replied Robert.

"Okay," said Henry, "here's the revised deal. For the next year, you work full time, and we'll double your salary. You finish the building work here in twelve weeks and for that you'll get a lifetime interest in your cottage at Rabôut Estate as you asked."

"Sixteen weeks," said Robert.

"Okay, sixteen weeks, and then you'll organise the refurbishment of your father's cottage so he's out of the Château by Easter of next year."

"Yes, I'll do that."

"Oh," said Henry shocked that it had been agreed so easily. "You need to come to three or four of our Matterers Lunches in London to see what we do."

"I've already been to one," said Robert.

"Well come to more. When I started, I thought this business was about wine and I was going to make it about the science of wine. I now know what it's about," Henry continued. "Relationships, this business is about relationships." He was speaking as though he had found the meaning of life.

Robert stopped in the street, whilst Henry walked on a few paces. Realising that he wasn't accompanied, Henry stopped too. He turned around to see Robert walking towards him with his hand outstretched.

"It's agreed, but I have a feeling that one year is going to turn into many," said Robert as the two men shook hands.

Back at Maison Gelina, Henry went through the drawings and his plans in detail. He walked the building, saying what he wanted, describing the lighting, the plugs, where the furniture would go, even the flowers. Just as they were about to start their third tour, Robert stopped him.

"Henry, I've got it, okay, I've got it! Now please leave, go and get some sleep, and only come back once a week." It was obvious to Robert that Henry was becoming incoherent from tiredness.

Henry agreed and then added, "a week on Monday, you have to come to Found House. Be there for 10:00 a.m."

"London 10:00 a.m.," repeated Robert. "I'll be there. Now, if you want to do yourself a favour, piss off and get some sleep!"

Henry walked to his car, which was not so far away. He was so exhausted he didn't know what he was going to do next. What the hell was he supposed to be doing? He didn't know. He closed his eyes and immediately fell asleep. It was eleven o'clock at night when he woke up. He was frozen to the core. He wanted to tell Sophie he was okay, but he didn't know where she was.

Henry went back to Maison Gelina which was all shut up. He phoned his mother who was still up.

"Sophie's staying with Imra. I spoke to her earlier," Victoria said.

"Whose Imra?" asked Henry.

"Imra Blanche, she's a model with the same agency. Sophie's renting a room from her when she's in Paris. Hasn't she said?" asked Victoria.

Henry didn't answer because he wasn't sure.

"Don't phone her now because she'll be asleep," continued Victoria. "She said she'll be there tomorrow evening and then, the next morning, she's catching the train from Paris to Bordeaux. Why don't you come with her?"

A phone call with Sophie's booker made sure that Sophie and Henry were on the same train to Bordeaux. They were pleased to be with each other and sat closely side by side, but it was strange for Henry noticed some very slight changes in Sophie. He couldn't say exactly what they were apart from one thing. On the train journey she ordered a vodka and tonic to drink. He had never known her drink alcohol until that very moment. He observed but said nothing. Somehow it didn't seem right that he did so.

Chapter 69

London September 1974

SUNETTA AND RICK honeymooned drug free in Casablanca and the Marrakesh in Morocco. It was in this spirit of freedom that Sunetta's relationship with Rick moved from one of lust to love. However, their summer holiday in Bali, taken in early September, caused immense difficulties in their relationship, because she found Rick was more in love with cocaine than her.

Although Indonesia drugs laws are some of the strictest in Asia, executing anyone involved in the trafficking of drugs and imprisoning anyone with drugs in their possession, Rick would search the bars to feed his habit. By the time they boarded the plane home their relationship was over, but Sunetta was not yet able to admit it to herself. Whenever she closed her eyes and thought of him, his Adonis body would fill her mind and she knew she could not let him go.

Immediately Sunetta and Rick walked into the gym on their first day back from their holidays, it was evident that there was something wrong. In Rick's office there was a team of people from head office waiting for them. Two of the head office team peeled Sunetta away to interview her. For ninety minutes she was asked questions which she could not answer because they had no relevance to the work she had been doing, or her experience. Rick on the other hand, after just under an hour of being quizzed quite intensely told his interviewers he needed to go to the men's room. He never returned. He just went through the back door and walked away. He had been stealing money, a lot of money and Sunetta, as his wife and work colleague, was assumed to be an accomplice.

Rick's method of stealing had been so breathtakingly simple that the internal auditors wondered why they hadn't included safeguards to stop what he did in their procedures. For every fourth or fifth new customer who signed up as a gym member, Rick gave them not a gym direct debit form but a bank standing order form which had an account name, bank sort code number and account number which he had set up. Every month, money poured into this account which Rick then emptied to fund his lifestyle. His deception would have gone on much longer except some of the standing orders which went to his bank account included payments for locker hire; and with one hundred percent of the lockers hired out there had to be some reason why locker income in the monthly management accounts was below budget. It was when the auditors searched to find the answer that Rick's crime was discovered. As they investigated, wads of Rick's photocopied standing order forms were found.

After five hours of interviews, in which Sunetta was bullied unmercifully, the Gym's owners concluded that she probably had no idea what Rick had been up to. However, they argued that since she had been a direct beneficiary of his crime she should pay back half of what they estimated Rick had taken. Completely overwhelmed, she signed a direct debit agreeing that one quarter of her monthly salary would be used to pay back half of what Rick had stolen. As soon as they had this agreement in their hands, they fired her for not having the right qualifications for the job she was doing.

It was a visibly destressed and angry Sunetta who got home that night. She was very scared of the argument she was about to have with her husband. Instead, she found that Rick had packed up all his things and left, taking the car, on which she had signed the HP agreement, with him. All she had was a note which read: 'Sorry, but you have to admit it was all such damn good fun. See you. Love. Rick x.'

If this was a low point for Sunetta, it was about to get worse as two thugs, sent by Rick's drug dealer, threatened to 'cut her' unless she paid what he owed. When she argued that she had no money they simply gave her the name of a local Madame reckoning that, with her figure, she could earn what they needed in one week working in a brothel. It was then that she got the phone call from her landlord asking why the rent hadn't been paid.

In haste, Sunetta packed a few things and went to stay with Big Joe in his studio apartment telling him no more than Rick and she had separated. Sunetta slept in Big Joe's bed, as he manfully volunteered to sleep on the couch.

That first night in Big Joe's flat, as Sunetta struggled to get to sleep, she thought about men. How she hated them. They mess with your body and mess up your brains, and yet their touch was so magical she knew she would never be able to live without one in her life. How could they make life so ridiculously complex, she wondered?

In the early morning, just as sunlight was breaking through the windows, Sunetta contemplated her options. It seemed as though they were very few. She contemplated asking her parents for money, but that would mean admitting defeat which she wasn't prepared to do. However, she accepted that this was a better option than working as a prostitute, but then she wondered how hard that would be?

It was while these thoughts were going through her mind that Sunetta remembered something her father would say to her: "Girl, it was a lack of thinking that got you into this mess, and it will only be clarity of thinking which will get you out." These were wise words for they helped Sunetta summarise her problem in two parts. She needed both money and a job now. She solved her immediate money problem by applying for two credit cards, which she had never had before.

The job problem was more difficult for, without a clean reference from the gym, she was almost certainly unemployable. It was then that she remembered her father's agent; the man who sold New Found Estate's wines into the English market. She would go and find him and get a job there. Her references would be courtesy of New Found Estate.

Chapter 70

France Easter to September 1974

EACH DAY THAT went by Henry was getting more and more worked up at the lack of progress in recalling every bottle of Château Rabôut sold by Maurice Rabôut over the previous five years. He was certain that any moment now the secret would be in the public domain and with it they would be finished.

Ainsworth had calculated the liability at around FFr 3.5 million, FFr 1 million higher than calculated by Juliette. Slowly, but surely, the liability was rising as more information became known.

Henry very quickly contacted his investors telling them he would be happy to buy back their Château Rabôut wine making the excuse that there had been a bad batch of corks which made some wine taste sour or vinegary. Some wondered whether it was a con intent on buying back their investment cheaply but most agreed because they realised that, once the problem was widely known in the investment market, their vintage wines of Château Rabôut would rapidly fall in value. He didn't dare contact anyone else until Maison Gelina was completed.

Henry devised a refraction system which looked through the glass into the contents of the bottle to spot the counterfeit wines. This meant that no bottle had to be opened. The original plan had been to destroy the counterfeit wine but Henry, ever the entrepreneur, set off a secret operation in a rented warehouse where the labels were soaked off, and a posh-looking label with no claim as to provenance were reapplied. These bottles were then sold in job lots to Henry's supermarket customers as a cheap table wine. It amused him when one of the newspaper wine columnist's wrote this recycled wine up as their purchase of the week.

The release of the money from Sophie's trust and the money she was earning from the modelling work had meant that good progress was made with their Vaults project near Folkestone. Henry had been able to agree a mortgage on Maison Gelina property in Paris to pay for the refurbishment work, but to Ainsworth's frustration no one was prepared to lend any money against either Château de Gressier or Château Rabôut. In fact, the Château Rabôut's bankers were demanding that their loan be repaid in such a manner that all the running costs for Rabôut's Estate were having to be paid by Château de Gressier and Henry's wine trading businesses. Everywhere was very short of cash. There was a constant pressure to find money to pay people, and the wine buyback programme was making everything very much worse.

It was a furious Ainsworth who phoned Henry to complain. "Did you know Serge Michaud has been telling the banks about the problems at Rabôut and the buyback programme?" he shouted down the phone.

"Whose Serge Michaud?" asked Henry, not immediately recognising the name.

"The former President of the Syndicate des Vins de Bordeaux overseeing the buy-back process," shouted Ainsworth, now frustrated that Henry didn't understand the problem. "It's why we can't borrow any money. We've effectively been blacklisted."

In a long conversation Henry learnt how Michaud's wife had boasted to her sister of her husband's very important new appointment. The only trouble was that the sister was the wife of the chairman of the bank which lent Château Rabôut its money. Within days the news had travelled throughout the top echelons of the French banking industry with the result that Château de Gressier and Château Rabôut's credit ratings were shot to pieces. No one would lend them a centime.

Henry protested long and hard to Jacques Chirac, who was the Minister of the Interior, about Michaud. Chirac agreed that Michaud should be dismissed straight away but counselled Henry against an angry sacking, warning that the man still had the capability to do de

Gressier, Rabôut and the wine industry of France tremendous harm. Chirac agreed to speak to a couple of banks to try and persuade them to provide the lines of credit Henry needed, but his promise of help turned to be nothing more than a politician's promise - worthless.

To make matters worse it was now obvious that, after a warm and dry May and June, the cold wet weather in August and for the rest of the growing season meant that the 1974 vintage was going to be one of the worst for very many years, with prices and sales reflecting the poor quality of the harvest. However, if things were bad, they were just about to get a whole lot worse.

Chapter 71

London October 1974

IT WAS VINCENT Ainsworth who interviewed Harriet Bussell, née Sunetta Daunier. The letter from New Found Estate which accompanied Sunetta's letter was a master in discretion for it said that, if there was a job opening available in Found Vintner's, then David Daunier would be grateful if Harriet Bussell could be considered for the post, as she had proven to be an excellent and reliable employee when she worked for them.

There had been no thoughts of a employing anyone else, for one reason, cash flow did not permit it, but as Ainsworth interviewed Harriet he concluded that it was Henry who was creating the block. His workload was creating an inefficiency which was stopping things from progressing as fast as they should. Harriet Bussell had the potential to make a good assistant to Henry. Her only weakness was she did not speak fluent French, but with 'A' level French included in Harriet's curriculum vitae, he hoped that she should be able to manage.

Sunetta recognised Henry as Hank the moment she saw him, and her heart jumped several leaps; except his name was different. She had known him as Hank Bellanger and yet now he was called Henry Guégan. This name change caused Sunetta to doubt her first thoughts as Henry clearly didn't recognise her. He was no taller than when they first met, but his body had filled out. Further, the long hair of his youth had now been cut 'executive-short' which changed the way his face looked, but eyes never changed. Each time she looked into his eyes she knew that this man was Hank Bellanger and her first love. However, her need for this job meant that, at that moment, Harriet, nicknamed Sunetta, said nothing as she thought if she did it might put her job at risk.

Henry's mind was a million miles away from the briefing he was supposed to be giving Sunetta as phone call after phone call, and interruption upon interruption disturbed his day, and every other day. He would admit much later that he found her stunningly attractive, and therefore a pleasing sight around the office, but with the pressure he was under Harriet's physicality was the furthest thing from his mind.

For a week Harriet shadowed Henry. Not once did he give her anything to do as he'd never had a personal assistant before. Everyone else who worked for him had a specific purpose with a job description which he had created. It was only when Henry was out of the office, and with the help of Ainsworth, did Harriet organise herself a desk with phone and typewriter in the main office where everyone else sat. She started by taking every one of Henry's incoming calls. She soon found that by asking around she could deal with about three quarters of everything he was being asked. Very slowly Harriet was making herself indispensable.

Chapter 72

Folkestone November 1974

"I HAVE A message from Vincent. He says it's urgent and you're to phone him at home immediately," said Harriet to Henry, when she eventually spoke to him at Maison Gelina. It was 10 pm and Sunetta was still at her desk. She was trying to work through the piles of paper which Henry had to deal with. Much of it had been superseded by other paperwork so it just needed filing. Without the clutter, Sunetta was certain that order could be created out of Henry's chaos.

Henry phoned the accountant at home. He was obviously in bed.

"Our problems have just got much bigger at the Vaults," exclaimed Ainsworth. "Bookham's solicitors have just served a letter-before-action on us over the access road. They've written on behalf of the farmer we bought the land from. He's claiming three hundred thousand pounds in damages, demanding that we restore the road to its earlier state within twenty-one days, and to make it worse, there are a couple of trailers loaded full of hay now blocking the road, so the contractors can't get in or out."

"What are you talking about?" said Henry. "All we've done is tart up a fucked-up old track."

"But that's the least of our worries," continued Ainsworth. "We're being told we've built a complete white elephant unless we install ventilation from top to bottom."

"Don't be ridiculous," said Henry. "We've spent weeks with the planning people to make sure we got this right."

"Well it appears Kent County Council have changed their minds."

"They can't do that, can they?" asked Henry.

The contractors are saying they've never seen anything like it," commented Ainsworth. "They say it's as though someone has set the whole of Kent County Council against us."

"Has our lawyer seen the letter from the farmer?" asked Henry.

"Yes, they're getting their files out and will report back to me in the morning."

"Okay, I'll be at the Vaults in the morning," said Henry.

"What about the lighting," Henry asked. He had, the week before, discovered he had commissioned the whole building without specifying where the lighting and electrics were to go.

"Our fault," said Ainsworth.

"Fuck, No!" exclaimed Henry, "how?" It was not the answer he wanted. It meant he had to find another £76,000 if he was to complete his Folkestone project.

"Apparently you said you didn't want to make up your mind how the storage was going to work, and therefore where the lighting was to run, until you saw the actual space, so all that was agreed was three phase electricity coming to a distribution board on each floor" answered Ainsworth.

"Oh God yes, that's right. I forgot. For Pete's sake don't tell Sophie, not for a while longer, at least not until it's all completed, otherwise she'll go ballistic."

"Yeh, yeh," said Ainsworth, glad that it was a man and not a woman who was lying next to him.

Henry had planned to go to London the next day, but now his plans were changed. He drove through the night to Calais, where he caught the first boat to Dover, grabbing some sleep on the ferry.

At the entrance to the drive leading up to the entrance to the Vaults were two trailers loaded with straw bales. They went from one side of the entrance to the other, standing well over fifteen foot tall, making it impossible for anything to pass.

Henry's driveway up to the Vaults was all exactly as he had envisioned. It had been designed as a double-width road capable of taking the heaviest of lorries, laid with drainage and carefully edged kerbstones, just waiting for its topcoat of tarmac. The newly laid grass seed had taken to give the wide verges a light green velvet look, and with an avenue of trees planted equi-distant on either side of the road there was a feeling of majesty about the entrance. The farmer's old fencing had been destroyed years before, so Henry had replaced it with strong, ranch-style fencing all the way up and around the old chalk pit. He was certain that putting up the fencing was in the purchase agreement for the land and, as he surveyed all that was before him, he was really pleased for he was seeing what had been in his mind's eye.

The huge concrete box was built with only one entrance high on the top floor to the right. The biggest task remaining was to backfill the land and cover the roof so that no one would ever know that there had been a quarry there. The road, to which the farmer was objecting, could then be linked up to the entrance of the Vaults and it would be ready to be opened. How could anyone object to this? he asked himself.

Henry drove into Folkestone and took a room in the Burlington Hotel where he started to work the phones. His first call was to the contractor, to tell them to move the hay bales.

"We can't get involved in a civil dispute," he was told by the contract manager, who promised to be back on site as soon as the bales were cleared, adding that every day there was a delay was adding to the cost. The call was just about to end when the contract manager said, "Can you hold? My boss wants to talk to you."

"Hello, I'm Fergus McDonald," said a voice on the phone in a very English accent, belying the obvious Scottish name. "I'm the chief executive here. Do you mind if I ask you a question?"

"No, go ahead," said Henry, a little puzzled by the interjection.

"Are you a Mason?" he asked.

"No, why?"

"Because there's something that smells about this whole thing. It's as though a gang has come together to stop or blackmail you."

"What do you mean?"

"We hate working in Kent, as we always get this kind of problem. Most of the county's designated a deprived area, and gets extra government grants because of it, but believe me, it's only sodding deprived because the council employs some of the most incompetent jobsworths in the whole country."

"What's being a Mason got to do with it?" asked Henry.

"Because you'll find it a darn sight easier to sort it out if you are."

Henry was stunned by this remark. "Are you sure?" he asked.

"Yes. Just let us know when we can get back on site," said McDonald, finishing the call.

Henry moved constantly from his bed, to the armchair, and back to the bed again as he contemplated what he'd been told. Could it be that a local farmer had such political influence that he was able to stop work and force him into paying a ransom to settle the problem? In France, the Mayor is everything; displease him and your life is purgatory; but a Masonic farmer in England wielding such influence? He'd never heard of such a thing.

His next call was to Pierre at Château de Gressier and then Thomas at Château Rabôut. They were to hire mini-vans and get every one of their male workers, including the part-timers, to come to Folkestone immediately. The two men who had worn the black suits at the meeting in the George Cinq Hotel were told to bring their 'uniforms' with them.

Henry's next call was to the private detective he'd used on the counterfeiting investigation. He was to get down here as soon as possible and investigate what the hell was happening.

After that, he phoned Sophie's PR agent. "Get down here fast," he ordered. "We have one hell of a story breaking."

His final call was to his solicitors. "We now know what this is all about," said the senior partner. "I've spoken to Bookham's lawyer. They say he is prepared to sell you the land within the fencing for a hundred thousand pounds."

"But that's more than I paid for the whole sodding site. What did I pay? Sixty thousand pounds?"

"Including the option, fifty-five thousand pounds plus a bit," answered Henry's lawyer. "I can tell you how they've come up with their figures. They're saying that the land, with planning permission, is now worth three hundred thousand pounds, and their ransom-strip is worth about one-third of the land value."

"What about the wayleaves?" asked Henry.

"Under the contract, you have the right to run water, electricity, and all services, telephones, under the road right up to the edge of his land, which goes up to the footpath next to the road, but he's claiming a right to the land which is the other side of your boundary. We think, well, we know, this land belongs to Kent County Council, but he says it's his and he has the right to fence it in. He also says you have no rights to plant the trees, nor any rights to lay the road, which you've done."

"So what? I either dig up the road, tear down some trees and have no services or I pay him a hundred thousand pounds. Is that it?"

"That's about it," said Henry's lawyer.

Well fuck 'im," said Henry. "I ain't driving millions of pounds worth of wine over some shit potholed road because of some fuckin' farmer. I'll come back to you as soon as I've decided what to do." He put down the phone firmly and leaned back in his chair to absorb what he had been told.

The next hour was spent on the phone to his new architect, the first was sacked when they'd forgotten about the basics of water and electricity, let alone where it was to go.

"We thought about ventilation," said the associate partner responsible for mechanical and electrical work who was on the conference call with his engineer. "We raised this issue with you. It's in the minutes of a meeting which were sent to you immediately afterwards."

Henry did not remember.

"We were certain, in fact we all agreed that the activities you were undertaking inside the Vaults were outside the likely scope," said the associate partner, not making himself clear.

"Can you remind me why?" asked Henry.

"Now we are in the EEC we're going to have to obey their regulations, and those responsible for planning in Folkestone are insisting we future-proof this site," said the Partner.

Henry started to remember a conversation about how British Civil Servants were gold plating all regulations which came out of Europe.

"It's thought that there will be a regulation which will require all premises involved in the processing of fermented products to have ventilation," said the Associate Partner.

"Nitrogen and certain dioxides are heavy and force out oxygen, which means that anyone working in these environments could suffocate," continued the engineer. "They're now making it a health and safety issue for the Vaults,"

"But we are not processing fermented products," said Henry, despair in his voice.

"Yes, that may be the case," said the partner, "but your choices are simple ones: you either manage to persuade the council to change their mind, or my bet is that on your first delivery of wine they will stick an enforcement order on you to stop anyone working there."

"That's not the big problem. It's the banks," said the engineer. "We have to provide a certificate that the building complies with all local building standards. With Folkstone and Kent Council unilaterally creating safety standards we will never be able to get it signed off. It means that the bank won't release the money to make the final payment."

"Jesus," said Henry, "this nightmare has got to end. At every stage this project is costing more money."

"Henry," said the engineer. "Can I suggest we change the spec now to include ventilation? We can vent through the front wall, not the roof, because we've started to seal it and we don't want to do anything which affects the waterproofing. Now is the time to cut through the concrete close to the entrance so it doesn't affect the aesthetics too badly."

"So all that effort I put into having a constant temperature is going to be destroyed by hot air being pumped in during the summer, and cold air pumped in during the winter," said Henry, his voice showing signs of defeat.

"We could probably design some sensors which only switch on the ventilation based upon changes in the air mix. Too much carbon dioxide, etcetera, and it switches on," said the engineer.

"Let's install the vents," said Henry. "We'll work out later when they're used. Personally, I think it's a nonsense, but if Mr Jobsworth needs to see the vents and tick them off his list, then it seems I have little alternative. What's the cost?" he asked, as a throwaway line.

Henry swore as huge figures were bounded around. He didn't know how he was going to find the money to make the payroll at the month end let alone this extra cost. All this did was add to what was slowly becoming an insurmountable problem.

Chapter 73

Folkestone November 1974

IT WAS AS a cub reporter for the Birmingham Evening News that Lucy Lite had first gone to court to report on a high-profile criminal case. It was here she decided she wanted to be a lawyer. A brief affair with an unmarried junior partner in a Birmingham firm managed to get her an articled clerkship to train as a solicitor. As she studied, so she found that it was the barrister, and not the solicitor, who did the exciting advocacy work, whilst she was stuck just moving bits of paper. It was a miscarriage of justice case which took her back into journalism. She wrote up a story, took it to The Daily Mail, and, after a couple of bottles of wine and an afternoon in a bedroom in a nearby hotel with one of the deputy editors, she was on the staff, back as a journalist. Another hotel tryst with another sub-editor and she was with the Telegraph, where her amour guided her to the financial desk and then into the soul-destroying world of corporate public relations.

She quickly discovered that PR firms paid twice the pay of a journalist, but with half the work and one tenth of the pressure. She found a role in one of the big agencies where she excelled by power-dressing, leaking the occasional exclusive, and by drinking and shagging her way through Fleet Street. She had become the 'go-to' girl if you had a serious PR problem.

Henry and Lucy greeted each other with Henry kissing her on both cheeks.

"Didn't we do a great job on the fire? Kept that one really under control, didn't we?" said Lucy making her first sales pitch.

"Yes, thank you," replied Henry.

Henry knew that speaking to Lucy was like speaking through a megaphone to the world, so he briefed her carefully on the story, choosing his words with precision. She listened, took notes, and said nothing. She asked a few questions and then said, "Okay, I must go to work. Do you have any photographs of the haystack?"

"No."

"Then go and get some now; back within the hour," she commanded.

A trip to the local camera shop, a rushed trip to the entrance to the Vaults, saw Henry present Lucy with two rolls of undeveloped film.

"I've written the story for you," she said.

"Can I read it." He asked.

"I'll read it. The headline reads: "Forced out by Arson, Forced out by Extortion. The first paragraph then says:"

"Sophie Elleswell, the million-dollar-a-year supermodel, who was forced out of her home just over a year ago by arson, is now being forced out of her new business project by a local farmer with the support of Kent County Council. They have stopped her working on her newly constructed wine vaults and, in the process, they've threatened the future of a £30 million investment project."

Lucy looked up, and Henry nodded for her to continue.

"Commenting on the situation, Sophie said, 'Last year my children and my home were attacked and now my business is threatened with extortion over land rights and by a planning decision which defies logic. Those in charge of the UK have to decide whether this country wants law-abiding, tax-paying citizens like my husband and me. If it does then it's going to have to find a way to support us, rather than destroy everything that we have done by using practices more suitable to the vagaries of a Third World dictatorship."

"Wow," said Henry, when Lucy had finished reading, "it's a bit tough. Will you get that published?"

"It's what you said," answered Lucy in defence.

"Will you get it published?" he asked again.

"For sure. An exclusive interview with Sophie with personal family photographs' is a take in any editor's books. It'll be in The Mail or Express either tomorrow morning or the next day. I'll get something different, not exclusive, in The Telegraph and may be The Guardian for the day after. They'll have different angles because the story will be written for different audiences."

They talked of TV and the timetable for the six o'clock news. "When they come, it will probably be the time when the bales are being moved," said Henry.

"Just as long as you're available for an interview," said Lucy. "And for God's sake, get yourself washed, shaved, and buy some decent clothes. You need to look like the husband of a supermodel." With her rebuke, she took Henry's hand, kissed him on both cheeks, and left. Like every man she dealt with Lucy had successfully crushed his balls without going anywhere near them.

Henry returned to his room and lay on his bed. Once the story was out there, he was going to need an emissary to ask favours. He couldn't do it himself. He opened his contact book and vacantly turned the pages. He suddenly knew the answer.

Diana Pickford was a newsreader for one of the major broadcasters. She was one of the women that Henry had started to pay to come to his Matterers Lunches after Sophie fell ill and he could no longer be sure she would be there. The first couple of times Diana came as a guest, but the third invite was followed by a phone call from her agent and a fee was agreed, but also a critical term: she wanted to sit next to the most important guest at the luncheon, a request easily accepted, as Diana had a thing for powerful men. Just before each Matterers Lunch Diana would, unknown to Henry, book a local hotel room with the aim of making a conquest. Just once, maybe twice if they pleased her, but never more than that. What amused Henry was how these trysts were added onto her bill; firstly, the cost of the hotel room, and then her time for entertaining the named gentleman in question.

Henry phoned Diana, and without any small talk, he explained the situation. "When the story breaks tomorrow, I want you to phone the top politicians you know," he said, "and I want them to phone the people they know, both at Kent County Council and Folkestone District Council, saying that Sophie's project is in the best interests of the UK, and they should get out of its way."

"What about the chief constable?" asked Diana. "I could get the home secretary to phone him."

"You know Roy Jenkins?" asked Henry. "He's not one of your er...?" Henry stopped, as he didn't know the word.

"Good God no! but he was at university with my elder brother. We've met a few times. He'll take my call." Diana paused and then continued. "I tried to have a thing with your Chief Constable once, but alas it was not to be."

"Oh," said Henry not knowing what else to say.

"It's rare you become a chief constable if you've slept on the other side of the sheets," she added, making their relationship clear, "but I've interviewed him since then. I'll talk to him too."

"Okay, perfect. Thank you"

"By the way," said Diana, "Dervis is pathetic." She was referring to her most recent after Matterers Lunch date.

"Oh, really?" said Henry once again lost for words.

"All his testosterone must go into running that wretched bank of his, for he's no bloody use at anything else."

"Ah, well, I'll do better for you next time," said Henry.

"Must go," said Diana suddenly. "Love you," she said, and then she was gone.

That night, Henry sat in the restaurant feeling very conspicuous as he ate on his own. He contemplated the very poor choice of non-alcoholic drinks, convincing himself that one day he would enter that market. He looked around and spotted a bookshelf full of guest books. He browsed through it without much attention, choosing at random Charles Dickens' A Tale of Two Cities. He opened it and read the opening words:

> It was the best of times; it was the worst of times,
> It was the age of wisdom; it was the age of foolishness.

Henry reflected on these words. They seemed appropriate given the circumstances he was in. They probably applied to every epoch, he thought. Nevertheless, they grabbed him and quickly he became absorbed. He had not read a novel since his O-levels all those years before.

Chapter 74

THE TRANQUILLITY IN the restaurant of the night before was destroyed by the raucous noise of twenty-six Frenchmen demanding petit déjeuner. Instead, they were offered a full English breakfast which they ate with relish, whilst disapproving loudly about the quality of the coffee.

Twelve had come from Château de Gressier and fourteen had come from Château Rabôut. It was a bigger army than Henry had expected, but nevertheless he was delighted. They would make short shrift of the work.

Henry scoured the morning newspapers and read word for word the report that Diana had written the day before. He was pleased with the story and the picture of Sophie and the children playing which accompanied it. He was now ready.

Henry phoned the contractor and told them that they could be back on site after 10:00 a.m. He then gave instructions to his two bodyguards to change into their navy suits and come with him, whilst ordering the rest back to their vans and to follow him to the entrance to the Vaults. There he gave instructions for the straw to be unloaded from the trailer and stacked on either side of the entrance road. The trailers were moved onto the verge and then he gave instructions for the two drivers to fill up their vans with bales of straw and to follow him.

The entrance to Mountleigh Farm was unimpressive and, the closer he got to the farmhouse, it was clear that the owners took little pride in its appearance. How could the owner of a place like this wield such power locally, he wondered, but then the expensive cars parked in the open barns to the side of the house indicated a wealth which the rest of the property denied.

As they parked outside the front entrance, Henry gave instructions for the two suited men to leave the car and come and stand behind him, one to the left and one to the right. His heart was pounding when he knocked on the door. He hated confrontation, but sometimes it had to be faced. At last, the door was opened. Henry didn't offer a handshake.

"Mr Bookham?" he enquired.

"Yes."

"I am Henry Guégan," he said introducing himself. "I bought the chalk-pit from you a couple of years ago and now you have deliberately blocked my access. I've come to tell you that your barrier is being removed right now and its not to go up again."

"Well, you shouldn't have dug up my road. You had no permission to."

"I have a right of way and you're blocking it," said Henry "Right now, your bales are being removed by twenty-six of my men. I don't think even you can muster an army of that size to stop them doing that work."

"Look I own the land between the drive and the road. It's mine and you have no rights to cross it," argued Bookham.

Henry moved away from the front door into the middle of the drive.

Bookham followed as he continued, "And you've run your water and electricity across my land without permission."

Henry turned and stepped up to stare at Bookham very closely in the face. Just as quickly, Henry's navy-suited bodyguards came up and flanked him. "I will be very clear," said Henry. "Today my lawyers are filing an injunction to stop you interfering with my pit. They're claiming damages against you for thirty million pounds. I just wanted to make sure that you heard it from me personally."

There was then a pause as Henry walked away, and then he turned around. "You know, my wife and I were burnt out of our house," he said.

"Yes," said Bookham. "Sorry about that."

"Yeh, well, I'm fed up being fucked about," said Henry as he moved closer to Bookham, held him firmly by the arm, looked deeply into his eyes, and then looked up and at the outside of his farmhouse. His eyes slowly moved from one side to the other. He then looked back straight into Bookham's eyes and said, "Believe me. I know what it feels like to see one's house burn to the ground. It's a real shame you're putting all this at risk." It was said in a tone deliberately designed to be threatening. Henry let go of his arm. "You fuck with me once more," he said, "and I promise you, you'll seriously regret it." There was controlled anger in Henry's voice.

Bookham moved forward ready to take a swipe at Henry, but as he did so, Henry's bodyguards moved forward too, causing Bookham to back off abruptly.

"You're going to get an offer from my lawyer this afternoon," said Henry, now with fury in his voice. "I'm going to buy the road land, all of it, everything within the boundary of the current fence right up to the edge of the road, every single inch! You'll get ten grand now and, provided I get no interference, you'll get another five grand in one year's time and another five grand a year after that. That's it – nothing more. I suggest you take it, for believe me, you'll regret it if you don't. I'll bankrupt you and God knows what else. By the time I've finished with you you'll be left with fuck all. Do you hear, goddam fuck all!"

"Get off my land," said Bookham, as he poked Henry in the chest two or three times. "You don't fucking tell me what to do and not to do," he continued.

The navy-suited bodyguards moved forwards, ready to protect Henry, who already held Bookham's hand firmly, deliberately twisting his fingers.

"I'm not telling you what to do," said Henry defiantly. "I'm advising you 'cause the consequences of not ... well. They'll be bad." Henry moved towards his car. "Have you read the papers this morning?" he asked. "I suggest you do," said Henry not waiting for a reply. "I think you'll find it difficult to buy a cup of coffee around here for a little while!"

Henry climbed in and closed the car door, ignoring the abuse coming from Bookham. As soon as the two navy-suited men had jumped into Henry's car he drove off, leaving Bookham standing in his drive, shocked by his experience. He had never been threatened or out manoeuvred like that before.

At the end of the drive Henry stopped for there were already three van loads of bales of straw piled up either side of the entrance.

"Okay," said Henry, "Let's give this guy a taste of his own medicine." With that the three of them stacked the bales across his drive to make a roadblock and, with another couple of trips with both his mini vans full of hay, Bookham would be going nowhere quickly.

Henry drove back to the entrance to the Vaults to find it clear as he'd expected. Two stacks were either side of the road. He thanked his men and arranged for them to go back to the hotel for showers and lunch before heading back to France.

Meanwhile the phones had been ringing from Whitehall to Kent as Permanent Secretaries from the Home Office and the Department of Trade and Industry were phoning the chief constable and the chief executives of the county and district councils respectively, telling them that the Vaults were important to the country, its relationship with France and Germany and they had to work with, rather than against Mr Guégan and Ms Elleswell.

Immediately Henry was gone Bookham phoned the chief constable to report Henry's threat, both to his life and to his property earlier that morning, but he found he got short-change.

"It's a civil matter," said the chief constable, "We can't get involved. But, I've discovered something this morning, Sophie Elleswell has got friends in very powerful places. If you haven't seen the papers look at them and I suggest you settle with him fast, for no good is going to come out of it otherwise. It even appears that there might be lobbying on his behalf from the French Government and on her behalf by the German ambassador."

Bookham hung up the phone and pondered the advice. £20,000 was better than nothing, he thought. His next call was to his lawyer to tell him to take Henry's offer. "Not a bad day's work for a bundle of straw," he said to himself out loud.

That evening Harriet took a message for Henry. It was from Fergus McDonald the CEO of the Vaults construction firm. "Tell Henry," he said "we've had phone calls from the planning departments of both Kent and Folkestone Councils offering to co-operate to find a solution to the ventilation problem in the Vaults. I don't know what he did but tell him well done from us."

Chapter 75

Paris November 1974

LA MAISON GELINA shop was opened in September under its old name of Maison Rabôut. It was much later than the date planned when Robert and Henry had struck their bargain. Robert had taken the precaution of having a surveyor take a tour of the premises immediately after his appointment as project manager for the refurbishment. This had revealed, thanks to the Paris Metro, some serious structural faults in the basement which had to be tackled before anything else could be done.

Henry was thrilled as the retail space of the basement and ground floors were better than he had envisioned. The flagstone floors had been painstakingly cleaned and were now covered each day with fresh sawdust. The wines were displayed and stacked in beautiful racking, made from recovered mahogany. The heavy brass lights had been cleaned, polished and re-hung and these were enhanced by the most discrete display lighting. At the back of the store there were two upended wine barrels, to make a place where wines might be tasted. However, the 'pièce de résistance' was the mahogany counter which had been carefully halved in size, enabling something very old to have a new lease of life. At last, with the shop open they could start taking much needed money.

Eight weeks later the top three floors of Maison Gelina were completed and ready to be used. Robert had hired a designer who, following instructions from Sophie, had done a wonderful job on the rest of the house. They consulted with Sophie on the style. "Exactly the same as London but with a few top-quality French antiques making it suitable for the Paris market," she had said but then paid little attention after that. Even the laboratory in London had been copied installing the very best of the latest equipment for Henry's wine analysis work but, with a department doing that in London and Henry having such little time everyone, including Henry, doubted whether this was something which was ever truly coming to Paris.

Henry had been desperate to get Maison Gelina finished so that Sophie and he could have somewhere to live when they were in Paris. He had been living out of a suitcase in any hotel he could get, whereas Sophie had settled into Imra's apartment in an arrangement which made him feel estranged from his own wife, for he was never invited there.

It was Rosalind, Sophie's booker who had suggested that she should stay with Imra. Immediately the two women met, they became soul mates. Each was convinced that the other was the most beautiful woman the other had seen, Sophie had two young children, Imra had one; both had their children living with their grandparents in the country, both knew the pain they suffered from missing their children, both were working every hour God gave and both had a passion for fashion. They swopped clothes, swopped stories, and sweated together in the gym to keep their bodies in shape.

There were two big differences between the two women. Imra was from Somalia and her dark skin drove her to wear the brightest of colours which Sophie just loved, for they radiated a joy which she was unable to bring to what she wore in the same way. Secondly Imra was divorced from her husband. He was the lead guitarist in a French rock band. They toured together in the early days of their relationship but, with each groupie her husband took to his bed, their marriage dissolved just that little bit more. However, with Henry's long absences Sophie was beginning to feel as though, she too, was separated from her husband.

On the afternoon of the formal re-opening of La Maison Rabôut, Henry paced up and down between the back of the shop and the pavement. He was distinctly nervous, for this was the first time Sophie had been to Maison Gelina for about a year. He knew she had driven past it but she had never been inside. He was desperate for her to be pleased. His mind was only on her. He was feeling the same rush of expected excitement he felt on their first date. He cast his mind back to their first meeting and he kept wondering how he could have been so casual about the whole thing. She was truly gorgeous then and now she was just perfect.

So much had gone wrong since their London home had been set on fire that Henry could sense their relationship was under strain. They had not made love for months and he was desperate to take her back into his arms and not to lose her. Today, he was going to make it all better.

Sophie's car pulled up outside and, like Tigger, Henry bounced to open the door. He looked into the car expectantly, but she didn't look at him. She was giving instructions to her driver and only when she was finished did she look up and smile weakly. Instantly, Henry saw tiredness in Sophie's eyes but then, ever the consummate professional, she alighted with grace, wearing a tight, knitted, woollen warm-blue trouser suit with faux-fur around the lapels and around the hood. They walked together through the shop which now spread uninterrupted from one side of the building to the other, and from the front to back, with only the wide staircase in the centre of the building, around which everything else circulated.

The sales staff tried to move discretely aside as Sophie made her tour of inspection, but she went to each of them, shook their hands, asked them their name, which she repeated, and thanked them for their work. She had a unique touch which each would remember.

Henry led Sophie to behind the staircase and then the entrance to the stone steps leading down to the cellar. It had been newly whitewashed, with boxes of wine neatly stacked. Excitedly, he pointed out to her the cases of extremely expensive wine that they had found just lying there, forgotten.

Every time Henry entered a floor, he felt a fresh sense of achievement. "Robert has brought this place back to life again," said Henry. "He must have been held down by his father. When I think about it, maybe I was lucky not to have a father," he added, in an effort at conversation.

When it came to going upstairs, Henry fell back slightly, allowing Sophie to climb the steps first, as he'd always done, but then, on this occasion, something made him stop and watch her climb the rest of the steps alone. He noticed her figure had changed. She was now much thinner and more toned than she'd ever been. Her narrow waist and slender thighs were slimmer than before, the tops of her legs no longer met, and her buttocks had lost their roundness, such that her bottom no longer filled the seat of the trousers she was wearing. She still looked good but was now too thin, which made him wonder where his wife had gone.

They climbed the stairs to the first floor which was neatly divided into two offices on the left-hand side. On the right-hand side of the building were the kitchen and the large dining room, where the table had been laid ready for a Matterers' Lunch.

They climbed one more flight to Henry and Sophie's private quarters. Again, Henry stood behind her as she climbed each stair, but this time he was fascinated by her golden hair which hung in a perfectly cut curve along her back.

As Sophie entered each of the rooms, in what would be their apartment, she found it was exactly as she had instructed in her brief meetings. Everything was in place, but somehow it did not make it her home. It was so impersonal; it felt to her as though she was in a hotel. In the kitchen, she opened the cupboards. It was stacked with the same crockery they had at Found House, even the oven, fridge and washing machine were the same make, but there Sophie had unpacked every piece. She had touched it and put it away. This simple act made it hers. She looked in the fridge and found it full; nothing had been forgotten.

"Have you stayed here the night yet?" was Sophie's only remark.

"Not yet, I wanted you to be here the first time. What do you think?"

"It's just as I envisaged," she said, for it truly was.

They climbed another set of stairs. This time Henry did not watch Sophie with the intensity of before, as he sensed an unhealthy anxiety had befallen his wife. Once again, the floor was designer-perfect, as though it had come off a film set. In Sophie's dressing room, laid out on her dressing table, were the make-up and styling products which she used.

"Did you do this?" she said, pointing to the tins and jars.

"Yes," said Henry, "I wanted everything to be perfect for you."

She kissed him gently on the cheek and squeezed his arm.

"Thank you," she said, "it's just perfect," but that was the problem. It was all too perfect, and that made it all wrong. The fact was that Sophie didn't want the place. She didn't want to be there. She wanted her life before the fire. She wanted her mews home in London. She wanted a home, and this was not a home. Although she never said this, it was the way the stairs went from the shop floor to their living quarters, to their bedroom, without a break which she didn't like. It made her feel as though her whole life was on display in this building.

"Have a look around and I'll get your cases," said Henry.

He returned a few minutes later with two heavy cases which, short of breath, he heaved into her dressing room.

"We've about two hours until the party begins," said Henry. "What would you like to do? Are you changing or are you going like that?" he asked innocently.

"Going like this," she replied. "Why? Do you think it's wrong?"

"No," said Henry defensively, "I think you look lovely. It's perfect."

"It's warm," she responded, by way of self-defense.

"Let's get something to eat," she said, desperate to get out of the showroom, where she felt afraid to touch anything, and into the real world.

"There'll be food at the party," said Henry.

"Yes, but you know when we're hosts, we never eat."

They sat in a small, innocuous cafe around the corner, and ordered mindlessly. At first, they chattered like they used to. It seemed such a long time ago. They talked about their children and their parents. They shared each other's news. It was when he told her about the problem with Farmer Bookham at the Vaults and the way he had dealt with him that Sophie became physically agitated.

"Why didn't you tell me?" she said, in an accusatory tone.

"Because I didn't want you to worry," said Henry calmly.

"So you thought it better I read about it in the papers?" she added.

Henry said nothing more. He wanted to tell her about all the extra-costs that had been incurred as a result of the lighting and ventilation issues, but it was the way she reacted and spoke which stopped him.

Secretly, Sophie was pleased and proud of him, whilst remaining totally perplexed at the situation. "You come from a strange country," she said.

"Stranger than Germany?" he asked.

"No, but strange all the same. You English, you welcome people from all over the world into your midst. You are polite and courteous, but you never, ever, allow them to belong."

"I'm not really English," said Henry shocked that he was being considered as such.

"Your grandmother was English, and you are a product of the English public-school system; that makes you English in my books," retorted Sophie.

Henry said nothing for, given the force with which Sophie was speaking, he thought it wise to remain silent.

"You allow foreigners to buy the best houses, their kids go to the best schools, membership of your precious clubs, even to polo, Ascot and shooting, but you never ever invite them to Sunday lunch. That is the reserve of those whose families have been to the same schools and same universities for generations. That's where the power is, and where it remains. It's when and where they conspire."

Henry looked perplexed at the outburst because it was unlike Sophie.

"I don't think you realise it, but England has an impenetrable class system which you are not part of. You could have been once, but you lost your place when you didn't get into Oxford or Cambridge."

"That's nonsense," said Henry defensively. Look how Lucy Lite and Diana Pickford were able to influence things for the better."

"Yes, it was the Matterers Lunches which gave us some contacts," agreed Sophie, "and our Vaults problem would not have been solved without them, but they don't have power. They just influence power, that's all."

"Well it worked."

"Until the next time," retorted Sophie "This time they came because you had the power of money," she added to prove her point.

"And a pretty wife," added Henry, trying to make light of the serious conversation Sophie was having.

"You were just lucky; your gang was bigger than his gang this time, but you might not be able to do that the next time." There was an ominous tone in Sophie's voice.

"You think money buys you influence, but it does nothing of the sort. It buys you weekday access, that's all. It's on those days when the powerful take your money for their own ends and spit out a few crumbs from their plates to keep you happy. I'm telling you the real decisions, the big decisions, are taken in the country houses of the oldest money in the land."

Henry shook his head in frustration.

"Look, we've had some of those people around our table," said Sophie. "It's obvious how it works. I can't see how you can't see it!" Her frustration was clearly displayed in the tone of her voice.

"We're helping them. They're helping us. It's just business," said Henry, trying to calm Sophie down, but it was not to be.

"You're so damn busy being a sycophant, trying to suck up to them that you can't see what they're doing," shouted Sophie, getting quite agitated.

"Come on Sophie, said Henry, trying not to rise to her insult, which had hurt his feelings. "It's not as bad as that."

"Believe me, however posh you speak and however much you pay, it will never be enough to get you into the room when the important decisions are being made."

In a five-minute conversation, Sophie had articulated why she would never go back to England, but Henry didn't get the depth of the message, or understand the effect that this newly expressed paranoia would have in the weeks ahead.

Chapter 76

Paris November 1974

WHEN HENRY AND Sophie got back to Maison Gelina, they found it was well prepared for their opening night's guests. All the staff looked incredibly dapper, but it was the lady that Robert Rabôut had on his arm which left Henry completely speechless. Pascale Verderi was an incredibly sexy French singer from Henry's school days. He had bought all her records which were catalogued and stored in the loft at his mother's house. He had covered his schoolbooks with pictures of her cut from magazines. This goddess from his youth, on whom he had had the biggest of fantasies was now in front of him in the flesh. Although older, she still looked quite remarkable, and his infatuation came flooding back.

"You're ..." said Henry, unable to finish his sentence, even though her name was engraved in his memory. He held her hand longer than was polite.

"Yes," she said.

"Forgive me," said Henry, "but I've had the most amazing crush on you since I was at school. I have all your records." Suddenly, he found the word 'record' made him feel extremely old.

"And it looks as though that crush hasn't gone away," interrupted Sophie, taking Pascale's hand.

"I'm Sophie. It's good to meet you."

Pascale smiled back. "And you too," she said, "I've admired your style for a long time. You choose so well."

"I'm lucky to have the best to choose from," said Sophie, repeating a line that she'd used many times.

"I had that once," said Pascale, "but the skill is to mix and match from everything they produce and, as I well know, it's not easy."

"Well, you do it very well," said Sophie.

"The trouble with the singing game is that in any photo shoot, if the guys had their way, they'd either have you wearing nothing at all, or every dead-end range to make the shot interesting."

Sophie laughed as she agreed with the observation. She then linked arms with Pascale and said, "Come on, let's tackle this together."

"Yes," said Pascale, "better in numbers."

At a quieter moment in what was a very hectic evening, Henry asked Robert how he knew Pascale.

"We live together. We've lived together for the last ten years or so," he admitted.

"Married?" asked Henry.

"To her? Sadly, no, I'm a catholic and married to somebody else. It means I have no chance of a divorce."

"I'm sorry," said Henry, "but then you are a very lucky bugger to have her," he said referring to Pascale.

"And so are you," said Robert, "to have Sophie."

"Yes, I am," acknowledged Henry.

They both looked at Pascale and Sophie together, and smiled. It appeared that a friendship was developing between the two women.

By all accounts the party was a great success. As a non-drinker Henry found it as tedious as he always found these events, particularly when the noise became so loud you had to shout to be heard, and with it, sensible conversation died. Sophie however, with a gin and tonic in her hand, and Pascale at her side, moved effortlessly amongst their guests as the perfect host.

It was quite late when Henry led Sophie away from the party to the top floor and their own bedroom, where they noticed the smell of stale cigarette smoke had reeked in to their clothes.

"Henry," shouted Sophie, suddenly. "We've no lock on our bedroom door. Anyone can walk in." She was clearly angry. Henry had never seen her turn so quickly. It was unlike her. He was shattered by the suddenness of it all. "And, as we've got no damn front door it means anyone can walk from the street up here."

Henry didn't know about the lock on the bedroom door, but he had the same concerns about the lack of a front door to their apartment. It was an absence which had worried him from the outset, but he didn't know how to solve the problem, and foolishly he had not asked the architect for advice.

Henry was affronted and then hurt by Sophie's assault. He had tried his damnedest to make it home from home for her, even to making sure that all the soaps, creams and cleansers which filled her dressing room were her usual brands.

"There's a lock on your dressing room door," said Henry defensively, "and tomorrow I'll get one put on our bedroom door."

In bed, between the roughness of the new sheets, Henry tried to hold Sophie, but she was not interested in him. Normally, in his arms, she felt unafraid, but somehow, in this house, in these circumstances, she knew she wouldn't be able to sleep. There was something wrong and Henry knew it. He just didn't know how to put it right.

Over the next two days they held their first Parisian Matterers Lunches. The formula was identical to London, important men and women, with pretty and intelligent girls. No talk of wine, simply good food, good wine and good company, and with an agenda that covered current politics, art and gossip. Robert and Pascale turned out to be the best of co-hosts.

At each of these two lunches there was a serious wine investor, to whom Henry showed his laboratory. He then quietly explained that there was a problem in some of the corks in the latest Château Rabôut vintages and, as a valued customer, if they would like to return their wine for checking and, if found faulty, he would be delighted to swap their spoiled bottles for this year's vintage, provided, for each bottle swapped, they also bought one of this year's vintage too. Alternatively, he also offered them their money back. In every case they accepted the swap deal.

It was whilst watching Henry at the Matterers Lunches that Robert realised that he had the same ability to sell in a non-selling way. For the first time he discovered that the less something was for sale, the more people wanted to buy it. He would simply promise to put people on a waiting list or agree that he would check their cellars as a favour to see if there was a special deal which could be done.

Like Henry, Robert couldn't bear the pretentiousness of the wine connoisseur, but unlike Henry, he had that rare gift of making everyone seem special. In London, it had been Sophie's gift which had made Found Vintners successful. It was now Robert's gift which was going to make Maison Gelina the place where serious people would come and spend serious amounts of money on wine. As far as Robert was concerned, the Rabôut family was back in the wine business.

On Friday afternoon, Henry and Sophie left Maison Gelina to drive to Château de Gressier. Henry did not notice that Sophie hadn't unpacked anything as she always travelled everywhere with a load of luggage. Without a word, she was moving out of Maison Gelina without ever having moved in.

Chapter 77

Château de Gressier November 1974

SOPHIE AND HENRY tried to enjoy the weekend at Château de Gressier. Sophie was so physically exhausted that she stayed in her pyjamas nearly all day. She played, just occasionally, with their children for although she was there in person she was not there in mind.

Henry insisted they tour the perimeter of the Estate last thing on the Saturday night, as they had always done. As they walked, he tried to persuade Sophie that everything was at last under control and moving in the right direction. The Château de Gressier and Château Rabôut estates were both calm. Gaston Rabôut had moved out of the Château into his Cottage. The wine recall was going well with no one making any complaints. Even the counterfeit wine had become a brand in its own right making Henry think of trying to trace the winery to keep the supply going.

The Folkestone Vaults were progressing well. An affordable solution to the ventilation and lighting problems had been found, and lorry after lorry was backfilling the walls so that no one would ever have known that quarrying work had taken place, or that a chalk pit, had ever been there.

Robert and Pascale had taken over the Parisian Matterers Lunches, as though they'd invented them, and La Maison Rabôut had suddenly become the wine shop for the fashionable classes of Paris.

Henry was feeling more confident than he had been for a very long time and he tried to persuade Sophie of this, but she would have none of it, only seeing black clouds ahead. In bed at night, he would try to persuade Sophie into his arms so they could make love. She wanted nothing to do with him. Her mind was racing and obviously elsewhere, but where Henry could not imagine. As he lay on his side of the bed, he started to wonder whether Sophie had taken a lover and that her depression was created by her desire to be with another man. These thoughts frightened him. If she went, he knew she would take Andrew and Peter with her, and the thought of his children being raised by another man meant that he got no sleep.

Chapter 78

Paris January 1975

SOPHIE, HENRY AND Victoria spent Christmas at Château de Gressier where Walter and Inga joined them for New Year's Eve. It was a happy time with all their efforts focused on keeping Andrew and Peter entertained but, as so often happens in life, just as you think you have everything under control, the crocodile leaps from the water and bites you on the backside. This is exactly what happened to Henry as he and Sophie went back to work after Christmas.

Sophie had agreed to join him in a Matterers lunch which made it rather special as she had only attended in the week after the Paris shop opened and not once since then. When they arrived at Maison Gelina Henry was surprised to see Ainsworth there. He had come unannounced knowing that Henry would be there. He was clearly very agitated.

"We can't pay the wages at the end of the month," said Ainsworth abruptly, as soon as the two men met. It was a remark overheard by Sophie who froze in her tracks.

"What?" said Henry, "that can't be possible. We're due to be paid by the supermarkets before then. In fact, everyone pays us before then. Hell, we financed the whole of their bloody Christmas. They've now got the cash in their bank, so they've damn well got to pay us."

"Didn't you see the notice?" said Ainsworth.

"See what?" asked Sophie, now joining in the conversation.

"The letter which they sent, extending their payment terms from 30 to 90 days."

"I ignored it because it's not per our contract," protested Henry.

"No, but it's what they've done," affirmed Ainsworth. One did it one week and then the two other biggies did it the next. When I phoned yesterday to make sure it didn't apply to us I was told it did."

"How can they do that?" Henry asked, aghast.

"It's simple, they just don't pay us."

"Oh Christ," said Henry completely deflated. "We're totally fucked if that happens."

Sophie froze on hearing those words for Henry had been so sure everything was going to be alright. The three of them moved up to the first-floor office where Ainsworth had already spread out his papers.

"We have two containers of South African wine, and one container of Argentinian wine, which are arriving this week, on which bills of exchange will mature. Without the supermarket money we can't honour either of those.

"Oh, Jesus," continued Henry, only slightly changing his invective. How much do we need in all?"

"About a hundred and fifty thousand pounds, maybe a quarter of a million"

"Noooo," said Henry elongating the word, "our wage bill can't be that big."

"It isn't, but we've got a host of other bills to pay as well."

"And the banks, will they lend us anymore money? When our debtor book includes three of the top five supermarkets they must surely be satisfied with their security?"

The thing is, Henry, our UK banks also know about the huge liability we have on the counterfeit wine too."

"How the hell do they know? I thought that problem was confined to the French banks."

"They were told by Constance who says he found out as part of their usual analytical tests on their stock."

Constance was one of London's largest wine dealers who constantly tried to emulate what Henry was doing in an effort to stop customers moving from them to him.

"That's bollocks," said Henry. "I don't buy that. They've never done any testing on any wine in their lives. They don't know how. No, the banks have found out another way."

"They do Henry," replied Ainsworth. "They discovered what you were doing and have tried to copy it; at least that's what our bank told me."

"I thought these people were supposed to be confidential," protested Henry. "They're no better than old women in a fucking corner shop!"

Ainsworth snorted in agreement. He'd worked with bankers all his adult life and he could honestly say he had not found one who was anything but a company man.

"I know that can't be right. We know where every bottle of counterfeit wine went, and none went to Constance".

"I thought that problem had been solved, or at least if not solved, it was under control," said Sophie her voice cracking with emotion.

"It is Sophie," said Henry reassuringly. This is a different problem."

"The bank told us that Constance was laughing at us, saying that we'd bought a pup because we didn't do our due diligence properly," said Ainsworth unhelpfully.

"Well that's the first damn true statement I've heard for a very long time," said Sophie furiously. "I warned you about this Henry. I bloody well warned you. You're not big or powerful enough to be in the bloody room when the big decisions are taken. She turned angrily and left the two men facing what appeared to be an insurmountable problem.

There was an empty place at the Matterers Lunch because Sophie was not there. She had phoned her driver, collected her numerous bags from their car and was gone. She did not say where she was going.

Chapter 79

London January 1975

IMMEDIATELY AFTER THE Matterers Lunch Henry flew to London, as it was only in Found House that his business could be saved. Ainsworth had returned to London immediately after he had parted his message of doom to Henry.

Henry desperately tried to find Sophie before he left. He phoned and left messages everywhere. Eventually he tracked her down to Imra's apartment who confirmed in a phone call that Sophie was staying with her but was fast asleep and couldn't talk.

"Please tell her I love her," said Henry to Imra, "and say that I've had to go to London. She'll know why."

It was late when Henry arrived at Found House. Ainsworth and Harriet were still there worrying what was best to do.

"The bank has to lend us more money," said Henry firmly, as soon as he and Ainsworth had settled down to review the precise situation.

"I've asked but they want more security," responded Ainsworth.

"Hell's bells," he said, "they have everything I have."

"They've suggested secured personal guarantees from your wife," said Ainsworth.

"They know they have everything, the whole of her trust fund has gone into financing the Vaults."

"Yes, but not her London mews house."

"Hell, what are we going to do?" said Henry in despair. "I can't ask Sophie for that. I can't." Henry paused, "after the fire and the trouble with... well, things are different."

Ainsworth said nothing for it was obvious to him from the way Sophie had reacted to the news that their relationship was under strain.

"I'll talk to my mother," said Henry. "She's offered me some money in the past. Perhaps she'll be able to help now."

"Can you make any rapid sales of some investment wines?" asked Ainsworth.

"Of course, but I'm not sure we have anything special to sell, do we?" said Henry.

"I think we could source some on decent credit terms," said Ainsworth.

"But we're not going to make much margin on it are we?"

"No, but if we sell today for cash delivery today, and buy on 90 days credit, we can create some time until we start getting paid again."

"Oh, I see," said Henry. "I'll make some calls. Give me a list of what I can sell and where it's from."

"Don't ask where it's from," said Ainsworth. "It will only piss you off."

"Okay," said Henry.

There was a pause as Ainsworth opened his folder.

"What do you know about these?" he asked, as he handed over five invoices from Curzon Studio Models. The first three invoices were addressed to Sophie's agency and in particular her booker. The last two were addressed directly to Henry's company. Henry looked at them. On each there was a list of names, all of whom he recognised. They came to his Matterers Lunches. Against each of the names there were different lengths of times and charges.

Henry pulled a face. "Nothing," he said, shaking his head." I know the names on the list, don't I?" he asked, curiously.

"Do you know Curzon Studio Models?" asked Ainsworth.

"No, should I?" asked Henry.

"I've done some work. They provide hookers, call girls, escorts, prostitutes, call them what you will," said Ainsworth.

"What, for us, why?" asked Henry.

"It's complicated."

"How did Sophie's booker know them?" asked Henry.

"It's complicated," repeated Ainsworth, "but apparently their PR arm uses them when fixing dates for Arabs and others from all over the world."

"Oh, Jesus," said Henry, "and this week?"

"Yes, they've all been from Curzon," replied Ainsworth.

"And they're all ...?"

"Yes."

"But why have they come here? I don't understand."

"You know Sophie used to arrange for all the guests, particularly the female ones."

"Yes."

"Well, when she fell ill she asked her booker to take over the task."

"What!" exclaimed Henry.

"Yes"

"Well, she ran out of ideas so she decided she'd get the girls from another modelling agency."

"Oh, hell," said Henry, not knowing what to say, "but they can't be, they're all, well, lovely women, sort of posh, not a thickie amongst them."

"I suppose that's why they charge us so much."

Henry looked at the invoices, "Why are the times different?"

"It depends on whether they were involved in afters."

"Afters?" asked Henry.

"Please Henry, don't be so thick. Yes, afters ... whether they went with one of our customers back to a hotel or somewhere."

"Jesus, one of these girls is charging for a night what we pay a secretary for a whole month," exclaimed Henry, as he looked in greater detail at the invoices."

"They don't get all of that."

"Uh?" Henry shook his head.

"The agency gets between twenty and thirty percent."

"You didn't know?" asked Ainsworth.

"I didn't know," said Henry emphatically. "How the hell would I? How did it come to light?"

"After paying the first few invoices from Sophie's account, Rosalind thought we should pay them directly, which is why the last two invoices came to us."

Henry put his head in his hands and sighed, "What do I say to Sophie? Do you know you've been procuring hookers for me?"

"Not the best conversation a man has with his wife," agreed Ainsworth.

Henry stared at the list of dates. "Didn't we have the CEO of Deata Stores on that day," asked Henry, pointing to the invoice. "Hang on, maybe we have a get out of jail card here. Quick, let's match the guest list with the girls, and work out ..."

Henry set Harriet the task of matching escorts to diners and diners to customers, whilst Ainsworth created a list of all the wines that Henry might sell to generate immediate cash.

By the time Ainsworth and Harriet went home, and Henry retired upstairs, the three of them were pleased with their night's work.

Chapter 80

London January 1975

ALTHOUGH OFFICIAL OFFICE hours in Found House were from 9.00am, everyone always arrived early, between 7.00am and 8.00am. Whenever he was in Found House, Henry always made it his first job to tour the offices and chat to everyone, exchange light-hearted banter, and pick up the gossip in the market. This time he spent longer with each of the supermarket account managers, who had now heard of the change of terms and were worried.

"Sell the three supermarkets nothing and certainly make sure they get delivered nothing," he ordered. Tell 'em' they're on stop until I have spoken to their boss. Look after your other customers. Give them discounts on the stuff we were selling into the supermarkets. Call it an excess stock clearance, whatever."

Back at his desk, Henry phoned each of the main supermarket suppliers. Some of them were so huge that the effects of the delay in payment to them would have been little more than a rounding difference in their cash flows, but to Henry, and businesses like his, this decision not to pay was not just hurtful, it was life or death. He got little satisfaction.

His next call was to the managing director of Constance. "I want you to join me in a ban on supplying all the major supermarkets until they revert to their original terms of trade," said Henry.

"Why would I do that?" he asked.

"Because you need to, you're hurting too," said Henry, and then added threateningly, "also, you won't get any product from Château de Gressier, nor Château Rabôut nor any of my new world vineyards and, by the time I've finished phoning around half a dozen more vineyards, I think you'll find you're a little short of wine for next year too."

By eleven o'clock, using the same tactics that he had used when talking to Constance, Henry had all the major suppliers agreeing to an informal boycott. He and Ainsworth then turned their attention to the list of escort women which Sunetta had created the previous evening.

"Diana Pickford's not on the list," observed Ainsworth, hoping she would be there.

"No," said Henry. "We've had a separate arrangement with her for a long time. I thought about Diana, but I don't think she'll be able to help this time. She fucks anything as long as he's powerful. Her interests are senior politicians mainly, top civil servants sometimes, the occasional editor or vice chancellor of a university, but not businessmen. They're not her scene."

Henry and Ainsworth studied the list carefully not really knowing what they were looking for. After a little while Henry said to himself out loud "Magic, just magic." He then opened his very scruffy phone book and dialed as Ainsworth watched on.

"John, Henry, how are you? Vicky said how much fun you two had when you were last here. It's just that she's one of our guests for lunch one day next week, and I was wondering whether you would like to join us."

There was then a discussion as to dates in diaries until Henry added "but that's not my main reason for phoning. I thought you ought to know that all the major wine suppliers are about to put you on stop because of the way you've imposed a change in the terms of trade. We're being forced to do the same, otherwise we'll get struck off and will not get any supply of wine from their vineyards. Given our friendship I wanted you to be the first to know in case you wanted to do something about it."

Ainsworth didn't hear what John was saying, but he heard Henry continue.

"Yes, the likes of Diageo, Guinness, they're all in on it. It's coming from the major producers. We're a minnow, just piggy in the middle. The thing you really need to know is that the stock which was going to the three blacklisted major supermarket companies is now going to others, to support a huge discounting campaign. So while you will have nothing, or very little stock, they will have ..." Henry stopped.

He listened intently.

"Yes, I know it hits our profits, but they are all worried about generating cash flow." There was a pause again while Henry listened some more.

"One supermarket might have got away with a change of terms, but when it is followed rapidly by two others then its stinks of a cartel," said Henry, "and the big boys aren't going to allow you to get away with it."

Suddenly John became very agitated for to even hint he was involved in a cartel would destroy his reputation with the City of London, and it was something which he valued highly. Although, it was accidental, the word cartel was one of the best words Henry could have used to bring things back to normal.

"Can I suggest you try and get your buyer to get a shipment for the weekend? said Henry. "My bet is that you won't be refused outright, but on Thursday there will be shipment or transport problems, so your shelves will be left short for Friday and the weekend."

Henry listened again.

"I think it breaks this Thursday a.m. with BBC's morning news, with two or three blacklisted firms being named. I am told there will be a TV advertising campaign on Thursday and Friday promoting weekend wine deals in those un-blacklisted supermarkets. We've been asked to contribute to the campaign. Oh, and by the way, it's been explained to me that since everyone's contracts will have been terminated by the supermarkets for non-performance, all those on the blacklist are going to have to pay much more for their wine after that. It's the extra price which will pay for the TV ads saying wine can be bought in your competitor stores."

Henry listened a bit more.

"I don't know who organised it," he lied. "I heard the news from my account executives, and I thought I should let you know straight away."

They said their farewells. Henry looked at Ainsworth who smiled
and rubbed his hands together in glee. "I think I'll call you Pinocchio
after that performance," he said.

Henry immediately phoned back his fellow merchants one by one.

"It's working," he said. "Don't refuse to supply, but make sure they
know that there will be a delay, and it's unlikely that they will get a
shipment before the weekend."

The senior wine buyer from Stalm Stores phoned Henry. They
were one of the large supermarkets on the blacklist. The grapevine
was working. "What do we have to do to make sure we're not on the
blacklist?" he asked.

"I don't think you can be if you've paid all your invoices up to date
by tomorrow, and confirm the original contract terms," answered
Henry. "We certainly won't blacklist you. We'd be foolish to do so."

Henry then phoned the CEO or the chief buyer of the other two
blacklisted supermarkets pretending to be their inside guy, telling
them that Stalm Stores had buckled and were going to honor their
existing terms of trade. "Pay all your invoices up to date by tomorrow,
and confirmed the reinstatement of the original contract terms," he
said repeatedly.

Ainsworth sat in awe. "It's a bit of a coup if you pull this off," he
said. "They think someone else has orchestrated the whole thing, and
you, 'as a friend', are tipping them off."

"Yes, I know," said Henry. "At some stage I'm going to blame
Distillers, saying that they thought that if the supermarkets got away
with it with wines, they'd move onto spirits and beers next."

"By the way," said Ainsworth, "I think you've just broken the law."

"How?" pleaded Henry.

"You've formed an anti-competitive cartel. I'm sure the Monopolies
Commission would have something to say if they knew."

"Fuck 'em," said Henry, "none of those wankers have ever run
a business in their lives." He picked up the stocking list which
Ainsworth had brought him. "I need to sell some wine," he said, "with
cash in our bank before Friday."

With that, Henry reached for his phone book and started dialing
New York, then Chicago, and finally San Francisco. Japan he would

tackle in the morning. By 9pm he'd finished his calls, and if everyone paid in the next couple of days as promised, he would have been saved, irrespective of what the supermarkets did.

Chapter 81

London January 1975

THE NEXT NIGHT, as Henry climbed the stairs of Found House to his apartment, he was enjoying an adrenalin rush for he knew that his business was saved. Ainsworth had heard that every one of the supermarkets had promised payment. Cheques would be couriered to them, as they would to every wine supplier, the very next day.

Henry's pleasure turned to anxiety when he tried to phone Sophie as she wasn't at Maison Gelina as he'd expected. He phoned his mother, her mother, her booker, but no one knew where she was. In desperation he phoned Imra Blanche and found she was there.

Sophie came on the phone. He asked how she was. She reported a hard day, working on shoots for magazine campaigns, but there was no coherence in what she said. Her voice was drifting, lazy, lamented. Henry raised the delicate issue of Curzon Models, but Sophie paid no real interest to the issue. Her only question was, were they nice?

"Nice?" repeated Henry.

"Appropriate," Sophie replied.

"What do you mean, appropriate?" asked Henry again.

"Could anyone guess they were ...?"

"Hell, no, well, I don't think so."

"Then what's the problem?" asked Sophie.

Henry couldn't believe what he was hearing. "Are you okay Soph?" he asked, but Sophie was far from okay. She was slowly getting stoned on marijuana, and every care she had in the world was disappearing with each cloud of smoke she was inhaling into her lungs.

Henry told her about the supermarkets and the problems they caused, and his solution, but she paid no attention to what he was saying.

"They're going to kill us, Henry," she said. "Don't you see? They're trying to kill us."

Henry didn't see. "I don't think it's like that. It's not like that at all," he said, bewildered.

"It is like that," Sophie shouted, her temper turning in a flash. "It's just like that. They're trying to kill us. Every day, they want us dead."

"Are you okay Sophie?" Henry asked again.

"Why aren't you here?" she asked. It wasn't said as a rebuke, as it otherwise might, it was as though she had forgotten where he was.

Henry explained, but while Sophie was listening, her mind was disconnected from reality. Instead, she absentmindedly hung up the phone.

Chapter 82

Château de Gressier June 1975

OVER THE NEXT few weeks Henry travelled extensively to London, California, South Africa, Peru and Argentina, doing his damnedest to make sure that, on Sunday mornings when his kids woke up, he was back at Château de Gressier. Meanwhile, Sophie was changing in front of his eyes, not just her physical appearance for she was getting considerably thinner, but slowly her confidence was collapsing with each joint that she secretly smoked.

The first notable change was how Sophie was never ready when the time came for her to leave de Gressier on Monday mornings. If she was taking the train into Paris, she would never catch it. She'd have been awake all night, only falling asleep when the morning came. After the third or fourth time of not attending an event she had been booked for, Cassie, her new Paris booker arranged for Sophie's driver, John Chabani, to arrive two hours before she was due to leave. This was to make sure that Sophie was up and about and getting ready.

John Chabani was a French Algerian. He was a big man in his mid-thirties with huge hands and without a shred of hair. He invariably moved very slowly, as though the heat of the day was wearing on his body, even though it might be freezing outside.

It was Henry's mother who, in an earlier phone call, first articulated the changes in Sophie which Henry had been quietly and anxiously observing. He had left Château de Gressier very early on Monday morning, before anyone was up, to fly to Naples where he met a consortium of winery owners about representing them in the UK market. The initial meeting had gone well and as is typical in Italy, business flowed into the evening and a large family dinner under the olive groves. It was therefore late Monday evening when Henry phoned Château de Gressier to speak to his mother to say that he had arrived safely and enquired after the children.

"Henry, you have to come home straight away," said Victoria, immediately after Henry had said hello. "You must catch the first plane back. Sophie's having a nervous breakdown," she said.

There was silence on the phone as Henry absorbed what his mother was saying.

"Henry, you must be seeing it, she's unwell, very unwell," Victoria repeated.

Henry sat on the bed listening to his mother's words, but not really hearing them. They made no sense. She was fine when he had left, except he knew she wasn't. Henry accepted his mother was right. It was like those dot-to dot-pictures; once you've drawn the lines between two, three, and four dots it becomes easy to follow the rest of the pattern; but even then, the picture Henry had drawn of the situation didn't make sense. Why the change? Why would she now stay in her pyjamas and be generally disengaged when she was exactly the opposite before? Why was she incessantly cuddling her children, as though she was trying to protect them, until they were asleep, after which she would sob with worry, whilst wandering around all night saying virtually nothing?

Henry got back to Château de Gressier late Tuesday evening, where he found a very painful sight. Sophie was in bed, unkempt, rolled into a fetal ball and crying. She had been like that since he left, on Monday morning, only moving from lying on her left side to lying on her right side. Sophie was just as she had been when she had post-natal depression, just after each of the children had been born.

"John came on Monday afternoon to take her back to Paris, but she refused to go" said Victoria as she put on the kettle. "Sophie just wouldn't get ready. I got John to speak to her but all she would say to him is that: 'people are trying to kill me,' and when John said he would protect her, Sophie became adamant, saying they were talking about her all the time, plotting against her. She is suffering from paranoia Henry, you must see that," continued Victoria in a lecturing tone.

"Did you call the doctor?" asked Henry.

"Yes, he's suggesting a sedative, the same as before, but I've not given it to her."

"Why?"

"Because it's not the solution."

"Why?" said Henry, in all innocence.

Suddenly, Victoria got cross with her son. "For Pete's sake, Henry, can't you see it? Sophie's addled her brain on hash, or what do you call it, pot?"

"What?" exclaimed Henry, "that's not possible."

"For Christ's sake, she uses marijuana and she now drinks. She never drank before!"

"Don't be silly," said Henry. "She doesn't smoke."

"Henry, she smokes grass," said Victoria with as much factual force as she could bring. She then stood up, walked over to her handbag, and produced a plastic bag half-full of marijuana. "This is hers" she continued. "It was hidden in her dressing room."

Henry shook his head.

"The depression, anxiety, paranoia and suicidal thoughts are all the effect of this bloody stuff," said Victoria, waiving the plastic bag in the air.

"Suicide?" asked Henry.

"Yes. She's saying she doesn't want to live."

"Oh God. It's like when the children were born," said Henry as he absorbed the seriousness of what he was being told.

"No Henry, its worse. She could get better from the baby blues but she's not going to get better from this."

The silence in the room was only broken by the click of the electric kettle switching itself off.

"Do you remember Justin Pearlman and Seth Waters, at your school?" asked Victoria.

"No," said Henry.

"They were at school with you. Both became schizophrenics as a result of hash. The possibility that you might start taking this stuff was my biggest worry when you were growing up for that very reason."

"Hell Mom, Sophie's grown up."

"Don't be ridiculous," said Victoria angrily. "Hash doesn't choose its victims based upon age. I just hope you don't take this poisonous stuff," she continued, shaking the bag in front of him.

"No, I don't," said Henry firmly. "In fact, that's the first bag of the stuff I've ever seen."

"You need to phone Sophie's booker and tell her she's not coming back to work. After we spoke yesterday, I phoned Cassie and told her to cancel all of Sophie's engagements for the next six weeks. But Henry, they need to be told she's never going back. Have you got that, never!" said Victoria.

"Never?" repeated Henry.

Henry's mother nodded. "Never, ever," she said quietly.

Slowly Victoria got up, touched Henry on the shoulder, as she went to deal with a child screaming in the background.

This couldn't be happening to his Sophie. His beautiful, intelligent, wise and loving Sophie and, if it was, then it was his job to find a cure. For the sake of Sophie, Andrew and Peter, he had to find a cure.

Chapter 83

Château de Gressier June 1975

EARLY THE NEXT morning Henry phoned Cassie to report on Sophie's state of health. He'd decided he wasn't going to say anything about Sophie not going back to work; for one thing her income from her contracts was vital to pay for the Vault's building work.

"Henry, the market doesn't want her anymore," said Sophie's booker candidly, immediately after Henry had said Sophie remained unwell. "They say the thing that made her special has gone. Photographers don't want to work with her. She's always missing or late for her appointments. Both La Goviette and Circum are talking about cancelling their contracts with her early."

The report Cassie gave was truly upsetting for it was the first time Henry had ever heard anything unpleasant said about his Sophie, and he hated it. How could he protect her from people saying things like that about her, he wondered.

"Speak to John," said Cassie. "He's really worried about her too."

"John?"

"Yes John, Sophie's driver," said Cassie. "He'll tell you what's been going on."

Henry walked across the Gallery from where he had made his phone call to look out of the window towards the drive. There, parked neatly, was Sophie's large black Mercedes with John Chabani at the wheel.

Sophie's agency had hired John as her driver immediately she went back to work with the instruction that wherever Sophie was, he was to be there too. He would leave occasionally to fill up with petrol, get something to eat or to have a wash and shave, but otherwise if he was on duty he would stay by her side and he would only come off duty when instructed by Sophie or Cassie. For his role was not just as her driver but, unknown to Sophie or Henry, her bodyguard too. It was the same for all supermodels; there were far too many men who obsessed and fantasized about these high-profile beautiful women that they had to have their own security.

Henry walked down to Sophie's car and climbed into the passenger seat. Each man knew who the other was, but they had hardly ever exchanged a word. If the truth were to be known, since he had started working for her, John had spent far more time with Sophie than Henry had done. The two men shook hands.

"She's not well John," said Henry as his opening remark. "In fact, she's very poorly, he added."

"I know boss," said John, getting highly emotional.

Henry found is strange to see such a big strong man well-up with tears like that.

"I'm sorry boss but it's 'cause I love her," he said. "I hope you won't mind me saying that, 'cause there weren't anything wrong between us. But she was so good to me."

"I understand," said Henry comfortingly. "There's nothing wrong with that. She affects a lot of people like that, including me," he added, trying but failing to be lighthearted.

"You know, like family, she was like family" said John, trying to explain himself.

"Its how Sophie wants it to be," said Henry. "Everyone who works *for* ..." He stopped and corrected himself ... "works *with* us, is part of that family. It's the way it's been at Château de Gressier for two hundred years. It's been the same in Sophie and my business."

"Yes boss. She said the business in London was a bit like a topsy turvey partnership, where no one was in charge, but it did well because everyone did their best."

Henry thought about what John had said. It seemed to him to be a very fair summary.

"John, Sophie won't be going back to work."

"I guessed that boss."

"Would you like to come and work with me? Will you do that?" asked Henry, almost pleadingly.

"Driving?" enquired John.

"Yes, ... no, ... It's whatever needs to be done. That's the only job description you're going to get.

"Yes boss," said John. I'd like that.

The two men shook hands again, as though they were sealing a deal.

"Excuse me, boss, but you know this is the fault of Imra Blanche, don't you?" said John.

"Why?"

"You know she smokes cannabis?"

"Who, Sophie or Imra?"

"You couldn't go into Imra's place without smelling the stuff. Until Sophie stayed at Imra's she didn't drink, and she certainly didn't smoke weed."

Henry thought for a little while. John was right. It was only after Sophie had stayed at Imra's flat that she started to drink, first vodka and then gin.

"It was Imra who introduced Sophie to her drug dealer, Patrice Gevais," said John assuredly. "If that hadn't happened then she wouldn't be poorly now."

Henry was surprised at how much John knew, but as he reflected, he realised he shouldn't have been.

"John, your first job is to go and get whatever Sophie has left at Imra's flat and bring it back here," said Henry. I'll go and arrange it," and with that he was gone.

His call to Imra was curt. "Do you know who supplied Sophie with marijuana?" he asked immediately, without the usual generalities. He wanted to check on the name given to him by John.

"Why?"

"She's poorly, and needs some more," said Henry. "I need his name and number?"

Imra left the phone for a moment and then came back and gave Henry, Patrice Gevais' telephone number.

"Does Sophie have much stuff at your flat?" he asked.

"Almost a whole room full."

"Okay, John, her driver, is coming to collect it," said Henry. "She's moving out and won't be back."

"Oh, no! why?" asked Imra.

"As I said, she's very ill, very poorly. She won't be back."

Henry put down the phone, as anger welled up inside him.

His next call was to Walter and Inga. They had to know how poorly their daughter was.

Chapter 84

Château de Gressier June 1975

HENRY STAYED CONSTANTLY by Sophie's side over the next few days, coaxing her to get up and shower, to get dressed and even put on some makeup. When he was with her Sophie didn't cry. His presence gave her the feeling of security she desperately needed, but whenever he was gone, she would wrap up in a little ball and cry tears of desperation. Henry walked her down to the river, through the fields of both de Gressier and Louis Estates. He chattered away, talking about everything. But the only time Sophie spoke was to talk about herself, and most importantly her fears. She could not accept that her children were safe.

When Walter and Inga first arrived, they wondered what the problem was for, when they first saw Sophie, she was clean, dressed and pleased to see them. But over the next forty-eight hours, as they observed her and the nursing she required, they first became distressed, and then very angry. They blamed Henry, arguing it was the building of the Vaults which had caused all the problems for, if it had not been for that, Sophie wouldn't have gone back to work.

Victoria, seeing how the attack hurt her son, came to Henry's defense, saying that it wasn't the Vaults that had caused the problem, but his grandmother's purchase of Château Rabôut.

"A problem made much worse by the hugely extravagant refurbishment of Maison Gelina" added Walter curtly.

Henry had already admitted to himself that the costs to refurbish Maison Gelina were horrendous, but if he was going to get the counterfeit wine out of the market through a bottle-swap, he had to have his Matterers Lunches there, for it was only in discreet conversations that deals of this sensitivity could be done.

At first, Henry was surprised at the depth of knowledge Walter had of his problems. But then he realised that, in Walter breaking Sophie's trust fund, he would have discovered what it was for and what the money was being spent on.

Henry and his mother wanted Sophie to go to England for medical attention. Her parents wanted her to go to Germany. Neither of them trusted the mental health services in France, not because they were bad, but because they both carried a preference for their own nation. To be frank, both Victoria and Henry thought the mental health services in the UK to be a bit of a cinderella service, and both dreaded the responsibility and risk of complaints from Walter and Inga if things went wrong.

The catalyst for action came one evening at suppertime. They were all in the kitchen. Victoria had cooked and there was general chit-chat around the room as she was about to serve up. Sophie was looking around vacantly.

"I suppose it's best that I kill them" she said, matter-of-factly, but not to anyone in particular.

Inga picked up on her daughter's words immediately. "Kill who?" she asked in German.

"Andrew and Peter, it's the only way I can keep them safe," replied Sophie also in German.

The room froze for the two boys were sitting at the table. Henry had heard her say this two or three times over the days before, but he hadn't mentioned it to anyone else. For Inga and Walter, it took them right back to the days immediately after Andrew was born when Sophie discussed with them her need to kill her child.

"Keep them safe from whom?" asked Sophie's mother, again speaking in German.

"The people who are trying to steal them," said Sophie.

"Who's trying to steal them?" asked Walter, very quietly and gently, recognising the delicacy of the discussion."

"I don't know. If I knew that I could stop them," said Sophie.

"Please, can we not have this conversation in front of ...," said Henry, his voice draining away, as it was obvious who he was referring to. Although the conversation was in German, he was anxious that his children would hear, as Sophie always spoke to them in German.

"Why are they trying to steal them?" asked Inga.

"To get money."

No one else said anything. They let Sophie and her mother talk.

"Kidnap them?" asked Inga.

"Yes, but we don't have the money to pay. We could pay once, but we can't pay now."

"Sophie," said Inga, "I don't think anyone's trying to steal Andrew or Peter."

Sophie looked at her mother and then looked at the table.

"Please, can we not have this conversation," insisted Henry. "Not here and not now!"

"Oh, they are, mother," said Sophie, ignoring Henry's instructions. "If we can't pay, they will sell their kidneys, liver, eyes, hearts in organ transplants. I've read about it. They can make hundreds of thousands by selling their organs."

"Sophie, that's not going to happen" said her mother, matter-of-factly.

"For Pete's sake stop," demanded Henry. "We're not having this conversation."

"What's not going to happen?" asked Sophie, as the patterns of conversation became befuddled in her mind.

Everyone who heard it found the fact that Sophie could articulate her reasoning, albeit illogical, completely frightening.

It was Victoria, also worried at what the children were hearing, who deliberately stopped the conversation by serving up, and, as the plates moved around the table, the tension in the room palpably lightened.

After supper, Henry and Sophie toured the estate in their usual evening walk while Victoria put the two boys to bed. Walter and Inga went into a mild panic.

It was much later, when Victoria took Sophie to get ready for bed, that Walter made an announcement.

"She's coming home with us" he said firmly.

Henry looked at Walter, weighing up his response.

"I'm not asking. I'm telling" said Walter.

"Walter, you have no right to dictate Sophie's life. You lost that on the day I married her. So please, there's no telling in this. We discuss it and then we decide."

"Discuss ahead" said Walter arrogantly. "As long as you agree with my decision I don't give, as you English would say, a shit."

There was something very comical about Walter saying the word shit with a strong German accent which made Henry smile. It was odd, given the anger being shown towards him.

"Actually, I agree with you," said Henry. "I think it would be best that she goes into a nursing home near where you live, at least for the moment. But nothing, and I stress this Walter, nothing is to happen to her medically without my consent. Do you understand? I'm going to get her well again if it's the last thing I do!"

This compromise was agreed between the two men, who unconsciously uncrossed their swords and moved away from each other. Except Walter's English was not good enough to understand the condition Henry had set!

Chapter 85

Château de Gressier July 1975

THE NEXT MORNING, Henry was up in the Gallery trying hard to keep his business show on the road at the same time as organising for Sophie and her parents to be taken back to Bamberg. In all the circumstances, it was thought best that she didn't fly. The plan had been to take the train to Paris where they would be met by John Chabani who would then drive them all the way to Bamberg. Henry was on the phone to the station, booking the tickets, when there was an almighty scream from the kitchen, followed by a yell from Victoria shouting for Henry to come quickly.

Henry dropped the phone mid-sentence, ran down the stairs into the kitchen of the Cellars, where he found his children screaming and with Victoria fighting Sophie, as she wrestled to hold her hand flowing with blood under the tap.

"She stabbed herself in the hand" said Victoria in a panic. "I don't know how many times, three, four. I just don't know. Straight into the back of her hand."

Henry moved closer to Sophie. The pent-up anger which Sophie had felt earlier was now replaced by shock, as she watched the blood streaming out of her hand held under the pouring cold water and into the sink.

"It suddenly happened," pleaded Victoria.

Henry reached across and grabbed a clean tea towel, and as he was wrapping her hand, Walter and Inga arrived which added to the confusion as they sought to find out what had happened.

"Walter, Inga please take the children next door," commanded Henry, as he sat Sophie down into a kitchen chair as she was now feeling faint from her actions. They did as they were told.

With Sophie seated, Henry unwrapped the towel from her hand and immediately blood oozed from the three round entry holes, so he quickly wrapped it up again, keeping the wounds under pressure to control the bleeding.

"What did she stab herself with?" he asked.

"One of the pencils. The black one, I think."

Henry un-wrapped her hand once more so he could carefully study it. He saw that two of the three stabs had gone through the back of her hand, piercing the skin on her palms on the other side. Keeping the cloth pressed firmly over the three holes, Henry encouraged Sophie to wriggle her fingers and clench her fist.

"That's good" he said. "No bones broken. But those wounds are going to need stitches."

Henry and Victoria looked at Sophie. It was clear to them that, although she knew that her hand was hurting, she had no idea that she had deliberately damaged herself.

"Do you think Doctor Botrel will do the stitches?" asked Henry. "So much better we go there than to the local hospital. Someone is bound to sell the story to the press otherwise."

A phone call to the surgery resulted in Botrel driving out to Château de Gressier. He was there in minutes and, using a local anesthetic to relieve the pain, he stitched both deep inside the flesh and on top of the skin. Finally, he gave Sophie a sedative and, very quickly, she fell asleep on the settee.

It was the first time that Victoria was able to explain what had happened.

"The children were at the table. I'd given them some paper and crayons to write with, and Sophie was sitting with them doing sweeping arrows and daggers and angles with sharp points. She was filling in the areas with heavy black crayon."

Victoria showed Henry the pictures which she had saved. He was shocked by what he saw. When Sophie had doodled in the past, she had drawn curves with soft lines and very delicate shading.

"That's not Sophie" said Henry.

"It is now" said Victoria mournfully. "I'm afraid, it is now."

"She was writing fiercely on the paper when she picked up the pencil, held it firmly in her fist." Victoria demonstrated, "and then, bam. She brought it down, bam, bam, bam, on the back of her hand. I simply couldn't believe it. She said nothing. It was just, bam, bam, bam," Victoria repeated, making the sound of pencil hitting wood.

Chapter 86

Château de Gressier July 1975

SOPHIE'S PATH TOWARDS self-destruction meant a change of plan. Sophie and her parents would no longer go by train to Paris. It was thought best that no one should see her in her current state. Both Sophie, and her image, needed to be protected. It was agreed that Henry would drive Sophie, Walter, and Inga to Geneva where they would meet John who would be in Sophie's Mercedes. He would take over and drive the three of them through Switzerland to Germany and back home to Bamberg.

In the morning, Andrew and Peter watched from the Gallery window as Victoria held them protectively. "Wave to mummy," she said, as Sophie bent down to climb into the car. She didn't look up at her two scared and confused children. They had seen their mummy leave many times but this time they instinctively knew something was wrong. They were too young to understand that so called 'recreational' drugs had consigned their mother to a living death.

Henry and John rendezvoused at a small hotel just outside Geneva where the five of them spent an uninterrupted night. As Sophie and he lay side by side, it felt to Henry that he had his old Sophie beside him. She felt the same, smelled the same, and even looked the same, for the few days that Victoria had been looking after her she had managed to put on some weight. It was when they spoke that Henry knew that the old Sophie wasn't there. The confident woman she had once been had gone and was now replaced by someone confused and very scared.

In the morning, Henry, very patiently, helped Sophie shower and dress. Comfortingly for Henry there was something very normal about the way they had breakfast together, just the two of them until, much later, they were joined by Sophie's parents.

The luggage in Henry's battered old car was transferred into Sophie's immaculate Mercedes. Henry kissed Sophie goodbye and watched as, with John at the wheel, her car drove away. Sophie took no notice either of his presence or of her going. Henry's mouth was tight and sour. His eyes filled with tears. His heart was breaking, and the knot in his stomach meant he was physically in pain.

Henry returned to his room and did something he never did. He went to sleep in the day. He slept undisturbed for nearly six hours, waking completely refreshed. For the first time, in what seemed an age, he felt his head was clear. In the hotel lounge, as he was served afternoon tea, Henry prepared a new jobs list. He made his plans under three headings - Sophie, the Boys and Work. He had written some very clear objectives, but he was far from certain as to how he was going to deliver on these.

In the late afternoon Henry phoned Château de Gressier and spoke to his mother. The pleasantries were very few, for Victoria got straight to the point.

"I'm taking the boys back to Hertford to live with me there. They are not staying here," said Victoria firmly.

"Why?" protested Henry.

"You can't look after your children, and Sophie's parents are too old," said Victoria. "I have to do it and I can't do it here. In England I know the system, here I don't, so they're coming home with me."

"But your house is let," protested Henry.

"Not anymore. I didn't like it being let out, so I stopped it after six months. It's empty and we're going back, and if you've got any sense, you'll settle in Found House again and stop running around like a mad thing," scolded his mother.

Henry protested, arguing that Château de Gressier was where Sophie wanted Andrew and Peter to make their home.

Victoria argued back. "That's nonsense and you know it. The boys can come here in the summer just as you did, but they need stability. They need England and that's where they're going, tomorrow. If you want to see your boys, they will be at home in Hertford," she said. With that she hung up.

Henry dialled back, but the phone just rang. Hell, how it irritated him when she abruptly stopped having a conversation; just like her mother, he thought, not realising that it was a habit which he was well versed in exercising. At least Henry now had clarity. He knew which way his car was heading. He was going back to London.

Chapter 87

Found House, London July 1975

HENRY ARRIVED AT Found House feeling tired but very buoyant. He had driven through the night taking 16-hours to journey from Geneva to London, stopping only for fuel and the channel crossing. He was only calling in for a shower and a few minutes rest before he continued to Hertford. The reason for his newly found confidence was his decision to sell the Vaults.

He had contemplated his business problems from every angle as he travelled, and it was the solution. Finally, he was prepared to agree with Sophie and Ainsworth that building the Vaults had been a damn silly vanity project, but now it was nearly finished and once his wines, which were in storage all over the place, could be moved there, it would start making a profit.

During his journey he had worked out the expected rental income from storage fees, deducted a few percent for costs and capitalised the net rental stream at 7%. The place was worth a small fortune, he concluded. 'In one bound I'm free,' he thought to himself, remembering a line from one of the comic strips of his youth.

As was normal, when Henry made an appearance at Found House, Ainsworth collared him. "We've a bit of a problem," he said. "We've had our answer from HM Customs. They've turned us down. They've refused to give the Vaults bonded warehouse status. We can't ship our wine from France to the UK and into the Vaults without paying VAT and duty. It's going to mean an upfront tax bill of between one and five million pounds.

Henry frowned. "They can't do that," he shouted. "Why the fuck have they done it? There are bonded warehouses all over the fucking country!" he yelled, before collapsing into the settee in his office.

"Don't shoot the messenger," pleaded Ainsworth, who was becoming pretty good at being a bearer of bad news. He was like one of those punch bags that hang from the ceiling. However hard you verbally slogged at him, you could be certain that, at the end, he would be hanging there still and in the central position, while his assailant was exhausted and defeated.

Halfway through building the Vaults, Henry had discovered that, if they brought the wine he had in storage in France into England and the Vaults, there would be an immediate charge to excise duty and value added tax, unless they could get it designated as a bonded warehouse, in which case these taxes would only be payable when the wine left the Vaults. He had not worried as he'd assumed bonded warehouse status would be a formality granted to him once the Vaults were nearing completion, which was about now.

"Customs are concerned that, between the port and the Vaults, there might be some leakage into the market," Ainsworth explained.

"Cigarette manufacturers store their finished cigarettes in bonded warehouses, so do all the brewers," he answered hastily.

"Yes," said Ainsworth knowingly. "The thing is that those bonded warehouses are at the end of the manufacturing process. We are not."

"Vincent, that's bollocks," exclaimed Henry. I'll find you bonded warehouse after bonded warehouse scattered throughout the country. In any case goods are flowing between here and Europe on a just in time basis every minute of the day."

"I know," said Ainsworth, "but it's the reason they have given. Interestingly, they've given us permission to take it to appeal in front of the Commissioners. I think we've got a good chance of getting it overturned."

For the next hour, Henry quizzed Ainsworth on the tax rules. It was clear he had investigated the issues thoroughly.

"How long is it going to take to get to an appeal hearing?" asked Henry.

"One year, maybe two, sometime, never," said Ainsworth.

"Never?" said Henry frustratingly. "Jesus, I've spent millions on a place that's probably going to be worthless." As he said these words, he knew his earlier plan of selling the Vaults, and getting out of his financial problems had disappeared into thin air.

"Yes, the worst scenario is that it might need a statutory instrument placed before parliament," explained Ainsworth, "and getting that done, who knows."

"What, involving parliament? That's ridiculous." Henry's voice yielded total despair. "Who do we know who might help us?" he asked himself out loud.

"Will the Chairman of the Board of HM Customs come to one of your lunches?" Ainsworth asked.

"No, he was invited but decided not to come, but his subsequent order was wise. It showed he was a shrewd investor."

"Then we should invite him to lunch again," said Ainsworth.

"We should definitely not," responded Henry. "Until this is all over, or unless he's an old Etonian."

"What's Eton got to do with this?"

"If he was from there then he'd be so fucking arrogant that he'd assume he was immune from criticism and do the hell he wants. Everyone else will want to act inscrutably. For the middle-class Englishman this means acting tougher on their friends than anyone else. They do it to prove how incorruptible they are."

Ainsworth nodded his agreement and then added, "unless of course you're a Mason."

"Yeh, unless you're a Mason!" repeated Henry desolately.

There was a pause in the two men's conversation as they thought through their predicament.

"If we can't get it designated as a tax-free zone then we have to accept that we're not going to be able to fill the whole space with wine," said Henry. "That means we're going to have to rent some of it out for general storage. I think I know a legal storage company who will rent half a floor from us, and I'm sure there will be others. Could you ask one of your surveyor contacts to make some enquiries?

"We'll get nothing like the yields per square foot we need to make the economics work. The bank's not going to like it," warned Ainsworth.

"They're going to be far less happy when they learn we're going to have to redesign the front with two entrances and not one. When I did my original sums on traffic movements with wine, I reckoned we could manage with one entrance dealing with movements both in and out. If we change plans to cater for general storage, we're going to need two entrances, one for in, and one for out.

"Henry, that'll cost a fortune," protested Ainsworth. "It'll mean removing part of the bank of insulation soil which has already been deposited around, and then using grinders and oxyacetylene torches, to cut away the concrete that's already there, let alone the delays in getting planning permission. What do you think it will cost?

"I don't know. Another fifty k, may be a hundred."

"The bank will never approve," said Ainsworth sharply.

"That's why we're not going to tell them. And it's why we're going to get it done before we've got planning permission. Sometimes in this life it's a darn sight easier to get forgiven than it is to get permission, and this is one of them."

"Are you sure?" asked Ainsworth cautiously.

"What's the bank going to do, foreclose?"

"They might."

"I doubt it. Do you remember the meeting just after Juliette died and we were wondering what to do? It was Sophie who insisted we got on with finishing the Vaults because she didn't want other people putting our lives on hold. It was a good decision then, and I think we should do the same again. We've always made decisions in the best interests of the project, and if the bank don't like it, then tough," Henry nodded his head firmly downwards as though he were adding an exclamation mark to his words. Is there any more bad news?" he enquired, sarcastically.

"Afraid so; Sophie's agents won't be sending us any more money to pay for the Vaults. They say she needs it."

Henry knew that this would be happening. With her contracts being cancelled, it was obvious that the money would start drying up.

"You've got a problem there," said Ainsworth.

"With what?" asked Henry.

"Well if Sophie is, as you say, without the mental capacity to make a decision, it means that you cannot act on her affairs unless you've got a Power of Attorney."

"At last, something I've done right," said Henry dejectedly. "Yes, I have one of those. We did it before Peter was born. We were frightened about Sophie getting a bad case of the baby blues as she did when Andrew was born."

"Thank God for that," said Ainsworth. "You would have been in a genuine nightmare without it. You know the courts would have taken over managing her affairs if you didn't have one?"

Henry nodded. "I guess we have to accept that it's the end of her money."

"In that case, I need you to sell some more investment grade wine. This will be the last lot." said Ainsworth. "Just to tide us over until we start taking cash flow from this year's wine production."

"How's the buy-back going?" asked Henry.

"Counterfeit wine has cost us about two and a quarter million francs so far, but the discoveries and returns are slowing down markedly. I think it will all cap out at about two and a half million."

"Pounds or French Francs?" asked Henry.

"Francs," answered Ainsworth. "That first assessment of your grandmother's was pretty accurate."

Henry nodded appreciatively, as Ainsworth and he wandered off into a general discussion which was all too easy, as gossip abounded within the wine industry. They wondered at the rumours they were hearing because it seemed that everyone else was doing much better than them.

Henry suddenly asked, "Is there anything else?"

"Yes," said Ainsworth, "I have one more bit of bad news for you."

"Oh, what else? It can't be as bad as everything else."

"No, it's smaller but much nastier, I'm afraid."

"OK go," said Henry, by way of a prompt.

"I'm afraid Harriet has been stealing from you, us."

"What? How? That's not possible," protested Henry.

"Yes, about £6,824," said Ainsworth.

"About," said Henry mockingly, given the accuracy of the number.

"It's what I've discovered so far, but there may be more."

"Oh, for fuck's sake," said Henry. "How the hell did ..."

"Personal use of your credit cards, etc."

"How did you discover it?" asked Henry.

"You know your top apartment is on a separate electricity meter."

"Yes."

"Well, they came to cut off the electricity for non-payment the day before yesterday and I happened to hear them come. I knew the bill had been paid because I'd signed the cheque. Well, she used the last couple of cheques I wrote to pay your electricity bill to pay hers."

"Hell, why?" asked Henry. "Isn't she damn well paid?"

"Yes, but why, I don't know. But since she came via David Daunier and New Found Estate, I thought you should deal with it."

"I didn't know, really?" said Henry in shock.

"Yep."

"That'll make it hard to sack her, won't it? They're far too big a supplier," protested Henry.

"Welcome to my world," said Ainsworth. "I'll make sure you have the evidence. When do you want to see her, tonight?"

"No, I'm going to Hertford to see my mum and my kids. Oh fuck," added Henry, "a cheating woman is the last thing I need to deal with right now.

Chapter 88

Hertford and Bamberg July 1975

HENRY WAS EXHAUSTED when he eventually pulled up outside his mother's home. As he walked through the front door, opening it using the key which had never come off his key ring, he immediately saw that the previous tenants had not looked after the house well. Nevertheless, he was delighted to be there for it had the security and comfort of home.

Henry's first action was to see his children who were asleep in his old bed, lying top to tail. He sat on the floor with his back to the wall and watched them breathe. They were so calm and peaceful. His thoughts were of only one thing, love. He tried to analyse the difference between the love he had of his children and of his wife. It was so very different and yet so much the same. The same was the pain and the anxiety that Henry knew he would feel if anything were to happen to either of them.

It was a long time later when Henry came downstairs. His mother was in the sitting room ironing. She rarely had the radio or TV on when she ironed clothing. It was the time she set aside to think.

"I can do this here," said Victoria. "I can look after them here. This is my home. I know how it works. I couldn't do this anywhere else." She spoke almost apologetically.

"I know, mother," said Henry. "And thank you. I understand. It's all much the same in France, and yet, at the same time, so very different."

"I wondered about doing this at my age, but you know, they make me feel young. Before, when I had you, I was working. This time, I'm retired. It will be very much easier. Also, I'm sure I'll be able to get some help."

Henry nodded. "Mum, I'll try and come as often as I can, but it won't be often, at least not for a little while." He told her of the tax problem with the Vaults and the fact that there was no more money coming from Sophie's contracts to help pay for it.

Henry stayed at his mother's house for the rest of the week. He updated his old bedroom, making it fit for his children with new bunk beds, whilst hogging the phone as he did as Ainsworth asked and sold vintage wines into the investment market for immediate delivery and payment.

On Saturday Henry flew to Nuremberg and then hired a car to drive to Bamberg to see Sophie. Her parents had found a lovely sanatorium for her to stay in. A huge hospital style building set in acres of lawn surrounded by fields and then wrapped in a valley of pine trees. It was a place of peace and tranquility. The ideal place to convalesce.

Henry sat for an hour with Sophie. Everything about her was the same as it used to be. She looked beautiful once again. Her hair perfectly styled, make up delicately applied and her clothes were as immaculate as a super model's should be, except her mind had gone. She was no longer capable of focusing on any issue and could only very vaguely remember the past.

"We have a problem nursing her when she gets cross," said the matron, "because she then gets very violent and she's far too strong for us."

But Henry didn't see any of that. He simply saw a placid person with all the fight taken from her.

"I'll bring the children in the summer holidays," was his parting shot, as Henry left at the end of his first day visiting.

In the car park, he saw a black Mercedes which had something about it which made him look twice. He went up to the driver's window and tapped. "John, what are you doing here?" he asked.

"Mr. Lemberger said I had to stay with Sophie and so that's what I've been doing."

"Since when?" asked Henry.

"Since she arrived.

"Do you see her?" asked Henry.

"Yes, I'm allowed to go in for twenty minutes, maybe half an hour in the morning after she's dressed and then another half hour in the evening before she goes to bed."

"We've already agreed that you're working for me, haven't we?" said Henry.

"Yes, I know. I'm just waiting for you to tell me what to do."

John was right. Henry had forgotten that he needed to give him instructions.

Henry moved around to the passenger side of the car and climbed in. He sat next to John. The two men looked straight ahead and said nothing.

"John, Sophie's going to be here for a very long time," said Henry. "I think you better come to London where I'm based.

"What are you going to do about this, boss? It can't go, just left."

"What do you mean?" asked Henry.

"The bastard who sold her the shit. He needs sorting."

"We'll have to do something," agreed Henry. "We can't allow people to go around doing this kind of damage. It's not fair."

"Well, if not him, we need to give Blanche a bloody good smacking," said John. "We can do no more than that 'cause she's got a kid."

"We'll think about it," said Henry. "In the meantime, can I suggest you give this car back to whomever it belongs, and you get to my office in London."

"This car is Miss Sophie's," replied John. "I did the buying. It was paid for by Sophie through her agent, I'm certain of it."

Henry absorbed the information. He knew nothing about Sophie's business arrangements. He had no need to, until now.

"Tomorrow, we go to Paris," said Henry. "See you here then.

"Yes, boss," said John nodding.

Henry got out, drove in his hire car to Walter and Inga's house where he had been staying. He saw nothing of the journey. His mind was on Sophie's agency and Imra Blanche and the conversations he was going to have with them.

Chapter 89

Château de Gressier July 1975

"WHAT DID YOU do before you were a driver," asked Henry, as they started their journey to Paris from Nuremburg, where Henry had dropped off his hire car.

"Army Boss, British, then Legion and then jankers[14] for being AWOL[15] and discharged from both.

"Jankers?"

"Yeah, well, I left the Brits to join the French because I missed out on the SAS.

"Can't complain – learned an awful lot of shit from that lot."

Henry shook his head in bafflement for John Chabani summarised his military career without a hint of emotion or, given how tough his experience must have been, without bitterness.

How did you get into the British Army?

"I was in London on hols, met some lovely army lads in a pub and joined. It was easy."

"No problem, you being a French national?" asked Henry being under the false impression that the British army only recruited British citizens.

"Nah, couldn't have been nicer. Good bunch of killers in the British Army. Good discipline."

They drove on a little way in silence. Henry was finding it strange to be chauffeured and John, knowing his job, only engaged in any

---

[14] Military Prison

[15] Absent Without Leave

conversation started by his boss. It was a golden rule of chauffeuring that the driver never started the conversation.

"What would you do to Patrice Gevais?" asked Henry.

"Gevais, the drug dealer, I'd break 'is fucking kneecaps, both legs. He'd walk with a limp for the rest of his life," he added.

"And how would you do that?"

"I'd jump him with a sawn down scaffold pole."

"He'd fight back," said Henry.

"They'd be a couple of us. My mate would hold him down while I whacked him."

"So you've doubled your chances of being caught, because every time you work with an accomplice you double the risk that the secret gets out. For no reason he could well snitch you up. No, there has to be a better way," continued Henry. "A broken kneecap, whatever, he's back in the game in six months. We need him dealt with for much longer than that. Sophie's going to suffer for years and he needs to suffer for years too."

"Break his kneecap, boss, and he will struggle to walk for the rest of his life."

Henry nodded, acknowledging that John had a very good point. They sat in silence for another few minutes and then Henry asked, "Can you get hold of any drugs?"

"Why?"

Henry repeated the question.

"Yes, boss. It costs more, but it's easier, less risky, bought on the streets."

"And a gun?"

"Possibly, boss. Depends on the kind."

"A pistol, a revolver, something small."

"Oh, that's easy. Again, it's just money. Are we borrowing or buying?"

"It's not going back," said Henry emphatically.

"I think we should work out a plan to send this guy down for ten years, hopefully fifteen and, in the process, we'll stitch up his supply chain too."

"How are you going to do that, boss?" asked John.

"We're going to buy a dealer's worth of drugs which we will plant in his flat with a gun and a few thousand francs, and then we'll phone the police. They'll do the rest. The risk to us is very small, maximum 48 hours possession of a gun. There's also possession of drugs but each time the amounts will be small so we can argue they are for personal use minimising the risk to us."

"I'm in," said John, "if you are?"

"How much would a drug dealer have as a stock of drugs?"

"It would depend how big he is."

"Reasonable size, intermediate dealer?"

Fifteen, maybe twenty thousand francs worth at say street value," replied John.

After this, they virtually sat in silence until they reached Maison Gelina where Henry's final parting words were, "One thing please, navy suits, white shirt, black tie, black shoes, it's the uniform."

"Can't do the tie, boss, if it's more than 90 degrees in the shade. Cap?" John asked.

"No cap," said Henry.

"Good, 'cause that would have been the real deal breaker."

The two men smiled. Their relationship was going to work.

Chapter 90

Found House August 1975

HENRY HAD PUT off and put off his meeting with Harriet. He knew it would be confrontational and unpleasant. However, he was taking his children to see Sophie the next week and the problem had to be out of the way by then. He didn't want to sack her because he needed her, but then he had to be able to trust her and she had broken that trust. She had to go!

Harriet's fraud was easy to commit. Her rent was months late, her credit cards were full, and the bank wouldn't extend her overdraft. She knew exactly where her money went. It was going on paying the HP instalments on a car which she had no idea of its whereabouts, paying off half of Rick Bussell's theft from the gym and the last of his debts with his drug dealer where the accumulated interest never seemed to end.

When it came to paying Henry's credit card or utility bills, she just put her payment slip in the post with his cheque rather than hers. On payday she intended to pay Henry's bills from her own account. No one would know, or that was her plan. However, paydays came, and she made no payment. It was always something Harriet was going to do tomorrow. With access to his credit cards, it became easy for her to pay for the things she wanted.

Harriet had a premonition that something was wrong when, at lunchtime, she saw a message on her desk saying that Henry wanted to see her that evening. He would be back in the office late and she was to stay. Although their rooms were not far apart, she did not hear Henry come into the building. The first Harriet knew that he was back was when he phoned to ask her to come into his room. As she entered, the expression on Henry's face said everything. Her heart went into her mouth. She looked at him and glanced at the table. Laid out were his credit card statements and photocopies of the paid cheques.

"Vincent has given me a dossier of evidence on your activities," said Henry. It looks as though you've stolen well over £6,000 from me." He spoke calmly, deliberately controlling his anger. It wasn't the deceit which upset him. He'd been in business long enough to get used to that. What he hated was confrontation. That had to be reserved for suppliers and truculent customers, not with those whom he worked.

"Six thousand" replied Harriet incredulously. "That's just not possible."

There was no denial of the fundamental charge.

"£6,800 to be precise, have a look for yourself," said Henry sharply leaning forward over his desk to push the papers towards her. "I've checked. It's at least that amount and probably more."

Harriet looked at the statements piled neatly into small stacks. She pretended to go through them, but she knew what she would find. Reading the statements was like reading a history book of a short period of her life. Her mother's birthday flowers charged to Henry's account. The weekend hire of a car in Bristol. It couldn't amount to so much. The room was silent. Harriet stared at the table glancing up to look at Henry every second or so. Henry said nothing. Suddenly Harriet's mood changed. She stood up straight, held her head high and looked at him directly. "You really don't remember me, do you, Hank Bellanger?" she said defiantly.

The words Hank Bellanger threw him completely. He suddenly felt he'd been found out doing something wrong, but he didn't know what.

"You were at New Found Estate for the harvest about ten, no, eleven years ago, weren't you?" said Harriet.

"Probably, yes. I've been there twice, once in my late teens and again about five years ago, why?" asked Henry.

"And you drove the trailer taking the fruit to the barn, didn't you?"

"Er, yes," he replied.

"And things happened there, didn't they?"

"Er," he said again. He remembered it very well but was not grasping the point being made.

"Do you remember a young girl in the packing shed at New Found Estate?"

"Yes," he said hesitantly.

"Do you remember her name?"

"Yes, of course, Sunetta, Sunetta Daunier," and with those words Henry froze. Suddenly, in front of him, Henry saw in Harriet the same gangly girl he had seduced all those years ago.

"That's me," said Harriet as soon as she saw Henry had, at last, recognised her.

"You're...... are you David and Satutu's daughter?" he asked.

"Yes."

Henry sunk back in his chair and looked at the woman in front of him. This news had taken the wind right out of his sails. "How come?" he asked.

"How come my name is not Sunetta Daunier?" questioned Harriet. "Is that what you want to know?"

"Yes, I think so," said Henry weakly.

"Sunetta's my nick name in South Africa. Harriet's my Christian name and Bussell is my married name, although I'm no longer married – well separated."

"Did you know I was just fourteen then" said Harriet, as she watched Henry gather up the papers on his desk and throw them together.

Henry didn't reply.

"Why did you leave without saying good-bye?" she asked, her voice clearly revealing her up-set at him going.

"The farm manager beat me up for, erm, getting too close to you. He hurt ... damaged me quite badly, actually." Henry paused as he remembered the moments. "He forced me out, sacked me. I tried to say goodbye, but you'd gone out. There was nothing I could do."

"Who, Lucky?" asked Harriet.

"Yes, that was his name." There was a pause. "I wrote to you after Little Joe died," said Henry defensively.

"Did you? I don't remember ... thank you," said Harriet.

"I thought your mother wearing red shoes was inspirational," he said.

"And her white gloves, ... both became quite symbolic for a long period of time," said Harriet, as they both reflected on the past.

"And this?" asked Henry pointing to the pile of papers left by Ainsworth. "Why this?"

Harriet sat down and slowly told her story. All of it; her affair with John Harrison, the married lawyer, falling pregnant by him, her abortion, her life with Rick and the debts he left her with. It poured forth as a narrative from a book told without any emotion. It was as though she was talking about someone else.

"Did you not know what your husband was doing?" asked Henry, trying to understand his fraud.

"No. I had no idea. Even the statements for the bank account he used went to his mother's house and not ours."

"So why are you paying back his debt? I don't understand," said Henry.

"I signed a piece of paper saying I would, and they take the money every month straight from my bank account. I can't stop it."

"Have you tried?"

Yes, I've told my bank not to pay it many, many times and to get the money back but nothing happens. They just take another repayment by direct debit the next month.

"You must have known you were going to get caught by doing this," said Henry, again waiving to the pile of papers in front of him.

"I suppose I did," said Harriet. "I don't know. Perhaps it was all done so as to ....."

"What do you think your parents will say when you, me, one of us tells them why you've been sacked," interrupted Henry.

"Oh, you won't be sacking me," said Harriet confidently.

"Why?" said Henry in puzzlement.

"You'll not want a discussion with my parents about what you did to me when I was just a kid. There's a long jail sentence in South Africa for that kind of thing."

"I suppose you'd say the same thing if I was to report this to the police," said Henry, testing her a little further.

Harriet paused. Her mind raced. The thought of involving the police was too frightening a prospect. As a mixed-race teenager, and from what happened with Little Joe in South Africa, she had learnt that there was no justice in a legal process over which you had no control.

"Oh no," said Harriet confidently. "I'd tell 'em how you've defrauded your clients by selling them about a million quid's worth of wine you don't own."

"Don't be ridiculous. I've done nothing of the sort," said Henry perplexed.

"So how come you've sold more wine than you bought or ever have in stock then?" she said accusingly.

"I haven't," said Henry without proper conviction.

"You have! It's in the records for anyone to see. Believe me, you don't want to be going to the police."

"So, what are we going to do about this?" said Henry, returning to the painful question of the missing £6,800.

"Well you pay those call girls, escorts whatever you call 'em almost a grand every time they come to one of your lunches, but we all know it's for more than that! Why don't I do the same thing, say six lunches and we'll treat the whole thing as quits."

"Harriet," he said in a teacher's tone.

"They get £300 for coming to lunch. They get another £500 if they've gone on somewhere with one of your guests, plus they get their expenses, but in most cases it's the men who pay for the room, so, six lunches and we'll call it quits," argued Harriet.

"It's more like sixteen or twenty-six times," said Henry, missing the moral point altogether, as he clumsily thought about the maths.

"Actually, I think it's no times," said Harriet, ever confident in her position. "Just think how bad it will be for you and your clients, oh and that newsreader girlfriend of yours, once her story gets into the press ..." Harriet stopped to allow the idea to linger. "I don't understand it," she continued. "Why's she screwing for money? She must be paid a fortune doing the job she does."

"Power" said Henry quickly, for he had thought about it several times. "She likes powerful men, and more so when she has power over them."

"What, she blackmails them," asked Harriet sensing something of interest.

"No, it's the power of her sexuality over them. Men are fools when it comes to a pretty woman, and by continuing to lay some of the most successful men she keeps proving to herself her attractiveness, her allure."

"Then why the money? Why do you pay her?"

"Her agent sends in the bill for coming to lunch. She acts as the hostess when Sophie's not here, that's all."

"Christ, have you seen some of the men she goes with; honestly, the thought of it makes you sick. I'd bloody charge you if I had to go with some of them," said Harriet, as disgust appeared in her voice.

There was a pause as Henry thought about something which Harriet had said earlier and with it his temper flipped.

"Christ I could kill you," he said, "really bloody murder you." The seriousness with which he now spoke worried Harriet, but it was the way that he came from sitting behind his desk towards her which she found really frightening. "You just don't get it, do you!"

"Why?" she asked not knowing what she had done to change his attitude and tone so suddenly.

"You really think you're going to blackmail an editor or two, or a cabinet member or two. You're fucking mad!" Henry was shaking his head in despair.

"I wasn't," protested Harriet.

"You bloody were, and you're a bloody fool. You think that some of these guys who run multinational businesses don't know how to squash someone like you. They'd squash you as quickly as they'd squash a fly!"

"I wasn't," said Harriet, again protesting her innocence while she got even more worried, as Henry laid his message on as thickly as he could.

"And some of the Arab sheiks, you'll embarrass them. Remember their religion and its ban on alcohol. They'll have you into one of their planes and then one of their jails or brothels before you've even noticed that your feet have left the London pavements. It's a bloody nasty world out there, and you've just decided to fuck those at the top. Well bloody good luck to you!"

Henry was now standing in the middle of the room, pacing as a trapped tiger. He realised that this girl had the power to make or break his businesses, and he didn't like it.

Harriet watched Henry move. He looked immaculate in his crisp white shirt, his dark tie and pressed navy trousers. She had observed how, sometimes his presence could go unnoticed and yet, on other occasions, such as this, he could fill and magnetise a room by just standing up. Henry was exuding power and when he did, it was captivating.

Why didn't he see it? she wondered. All he had to do was take her in his arms and she would make it all go away. Her threats, they weren't meant. They weren't real. Didn't he see, they were an attack in self-defence? All she wanted him to do was to want her and love her.

Harriet stood up too, for she found Henry's prowling up and down intimidating. The two moved about the room saying nothing. It was as though they were two boxers in a room stalking each other.

I'm sorry about the money," said Harriet after a little while.

Henry snorted. "You're right I can't sack you, not because of the fraud thing, that's nonsense. And if you're thinking of blackmailing the rich and powerful in this country then go and read about Profumo and Christine Keeler[16] first. You'll soon decide it's not worth it." There was a gap as Henry paused for thought. "No, the only reason I can't sack you is because of your parents. I couldn't hurt them like that," said Henry.

Harriet suddenly felt very relieved. She could put up with anything as long as her parents didn't find out. They would have been so ashamed and that would really hurt them.

---

[16] In 1961, John Profumo, the Secretary of War had an extramarital affair with 19-year-old model Christine Keeler who was, at the same time, involved with Captain Yevgeny Ivanov, a Soviet naval attaché. Profumo denied the affair but weeks later a police investigation exposed the truth, proving that Profumo had lied to the House of Commons.

"The thing is, I have to be able to trust you and at the moment I can't." Henry's voice was now much quieter, more considered, almost reflexive.

"You can. You can," pleaded Harriet, softening her voice to mimic his change in tone.

"I can't. There will have been no consequences. There's nothing which is going to stop you from doing it again."

"I won't, I won't. I promise," said Harriet responding in the same kind of whisper with which Henry was now speaking. "I'll pay back the money. I promise."

"Its not possible. You can't manage on what you earn now."

"I could if you paid me overtime," she retorted.

From the scowl on Henry's face, she could see that now was not the moment to be attempting to negotiate a pay rise.

Henry returned to behind his desk and fell exhausted into his chair.

Harriet felt a wave of sympathy for him, as he looked to be a man overwhelmed by events. All she now wanted was to make it all better, but she didn't know how.

"There has to be some kind of ... punishment, I suppose? said Harriet.

"Yes, but I don't know what, do you?"

"No," she said dejectedly.

Harriet sat down too. There was silence in the room as both were thinking about what to do next. Each was thinking about the other and how things might have been different. Why couldn't she have been Mrs Guégan she wondered and then, as she thought about Sophie's beauty, she answered her own question. She thought Sophie was one of the most perfect looking women in the world, to rank alongside a Bardot, or Hepburn or Brinkley, and with those thoughts she decided that, whatever it was these women had, she didn't have it.

Whereas, Henry was thinking exactly the opposite. He was wondering why he hadn't kept her in his life. There was nothing about the way Harriet looked or behaved that didn't appeal to him. In fact, ever since she had come to Found House, she had become his dependable right hand. She knew what he was thinking before he did. She couldn't leave. He couldn't bear it.

"You could spank me, beat me," said Harriet, saying anything to break the silence which she found unbearable.

"Don't be silly," said Henry, dismissively.

"It's happened before," said Harriet, "only no cane. I couldn't bear that," she added, thinking back to the time her father beat her.

"Oh," said Henry frowning and shaking his head.

"Men like that kind of thing, don't they?" pronounced Harriet.

"Do they?" responded Henry absentmindedly. He wasn't concentrating on what she had been saying. His thoughts were on her accusation that he been selling wine he'd not bought. Could she be right he wondered?

Suddenly Henry felt too exhausted to deal with the situation. "Maybe," he added. "We'll have to deal with this another time, but right now I can't think about it anymore. We'll deal with it after I'm back from taking my children to see Sophie."

"That's not for a couple of weeks," said Harriet. "Does this mean I'm not losing my job?"

"Not unless you want to go."

"No, I like it here. It won't happen again. I promise," said Harriet, not wanting to leave the man who she knew she was once again in love with.

"You're right about that," said Henry firmly. "By the time I've finished, you'll never think of taking even an apple that doesn't belong to you. Look, go home now. All of this is for another day. I'll see you in the morning." Henry smiled a strange leering smile she had never seen before and from the look in his eyes, Harriet guessed that her suggested punishment had been accepted, and her spine shivered with the thought.

Chapter 91

Found House August 1975

HENRY WANDERED INTO Ainsworth's office the next day at mid-morning and stood by his door. It was, as ever, clear of papers other than the ones he was working on. His ability to deal with paperwork never failed but to impress Henry who was always behind with his.

"I didn't sack Harriet yesterday," said Henry. "She said something which stopped me," he continued almost apologetically.

"I assumed you'd not said anything because she was here first thing this morning," replied Ainsworth casually. "She was looking very sheepish. What happened?"

"In fact, she said two things to me which made me realise, well firstly she knows about the girls from the agency and Diana."

"I'm not surprised," said Ainsworth. "She's an intelligent kid."

"Hmm," acknowledged Henry before he asked: "Have I ever sold stock I don't own, or have we ever not bought stock to fulfil one of our sales orders. For example, when we've done these special inventory sales to generate cash flow." Henry held up a list of wine stocks he'd been given to sell. When I've done this, we've always bought the stock, haven't we? You know, actually bought and paid for it."

"Haven't had to," said Ainsworth confidently. "I changed our terms of trade ages ago."

"How, why?" asked Henry, completely astonished.

"If you remember, we used to allocate storage space for each customer, and we'd keep all their stock together, but it was very inefficient in terms of storage and identifying and recording items in and out. It was a nightmare. We now store by type of wine so, for example, all the Château Latour are stored together, so's all the Château Lafite and then the Château Margaux."

"So how do we know which case belongs to which customer?" asked Henry naively.

"We don't. You need to think of it like a bank. When you pay a pound into your bank account you don't expect to get exactly the same pound note back, do you? You just want a pound note. We are doing the same thing."

"I didn't appreciate that," said Henry, "Do any of our customers mind?"

"Not so far."

"But I don't think it answers the question. Have I sold stock I don't own?" Henry repeated.

"Banks lend money which they don't own," said Ainsworth. "We are simply operating the same principle. A bank knows that not all their customers want their money back at the same time. It's what they've done for the last three hundred years; to take their customers' cash and then lend it on to their other customers. It's all we've done."

"You've done," said Henry sharply. "In any case, that's not a good analogy. You haven't lent it on, you've got me to sell it on."

"Henry," said Ainsworth in a tone which a parent might use when talking to a child, "look at the stock market. Every day people are selling shares they don't own with a promise to deliver the physical shares later when they buy them. That's all we're doing. Honestly, it's no different."

"How much wine have we sold which we haven't owned?" asked Henry, getting frightened by the possible answer.

"We've sold about £1,500,000 in options, give or take a bit. It's good, isn't it?" said Ainsworth smiling with pride.

"Christ," said Henry feeling physically sick.

"Does that include this £300,000 you've just given me to sell? What happens when they want their wine back?" asked Henry. His mind was in total turmoil. How the hell did he not know what had been happening.

"Henry, few of our customers drink the stuff. They just want their cash back so, when they ask us to realise the stock, we just give them their money back plus a profit. Sure, we must keep some wine for delivery but it's less than 15% of the amount we have in stock."

"Are you telling me I owe £1,500,000 for stock I have sold but not purchased? Is that right?" said Henry agitated as he tried to get his head around the issue.

"No. You've sold contracts to deliver a specified number of cases of wine at a date sometime in the future with a historic purchase value of £1,500,000."

Henry shook his head perplexed.

"You've not been selling wine, Henry. You've been selling wine futures."

"I've been selling wine," said Henry emphatically. "In any case, when you purchase an option to buy a stock exchange share you only pay a small percentage of the value, just a few percent whereas I've sold the wine at full face value."

"That's what you might have thought but I can assure you the paperwork says exactly what I've been saying. I've had it checked with our lawyers and accountants, both here and in France and they've signed off on it."

Henry palpably relaxed on the knowledge that it had been approved by his professional advisers. Further he had to admit the brilliance of its creativity. It made so much sense.

"We would have been bust long ago if I hadn't developed this," said Ainsworth. "Your business is growing all the time. You're funding all the supermarkets stock off your balance sheet and you've got bugger all in bank borrowings. Henry, it's been our route to survival," said Ainsworth, almost pleadingly, as he could see Henry was uncomfortable with what he was being told.

Henry leaned against Ainsworth's door in awe. "I need to read the contracts."

"Why?" asked Ainsworth, almost offended that Henry didn't trust him.

"Because, I need to understand how it all works."

"Of course," said Ainsworth, "but don't worry. I can assure you; we've not done anything illegal."

"It might be legally okay but I'm really uncomfortable," said Henry. "It doesn't seem morally right to me."

"It's not moral when pension funds lend shares of their pensioners to people who then sell those shares only to buy them back later at a cheaper price, but it's what happens in the real world," said Ainsworth.

"Honestly Vincent, I don't understand," said Henry. "In every business unit we are profitable, in some we are very profitable, but we never have any money. Surely we must be able to get some bank somewhere to lend us something?"

"Look Henry," said Ainsworth patiently. "I've found a legal gold mine. Let's continue to use it until the Vaults are built and the tax problem is solved. Once we've managed to get the Vaults classified as a bonded warehouse then we can borrow all the money we need on mortgage and, if you want, you can buy out all the options then."

Henry stood still, staring at the floor.

"We don't charge those who we've sold wine options storage charges for storing their wine which we don't have, do we?" asked Henry as he was having second thoughts.

"Of course we do, but we no longer call it a storage charge. If we had done that it would have been false accounting, and that would have been illegal. Instead, we call it a facilitation fee. I wasn't going to miss out on the income. We need it," replied Ainsworth looking particularly pleased with himself.

Henry reluctantly nodded his agreement and returned to his desk. He thought about his conversation with Harriet and what he was going to do about her. How had she worked out what was happening, he wondered. She must have a better understanding of this business than he'd thought. What he did know was that, until the options were unwound, he was not going to think about trying to sell the Vaults.

Until then, they needed three hundred thousand pounds of extra capital, so he had to go and sell some wine options!

At his desk he called Harriet to come and see him.

"I've checked with Vincent," said Henry confidently to Harriet. "It's just as I thought. You've confused the selling of wine with the selling of wine call options, two very different things. One is a physical asset, and the other is an investment instrument." He was pleased with his explanation. "There's no reason why you should have known the difference," he added, so that Harriet could feel better about herself.

"Oh, thank you, sorry," said Harriet demurely.

"I'm telling John he's got to go and sort out your ex-husband's drug dealer. He can't bear the bastards. He'll make sure you're not bothered again."

"Oh, thank you," repeated Harriet.

"And I need you to make an appointment for me to see the chairman of the gym you used to work for. We need to get your money back."

Harriet looked shocked.

"Not Dan Boyd but the chairman. Boyd's a narcissist so we'll get nowhere with him. I have to see the chairman" he added for clarity. "It's a public company so he should be quite easy to track down, but don't say what it's about. Just say I want to see him."

"Are you sure?" Harriet asked.

"Yep, provided you give me a complete dossier of all the evidence beforehand. I'm not going in to fight your corner unless I fully understand what the hell had been going on."

"Okay, yes of course, thank you," she said, surprised by Henry's apparent change of personality.

"You are part of this team, and this team fights together," he said. "But you won't be thanking me when this is over, believe me," and he smiled the same horrible leering smile of the night before.

With that look, had Henry confirmed her punishment, she wondered.

Very quickly, Henry threw a few things from his desk into his briefcase and was gone. He had one last job to do before he took his children to see their mother in Germany.

Chapter 92

London August 1975

HENRY'S LAST JOB before his summer break was to have a meeting with Sophie's London and Paris agents. The aim of the meeting was to get an understanding of her business affairs. Although Sophie had, right from the start of their relationship, an intimate knowledge of the finances of Found Vintners, and the three vineyards, he had always thought it impertinent to enquire into Sophie's finances. Perhaps it was because Sophie's father made him feel that way.

"She won't be coming back," said Henry to Rosalind and Cassie, after they had settled down in the board room of their Knightsbridge offices. "She's very poorly," he continued.

"Is that forever?" asked Cassie, her tone revealing obvious concern.

"I'm afraid it is," said Henry firmly. "It's not like when she was pregnant. I'm afraid she's now very poorly and unlikely to recover."

"What happened when Sophie was pregnant?" asked Cassie.

Rosalind explained and, as she did so, Henry started to get upset by her reaction. It was clear from the way Rosalind spoke that the care which she had once showered on Sophie was at an end. The young enthusiastic booker, who had taken Sophie under her wing, was now jaded, jaundiced and bitter. She had lost the energy which a top booker needs. As a result, she no longer had the charisma to nurture the careers of the bright, young, new talent.

The directors from the agency were late in joining the meeting so Rosalind, now less familiar with Sophie's affairs but the more senior person in the room, tried to explain the situation. As she spoke it became clear that, for them, their golden goose was now dead and the quicker that goose could be buried, and a new golden goose found, the happier they would be.

It was when the directors of the agency joined the meeting that Henry began to despise these people. Until then he thought they worked for Sophie. Now, he realised that they work purely for themselves. The more these middle-aged women created insecurity with their models, the more anxious they became, and the easier it was to manipulate them. Sophie's father had done a good job in controlling the 'Hound of Hades' as Walter used to refer to them in German.

Henry started to despair at their conversation. To each question he either got no answer, a banal answer, or a promise that they would come back to him. It was clear that no one in the room knew anything about Sophie's contractual or financial position.

In an attempt to assuage Henry's obvious displeasure, it was agreed that the London and Paris offices would make available to him all of Sophie's contracts and papers so a complete review could take place, with a statement of affairs produced at the end. Ainsworth didn't know it yet, but he was about to be given another job.

After the meeting, Henry walked into the grounds of Kensington Palace. He sat down on a park bench and aimlessly watched the tourists enjoy London. It was a beautiful bright summer's day. It was another chapter of their life over, Henry decided. He had to concentrate on the future, and that meant getting Sophie well again. She had to come home. He couldn't live without her. It was as simple as that.

Chapter 93

Bamberg August 1975

ANDREW AND PETER were excited to see their grandparents, as were Walter and Inga thrilled to have their grandchildren in their midst. With his children settled down, it was early evening when Henry went on his own to see Sophie in her convalescence home. He had a feeling that everything was going to be alright.

It was with a bounce in his step that Henry walked into Sophie's room in the sanatorium with a bag of carefully chosen and wrapped gifts, but the scene before him thrust a dagger into his heart. Sophie was sitting slumped in a chair, her head fallen forward, with saliva dribbling slowly out of her mouth. Henry squatted down to look at her face but there was no expression. Her face muscles no longer held any tension. He held her hand, which was cold and clammy to his touch. Henry touched her hair, which was now long and lank, separated by a simple centre parting. He stroked her cheeks as he spoke softly, trying to coax some recognition from her. What had happened to his most beautiful Sophie? Henry squeezed her hand hoping that there would be a response. A flicker of an eye, anything to say that she knew he was there, but there was no reaction.

Henry pressed the call button once, and then again, and then he held on to it hoping that an alarm would ring somewhere, as anger took over. What the hell had happened. At last, a nurse came, walking quietly and calmly.

"What's happened to Sophie?" Henry demanded.

"What do you mean?" said the nurse. "She's sleeping as a result of a sedative."

"What sedative? How can she have a sedative before she's dressed for bed?"

"It's what she's prescribed" said the nurse defensively.

"For god's sake get me matron, immediately," demanded Henry. "This isn't right."

The deputy matron arrived, neatly turned out in a pressed blue uniform and a white crisp nurse's cap.

"What's happened?" asked Henry in his best German, finding it hard to contain his civility.

There was an immediate denial that anything was wrong, but in the conversation, during which Henry got crosser and crosser by the moment, he was told that Sophie had been fighting other patients and staff. As a result, she had been prescribed a sedative to relieve her anxiety and calm her down.

Henry would never know what made him do it, but he demanded to see Sophie's drug chart. He paced up and down Sophie's room without her noticing his presence, as the deputy matron scurried to find documents which should have been readily available.

On her return, Henry studied the list, which was neatly typed up, but all in German.

"What are all these?" challenged Henry, pointing to a list of eight or nine drugs.

"This one's the sedative," said the deputy matron, pointing to an unpronounceable name. "This is an antibiotic. It stops a lung infection. We put everyone on it as a preventative because our patients don't move about as much..........."

"And this one?" interrupted Henry, pointing to the fourth on the list.

"It's an anti-psychotic."

"What's an anti-psychotic, when it's at home?" asked Henry.

"It's to stop Sophie hallucinating. It's designed to treat her schizophrenia. They've been prescribed by her doctor" said the deputy matron defensively.

"Yes, and whose permission did you get? You didn't get mine."

"Herr Lemberger said that it was okay" said the deputy matron. "I'm sure we have his signature."

"As you well know, Herr Lemberger has no authority in this matter. It is on your file. It clearly states that, if there are to be drugs prescribed, you are to consult with me. Where is Sophie's file? I need to see it now." He was intensely angry.

Henry's request was immediately denied, but when an intractable force meets a stationery object something is going to have to give, and in this case, it was the deputy matron who yielded. Having carefully removed Henry's letter of authority from the file she handed it over. As he studied the form on the front of the file all written in German, he saw his name against the words Nächste Angehörige which he happened to know translated into next of kin.

"Look," he said. "You will see I'm the next of kin, and the only one authorized to deal with drugs. You have not consulted me. I'm telling you now, this stops immediately."

Henry turned away and walked towards the window. "Fucking quacks," he said out loud. He turned to face the deputy matron. "You've used a medical cosh on her," he said aghast. You've damn well drugged her to the eyeballs to make it easier to manage her. No, fucking no. Do you get me? Fucking no.!" he yelled.

The Deputy Matron didn't answer. She simply turned and walked out of the room, her expression as cold as the steel in her emotion.

What the hell was he going to do? Sophie couldn't stay here, they'd kill her.

Henry undressed Sophie to put her to bed. As he did so he noticed that the muscles she once had were wasted and her skin was loose to the touch from a loss of weight. Through the night the nurses tried to encourage him to go home, but he wouldn't. He stayed sleeping on the floor.

In the morning there was some slight improvement in Sophie's condition. She was less sleepy but still she didn't recognise him or what was happening to her. He fed Sophie sweet milky tea through the spout of a tea pot. He found that was the only way he could get her to drink. He wanted the chemical muck swilling about Sophie's body and shutting down her mind washed out as fast as possible, and drinking was his only solution.

As soon as he thought it respectable, Henry phoned Walter and had angry words, but it became obvious that he didn't understand what Henry was going on about. Disturbed by the phone call, Walter drove up to the sanatorium, where it became clear to Henry that he'd no idea of the drugs which had been plied on his daughter.

"I gave no instructions for this," said Walter, after Henry had shown him the list.

"Well someone did," said Henry. "And she was in your charge."

"Not us, we don't even take ..." He paused as he searched for the word 'headache pill'.

A few hours later, Inga arrived with the two boys, and as Walter supervised a game of football with them in the mown grounds, the scene repeated itself with Sophie's mother, who gently wept as she held her daughter's hands and combed her hair.

"My beautiful daughter" she kept repeating. "My beautiful, beautiful daughter."

By lunch time Sophie's family had gathered in one of the residents' sitting rooms. Her sisters and their husbands were with them. Sophie remained semi-comatose in a wheelchair. She watched as her boys played happily on the lawn but didn't recognise them. Likewise, the plight of their mother was lost to their young eyes.

"I'm going to take Sophie home to England," said Henry. "She's not staying here."

There was silence.

"She can't stay here," he repeated firmly.

"But not England, please, not England" said Sophie's mother. "I need her here. I need to look after her."

"But you haven't, have you," rebuked Henry. "Look at her. When were you last here?"

"Where will she go in England" asked Walter.

"I don't know" he admitted, not having a clue about mental health hospitals in the U.K.

"I will find somewhere else close by," said Sophie's mother. "It will be much better. In the meantime, she comes home to us."

Henry had no argument with that, and so, under the guise of telling the sanatorium they were taking Sophie for a drive, her family sprung her free, and back into their arms.

Over the weekend, Sophie drank more and started to eat again. Sophie's mother, using all of her influence and pulling favours accumulated over many years, arranged for her hairdresser to come out on Sunday and, using a picture taken of Sophie when she was sixteen, gave instructions for her hair to be styled like that. It was the first sign that the poorly woman in front of his eyes really was his Sophie.

Any plans which Henry had of taking Andrew and Peter to Château de Gressier for the summer were abandoned. Instead, over the next five weeks, whilst Walter and Inga looked after his boys, Henry dedicated his time to Sophie. As the effect of the drugs abated and, at first with one of her sisters on one side and Henry on another, Sophie was encouraged to walk. It was a few yards at first. By the end of the five weeks she was doing walks of three or four miles in both the morning and the afternoon.

By the time Henry had to leave to take his children back to England and school, Sophie's strength had started to rebuild. She had put on weight and her muscle tone was back, even in her face. With her hair trimmed and in her proper clothes, even without make up, Sophie still looked as though she were one of the most beautiful women in the world.

Nevertheless, her brain remained scrambled such that she was unable to put a sentence together. If marijuana had addled Sophie's brain, the anti-psychotic drugs had killed it completely. It left Henry feeling crushed as, with her mind broken, he knew his hope of getting her better had vanished.

As Henry looked after her, he realized that theirs was no longer a two-way relationship, just a one-way duty of care. But that didn't matter, he loved her, for all she was and all she had ever been. He was never going to abandon her. Not now, not ever.

Chapter 94

Paris September 1975

HENRY AND JOHN sat in the café, at the table nearest the window, staring out over the road towards the door of a set of apartments in which Patrice Gevais had a flat. The coffee cups had been drained and refilled many times without a word being spoken between them. Much earlier John had phoned the police reporting that a drug dealer had just taken possession of a gun and was about to go out and shoot someone.

"How do you know," said the policeman who answered John's 112 phone call to the emergency services. "I've just come from there," he replied with his voice muffled over the telephone mouthpiece before hanging up. The check of the police database confirmed Gevais as a known small-time drugs dealer and, on this news, the wheels of the Paris gendarmerie started to turn.

Hours of planning and risk-taking were now dependent upon what happened next. From the moment Henry discovered that Sophie had been prescribed anti-psychotic drugs, John had been travelling the nightclubs of Paris buying small quantities of a variety of drugs, heroin, cocaine, ecstasy, cannabis. He had spent about £25,000 in all of Henry's money buying wraps already prepared for the user market. He could have acquired the same quantity more cheaply through one of his contacts but then someone would have known. This way no one took any notice of a man appearing at nightclub cloakrooms spending a few francs as he left. He also bought off the street, making sure the deal was always done away from the dealers' usual grounds. He always bought just enough to argue that it was for his personal use and no more.

After each buying round, John would journey to an old Citroen car, parked in a multi-storey carpark around the corner from Gevais's apartment. John had purchased the car for cash from one of those dodgy, ask no questions, dealers' yards on the outskirts of Paris. He'd registered the car with Gevais's name and address. It was in a holdall, in the boot of the car, that John would decamp his nightly purchases, making sure he left no fingerprints, avoiding the CCTV and always ensuring that the parking ticket was in date. John took inordinate care not to arise suspicion.

As soon as the holdall was full, John went in search of a gun; preferably a used one with a history in which the police would have a serious interest. It was part of the job which John knew he would hate most. It meant dealing with an underworld and underclass, dominated by people who he would happily describe as pieces of shit. He loathed everything about them. Their laziness and stupidity but mostly, having grown up amongst them, he knew how gutless they were when they were without their gangs to protect them.

It was in the back streets of Marseille where John found what he was looking for. In a non-descript hire car he watched the comings and goings of seedy nightclubs occupied by pimps, hookers, drug addicts and their dealers. He made sure he never stayed outside any one club too long to be spotted. Nothing had changed since he was a boy living around these streets; not even a coat of paint had been applied in the last twenty-five years.

John knew he had to choose his victim carefully as much depended on it. He was contemplating the ideal profile when a youth came into his focus. He studied the boy carefully as he was different from all the others. John wondered what it was that made the boy stick out. It wasn't just that he was very thin and gaunt, nor that his foot dragged as he walked. He looked as though he rarely washed or combed his hair. Unlike the jeans and T-shirts around him, this boy wore a badly fitting suit, complete with shirt and tie. It was as though, through his dress, he was aspiring to be someone else and then it dawned on John; this was a young white boy in a black man's world.

The boy was constantly walking, always with great purpose between about nine or ten bars and strip joints. He never stopped in each for more than 10 to 15 minutes. It was as though he did not belong to anyone or to any place.

Henry parked his hire car halfway between the longest of the boy's walks and waited. Just as the boy appeared, he opened his passenger front door and blocked his route. "Get in," he said.

The boy looked up at John and immediately realised that there was no match, so he climbed into the front passenger seat as instructed. John climbed into the back seat so he could not be seen.

"Gendarme?" asked the boy turning around.

"Look straight ahead," instructed John, pushing the boy's head forward.

"You're not from here," said the boy, "otherwise you wouldn't be so stupid."

"To do what?" asked John innocently.

"Ask for information. The gendarmes are paid to keep away, well away."

"That's good," said John, "'cause I don't want them here." It was at that moment John worked out what the boy did. He was the bookie's runner, setting-off and settling bets. It meant he was trustworthy and had a brain about him, but it was a brain which only worked if the boy had his regular fix of heroin.

"I want you to do me a job," said John.

"I've got a job," replied the boy.

"Yeh, but not this job. Not such a well-paid job," said John, still testing the ground.

"To do what?"

"To buy me a gun."

"How d'you know I can get a gun?"

"I know," said John. "I was once from around here."

"What kind of gun?"

"Pistol, revolver, small, handheld, working, must be no more than 10 years old."

What'll you pay?"

"$3,000," said John sharply.

"And me, what do I get?" asked the boy.

"You get the difference between $3,000 and the cost of the gun."

"I need $10,000," the boy replied.

"$5,000," said John, knowing he was offering five times the market price.

The boy nodded at which point John handed over an envelope containing $1,000 in French francs and a key to a locker at Marseilles railway station.

"You put the gun in there on Wednesday, day after tomorrow," instructed John, pointing to the address fob attached to the key. The rest of the cash 'll be in the locker." He then grabbed the boy around his neck and his fingers dug deep into his shoulders. "Cheat me and I'll break your fucking neck. One snap, not dead, just fucking paralysed .... get me!"

Two years in two military jails teaches you how to use your voice to threaten, with the result that the boy was in no doubt as to his fate if he failed to deliver.

John spent the next couple of days locked up in an old and undistinguished sea front hotel. He ran, he walked, ate and just lay on the bed. He knew he should go and see his mother and family, but somehow, he couldn't. Even now, after all these years, the memories were still raw.

On Wednesday from mid-morning, John started to watch the locker from a distance. There was no money inside, just a note with more instructions to follow.

At exactly 12noon just as he had been ordered, the boy opened the locker, took out the note and started to read. He stopped, looked around, shut up the locker and started to walk as he followed his instructions. John followed closely behind. The instructions made the boy walk around three separate blocks in a figure of two eights so John could see whether the boy was being followed.

Eventually, satisfied that the boy was on his own, John crept up behind him and tapped him on the shoulder. The boy jumped out of his skin. His nerves were on end and he was sweating profusely. His eyes showed that his whole body was in physical pain from a lack of heroin. "Good God," he screamed out loud

"Come with me," instructed John. They walked another three minutes to where John had parked his car. This time John got into the driver's side and with the boy safely on board he drove to a parking lot overlooking the sea front. John chose a spot where there was not a car close by and stopped.

"Got something for me?" asked John quietly.

The boy reached into the plastic bag he was carrying and brought out a folded grubby white T-shirt. He unwrapped it slowly to show a gleaming Smith and Wesson pistol. John put on some plastic gloves and began to strip the gun, revealing a degree of professionalism as he checked it's mechanism and made sure it had a firing pin.

"Bullets?" he asked as he saw that the cartridge was empty.

"You never said nothin' about bullets. They will be extra. How many d'you want?" said the boy.

"Bullets," said John angrily holding out his hand and clicking his fingers.

The boy looked at John and, in his desperation to get the deal done and his next fix of heroin, decided it was not a fight he was going to take. Instead, he produced a handful of loose bullets from inside his jacket pocket.

John, satisfied he needed no more than that, nodded to the boy and told him to drop the bullets, one by one, in to the white T-shirt alongside the gun which he then bundled up in a roll.

John reached inside his right jacket pocket and bought out a bundle of French francs. He did the same with his left pocket.

"We agreed dollars," said the boy beginning to physically shake with pain.

"When converted it's over the four thousand dollars we agreed. In any case it's all I've got," said John as he threw the two bundles onto the boys lap.

The boy started to count the money as John started the car and drove out of the car park back towards where the boy and John had first met. At some indiscriminate point, half a mile from the hellhole of Marseille where the boy lived, John stopped the car and threw him out. Within a few minutes, as soon as the kid had paid his dealer for the gun, his withdrawal symptoms were being relieved by a file of heroin. Until that moment, his dealer had deliberately kept the boy short of heroin to make sure that he came back with the money from the gun sale.

John dumped the car at Marseille train station, throwing the keys to the booking clerk, not caring that his credit card was going to get debited with extra charges. His only concern was to catch the next train to Paris. He would feel much safer once out of the city of his birth, and the gun was no longer in his possession.

John arrived in Paris late in the evening. He phoned Gevais's flat and found he wasn't in. He then went to the car, threw the gun and bullets into the holdall of drugs, which he then carried nonchalantly to the cafe where they were now sitting. He ordered an anise and water, which he threw down his throat to calm his nerves.

"May I use your phone," John asked the cafe owner waving a five franc note to show his willingness to pay. The café owner said nothing. Instead, he lifted the phone on the counter. John dialled Gevais flat. There was no answer. He put the phone down and checked the paper he had written the telephone number on and dialled again. There was still no answer. Leaving the five franc note on the counter top, John picked up the holdall and walked across the street to the front door of Gevais's apartment block.

A few days earlier he had shone a torch on the buttons on the access code, and by looking for wear and dirt, he already knew the four numbers to gain access, but he didn't know the order. He would have to try 256 combinations, but one was bound to work. Just as John was methodically typing in the numbers, he was let into the apartment block by someone leaving. Gevais's front door locks were no resistance to a man who, in the tedium of army life, had taught himself how to break locks.

Gevais's flat was neat and tidy. Everything was expensive with good taste. It was clear that the drugs business was providing its owner with a nice little income. John went straight to the kitchen where he chose a low-down corner cupboard. He took out the immediate pots and pans and then forced his holdall deep into the corner. He then put back the bits and pieces to make it appear as though nothing had changed. Finally, he placed a wrap of cocaine close to the front so that the drug dog would find it in seconds. As John left, he knew that everything had been set up. All he had to do was to make the early morning phone call which he had just done, but nothing appeared to be happening.

"We have to phone again," said Henry. "It's been far too long."

"We can't," said John. "The police record all their calls. Making one call was risky enough."

On this news, Henry contemplated what they should do. He said nothing.

After a little while, when the tension had become almost unbearable, John leapt up and left the table café, only to return in less than a couple of minutes. Henry looked at him quizzically.

"Just heated it up a bit from the phone box in the road, Boss," said John matter-of-factly.

The two men said nothing, even when the sound of police sirens screamed in from a distance. Suddenly a host of police cars arrived surrounding Gevais's apartment block. As the scene of organised chaos developed before the two men's eyes, they shared a secret smile. Henry and John watched carefully, enjoying the best cinema seats in their production, as the police, with semi-automatic guns, stormed into Gevais's apartment building.

The excitement was only minutes long and things quickly calmed down as policemen returned to their cars to wait for further instructions. Eventually John and Henry saw Gevais led out in handcuffs, and when they saw John's holdall following, the two men looked at each other and smiled a knowing smile. Still they had said nothing.

"Next time, he should pick on someone his own size, shouldn't he Boss?" said John, rationally.

"Well at least someone your size," said Henry as the two men shook hands. Once again Henry noticed how John's hands completely enveloped his own.

Chapter 95

Paris September 1975

HENRY SAT IN the little restaurant by himself, not knowing whether she was going to turn up. It was the same Paris café tabac that Sophie and he had dined on the night Maison Rabôut had its formal opening.

When Henry first proposed they meet that evening, Imra protested arguing that she had an existing appointment which she couldn't miss.

"Be late to it," said Henry, "this is more important to you." He paused then added, "and your daughter." He emphasised the last word.

At his table Henry studied the newspaper cuttings of stories and pictures which his office had put together about Imra. At the end of his reading, he thought he knew the woman even though he had never met her. Like everyone else, he thought she had a classically beautiful face. Her skill was to adorn her very dark skin with bright colours. This made her incredibly photogenic. It meant you were attracted to look at her not once or twice, but three or four times, as your eyes shot between the contrasts of the brilliant whites of her eyes, her dark skin and the colours she was wearing.

Her neat sculptured face, slender neck and neat shoulder line meant that there was no better model to show off exquisite jewellery. Despite her beauty Henry knew he didn't fancy her for there was no muscle shape around the top of her legs, which looked weak and pathetic as a result. Further, the clothes she chose for herself had a harshness of style which he didn't think worked with her skeletal frame.

Henry's concentration was broken when he noticed that, standing right next to him, were long legs in very tight jeans.

"Henry?" asked Imra impatiently. Likewise, she knew who he was. The husband of one of the world's most beautiful women is not immune from the attention of the world's media.

"Yes, I'm sorry," said Henry completely thrown as he had not seen her come in. He stood up and offered his hand, which Imra ignored as she moved to slide on to the bench seat in front of him. Her frustration of being summoned to the meeting was obvious.

Henry said nothing as he gathered the cuttings which had been spread across the table. Imra looked quizzically at him for she found it unsettling that he had been studying her.

Henry allowed Imra's face to take all his attention. It was more beautiful than the photographs had suggested. She had the darkest most expressive eyes he had ever seen; something which the catwalk simply ignored. There was a long silence between them.

"Thank you for coming," said Henry.

"How Sophie?" asked Imra, with concern in her voice.

"Very unwell, she won't ever be coming back to work. Thanks to you, she's a mental vegetable."

"I'm sorry.........." Imra broke off. "A vegetable .... thanks to me, why?" asked Imra genuinely confused.

"She can't talk because she can't remember for long enough what she wants to say. She doesn't know where she is. She doesn't recognise her children. How is she," said Henry. "She is in a living hell, thanks to you and your friend Mr. Patrice, fucking, Gevais."

"Why me, what have I done?" asked Imra, now totally confused.

"Gevais and you introduced Sophie to marijuana and God knows what else. It's totally scrambled her brain!"

"No," said Imra. "It's not possible."

"Yes, retorted Henry. It's very possible. In fact, it's not just possible. It's a fucking fact. It's fucking Russian roulette with schizophrenia as the bullets."

Imra shook her head, disbelieving what Henry was saying.

"Please don't swear. It's not very pleasant to listen to," said Imra, sensing that she should get ready for a fight, but she was still not sure what this was all about.

"Some brains can take it, some can't," said Henry. "What none of you dope smokers know is which of you can and which of you can't, but most importantly you don't know the strength of the bloody stuff you smoke."

Imra gently shook her head denying his words.

"Its fucking Russian roulette, but worse, 'cause with dope smokers, they're playing with two bullets in a gun with a five-hole chamber."

Imra still had no clear idea what Henry was going on about, except she noticed that he was getting angrier and angrier as he spoke.

"Gevais has been arrested," said Henry, changing the subject. "He's going to jail for ten to fifteen years."

"Why?" asked Imra. She spoke softly as she sensed that this was the real reason for their meeting.

"They found enough stuff in his apartment to put him away for a long time. They also found a gun."

"Don't be ridiculous," said Imra. "He only supplied friends. He was very small time. In any case, he didn't have a gun."

"He most certainly had a gun!" said Henry firmly. "I watched him being arrested."

"You watched him?" Imra asked, as she tilted her head to one side.

Henry smiled a knowing smile which conveyed everything which Imra needed to know.

"You fixed him, you framed him," Imra said accusingly.

"Don't be ridiculous. I couldn't get the amount of drugs he had nor a gun," said Henry. "I wouldn't know where to begin." His arguments were sufficiently strong as to allow Imra to accept his protestations of innocence.

Their waitress had left menus on the table as soon as Imra had arrived. She knew who she was, which had an intimidating effect on her, but it was the intensity of Henry and Imra's conversation which caused the waitress to come up to their table several times and leave again ignored.

"I'm not stopping," said Imra tartly when the waitress eventually gained their attention.

"Oh I think you are," said Henry. "We still have a lot to discuss."

"Really, I have to be somewhere else," said Imra.

"You'll be ninety minutes late," Henry instructed. "'We still haven't discussed how this will affect your daughter."

Imra looked up from the table into his eyes. If looks could have killed then, at that moment, Henry would have been a dead man.

"Oh yes, she is caught up in this mess," said Henry.

"How?" she demanded.

"I'll tell you."

"Touch her and I'll kill you," said Imra, venom pouring from her breath.

"Don't be ridiculous," said Henry in retort. He then deliberately quietened his tone. "Try and understand the mess you're in. Help me and I'll help you. Don't help me and you'll bear the consequences. It's a simple choice for you to make.

The two lined up against each other as two fighting dogs on their leads. One taught by the poverty of Somalia and the hardships of the backstreets of Algeria. The other taught by the rough-and-tumble of business. Both ready to be as tough as they needed.

The waitress interrupted. Henry looked at Imra and then at the specials board.

"Two dover soles, off the bone, with a mixed salad and a bottle of your house white," he ordered, without any consultation. The waitress left as quickly as she had arrived. "I've ordered for you," he said sharply.

Imra was affronted by his cavalier behaviour towards her. How dare he order on her behalf without asking! "No wonder she ended up hating you," said Imra in response to Henry's rudeness. "Sophie was so unhappy with you," she continued. "She loved you so much and yet you hurt her so badly, time and time again."

Henry heard the words, but they held no context.

"When you blame me for her drug taking, well you've got that well and truly wrong."

"Why?"

"We only take them to hide us from someone or something. It's the same with alcohol. It deadens the pain. Most of it's an unconscious pain, but it's a pain all the same."

"What do you mean?" asked Henry perplexed.

"Your bloody stupid detective work gets Sophie and her kids firebombed out of her home. You buy a business you can't afford which nearly bankrupts you. In the meantime, you're pouring all your money and hers into a pit somewhere in England which turns out to be worthless." Imra paused. "She only went back to work to save you from bankruptcy, and all you did was work harder for yourself."

Imra looked at Henry who was taken aback by the attack, but she wasn't prepared to stop there, and so fired the next barrel.

"She hated the house you have near here. She only stayed there once, didn't she? Do you know what she told me? She said it was a parody of your whole married life; that you hadn't even bothered to put a lock on the bedroom door; so the shop came into the bedroom,' that's what she said. You had so much and yet you abandoned the most beautiful woman in the world for your own greed and ambition and you have the nerve to blame me!"

The interruption of the waitress gave Henry a break from hearing what he found painful. She poured a small element of wine into a glass. He stared at it. He quickly sniffed the wine took the first sip and nodded. The waitress filled both glasses and Henry watched as, with her first couple of mouthfuls, Imra visibly relaxed in front of his eyes. Henry's wine glass would remain untouched as he only drank water.

Over the next twenty minutes Imra took swig after swig of wine as she told Henry how wonderful Sophie was, how kind, how beautiful and how much she loved him.

"Do you know, she'd never slept with anyone other than you, despite thousands of offers."

Henry nodded.

"I don't think you know how much she missed her children, every evening she hurt as they went to bed and she realised she was missing their growing up. All so your business could have the money it needed."

"I was doing it for us," protested Henry.

"No, you were awful to her," said Imra. "It was you who lost her. No one took her away from you. There's only one person to blame around here and it's you!"

The conversation paused as dinner was served. Henry was silent as he knew everything Imra had said was true.

"Sophie never said any of these things to you, did she?" asked Imra.

"No," said Henry.

"It's because she loved you too much. She wanted you to be happy, to have everything."

Still Henry said nothing.

"It's because she's a post war child of Germany," said Imra. "They learnt that they're not allowed to complain. It's their price for losing the war. I asked her once why she didn't tell you how she felt, and that's what she said."

As Imra spoke Henry answered each criticism and complaint in his head in a form of self-defence, but he knew what she was saying was substantially true, but now it was too late to do anything about it, because Sophie was lost to him forever.

Imra was pleased with what she had said and the way she had said it. She noticed that, sitting in front of her, was no longer an arrogant, accusing man, demanding that she do as he said. Instead, there was someone who was deflated and contemplative.

They both ate in silence. Imra enjoyed every morsel as, in a permanent battle to keep her weight down, food of this quality was a rare delight.

"You're right," said Henry, "I'm a complete bastard and let me prove it to you. You've got a choice. Your name's on the list of Gevais's customers so you're about to be interviewed by the police. You'll be exposed as a junkie. As a result, your flat will be raided, you'll lose your income, and your daughter will be taken into care. Believe me, if you think it will be bad, it will be worse than that. Or you can work with me and we'll keep you out of it."

"Are you threatening me?" asked Imra.

"No, I'm just making it clear to you the mess you're in and the options you have."

"God, no wonder Sophie said you're such a bastard."

Imra's words cut Henry in two. It was the vitriol with which she spoke, and the fact that Sophie had shared her thoughts about him with Imra, which truly hurt.

"Sophie said that?" asked Henry, leaning forward.

"Oh yes."

Henry sat back again as he reeled from this second verbal blow. He paused as he took time to reflect on his proposed strategy. He filled his fork and placed the contents in his mouth. He tasted nothing. His mind was on the girl who sat opposite. He still couldn't make out if she was sexy or not. He did know that he didn't want to sleep with her. Nevertheless, there was no doubting the beauty of her smile or the radiance of her dark brown eyes, but it was clear that, even with her porcelain looks, she was not going to crack easily.

"Here's the deal," started Henry.

"Here's the deal," mocked Imra, with sarcasm pouring out of her voice.

"This is what I want you to do," said Henry changing tack. "You will prepare a witness statement with the help of my lawyer," he continued confidently. "Your statement will say that Patrice Gevais supplied Sophie with drugs. You will report how those drugs badly affected her. Your statement will tell about your own purchases too, but the amount can be made very modest. Once your statement is prepared, my lawyer and you will go to the police together."

"Why are you doing this?" asked Imra

"Based upon the evidence the police have got Gevais will only get charged with possession of drugs and a gun. With your statement he goes down for supply with a much longer sentence.

"You fixed this, didn't you?" accused Imra, repeating her accusation.

"No," said Henry emphatically, "but Sophie has some dear friends who are very upset at what has happened to her.

"But this is unfair," protested Imra. "How was Patrice to know that she would suffer so badly?"

"He didn't, but in law the thin skull doctrine means that you take your victim as you find them. Sophie's frailty provides him with no defence," said Henry.

"I can't do this. Don't you understand, Gevais's suppliers will be after me! These guys look after their own. They don't mess around. They'll do me real harm." There was panic in Imra's voice.

"I'll look after you," said Henry.

"How?"

"You can move to London. You can live in Sophie's flat until you get sorted with a place of your own," said Henry.

"I can't speak English, nor can my daughter."

"You'll learn. It'll only take a couple of months. Sophie's London agency will take you onto their books," he continued. "Same agency, just a different office; they'll be pleased to have you."

Imra shook her head.

"Gevais's suppliers have only one concern; to make sure he doesn't say where he gets his drugs from. He'll know to keep his mouth shut if he wants to take a shower while in prison. He'll get spoken to and told to plead guilty."

"You can fix this?"

"No," said Henry, "but friends of Sophie's can."

"She doesn't have friends like that," said Imra

"I didn't think so too, but help comes from the most unusual places," said Henry.

"May my mother come?" asked Imra.

"What, to England? Yes, of course."

Imra looked at his glass of wine. "Do you not drink?" she asked.

"No, it was one of the things Sophie and I had in common."

"Don't be silly, Sophie had a vodka and tonic, or vodka and coke every night she came in," said Imra.

"Sophie didn't drink," said Henry emphatically. "In the whole time we were together, we never, not once, drank alcohol."

"You have a bloody odd job for someone who doesn't drink. You're right, she never drank wine, whisky or brandy. She didn't like them. Vodka was her drink, the occasional Gin maybe, but definitely Vodka. I promise you!"

There was a silence as Henry accepted that Imra would not be making this up.

"Do you know why she married you?"

Henry shook his head.

"You were the only man who kept coming back even after she made it clear she wouldn't sleep with them."

"She said this to you?" asked Henry.

"Do you know why she didn't sleep with you when you were in South Africa and after you'd asked her to marry you?"

"She wanted her parents to like me, to approve of us getting married," answered Henry upset that Sophie had discussed such an intimate matter with Imra.

"No, she was frightened."

"Of me?"

"Yes ... no ... of all men. She was frightened of going to bed with any man."

"She said that, why?" asked Henry.

"Her mother was one of the Berlin women."

Henry said nothing, for he didn't know what it meant.

"Her mother was raped many times by the Russians during the war, after Berlin fell," said Imra without any emotion.

Henry didn't know how to react. He felt embarrassed because the news had been served to him as though it was just another item which could be heard without emotion, but he found this far from the case.

"Her mother's fear of men was deep inside Sophie's psyche. You want to know why she took drugs. I'll tell you. Her family were screwed up. She eventually found strength and security in you and you abandoned her," said Imra.

"I didn't abandon her," pleaded Henry.

"You bloody well abandoned her." Imra could not have been more emphatic in her statement.

"I thought we were working..." Henry didn't finish his sentence. It didn't seem necessary.

What, at one time, seemed straightforward had suddenly become complicated. From Henry's demeanour Imra detected that she now had the psychological advantage.

"Never mind," said Imra sarcastically. "Sophie said you were a great lover when you put your mind to it." Henry started to smile, so Imra added, "it just wasn't often enough. Sometimes she wondered if you were gay. Are you gay?"

"No," said Henry, getting even more disturbed by the fact that Sophie and Imra had these kinds of conversation.

Imra nonchalantly smoothed her hair away from her face and behind her shoulders. "I just wondered as you haven't tried to flirt with me."

"Do all men flirt with you?" he asked, perplexed at her arrogance.

"Yes, of course, apart from gay men."

"Perhaps your turn will come," said Henry. "But at the moment I have other things on my mind other than your seduction."

"Of course," said Imra, but don't worry your turn will never come!"

"Why not, are you gay?" asked Henry, taking his cue from her earlier question.

"No. It's just I'm much better off without a man and their revolting ways." Imra shook her head as though she was trying to shake thoughts out of her mind.

Henry noticed that the wine bottle was empty. Imra had consumed almost all of it and in the process had forgotten she had to be elsewhere. Henry would normally have offered coffee, but he was feeling quite deflated by their conversation. It was time their dinner ended. He signalled for the bill.

"Marijuana causes schizophrenia, particularly when it's very strong," said Henry. "This is not a matter of debate, it is a medical fact. We have mental hospitals full of kids whose brains have been blown apart by the stuff." Henry paused. "This is what's going to happen. John, you remember John, Sophie's driver?"

Imra nodded.

"John will take you to see Sophie. He will also take you to see Sophie's London flat so you can see where you will live".

"Might live," corrected Imra.

Henry ignored her remark and continued. "After that you will tell me whether you're with me or against me."

"We'll see," said Imra not being prepared to give Henry an inch.

"If you haven't seen Sophie and come to London within ten days, I shall assume you're against me."

The bill arrived at the table. Henry ladled out French francs. He stood up and started to speak but stopped himself. "John will be in touch tomorrow," was all he said.

Henry moved to the bar to pay his bill and to say thank you to the proprietor and waitress. He expected to return to the table to say goodbye to his guest, except it was not to be. The three of them watched as Imra flounced out saying nothing as she went.

"She's very pretty," said the waitress.

"No," said the proprietor. "Too skinny, her arms and legs have no meat on them, and look at her arse. Her back goes straight into her legs without going into a bum."

Henry looked again and had to agree. "At least she's had one good meal this year," said Henry, just before he followed her out of the café.

Chapter 96

London October 1975

HARRIET NERVOUSLY SMOOTHED the front of her pleated skirt. She had chosen it especially for this meeting but now, having seen in the reception hall mirror its hemline hung longer in the front than at the back, she was feeling decidedly uncomfortable. She cursed her mother's genes for her protruding bottom and then herself for not wearing a trouser suit as she usually did. Surreptitiously she rolled up the waist band of her skirt by one notch in the front in the hope of bringing the hemline level.

Despite being well prepared Henry felt nervous too. Harriet's sworn statement had been tested and verified as best it could be by his lawyers. They had assured him that Harriet and he were on strong grounds. However, he couldn't help but remind himself that, should the case come to trial, one of the lawyers would be right and the other one wrong.

As they were shown into Patrick Tracks' more than ample office, he rose from his desk and, in a warm welcome, he invited them to sit at a round table which was placed in one corner of his wooden panelled room.

"How's Sophie?" asked Tracks.

"I'm afraid she's not too well. She's probably going to have to give up work," replied Henry.

"Oh, I am sorry," said Tracks, sincerely. "I met her when she very kindly attended an NSPCC charity event for one of my companies. She was quite brilliant as master of ceremonies."

Tracks was a serial public company chairman who was so infamous in financial circles that the newspapers had created the nickname of

'Tictac' for him. It explained why their meeting was in the offices of Haverings Merchant Bank, where Tracks was one of its Managing Directors, and not at the head office at Boyds Gym, which is what this meeting was all about.

Henry spoke quietly, respecting the sombre tone of the room. Very carefully he explained how Harriet had worked at Boyds Gym, the circumstances of her dismissal and the repayment by her of the money stolen by her husband, even though at the time she knew nothing of his crime.

"The thing is," said Henry, "Harriet was unfairly dismissed and the agreement she signed with Boyds Gyms to repay Mr Bussell's debt was improperly obtained. She is due compensation for her wrongful dismissal and the money you have been taking from her account has to be repaid with interest."

"As you can imagine," said Tracks very smoothly. "I know nothing of this. These are day to day operational issues which would not normally come to my attention."

"Of course," said Henry in a conciliatory tone. "My lawyers have prepared a statement of claim and a witness statement." He handed over a sealed white envelope. "These are all marked draft as I hope we'll be able to settle this matter amicably."

"Thank you," said Tracks. "We'll consider it carefully."

"I am hoping we can settle this matter discretely as there is one important issue omitted from Harriet's witness statement which would be included if this matter ever came to trial. Its been excluded at this stage because, if it ever got out, it would cause enormous damage to the Boyd Gyms' good name" said Henry. "It's why I wanted this private meeting with you, rather than my lawyers just sending a letter."

Tracks leaned forward to listen carefully, as though he were about to be part of a conspiracy.

"Sadly," said Henry, "instead of just sacking her, the senior managers at Boyds Gyms subjected Harriet to a prolonged period of corporal punishment. Not only was it exceptionally painful, but it was both degrading and humiliating."

Tracks stared intensely at Harriet, who blushed under his examination, because not a word of what Henry had said was true.

"I'm very sorry," said Tracks who prided himself on his judge of character. He was convinced by Harriet's reaction that everything Henry had said had happened.

"For this reason, I think it best that we settle this matter privately, don't you?" said Henry.

"How are you involved in this?" asked Tracks, beginning to ponder on Henry and Harriet's relationship. Were they sleeping together, he wondered; quickly dismissing the idea when he thought about Henry's wife.

"Harriet's mother and father are very good and long-standing friends of mine. They live just outside of Cape Town. When they heard what had happened, they asked for my help."

Tracks nodded. "We'll examine Mrs Bussell's claim and our lawyers will be in touch with an appropriate response," he said.

Thank you," said Henry as he handed over his lawyer's business card.

Harriet, Henry and Tracks stood up at the same time and they shook hands. The meeting was over. It had lasted all of ten minutes. Harriet was surprised at the civility of it all. It was as though there was nothing personal about what had happened. It was just another business matter which had to be dealt with, which is exactly how the two men saw it.

"Why did you say that?" asked Harriet when they were in a taxi on the way back to Found House.

"Say what?"

"About the corporal punishment."

"Because you told me about it," said Henry dismissively, as his mind was already elsewhere.

"No, I didn't. I said nothing of the sort," protested Harriet, angrily.

"Yes, you did. I remember it clearly! You said you'd been caned before and couldn't bear that again. I remember your words precisely!" retorted Henry rather annoyed.

"But that wasn't at Boyds. I never said that happened at Boyds," complained Harriet.

"Not at Boyds?" asked Henry, verifying what Harriet had been saying.

"No it wasn't there."

"Where was it?" he asked.

Harriet chose not to answer that question. "It was so embarrassing. Did you see the way he was looking at me after that?" she said.

"Yes, he fancied you."

"He's a dirty old man who spent the whole time wondering about us and whether we're sleeping together," she protested.

"Well at least it's not mentioned in your witness statement," said Henry, "otherwise we would have had a real problem."

"So what, you still said it!" said Harriet annoyed.

"Yep, it's a bit of a cock-up," admitted Henry. "We'll have to see what happens. My bet is that this aspect will not get mentioned directly in any correspondence, just alluded to."

"It was humiliating, Henry!" said Harriet having the last word. Nothing else was said between them until they arrived at Found House.

On the steps, as Henry sought to find his keys, Harriet took Henry by the arm and stopped him going in.

"It's a month now since ..." She stopped as she didn't know the correct words to choose. "It's not fair. It's the not knowing when; the suspense is agony. I walk around in knots. It's like its own form of torture. You either have to do it or not." There was almost a pleading in her voice.

Harriet released his arm and Henry opened the door. The two of them looked at each other waiting for the other to go in first. At that moment, there was the same unsaid spark of magic between them which they had first found in the barn at New Found Estate all those years ago.

"Seven o'clock my office," said Henry, still unsure as to what he was going to do.

Meanwhile Tracks had given his instructions. He needed to know anything and everything about Henry Guégan and his businesses. As Henry walked through the door of Found House, accountants, lawyers and private investigators in England were already at work.

Chapter 97

London October 1975

HARRIET WALKED BACKWARDS, turned quickly and darted into Henry's personal bathroom. She rapidly closed the door securing the solitude she desperately needed.

"Leave your knickers on," she heard Henry shout above the noise of the extractor fan.

The conversation with Henry had lasted but a few minutes. It was odd in so many ways, particularly as nothing explicit was said between them, but both knew what was going to happen. It was as though they were talking about a forthcoming business event, except it wasn't. It was very personal. The reality was that Henry and Harriet had got themselves into a position which they regretted. They both found it awkward, even ridiculous, but neither knew how to end their predicament.

Harriet stared into the mirror. She saw the Sunetta of her youth. A girl abased because of the colour of her skin and now, instructed to get undressed, humiliated by circumstance. By habit, she pulled at her face and examined her perfect skin for the flaws which were not there. She put down the lavatory lid, lifted her skirt, and wriggled from side to side as she struggled to pull her tights half way down, before sitting on its cold lid. Her tights, free of her feet, were discarded, as a bundle, into the corner on the floor.

Harriet placed her face into her hands. There were no tears. This was life delivering up her lot. Slowly, Harriet stood up and started to undress. She stopped suddenly. Did he want her to take off her bra when he had deliberately said she should leave her panties on, she wondered. Nevertheless, she unclipped it at the back, unsure at what he expected. She was mindful not to make a bad situation worse. Her hands moved to the front of her breasts squeezing and lifting them up. She took a few seconds to play with her nipples which were sensitive to her touch.

Harriet ran her hands down her hips and across her bottom. She always thought God had served her well when he had produced her nether regions. Her hips were slim, her bottom was round, but now she felt huge, wide and ungainly. She thumped the side of her fists against her hip bones in the vain attempt to make them smaller.

Harriet wrapped a light blue bath towel, which was soft and warm from the heat of the radiator, tightly around her body. She adjusted the towel carefully, so it was high under her arm pits and covered her breasts, and then pulled it down so it covered more of her bottom. He might have told her to undress, but she wasn't going to willingly parade naked in front of him.

Harriet looked again in the mirror and reached for the comb placed on the glass shelf. She removed the band which held her jet black hair in a ponytail. She combed her hair furiously and took care to create the perfect centre parting, but rather than put the band back, she allowed her locks to fall naturally behind her ears and over her shoulders.

Harriet returned to Henry's office just as he was reappearing. Music was now playing in the background. She shivered as she heard the strong rapid beat of Barry White's song, 'Never, Never Gonna Give You Up.' She wondered if it had been chosen by Henry as a rhythmical prop to her beating. But there was such uncertainty in their conversations that she had no real idea as to what was going to happen next. However, just the thought of what it could be was enough to turn Harriet sick with fear. Nevertheless, she kept her poise, erect and defiant.

Henry was now without his jacket and tie, but with a pressed white shirt, open necked collar and the double cuffs of his sleeves turned back, he looked like a man who was in command. Ever since she started working for him Harriet found his masculinity sexually attractive, but it was the way he held himself, when he sought to be master of all he surveyed, which she found an indefatigable aphrodisiac.

Henry had been wandering around the rest of the office looking for a suitable implement with which to chastise Harriet. Eventually he found a wooden spoon. There were many lying around the general office as they were given as booby prizes to the worst performing team in the numerous client entertaining events his account managers attended. It had become part of his firm's culture that they worked hard to come last in any corporate entertaining quiz, but it had to be wittily and cleverly done, for there was acknowledged shame in coming last from ignorance.

'Thank God,' thought Harriet, as she saw the wooden spoon. 'I won't get marked with that,' but her heart started to thump even harder, and she felt light-headed as she realised she was going to get hurt, and badly hurt at that.

Henry locked the door and looked at Harriet. He had studied her many times before, and had always thought how sexually attractive she was. Now, wrapped in a towel she looked alluring and available. 'Christ, she is stunning,' he thought.

Henry moved to one of the two sofas in his office, which were opposite each other, and sat down in the middle. He said nothing. He simply indicated where he expected Harriet to lie. She felt totally ungainly as she lay over his lap and along the length of the settee. Not wanting to see what was going to happen, she pressed her face into the cushion placed in the corner of the settee's padded arm. There was something secure and soothing from the chill of the cushion and its musty smell.

Henry's initial handling was kind and gentle, but suddenly he grasped Harriet's right arm and her hips, and with a sharp tug, he pulled her body tightly into his.

As Henry lifted the towel to reveal Harriet's bottom, she felt ashamed, and then as he squeezed the material of her white cotton panties between her buttocks leaving her cheeks exposed, she was overcome with embarrassment. Still nothing was said between them.

Slowly, Henry started stroking her, from the top of her legs to the base of her back. Harriet buried her head deeper into the sofa cushion. Every time he removed his hand, she braced herself for the first stinging blow. Except a blow didn't come. Instead, he continued to caress her, softly, preciously, rhythmically as though he were holding, for the first time, something of great value. There was a kindness in Henry's touch, allowing Harriet to start feeling calmer, her breathing less frantic.

After what seemed to Harriet like an eternity, Henry stopped what he was doing and tugged at the blue towel. Harriet leaned upright so that it could be freed from under her. Immediately it was free he threw it to the ground. Once again, Henry started to stroke her, but this time it was with both his hands and covered every part of her body, from around her shoulders and neck, down to behind her knees and her calves beyond.

Henry was fascinated by the perfection of Harriet's skin. It was so smooth and soft with different shades of brown as a result of genes and the effect of her sunbathing. He watched amused as parts of her body twitched involuntarily as he tickled her skin with the back of his nails.

The flow of Henry's hands, from her legs, over the hills of her buttocks into the valley of her tiny waist and back again, were interrupted by the waistband of Harriet's panties. Frustrated by the disturbance, he lifted the waistband over her bottom in an attempt to remove them. "Lift your hips," he commanded, in the now silent room.

Immediately Harriet raised her hips freeing her panties until they got stuck around the top of her legs. Henry's response was quick and decisive. He dug his fingernails deep into the cotton seam on one side of her panties and, with a sharp jerk, he snapped it apart. The other side was despatched equally as ruthlessly. Harriet froze. Not a breath could she take. The manner with which she had been disrobed took her back to the swimming pool at New Found House and the searing pain caused by Lucky Naidoo. Perspiration started to pour from her forehead as she remembered that time. Once again, she knew she should protest, shout out, say no but she did none of those things for she was first and foremost a woman, an African woman of colour, brought up by the demands of South African society to be compliant.

Henry immediately noticed the change in Harriet's body as she became rigid, like a statue. Her back began to glisten in perspiration as he heard her short sharp panicking breaths. His warm hands restarted their soft rhythmical journey of the whole length of her body. While calming her, it also left Harriet feeling confused, for she now felt exposed and, most of all, entirely vulnerable to his touch.

The fear of her thrashing subsided as she felt his now swollen penis push into her stomach. I told him men liked this kind of thing, she thought as her mind started to work again after it had been stunned numb. Instinctively, Harriet knew what she had to do. As the music changed to 'The Way We Were'[17], sung by Barbara Streisand, she pushed herself on to her elbows and half twisting she turned backward to look at Henry properly. In the process, she stroked her long fine hair from her face, behind her ear, so it fell across her neck and then in waves on to the cushion below.

Until that moment Henry's focus had been on one thing, an intense study of Harriet's body, but now his attention was taken by the side profile of her face, and her look of concern. It was a look he had seen before. With the shape of the mouth turned down, and her dark eyes, made darker by delicately applied make up, she looked frightened, apprehensive, but oh so beautiful.

"Oh Christ," said Henry out loud, as he recognised Harriet's expression from their first time together. There could be no punishment for the innocent schoolgirl from all those years ago. She was very precious to him then, and he felt the same way about the woman now prostrate, naked across his lap.

Henry bent down and leaned across to kiss Harriet on the lips, and instinctively she rose towards him allowing him to sweep her into his arms. They kissed as they kissed all those years ago, with passion and lust. Harriet smiled. She didn't care what happened next. Her man was holding her in his arms. This was her man. She'd had him, she'd loved him long ago, long before anyone else and now he was to be hers yet again.

With a tap and a few signals Henry persuaded Harriet to roll up in a ball and he slid from under her body to sit on the floor next to

---

[17] The Way We Were songwriters: Alan Bergman, Marilyn Bergman and Marvin Hamlisch Marvin. Copyright of the lyrics belongs to Arlovol Music, Colgems-EMI Music Inc.

her. She lay on her back, stretched out with her feet dangling over the edge of the settee. She was staring vacantly at the ceiling when her mind became attuned to the lyrics of the song now playing:

"When I had you there but then I let you go,
And now it's only fair that I should let you know,
What you should know.
I can't live if living is without you.
I can't live, I can't give anymore ...."[18]

Who's singing this?" she asked, identifying with the words of the song.

"Harry Nilsson, I think," replied Henry as he stroked her fine black hair away from her face and very gently stroked her forehead with the curve of his hands. Harriet found the effect very comforting.

Henry bent forward and kissed Harriet softly on the cheek and then the ear. She bent her head and shoulders so that her lips were ready to greet his mouth. Within seconds they were in another embrace kissing each other passionately. Henry started to work on Harriet's body with his tongue, kissing, licking, and sucking at her breasts, nipples, and tummy button, whilst his hands massaged every bit of her body. The eagerness with which Harriet thrust her pelvis backwards and forwards at his touch gave Henry the assurance he needed.

Henry undid his belt, removed his shoes and slid his trousers, underpants and socks off in one well practiced movement. He pulled Harriet from the sofa to lie on top of him. They continued to kiss each other passionately. Harriet stopped, sat astride Henry and started to undo his shirt. With the buttons undone, she lifted her weight from him and then slowly, with her hands as a guide, she lowered herself onto his swollen shaft until she had him fully enclosed. She leant forward, placed the palm of her hands firmly on his chest and as she did so Henry raised his buttocks. He pushed deeply into Harriet

---

[18] Without You songwriters: Peter William Ham and Thomas Evans. Copyright of the lyrics belongs to Songtrust Ave, BMG Rights Management

who gasped in response. Her eyes were closed. She rode him long and hard, thinking only of herself and her needs. She felt herself getting more and more aroused. The more aroused she became so she dug her fingers into his chest. She wanted to climax. She needed to come but was not yet ready. Despite the fantastic pleasure of feeling him inside her, Harriet's overwhelming sensation was of frustration as her body was not responding as quickly as she hoped.

She moved her hands to the floor each side of Henry's body, lowering her breasts so her nipples brushed up and down on the hairs of Henry's chest. Henry took her breasts into his hands and very gently massaged her nipples between his thumb and forefinger. His touch yielded a confusing mixture of pleasure and pain. Slowly, but surely, she felt her body go into spasm. Her face froze. She daren't move. "I'm coming" she whispered, "I'm coming."

Chapter 98

London October 1975

"HOW ARE THE English lessons going, John?" asked Henry, as he climbed into the back seat of his car.

"C'est difficile," said John, as the car pulled away from the kerb.

"In England we speak English; In France we speak French."

"N'est pas possible," continued John. "Boss," he said in all seriousness, "there's something you need to know about Imra before you meet her."

"What?"

"You know she has a kid," said John.

"Yes, she has a daughter."

"The thing is: I think the father of her daughter is Imra's grandfather."

"What?" said Henry not only confused by what he had been told, but because it challenged his preconception of her family arrangements.

"Say that again. I assumed her daughter was her husband's," said Henry.

"Yes, I know. It's what we all think," said John, before he repeated Imra's daughter's lineage.

"How old is her daughter."

"She's aged twelve."

"I thought she was much younger, say four or five. How old's Imra?"

"It's what everyone thinks," said John, then added: "Imra's twenty-five."

"Pardon," said Henry, "are you saying she had the kid when she was just thirteen."

"Her name's Xara. It's a shortened version of the Somali word for passion."

Henry pulled a face.

"It's worse than that boss," continued John. "Imra's grandfather committed suicide in jail awaiting trial. Immediately she said who the father was he was banged-up in France and then he topped himself."

"Is the kid okay, not mentally retarded or anything?" asked Henry, trying to work out why Xara was much older than he thought.

"No, Imra and her mother now think that the grandfather wasn't the father of Imra's mother."

"Hells bells," said Henry. "Is all this true? It sounds a bit fanciful. How did you get all of this?"

"It's a long way from Paris to Bamberg and then back to London," said John. "Immediately, she was out of France and with a couple of glasses of wine well ... I think she felt she could trust me."

"The girls a fool," joked Henry, taking a Morecambe and Wise catch phrase in an attempt to lighten the situation.

It all happened when, with her mother, brother and grandfather, she left Somalia and travelled across North Africa into Algiers, then to Italy, across Europe and into Paris."

"That's one hell of a journey."

"They had to leave because Imra's father and grandmother had been killed in Somalia. It was political gangsterism there. They were frightened for their lives. They were making their way to London when they realised Imra was pregnant, so they stopped in France and applied for asylum there."

"Then, she's done bloody well for herself, hasn't she?" said Henry admiringly.

"Boss, if you knew the half of it, you'd consider her a hero, but listen; it's worse, much worse."

The way John spoke gave Henry notice of the import of his next message.

"Boss, her brother committed suicide earlier this week."

"Fuck," said Henry quietly to himself.

"He was a bit older than Imra, and was messed around with, you know ... by her grandfather too. She was just eight or nine when her grandfather started on her. Her brother was so relieved it was no longer him he said nothing."

"Fuck," said Henry a little louder.

John looked in his rear-view mirror and watched as Henry leant back heavily and closed his eyes. He was trying to take on board what he was being told.

"Her brother blamed himself for not protecting her, but he was only ten at the time."

"Christ," said Henry, "the boy was just a kid. Surely, he's been told it was not his fault."

"Everyone's told him, but he couldn't stop blaming himself. Imra now thinks that every time he saw her daughter all the memories came flooding back. It was a never-ending nightmare for him."

"Oh shit, no," said Henry in despair as he suddenly realised the complexity of the dinner he was about to have.

"He was petrified he would turn into the same kind of person as his grandfather," continued John.

"There is no scientific evidence of that, is there?" asked Henry.

"Well, that's what appears to have triggered his suicide. In the weekend papers there was an article saying that a study had shown that sexually abused children went on into adulthood to sexually abuse their own children. It claimed that, unless it is deliberately stopped with pro-active counselling, the pattern continues through the family line."

"Is that true?" asked Henry.

"Who knows, but apparently in his suicide note he not only apologised to Imra for letting her down but went on to say he didn't trust himself to have children. The article was found open in his flat, so he'd obviously read it. All this, even the bit about Imra, is going to come out at the inquest."

"Bloody Hell," said Henry in a deeply sympathetic tone, before asking: "how did he die?"

"He hung himself in his garage," said John, matter-of-factly. "He put a noose around his neck, put on a child's set of handcuffs behind his back, and kicked aside the table he was standing on."

"How did you learn about her brother's death?" asked Henry.

She told me yesterday afternoon, just after we'd seen Sophie's flat. He was found in the morning and she knew almost immediately, but weirdly, instead of going straight back to Paris to be with her mother, she still went to see it, and then we have this evening. Don't you think that's odd?

"Jesus," said Henry out loud, as he contemplated what he was going to say to her when they met.

"Boss, it explains the way she is," said John.

"What?"

"The drink, the weed; she can't sleep without it." John paused. "Could you?" he asked.

Henry did not answer, instead he sat in silence until the car pulled up at Odins Restaurant on Devonshire Street, London.

Odins was owned by the highly eccentric Peter Langham; better known for his famous restaurant in Piccadilly. Like Langham's in Piccadilly, the food at Odins was always excellent, but as a place it was far more discreet, with less chance of the alcohol induced owner taking a very public, but unreasoning, dislike to you.

Henry was taken to sit at his favourite table where he would not be overheard. It was typical of Langham's disregard of anyone else's sensitivity that he had placed next to the table, at eye height, a painting of a man touching a young woman's breast. Pictures of a similar ilk were close to every table.

Imra was late, beyond fashionably late, to the point where Henry wondered whether she was coming at all. While he waited, he rehearsed what he was going to say, but none of the lines he practised seemed right.

Unlike last time, when she just presented herself at his table, Imra moved through the restaurant as though she were walking on air. Every deliberately sensuous sway of her hips caused her floor length skirt to float effortlessly from side to side. Other diners watched, as she slid into the seat opposite him. Imra knew how to make an entrance.

Imra offered Henry her hand, held slightly dipped downwards which, as he stood up, he could only hold between fingers and thumb. Henry had already ordered the wine and chosen what he was going to eat. He poured a glass for her and then with his taster portion he raised his glass and said, "Cheers, good to see you. Thank you for coming." He did not know what else he should say.

Henry looked into Imra's face. He was convinced she had aged since they last met. "I am so sorry about your brother," he said.

"Thank you. Did John tell you?"

"Yes"

"And the reason?" she asked.

"He did. I'm sorry."

"It's going to be in all the papers in France. Because of who I am, we're not going to be able to keep it out."

"The whole thing?" asked Henry.

Probably, of course most of it will be made up. Unlike here, the papers in France don't usually care who you sleep with. For them it's a boring subject, but this; it will be wild." Imra shook her head in anguish as she spoke.

"Did you see Sophie?" asked Henry, deliberately changing the subject.

"Yes, it was just dreadful. It made me feel so sad."

Henry nodded, for that is exactly how he felt.

"I don't understand it" said Imra. "She looks as beautiful as ever, but her mind and her personality have gone. She knows things but just can't remember them. She gets so confused and you can see this causes her to get incredibly frightened. It's written all over her face."

"How long were you with her?" asked Henry.

"I intended to visit for just the morning. I stayed all day and the next day too. She knew she knew me and wanted to say things but, as soon as she started to speak, she forgot what she wanted to say. I thought if I stayed longer, she might remember what she wanted to tell me, but she never did."

Henry nodded.

"Henry, I'm so sorry," said Imra, "I'd no idea."

The two were joined in a grief which, at that moment, they were only able to talk about because their own mental safety systems had temporarily shut down their emotions.

Henry raised his glass: "To Sophie and your brother," he said. "What was your brother's name?"

"Afrax, it means joy in Somali," said Imra.

"To Sophie and Afrax," said Henry, raising his glass again.

"Imra repeated the names before she took a sip of wine, which she followed by a mouthful.

"John's taking me to see your lawyer in Paris next week. I'll make a statement about Gevais. It's the least I can do for Sophie."

"Thank you," said Henry.

"And we're going to move in to Sophie's flat as you suggested ... until we find somewhere of our own. If that's alright?"

"Yes, good," said Henry.

"After my brother's ... well, Paris has nothing for us now. We need to start again, and this gives us a chance to do so," she said and then added, "Thank you." On that last word Imra smiled at Henry for the very first time. He smiled back.

"When will you move," asked Henry.

"As soon as possible after Afrax's funeral. There has to be an autopsy and an inquest first."

"Well it's yours to use from today. In fact, I will be glad when someone's in it. What did Afrax do?" asked Henry, thinking it would be helpful for her to talk about her brother.

"He was a chef in his own restaurant in Montmartre. He served the tourists during the day and then, after 8 o'clock, the menu changed and he would cook only one menu, which was what he wanted to eat. Every day was different. It became so popular that you had to book a long time in advance. Even I couldn't get a table without booking," said Imra proudly.

"Did you help him get started?" he asked.

"No, he worked two jobs to get the deposit to take the lease. Me and my friends going there might have helped by making it better known, but it was his genius which kept it going."

"What happens now?

"I don't know. I suspect it will have to be sold. I think some of his friends might want to buy it with the idea of keeping the concept of 'the one menu' restaurant alive."

This time Imra selected what she wanted to eat and, after ordering, they chatted generally about everything. Their animosity of the past had gone. Henry was interested when she talked about John, telling him new things about his chauffeur. She spoke fondly of him as though she had found a good friend.

Given its portent, the evening was far more enjoyable than either of them had thought it might be. Just as Henry was paying the bill, Imra reached across the table and took hold of his arm. "I am sorry about what I said last time," she said.

Henry looked quizzically.

"About what I said about you and Sophie," she added. "It wasn't nice. I am sorry."

"Perhaps I deserved it," replied Henry.

"Somehow I think not. There's always another side to every story and I don't think I'd seen the other side, not until tonight."

They both walked out of the restaurant into the chilly autumn air. Henry's car was waiting with John at the wheel.

"Will you take Imra back to her hotel," asked Henry. "I need to walk," he said, as he buttoned up his jacket.

Imra and Henry held hands. He kissed her good-bye gently on both cheeks. She responded by jumping forward and kissing him very swiftly on the lips. Then, in one move, she floated gracefully into the back seat of the car.

As the car drove away, John put his left arm around the seat and Imra took his hand. "It was good," she said, as the two of them looked at each other fondly through the rear-view mirror. "I think you're right. He's not a bad man."

Chapter 99

London October 1975

HENRY HAD EXPECTED Harriet's problems with Boyd Gyms to be sorted out between the lawyers. It meant he was surprised when he received an invitation to luncheon from Sir Patrick Tracks to discuss the matter.

Tracks had been awarded a knighthood in the Queen's Birthday honours list for services to the financial services industry back in the summer but, dubbed by the Queen the week before, and with his insignia in hand, what had been just an announcement had become very real to him. The Chancellor of the Exchequer was prepared to throw whatever trinkets were necessary into the City of London to keep them on side and lending to his Government. This was Tracks' reward for helping to fund a couple of North Sea oil rigs, so essential to the UK's economic future; a project for which his bank had been very handsomely paid.

Tracks was now basking in the joy of now being called Sir Patrick, instead of just Mr Tracks as he had been called before. As he climbed the steps of the City of London Club on Bishopsgate, where lunch had been arranged, Tracks was secretly hoping he would now get one of the better tables under the window so they would not be overheard.

The City of London Club is an exclusive private member's club for the power drivers of London's financial markets. It had just been fully refurbished thanks to a huge dowry from NatWest Bank so they could build their new head office block in the shape of their logo on the land next door. Its members were rightly proud that their dining room was protected by a Class 2 listing, for its shape was uniquely two perfect cubes placed side by side.

After the briefest of welcomes, the two men sat down at one of the better tables as Tracks had hoped. He studied the menu and then, taking a heavy silver pencil from his jacket pocket, he started to scribble his order on the pad which had been left on the table. Henry chose equally as quickly and was surprised when Tracks wrote his selection on the pad too. The waitress came up to their table took the pad and read it out to them before taking it to the kitchen. This practice was the same as in every one of London's old and hallowed private members clubs, but Henry had never seen it done before, and was surprised by the experience.

"I want to discuss with you the offer which Boyd Gyms is prepared to make to Mrs Bussell before it is made. As you said, we don't want any embarrassment in the matter, do we?" said Tracks.

Henry's heart sank as he was certain that his claim of Harriet being spanked by the Area Manager was going to be challenged and, at some stage, they would have to admit it was not true.

"This is what we are thinking about," continued Tracks, as he took a sheet of folded paper and handed it to Henry.

Henry looked at it hard. There was a number for unpaid salary and untaken holiday. There was a number for one month's notice, and another number for the repayment of monies improperly taken and a final number, called compensation, was calculated as being six months' salary. Within a few pounds it was the same amount as Harriet had claimed.

"Thank you, I'm sure she will accept," said Henry perplexed, for David Boyd had a reputation of not giving up anything, particularly a claim from an ex-employee, without a fight. If this was their only business, then it didn't merit a lunch.

"Good," said Tracks and then without a pause he asked: "Have you ever thought about floating your company on the London Stock Market." Tracks agenda was out in the open. He had just spent Boyd Gyms's money so he could have this meeting with Henry without Harriet's claim being an issue. What were a few thousand pounds paid by Boyd Gyms as compared to the hundreds of thousands his bank would earn from getting Found Vintners listed on the London Stock Exchange.

"No," said Henry. "I didn't think we were big enough."

"I've been looking at your numbers," said Tracks. "Your profits are certainly large enough, but your balance sheet shows you're undercapitalised. You are always short of cash as everything goes into funding growth. A float would put money into the company and into your pockets."

Henry listened as a very smooth salesman went about selling his wares.

"What about the vineyards?" asked Henry.

"You have more than one? said Tracks, surprised. His report said nothing about one vineyard let alone more than that.

"Yes, three in total."

"I'm sure the stock market would like to have a share in the ownership of the vineyards particularly when they are owned by a distributor," said Tracks, recovering his position quickly.

"You know we have a retail shop and a wholesale business in Paris," said Henry, as a statement and not a question. Tracks did not, but his expression neither confirmed nor denied what he knew.

"What would the stock market want for its money?" asked Henry knowing that everything had a price."

They'll want between 20% and 35% of your company, and two or three non-executive directors on your board.

"And who would these people be?" Henry asked.

"People who know about the stock market and the needs of the investors."

"Such as?" he pressed.

"Well, I am not proposing myself, but it would be someone like me," said Tracks.

"Not being rude, but you know nothing of my business."

"True, but when you sit on a lot of companies' boards you get to know a lot about business, and that's where we add value."

It seemed such an axiomatic answer that Henry decided to leave the point alone. He didn't know how he would get on being accountable to someone else. Instinctively, it felt anathema to him.

The lunch ended, the two men parted and, as John chauffeured him back to Mayfair, Henry thought about their conversation. He was wishing that Sophie was there so he could have her opinion when he realised she would say no, for no other reason than she would not have liked, and certainly would not have trusted Tracks. There was a smoothness and sincerity which was so window dressed in the image of the City that it made him seem wholly untrustworthy.

Back at Found House Henry told Ainsworth of the conversation he'd had with Tracks about floating the company.

"You know he's in the business of selling pounds for ninety pence, don't you?" said Ainsworth.

Henry looked shocked.

"The shares have to go up immediately on the first day of trading so those that bought them make an immediate profit. It's the name of the game. The guys that make the profits are Tracks' mates, his cronies. The guy who loses is you. Your loss is their gain," said Ainsworth disparagingly.

"Why does anyone float then?" asked Henry.

"Didn't he give you the cake argument?" asked Ainsworth.

"Well he told me that I would own a smaller percentage of a much more valuable cake, if that's what you mean," replied Henry.

"Precisely," said Ainsworth, as he nodded his approval of the answer.

"I don't think it's for us, do you?" asked Henry.

"Not this year," said Ainsworth. "We've got a lot of big things coming through and before they're visible we would be selling too cheaply; may be in a year or two."

"It was a decision which Henry liked, mostly because it came with a rationale which he could give to Tracks when he followed up with a phone call, which he almost certainly would.

Henry's next call was to Harriet's desk. "This is what Boyd Gyms have agreed to pay you," said Henry, as he handed her the slip of paper which Tracks had given to him.

She looked at it and then pointed Henry to the figure on the bottom. "This much?" she asked.

"Yes" said Henry, looking pleased with himself. "There'll be legal fees to pay but you will net over £15,000."

I'll be able to repay you what I owe," said Harriet.

Henry smiled. It hadn't occurred to him, but the fact that it had been her first thought made him feel good about her.

"Perhaps I could buy you dinner." Then, because of the concerned look on his face, she added, "not a date dinner, a thank you dinner?"

"Yes, that would be nice, thank you."

There was nothing like the same response being felt in Tracks' offices. The air was blue with his swear words and everyone was a victim of his vitriol. He had gone into the meeting expecting to know as much about Henry's businesses as there was to know. To find out he knew nothing about Henry's French operations was unacceptable. "How the fuck could that be," he yelled cursing anyone and everyone in his research team.

Chapter 100

London October 1975

HARRIET BOOKED A table at San Lorenzo for her 'not-a-date' dinner with Henry. It's a little Italian restaurant on Beauchamp's Place later to become famous as a favourite of Princess Diana.

Henry arrived punctually. He looked around the room as he gave his name to the maître d'. He was surprised he couldn't see Harriet as he had been told his guest had arrived. As he was guided to their table, he could see a woman was sitting there, but it was not the Harriet he knew. She had spent the afternoon at the hairdressers. Gone was her long black hair to be replaced by a pixie cut, sharp to her face.

"Do you like it?" she asked nervously, as Henry took his seat. "I asked for the same look as Mia Farrow."

"Er, why?" he asked. His frown gave away his thoughts. "It's like Audrey Hepburn's in Roman Holiday, isn't it? Except, ... your fringe is swept to the side, which is nicer."

"You don't like it?" she pressed anxiously.

"I do. I think I do, it's just, well, it's a surprise that's all."

"I'm starting again. It's the new me. Today, I start the rest of my life!" It was said with a confidence which belied Harriet's true feelings about her hair cut. It was why she had spent the second part of the afternoon fighting back tears as she purchased a new bra. Unable to stick her hair back on, she decided she would have to make something more of her embonpoint, so men looked there and not into her face.

"I can tell you one thing," continued Henry. "It makes your eyes look much bigger. I've always thought you had beautiful eyes, clear, sparkling eyes but now they're like ... well ... clear pools that draw you right in." He was pleased with his description as he sought to dig himself out of the hole he felt he was in.

Over dinner they chatted freely as friends do. There was little mention of work. Instead, Henry listened as Harriet spoke, which she did freely after her first glass of wine. Naturally, they talked of their first meeting, of her mother and father, and of Lucky's fate, without mentioning her involvement. At one moment, Harriet asked if Henry had ever thought about the co-incidence of her father's vineyard and his office having the same 'Found' name. He hadn't and the matter was not mentioned again.

Harriet talked at length of growing up as a girl of colour in an apartheid country. She spoke of Little Joe's death, of her father's strictness and his expectation that they serve others before themselves. She had very rarely spoken about these things before because it was hard to put anything into context for those who hadn't been to South Africa. Now she was finding it a cathartic experience because Henry listened attentively to whatever she wanted to say. It was she who set the agenda, not him. He was learning about a world which was a million miles from his own experiences. He knew for certain that he no longer saw the colour of her skin, but was he subconsciously racially prejudiced he wondered. It was a question he found impossible to answer truthfully and would never be able to do so.

There was a chill in the air as Henry accompanied Harriet on the fifteen-minute walk to her flat in Sloane Gardens. She shared it with the daughter of the owner from whom she rented a small bedroom. They walked side by side as colleagues. Not once did they hold hands or lock arms which might have suggested something closer.

"Would you like to come in?" asked Harriet nervously when they arrived outside her building. "It's still early," she added, seeking to justify her question.

It was an invitation Henry had been expecting, even hoping for, but as it was asked, he didn't know his reply. Without answering he followed her apprehensively up the steps thinking as he went, this far and no further. As she placed the key in the door, Harriet turned towards him and looked at Henry straight in the eye seeking an answer. It immediately struck him. He had seen that expression before. Yes, he had seen it in Harriet a few days ago when she turned naked on his lap to look at him. Yes, he had seen it years before when they were in her father's fruit sorting shed on New Found Estate. But now he truly knew where it had come from. It was a look made famous 300 years before, captured by Vermeer in his painting of the Girl with the Pearl Earring. It was a painting he'd loved from his school days when he had yearningly studied her face, wondering what she was thinking.

Harriet's and the girl's face did not look the same. Harriet's was far more beautiful, while the girl in the painting was more enigmatic, but their expressions were identical. Each adoringly, but nervously, seeking approval for the role they had assumed. Each uncertain in their relationship, wondering whether their unspoken expectation was reasonable, let alone valid. Each hoping to be spiritually satisfied. Each seeking more, while suspecting no more would come. Each frightened that they might be a muse for that moment in time, to be discarded later.

Harriet's look said so much that Henry had no hesitation in accepting her invitation. Together they climbed the stairs.

Neither would remember the moments between them going through the front door of her apartment, turning immediately left into her bedroom and lying naked arm in arm in her four-foot bed. Except Henry would recall the stale smell of the perspiration of her ex-husband from deep inside her pillow. It was a smell which created a challenge for Henry was not going to be outperformed.

Time and time again they made love until Henry was spent and then, as soon as he recovered, they made love once more. Not once did Harriet achieve the full orgasm she had enjoyed only nights before. It was an omission which caused Henry to work harder, more vigorously as he tried to please her. Eventually, Henry was capable of no more. He fell into a physically exhausted sleep. It was the moment when Harriet became equally as contented. He had pleased her but more importantly, she had serviced 'her man' in a way which proved he would have no need of any other woman.

Harriet didn't hear Henry get up and leave in the early hours of the morning. The only evidence that he had been there was a note on her pillow written on paper torn from his personally embossed pocket notebook. 'It was all too good to say I'm sorry', he wrote

Harriet stared at the note and immediately felt comforted by the words. He could have left and said nothing, but any joy she felt immediately faded as she thought about the consequences of the night before.

Harriet rolled across the bed and reached for her handbag on the floor. She took out her diary. She had stopped taking the contraceptive pill after Rick had left, determined she would never sleep with another man again.

She thumbed rapidly through the pages until she found the last circled date and counted forward. "Oh God" she said out loud as it dawned on her that last night was right in the middle of her cycle. The thought of being pregnant chilled her. Harriet laid still and contemplated the consequences.

If I'm pregnant I'll keep it, she vowed, as she swung her feet over the edge of the bed. I'll go back to New Found Estate and bring it up there. This time she knew her mother would understand.

As Harriet left the house early the next morning, Rick Bussell's pillow was discarded into the outside dustbin. She no longer wanted or needed in her bed the smell of her husband which, in the early hours of the morning, had previously given her comfort. She had a new man in her life. A man who she knew would not let her down.

Chapter 101

London October 1975

"I THINK I'VE found your get out of jail card," said Ainsworth immediately Henry and he had sat down for their weekly business review meeting.

"What jail are you springing me from?" said Henry, the irony of the efforts he had been making to put Patrice Gevais in jail not lost on him.

"I have been through all of Sophie's papers which her UK and French agency sent," said Ainsworth.

I'm sorry it's taken so long but it has been a bit like drawing hens' teeth because they would only give me things piecemeal. Eventually, I couldn't bear their mess of papers in my room any longer so I came and did it over the weekend."

Henry nodded as, given Ainsworth's obsession with neatness, it sounded just the kind of thing he would do.

"Did you know they charge a fee not only on all the money the model earns but also on every item of expenditure that they supervise being spent?" There was incredulity in Ainsworth's voice.

"No, but it sounds very unusual," said Henry, suddenly paying greater attention.

"Notably they got 15% on all her income, including recharged expenses, and then they got another 15% on everything they supervised of her spending. When they paid for an airline flight or settled her credit card bills, or even paid her tax lawyer's bills they charged her a 15% handling fee. Even the car Sophie bought, and John's invoices have been subject to a 15% surcharge. Can you believe it?"

"Is this normal? It doesn't sound like it to me," said Henry.

"I did some asking around. It would appear to be normal for the super-talent who can afford it. The 15% they charge on her income is normal, but 15% on expenditure is excessive. In London the rate is more like 5% but only again for the top earners. When Sophie's father managed her affairs, he point-blank refused to allow the London Office to charge a disbursement fee, but when she moved to the Paris agency and signed one of their contracts it was in there."

"So they're entitled to the money?" asked Henry.

Ainsworth nodded, "unless we want to challenge it on the grounds that the Paris terms should have been the same as London."

"They didn't charge 15% for paying her money into her bank account or on the tax she actually paid, did they?" asked Henry, suddenly waking up to the open chequebook possibilities created by the Agency's contract.

"No. ..." Ainsworth paused to give greater effect to his message, "but I thought it so unfair I thought I would have a hard look at what they'd spent her money on." Ainsworth paused again, as he contemplated what to say next.

"Well?" prompted Henry, beginning to get frustrated as he was becoming aware that Ainsworth was teasing him.

"They took out two important insurance policies," he said. "They were both group policies for all their super-talent and Sophie's was one of the names which was included. I think the agency signed the girls up to this policy purely because they would get paid 15% of the premium as part of their expenses management fee."

"And," said Henry prompting Ainsworth to go faster.

"Well, she has a permanent health policy which will pay her $10,000 a month indexed linked until she's aged fifty, provided the premiums have been paid," said Ainsworth, obviously pleased with himself.

"Have they been paid."

"Yes, even this month because it's a group policy covering all their top girls."

"Good God," said Henry, "that will go a long way to help pay for her nursing costs. Why didn't they say?"

Ainsworth ignored Henry's question. "That's not all," he said. "They've taken out a permanent incapacity policy which pays Sophie an amount which is equivalent to one year of her contracted income should she die, but these are the key words, or has to retire on ill-health grounds."

There was a prolonged silence. "That could be as much as three million dollars, or thereabouts," said Henry, not quite believing what he was being told.

The calculation's a bit complicated but I reckon it's about $3.365 million," said Ainsworth.

Henry knew Ainsworth's rough calculations. Even when dealing with millions, he would be right to the nearest ten thousand dollars.

"After the agency have taken their 15%, it's worth over $2.8 million to you and Sophie," said Ainsworth.

"Henry flopped back in his seat feeling that he had just won the pools.

"I suspect it will be paid tax free as Sophie didn't claim the cost of the insurance premiums as a business expense when doing her tax returns," continued Ainsworth pedantically.

"Is the agency entitled to its 15% on the amount of the pay out?"

Probably not, but if I were you, I'd do a deal where they get their fee on the Cabbage Policy."

"Cabbage policy?" interrupted Henry.

"Sorry, said Ainsworth suddenly realising the insensitivity of the term. "I meant the permanent incapacity policy. As I said, I'd do a deal where they get their 15% on the permanent incapacity policy but nothing on the monthly permanent health policy. It gives them an incentive to get the insurance companies to pay out."

Henry nodded. "Good advice," he said.

"Henry, you need to be very careful," warned Ainsworth. "If Sophie's mental health problems were discovered to have been self-inflicted, as it were, then the insurance company could try and reduce the amount for contributory negligence."

"You know?" said Henry surprised. "How?"

"I put John up against the wall and gave him the third degree. I wanted to know why you had paid him so much money personally. I thought he might be blackmailing you!"

"Blackmailing me!"

"Yes, I'm sorry, but my job is to protect the well-being of this business in all its forms."

"I'm surprised John said anything," said Henry, a bit shocked that what he thought was just John and his secret had been given away.

"You'd be surprised what a gay Jew can get out of people when they need to," he said proudly.

The message was not lost on Henry. For a long time, he'd known Ainsworth was Jewish, but this was the first time he had referred to his sexuality.

"My best guess is that if there is a contributory negligence counter claim then you could look at the pay-out being reduced to somewhere around £2 million, perhaps a little bit more."

Henry's mind was in overload. If Ainsworth was right, then the statement Imra was about to make to the French police saying that Gevais supplied Sophie with drugs could cost £1 million or more. He had to speak to her straight away.

"If you get this money then it means we could finish building the Vaults," said Ainsworth. "It would be one hell of a relief to get that done and for it to be income producing. It's way over budget, over time, everything."

"No, far more importantly, we buy back the wine we've sold which doesn't exist. Until that's done, I can't relax. I'm worried stiff about it all."

"Henry," said Ainsworth patiently. "I found you a gold mine. It provides you with all the capital you need for trading."

"I was reading about the new financial regulations which are coming into force," said Henry. "I can't believe selling financial futures, which is what you say we are doing, isn't a banking activity or something like it. If I'm right, then it means we are not regulated as we should be. I have this horrible feeling that it could all go terribly wrong."

For the first time, without saying so, Ainsworth secretly agreed with him. He too had been examining the regulation changes and they looked as though they could well stop his little scheme. Perhaps Henry's windfall had come just at the right time.

"I think it might take three, maybe six, months to get the insurance claims dealt with," said Ainsworth, without acknowledging that selling wine options might very soon have to stop.

"We'd never have known if you hadn't done that work," said Henry appreciatively. "Thank you."

"It wouldn't have happened if Sophie hadn't moved to the French branch," replied Ainsworth. "The UK office of her agency had never heard of the idea so didn't have such a policy for their models."

"Yeh, but then, if we hadn't gone to France she wouldn't be where she is now," said Henry, despondently.

The two men worked through Ainsworth's list of current business problems, but Henry wasn't listening. Once again, he realised that, without Sophie, he no longer had any interest in the day-to-day minutiae of his business. He'd started it to impress her and by being there and taking an interest in what everyone was doing, she had provided its heart and its soul. If you had asked any of Found Vintner employees, they wouldn't have said that they work for Henry Guégan. They would have said proudly that they worked for Henry and Sophie, with perhaps a little too much emphasis on the last name.

At lunch time on that day there was a Matterers Lunch which Harriet joined for the first time. She proved to be such an excellent hostess that her future place at the table was assured.

Immediately after lunch all Henry wanted to do was talk to John, talk to Imra about her statement and then go home to see his mother and be with his kids. It meant he was highly irritated when he went into a meeting, which had been arranged by Ainsworth, with a man Henry had never heard of, from a firm he didn't know, to talk of a job he didn't know existed.

To Henry's distain the smartly dressed overweight and balding man started to speak immediately the two men met. Henry heard all the words but had no idea what was being communicated by a man whose blandness made him instantly forgettable. The only thing that he could get from the meeting was that Dick Toucher, the chairman of Clydesdale International, wanted to meet him about a job. It seemed very strange to Henry because Toucher had been to a Matterers Lunch and could easily have picked up the phone to talk to him.

It was a later discussion with Ainsworth which decoded the meeting. Henry had been approached about being a non-Executive Director of Clydesdale International, one of the largest drinks' companies in the world.

"You mean someone thinks I'm employable," said Henry, summarising the discussion.

"Surprising, but true," said Ainsworth with a broad smile on his face.

Chapter 102

Folkestone June 1976

IT WAS A perfect summer's day when the Secretary of State for Trade and Industry came forward, made a speech about investing in the United Kingdom, cut the tape at the entrance to Henry's underground warehouse and declared "Found Vaults" open. He ignored the vitally important fact that HM Customs & Excise had still not approved it as a bonded warehouse.

At first Henry wanted to name it after Sophie, but somehow the sheer bulk of the building made it seem inappropriate. Sophie was a slender figure of beauty both inside and out whereas there was nothing beautiful about the huge utilitarian nature of his warehouse. He debated long and hard as to whether he should call it a vault or a cellar, but he felt there was something more attractive to investors if they thought their wine was in a vault.

With Sophie's insurance money, and benefiting from trial and error, sweat and tears and, above all, bloody mindedness, Henry was delighted with his warehouse. He invited everyone and anyone who had been involved in the planning, design and build of Found Vaults to the opening. He included the Chief Constable, the Chief Executives of the county and district councils, even the planning officers. Invitations went out to Pierre Hilaire at Château de Gressier and his mother Dominique, Thomas Cannen from Château Rabôut, Robert Rabôut from La Maison Gelina and Vincent Ainsworth from Found Vintners together with all their key members of staff. Harriet insisted that the guest list included her, which seemed only fair since she was organising the whole grand opening.

Invitations went to everyone who had ever been invited to one of the Matterers Lunches both in London and Paris, except the big wine investors. He didn't want to be in the embarrassing position of them asking to see their wine in storage as he still didn't have the money to buy back all the outstanding wine options. Harriet questioned whether the ladies from the escort agency should come. Henry thought that those who had attended three times or more should, provided it was made clear that it was a party, and they would not be paid for coming nor for any 'afters'. Harriet did not approve of the decision and she made plain her views.

As far as Henry was concerned, Found Vaults was as much Sophie's project as his. Although, it was he who had conceived the idea and had the drive to make it happen, it was she who he'd started doing it for. Above all else, it was her efforts which had enabled him to achieve his ambition. It was therefore important to him that, in Sophie's absence, her parents came to the opening. As the thought of a plane journey was too much for Walter and Inga Lemberger, who were beginning to feel their age, Henry arranged for John to drive them all the way from Bamberg, with stopovers in Cologne and Calais and then across the Channel to Dover. It was an un-rushed two-day journey which they both enjoyed.

Over 350 invitations went out and given that Found Vaults were outside Folkestone, and a long way from anywhere, Henry was absolutely staggered when well over 250 people accepted. He had expected far less than half that number. Suddenly, the catering had to change on a massive scale. All the wine on the top floor of the warehouse was moved down one flight. Just inside the entrance an enormous marquee was erected complete with a kitchen making it fit for any wedding reception.

After the buffet lunch, everyone was turfed outside and into the afternoon sunshine for the formal opening ceremony. Once the tape had been cut, Fergus McDonald, the Chief Executive of the contractors, formally handed Henry the keys, then everyone came back inside for champagne and Henry's speech.

Henry had only spoken in public three times before, and that was at his three wedding ceremonies when he repeated the same speech. To say he was nervous at addressing so many people was an understatement. Thanks to a script prepared by a well briefed comedy writer, Henry gave a very clever and witty speech which allowed him to say thank you whilst incorporating the many deserved digs in a light-hearted and teasing manner.

Throughout the day there was competition between Diana and Harriet as the person who should be seen as Henry's fellow host. It was behaviour which his mother noticed and strongly disapproved of, but besides this there were some lovely moments. Ainsworth introduced his boyfriend for the first time. Robert and Pascale held each other's hands as they moved through her adoring fan base, and the affection between John Chabani and Imra Blanche became obvious for all to see.

The only low light of the day was his conversation with the three bankers who he had fought all the way along to fund the project and get it to completion. They no doubt thought that they had been helping, but in Henry's view they had not an ounce of commercial acumen between them. Henry shook hands with each of them, thanked them for their efforts and apologised for being 'a bloody difficult customer.' It was when one of them referred to their lending risk being reduced on completion of the building, and they all laughingly agreed, that Henry realised the enormity of the cultural gap between them.

These bankers saw the project only in terms of their balance sheets and cash flow. He despaired. Could they not see it was far more than that? A scar on the Kent countryside had gone. He'd replaced it with a working warehouse which blended unobtrusively into the landscape; a warehouse which had been deliberately over engineered to give it a lifespan of several hundred years.

As he moved away from the bankers to speak to his team of happy wine growers from Château de Gressier and Château Rabôut he realised the difference. The wine growers didn't focus on today or tomorrow, or even the day after that. Their whole philosophy was about doing their very best to enhance, improve and preserve whatever was there. To make sure, as best they could, that their vineyard would still be there in a thousand years. Nothing was allowed on the soil or on the vines if it posed any risk to the *terrior*. I'm not the owner of the vineyards, thought Henry, just the custodian with the responsibility to look after them until that obligation is passed to the next generation.

The party continued well past its official ending time as those die-hard party goers congregated with the last few bottles of beer and wine in the summer evening sunshine on the grass banks all around the entrance to the Vaults. The fact that people didn't want it to end showed that the party had been a great success.

As Henry climbed into his battered old estate car to catch the last ferry to Calais, there was not a pair of eyes who watched him wave them goodbye who didn't see a lonely and lost man. Each wondered about his future.

Chapter 103

London August 1976

IT WAS A scorching hot day when Henry returned to Found House from his solitary pub lunch. His children were growing up and developing lives of their own such that, as on this Sunday, they had events which no longer involved their father. He was finding it strange and a little hurtful that, having focused much of his attention on their well-being, he was slowly but surely becoming a supernumerary in their lives. The glue which Sophie had so strongly provided to their family was gradually dissolving in her absence.

The humidity was so bad that, as soon as he was inside Henry went upstairs to his apartment, showered and slipped naked under a sheet with plans for an afternoon sleep. He was sleeping in the guest bedroom for, ever since Sophie had gone into the sanatorium, he couldn't bear sleeping in the room they had shared. Somehow it was their room, and without Sophie, it could never be the same.

As Henry lay in a state of semi-consciousness, he was thinking about Harriet. He enjoyed remembering their love making, but it was the rest of the relationship which he found complicated. He respected her work and her opinions and most of the time their relationship was of equals. At other times it became one of master and servant, where Harriet would test the obvious boundaries. In his eyes there was, and had to be, a clear distinction between the way they behaved upstairs and downstairs. He wondered why this had not been a problem with Sophie, and then he realised that her involvement in the business was only ever upstairs, and in the decisions of the board room, whereas Harriet was involved in the day-to-day minutiae of the business. There was also one other big difference. Sophie was always happy. He remembered she had a lightness of disposition which made her easy to like, whereas Harriet took the burden of the world on her shoulders.

Did he love her? Henry wondered. He knew he didn't love Harriet in the way he loved Sophie. There was something about Sophie's joie de vivre which added to his life in a way that Harriet could not. And yet he had to admit that he loved her too. He loved the way they made love; he loved the way that she looked after him, he loved the way she looked.

It was then, as he was recalling all the ways that he loved her, he realised the issue. Having been brought up as mixed race in South Africa she had been inculcated into considering herself a lesser person, always subservient to whites. It had been culturally driven into her psyche to be subordinate. Every now and again she would vigorously rebel against inequality or, being second, and would fight to be first. Further, the way Harriet spoke of growing up on New Found Estate, the jobs she had and the strictness of her father, he realised how desperate she was for her father's approval. In her father's absence she sought the approval of men generally, often going to extremes to get their attention and approval.

As Henry's thoughts returned to the sheer physicality of Harriet's love making, a movement in the shadows caused him to open his eyes, for standing next to his bed was Harriet. She was wearing a short summer shift dress with a light blue floral pattern. It had a low T-cut top with quite wide shoulder straps. She said nothing, just smiled as his eyes fell into focus.

"What are you doing here?" he asked, with a big smile.

"I saw your car parked outside," she replied.

Harriet reached behind her neck, unclipped and slipped down the zip to her dress which she allowed to fall to the floor. She was wearing nothing else other than white cotton panties. It was the most natural thing in the world for her to climb between the sheets and next to him. At her touch she was surprised, but pleased, to find that Henry was completely naked. Henry turned on his side, took her in his arms and they kissed as only lovers know how to kiss.

When she climbed into his bed the thought of getting pregnant was far from Harriet's mind, but within a few minutes of his touch she knew she wanted Henry's baby and she wanted it now.

There was something quite magical about that afternoon's love making. On every other occasion they had made love it was squeezed into their tight schedule or just before exhaustion came calling. But this Sunday afternoon, theirs was pure, unrushed, unpressured, exhausting, exciting, and enriching pleasure. The humidity of the day caused their bodies to slide so closely that they each felt that they had dissolved into the other. It was as though their two hearts had become one. He was in no doubt whatsoever. Henry didn't just love Harriet; he was in love with her. A love which he knew would last until the end of his days.

It was close to 7 o'clock in the evening when Harriet and Henry rose from their bed, showered together and, under the stream of tepid water, made love for the last time. It was as they were drying that Henry heard the phone ring.

It was Satutu. "Do you know where Sunetta is?" she asked, out of breath.

"Yes, she is here,"

"Working on a Sunday evening?" asked Satutu, surprised.

"Yes," lied Henry. "We've just won a big account and are way behind on the paperwork," he added, in the hope that this would make his lie sound more plausible.

"Can I speak to her please?" asked Satutu, not really believing him.

Henry handed Harriet the phone, who placed the receiver against her ear and allowed the towel, held by the corner in just one hand between her breasts, to hang to the ground between her legs. Henry wanted to freeze that moment for ever. With her hair scrunched high onto the top of her head, she looked the perfect model for the perfect statue to be cast in bronze and preserved for ever.

As she listened, the smile and rosy glow of contentment was wiped from Harriet's face. There was no conversation.

"I'll catch the first plane home tomorrow," she said. I think there is one first thing in the morning. I will be with you tomorrow evening. Please give Pa my love." With those few words Harriet put down the phone. It was the most abrupt ending of a family telephone call that Henry had ever seen.

Satutu and Sunetta had just applied the defence mechanism of the Xhosa tribe of Satutu's heritage. In a life and death crisis it is the custom of those from the Xhosa tribe to say the fewest of words with little emotion expressed until the outcome of the crisis is known.

"Pa's had a heart attack on Friday and today they've discovered he's got advanced pancreatic cancer," Harriet explained to Henry matter-of-factly. "The hospital says he's only got weeks to live. I must go home. Then she added, "now." There was an imperative in the way Harriet spoke.

"Of course," said Henry. "I am so sorry,"

"First, I need to have a cup of tea and make a list of the things I have to do," said Harriet. "It's what we always do in our family when there's a crisis." Her voice and demeanour were without emotion.

"So do we ..." said Henry, perplexed. Until then he would have sworn that this was only his families saying.

As the plane droned on through the sky, towards Cape Town, New Found Estate and her home, Harriet held her tummy and wondered whether she was pregnant; how she wished it so. Her only concern was whether the long flight might stop her from conceiving.

She thought about Henry in the barn, and then all the other men who had taken her, or who she had taken to her bed. Lucky, John Harrison and Rick Bussell had all used her and let her down. As she thought about Lucky she remembered his tortuous burns; nothing else. Long ago, she had blanked out any emotion of what he had done to her. She thought about John Harrison's aborted baby and her eyes welled up with tears of regret. Her daughter, she always thought of her baby as her daughter, would now be three years old. She thought about Rick Bussell and the risks they had taken and the relief they both too often felt when they learnt there was no new life on the way. It was a lucky escape she thought, for Rick would have made a terrible father.

Harriet compared Henry to each of these past men in her life. She was sure Henry was the right choice. Harriet worried about what her mother and father would think about her being pregnant and not being married, but she consoled herself with the thought that, once they knew who the father was and his situation, she was certain they wouldn't just understand, but be pleased for her.

Harriet was determined. She wanted her pregnancy to be confirmed as quickly as possible so she could tell her father before he died.

Chapter 104

London September 1976

HENRY AND SIR Richard Toucher, obviously known as Dick, met for lunch in the American Bar of the Savoy hotel. Henry was surprised to find Toucher, Chairman of Clydesdale International, already deep in conversation with Sir Patrick Tracts. As soon as Henry made himself known, Tracts and Toucher sharply ended their conversation, with Tracts leaving almost immediately after he had shaken Henry's hand and wished him well.

"You know Tictac?" asked Toucher using Tracks' nickname.

"Only slightly, we spoke once about his bank floating my company," answered Henry, casually.

Toucher just nodded and made no further comment.

Toucher was taller and broader than Henry had remembered. He always used his physical presence to take charge of any meeting he was in. He expected to get his own way and demanded others to get it for him.

Toucher's reputation was made in marketing. It was a well-known adage in the private equity community that you could fix money, fix management and fix technology but you couldn't fix the market. Being a marketing man Toucher couldn't have disagreed more. He pointed to the cigarette industry which had all the negatives in the world to face and yet, by careful packaging and marketing the product was made so attractive that people still wanted to buy them. Likewise, he would point to Perrier and the bottled water industry which should've had no place in a country with clean delivered tap water. Yet, as a result of its catching green bottle, it was now a multi-million dollar business.

Toucher and Henry walked through the dining room to a table for two overlooking the River Thames which had been reserved for them.

Dinner drinks were discussed, and Toucher was amused to discover that Henry was teetotal. Henry showed off by pointing to Château De Gressier wine in the Savoy's wine list. "It's been in there every year, apart from the war years, since 1920," boasted Henry.

"So I hear you want to come and work for me," said Toucher opening the conversation briskly.

"Who told you that?"

"Walter Whistler."

"Ah, your headhunter, I'm sorry they've told you wrong," said Henry. "They told me that you wanted me to join your board."

"Same thing," said Toucher cockily.

"I don't think so," said Henry perplexed. "We start this conversation with a different perception of our bargaining positions."

"Even so," said Toucher hurrying to get on, "I am told you were the person who organised the wine trade's response against the supermarkets cash flow squeeze of a couple of years ago."

"I had no alternative. The truth is that I either bluffed it out or was bankrupted, and thankfully the bluff worked."

"We reckon it saved us just under half a million pounds to date in bottom-line profits," said Toucher. "Someone who can do that should be working with us."

"What do you expect me to do?" asked Henry. This time he listened carefully taking notes as Toucher spoke. It seemed a very odd job he was being offered, made more disturbing by the large amount of money he was being offered to attend just a few meetings a year. Henry knew first-hand the complexities of running his small-business, Clydesdale International was huge. He knew it couldn't be managed on a part-time basis as Toucher was proposing.

"Wouldn't we have a conflict of interest?" asked Henry, "I certainly wouldn't want you sitting on my board learning my trade secrets."

The conversation stopped as both men ordered quickly and settled on a jug of tap water to drink.

"I was told that that might be a barrier, so my people came up with a possible solution," continued Toucher. He produced from his inside pocket a sheet of A4 paper neatly folded into three. It was exactly what Tracks had done at the City of London Club.

"I am told your business comprises, and he read from a list: "a vineyard at Château de Gressier, a vineyard at Château Rabôut, the Retail Shop in Paris trading as Maison Rabôut, Found Vintners trading from Found House in London, and a huge ventilated warehouse in Folkestone. Is that right?"

"We have a third vineyard called Château Louis," added Henry. It sells its wine to the local winery consortium.

"We will buy everything from you apart from the vineyards," said Toucher abruptly. "What are they worth?

Henry was taken aback by the bluntness of it all. "I don't know," he said. It's not a question I've been asked before. In any case, we've invested heavily in the past so our profits will be much higher in the future. It would all go too cheaply if we were to sell today," added Henry, remembering his conversation with Ainsworth when they discussed Tracts' suggestion that they floated on the stock market.

"We'd really like Found Vintners and the Kent warehouse," said Toucher. "Those are the real jewels in the crown."

"If you have those then you should take the Paris business too, because those three are all inter-connected," added Henry, being helpful whilst not seeking to sell anything.

"Of course, the Found Vaults still has to get classified as a bonded warehouse and I understand there's a group opposing your application," said Toucher.

How did he know that wondered Henry, noting the unveiled threat.

"Six months ago we thought that getting bonded status was essential but it's beginning to fill up nicely now we've started marketing it. Some of the major wine investors have decided its better to pay duty and have their wine properly stored with us rather than have their fine wines cooked in a shed in the summer and frozen in winter. We even have rubber on our racking to reduce the effects of any vibration. There are no better conditions anywhere," added Henry, proudly.

"What about the concrete dust? Isn't that causing problems?"

How does he know about that thought Henry?

"Not now, we've sealed the whole place, floors, wall and ceiling with concrete sealant. We've also laid a rubber floor on the main forklift runways," said Henry. "It was expensive to do but well worth it. We then installed some air scrubbers with good filters and the problem was solved."

Toucher was impressed.

"It was no more than the usual teething problems when dealing with a project like that," added Henry. "I think we've got real expertise in this now. I am looking for a site around Lille to see if I can do it again. I'll do it much cheaper next time."

"I gather your retail business in Paris is growing nicely since the refurbishment," said Toucher changing the subject, "particularly with the investor market from Saudi Arabia, North Africa, Germany and Switzerland."

Where is he getting his information from wondered Henry, beginning to get worried?

"Now Robert's free from his father he's turned out to have a real flair with the customers," explained Henry.

"No doubt helped a lot by Pascale Verderi," added Toucher. "There's not a wine investor out there who wouldn't have had a crush on his girlfriend when they were growing up."

Henry could only agree as he had been one of those with such a crush.

"London continues to grow," said Toucher. "I gather this year alone you've become European agent to another fourteen vineyards around the world."

This was too accurate information. Henry now knew someone had been telling tales.

"Your seven-year contracts, guaranteed minimum take-offs and 30% paid up front on signing helps you win the contract in the first place, but it must bash the hell out of your cash flow."

"It does," said Henry. "I never have any money; everything goes into growing the business. It is why you're paying the bill for this lunch," he teased. "The thing is, we are buying so effectively that the pay back on my 30% upfront payment is between 20 and 24 months so in the long run it's worth it. At the end of the contract term, if their wine has proved popular in terms of the UK market, then the price will increase and the terms of trade will change, but I think we will stay as their agent." Henry worried about what he had just said, wondering why he'd been justifying his business decisions to this man.

Toucher heard Henry's reply, but he was also studying his notes. "What happened with Château Rabôut and the boy?" he asked.

"You tell me," said Henry sharply. You seem to know an awful lot already.

"I'm told the acquisition was fixed by your grandmother when she knew the line of succession was about to be locked up in jail. By the way, scary about the fire, must've been very frightening."

Henry nodded.

"Was the attack really political?" Toucher asked. "One hell of a bad luck co-incidence if it was."

Henry looked blankly and ignored the question. He was delighted that Toucher didn't know the true background, and therefore not everything about his business.

"I gather your grandmother and Gaston Rabôut worked in the French resistance together."

Henry nodded. He had heard the rumours too. "They certainly knew each other very well, but the rumours, I don't know how true they are," he added.

The meeting paused as the two men ate and looked out of the window watching the boats go up and down the Thames.

"I won't be selling the vineyards nor the buildings; not Found House nor Maison Gelina." There was certainty in Henry's voice. "I am only the custodian of the vineyards, just for my life time. It will be the same for my sons. The two buildings, well those are their inheritance. I am happy for you to take a commercial lease on them, but they are not for sale. I am happy to think about the rest but like everything, it depends on the price.

"I don't do price," said Toucher. "I have a bunch of calculators who study numbers and tell me what I should pay. I then add some, because they don't understand the difference between value and worth. I promise you, we won't have a problem with money," said Toucher confidently.

Both men returned to the food on their plate.

"You'll lease me Found House and La Maisson Gelina?" asked Toucher abruptly, seeking to confirm what Henry had said.

"Yes, said Henry, equally as abruptly then he added, "but not for ever, say ten to fifteen years."

"How would we take this forward," asked Toucher.

"You'll need to have a conversation with Vincent Ainsworth," said Henry. "He'll give you the information you need to know."

"Is he your gay crooked accountant?"

"He's gay, if that's what you're asking," replied Henry, but the look on Toucher's face said he knew more about Ainsworth's background than he did.

"Because we're a public company will have to use a merchant bank to advise us. Since you know Tictac, I'll get him to speak to you."

"No, get him to speak to Vincent. I still have a business to run," said Henry.

There was a discussion about dessert or coffee but both men knew the meeting was over, so they shook hands and said their goodbyes. It was only a small victory, but Henry was pleased that it wasn't him paying the bill as it usually was.

"We have a security leak," said Henry angrily to John as soon as he was in the back seat of his car. "That man had information which can only have come from us."

"You sure Boss?" asked John.

"Yes, one hundred percent."

"Check the CCTV ... and check the phone logs for calls to either Clydesdale International and to Tract's Bank and anything which looks strange. There was a very odd meeting between Tract and Toucher before I arrived. It was as though Tract was briefing Toucher about us." Henry paused, "I've a horrible feeling I'm being set up."

Chapter 105

London September 1976

EARLY NEXT MORNING Henry told Ainsworth of his conversation with Toucher but said nothing about his suspicion of a security leak; the fewer who knew the better.

"Are we out of our wine option problem?" Henry asked.

"It's not a problem," said Ainsworth firmly, then added: "Not quite another month or so and it will be gone. Certainly, by the time you get to do a deal, if that's what you want to do, it will be over."

"Thank God, said Henry. I don't think I could think about selling if they were still outstanding.

The average yearly yield we've had to pay to date is 7.35% per annum which is damn good, but I think I might have to increase the investor yield to 8.5% may be 9.0% if you want to buy the whole thing out, but then again it might be cheaper to buy physicals in the market," explained Ainsworth.

"Please, Vincent, buy physicals, buy back the contracts, almost at whatever it costs. Let's get rid of the problem once and for all. Where are we on the Rabôut counterfeit wine problem?" asked Henry, changing the conversation.

"I don't think we've had anything back for months and everything we've tested has proven genuine. I think we are out of that one," confirmed Ainsworth.

"And the cost?" asked Henry.

"About FFr 2.9 million; that's FFr 350,000 less than the budget but its still a lot more than went into the recovery pool of FFr 2.5 million.

"So I owe Gaston and Robert Rabôut nothing more?" checked Henry.

"No, nothing," confirmed Ainsworth. "You know, you saved a small fortune thanks to the re-labelling exercise and putting the counterfeit wine back on the market. Without that I don't know what we would have done."

"So it turned out to be a good deal?" asked Henry.

"Yes, a very good deal," confirmed Ainsworth. "In my view Château Rabôut is now probably worth well over FFr 3.5 million, so you've got Maison Gelina for free."

"Not free," said Henry. "Look at what we had to invest in both businesses to get them profitable. It wasn't easy!"

The two men chattered aimlessly for a few more minutes.

"The thing is," said Henry. "By selling I can provide financial security for Sophie and the boys. You know, without her, this business has no fun for me anymore. She was such an important part of it."

"Henry," said Ainsworth sternly, "if we're talking about financial security for your family, we need to talk about financial security for mine. It's something which has been on the agenda now for four years and we've never done anything about it because ..."

"We'll need to do something for all the staff as well," said Henry as he remembered Toucher's description of Ainsworth. "Do you know why Toucher would refer to you as a crook? It's what he called you, a crooked accountant."

The colour drained from Ainsworth's face.

You don't know?" said Ainsworth.

"Know what?"

"Nobody's said to you?"

"Said what?" asked Henry, getting cross that his question was not being answered and suddenly wondering whether it was Ainsworth who had been providing Toucher with his information.

"You know I worked for Hermit Veritage before?" said Ainsworth.

"No," said Henry. He may have done, but if he did, he had forgotten.

"Sophie quizzed me about it for a long time, just after I joined, when I was in my probationary period."

"Did she, I don't know," said Henry speaking quickly. He was anxious to know what it was that everyone else knew but not him.

"All the directors there spent large amounts of company money having their houses done up, big extensions, swimming pools, things like that. Company cheques went out to the builders, but we never got invoices from them or anything. I first booked the payments in the accounts as loans to the directors, but it caused one hell of a row. One day the finance director told me to charge everything to repairs and maintenance in the company's books," so I did. Because I needed to have something to give the auditors to audit, I typed up invoices as though they were from the contractors we had paid. Then, as every cheque went out, so I typed up the invoices which I then put through the company's books."

"How were you benefiting?" asked Henry. "I don't understand."

"I wasn't. I didn't," said Ainsworth.

"One day the company lost a huge contract it had had for years. It was one hell of a surprise. The bank freaked out and appointed a receiver to sell the good bits of the business to get their money back. It was the receivers who discovered what the directors had been doing and reported the matter to the police. I was charged with conspiring to defraud, aiding and abetting fraud, false accounting, you name it. It was a bloody nightmare" said Ainsworth shaking his head.

Henry was shocked to hear Ainsworth swear for he rarely, if ever, did so, but with the swear word came the sight of Vincent being visibly distressed.

"In the end I did a deal. My solicitors got the police to drop the charges against me provided I became a prosecution witness, which I did. In fact, I became the main one. There were so many things they did wrong. I couldn't believe the extent of the Mickey Mouse accounting the auditors allowed this company to get up to so as to boost its profits. The share price would rise on each profit announcement; the directors would then sell some of their shares at the higher price, always getting more shares through a grant of options. For the directors it was a merry-go-round of fortune."

"So how come Toucher knows all of this?"

"At the trial the directors' lawyers argued that my evidence was unreliable because I'd been charged. This is how it all became public."

"So you did nothing wrong?" said Henry.

"No," said Ainsworth. "It would be wrong to plead the Nuremberg Defence."

"Nuremberg defence?" asked Henry.

"I was ordered to do it by my boss, so I can't be guilty," explained Ainsworth. "It was the main defence of the Nazis at the Nuremberg trials. No. I did something wrong. I just didn't benefit from it. It didn't occur to me that I was committing a crime. I was just trying to neaten the paperwork, that's all."

It was those words, 'neaten the paperwork' which said it all, as far as Henry was concerned. He could see that was exactly what Ainsworth had been doing.

"What happened to the directors?"

"They went to jail for between five and eight years. It was a pretty horrid time for everyone."

"So how did you come to us? I can't remember" asked Henry.

"I qualified in the same firm as Martin Sheds. If you remember it was he who knew my story and kindly recommended me," explained Ainsworth. Martin Sheds was the partner in the accountancy firm which did Found Vintners annual audit and tax returns. "I came on a three-month trial and have been here four years."

"Christ, it seems longer than that!" exclaimed Henry. "It seems like it was just yesterday and a lifetime all at the same time."

Ainsworth nodded. "It's why you can be sure there's nothing dodgy about the wine contracts you've been selling. I couldn't risk it. I couldn't afford to be caught up in something like that again," said Ainsworth, then adding, "everything, every penny is squeaky clean. I know it."

"If Clydesdale were to buy us then I'd be one of the first people they'd sack, not only because of what happened, but they'd expect to save money by consolidating the accounts department," and on those words Henry and Ainsworth started to negotiate.

Henry offered Ainsworth 5% of the businesses that Toucher wanted to buy. Ainsworth wanted 10%. They settled on the latter figure but only after all the money that Henry and Sophie's Trusts had loaned and invested in the business had been taken into account.

It meant that the 10% was calculated on the real profits made from selling the business, if it were ever sold.

Based upon Ainsworth's estimate of what the business was worth, Henry could quickly see that with 10% of the gain, as they had agreed, Ainsworth was never going to have to work again.

"You don't have a contract of employment, do you?" said Henry.

"No, no one does."

"Then draw one up. Make sure it says that if anyone other than me sacks you for any reason other than gross misconduct then you will get five years severance pay."

"You can't put a poison pill into your own deal," cautioned Ainsworth.

"I can and I will. I can't stop Toucher sacking you, but I can make it really, really expensive!"

"Do you think they'd count my boyfriend as gross misconduct?" asked Ainsworth coyly.

"For Christ sake Vincent, homosexuality was decriminalised ten years ago. It doesn't matter anymore, but if you're worried you know what to do. Just write into your contract that being a homosexual does not comprise gross misconduct!" Henry's stridency contrasted strongly against a subject which Ainsworth found immensely embarrassing.

"Will you join Clydesdale's board?" asked Ainsworth, deciding Henry's frustration with his coyness called for a change in subject.

"Yes probably, if invited but this deal needs to be done first ... before I think about that. We'll learn a lot about them as we go through this and that will help me decide. What's the likely timetable?" asked Henry.

"I'd say four to six months," replied Ainsworth.

"Good God what the hell will everyone be doing during that time?" demanded Henry.

"Due diligence, Henry, due diligence," said Ainsworth with such exasperation that Henry knew he was wearing his patience.

"You'll have to keep me out of the sales process until the deals virtually done, otherwise I'll go out and start spending the money."

Ainsworth nodded.

"Seriously Vincent," said Henry. "If you think this is a good deal then you need to make it happen. Remember, these businesses are my babies, and I can't be involved in committing infanticide!"

Chapter 106

Cape Town October 1976

DAVID DAUNIER'S FUNERAL was a well-attended affair with everyone speaking kindly of him. Satutu, Big Joe and Sunetta held each other tightly in support, wondering how they were going to live their lives without him. He had been the sun around which each of their planets had circulated.

David's Will was read in the dining room of New Found House after all the guests who had attended his funeral had gone home. As was expected New Found Estate was placed into a trust, which was to benefit Satutu in her life time, and afterwards it was to come out of trust and be owned by Big Joe and Sunetta equally. There were instructions that the Estate was never to be broken up; only ever sold as one unit. There were modest monetary gifts of equal size to each of his children and small monetary gifts to the servants and farm hands. Typical of David's mathematical background, the size of each gift was based upon a formulae involving length of service and the amount of weekly pay.

There was no surprise over David's choice of two of his Executors and Trustees, both of whom were highly respected lawyers; one from a black law firm, the other a Mr Creedon who was now the senior partner of Foure Chetty and Steyn. It was the choice of the third trustee which came as the real shock. No one had ever heard of him except Sunetta, as Harriet was known locally. His third trustee was to be Henry Stoddart Bellanger of Found House, Mayfair, London.

"Who's he?" demanded Satutu immediately his name was announced, upset that someone she didn't know was being thrust into her family's affairs.

"You know him Mama," replied Sunetta. "I worked for him in London before coming home to be with Pa. He's the Estate's wine distributor in London. You know him as Henry Guégan."

"Did you know about this?" demanded Satutu.

"No, how could I?"

"Excuse me, but if I may continue," interrupted Creedon. "I have a letter here which might help us. My instructions are that immediately after Mr. Daunier's funeral, not before, I am to open and read it and then give it to Mrs Daunier. There is another letter which is sealed. I am to give that to a Mr Bellanger."

There was a general murmur of agreement, which the lawyer ignored as, irrespective of what they said, he was going to do as instructed. The room fell silent as the envelope was opened. There was a nervous chuckle as inside was another envelope. This was opened too, and a letter extracted. There was a very heavy air of anticipation as Creedon read it silently. Not a muscle moved on his face to give any clue as to what was involved. This added to the tension in the room. He passed it to his fellow executor who read it too. He said nothing, but simply nodded as he handed the letter back. He too maintained a straight poker face.

"Shall I read it?" asked Creedon addressing his remarks to Satutu. "I think it best that everyone hears it."

Satutu nodded and Creedon started to read.

"My Darling Satutu

I want you to know how much I love you. I want to thank you for three wonderful children and for making all our lives so happy. I do not think you know what a truly wonderful and magical person you are.

You gave Big Joe, Sunetta, and Little Joe that most precious thing, the gift of life. You nurtured Big Joe and Sunetta into adulthood in the most loving of manners for which they, and I, are eternally grateful.

The grace and dignity with which you dealt with the loss of Little Joe provided an example to all the people of South Africa at its darkest hour. You are admired far more than you can possibly know.

For them, and for me, I say a sincere thank you. Such a small word which, hopefully you know means so much more.

Since I came to South Africa I have been living in disguise, and some might say under false pretences, for my real name is not David Daunier, but Penrose Victor David Dovingdon."

There was a gasp around the room which caused a momentary pause.

"...and, as you rightly guessed, I was born in England. My date of birth is accurate. I served as a Major in a Balloon Company in France during the First World War. There, I was charged with, and found guilty of many things, including murder.

There was a further gasp and this time a pause as the reader allowed the news to set in.

"In June 1918, just months before the war was to end, I was sentenced to death at a Court Marshall. I was not guilty. The sentence was not carried out because, after the war and with the help of people who believed in me, I escaped and became a French citizen and took a new name.

You may not recognise the name Henry Bellanger. He is our agent and distributor in England. More importantly, he is my sister's grandson and my father's great grandson. Found House, where he lives in London, was once my home. I discovered this only on the day he arrived, unannounced and by accident, seeking to work with us. He does not know of the connection, nor of my request that he be one of my Executors.

Henry will one day inherit Château de Gressier in Bordeaux from my sister Juliette Guégan (née Dovingdon).

He's already inherited it," interjected Sunetta. "She died years ago. He changed his name from Bellanger to Guégan at the same time."

Creedon coughed to express his disapproval at being interrupted. He continued:

It is from her vineyard that our vines originate. The very essence of New Found Estate comes from de Gressier. It is where I convalesced after I was blown up and badly injured during the war. While there, the spirit of de Gressier got trapped in my soul. I brought that spirit here. It is the inspiration of everything around you. The soul of de Gressier is now here, to remain forever in the lands of New Found Estate.

The papers which support my defence are stored with my sister, at Château de Gressier, in case you have any need of them. For me, and the British Government, the matter of my appeal against my sentence is now closed. No doubt they would have liked it much sooner. I am just happier that my death is at a time of God's choosing and not theirs.

If you think about it carefully, I have never lied to you. Every man can change his name. I might not have answered your questions as fully as I should, but then everyone is entitled to their secrets; aren't they!

I simply ask that you judge me, not on my deep past, but on the way I have lived since we met. I hope I have not been too disagreeable, and your judgement is kind, for it will be far easier to meet my maker knowing that you do not feel ill of me.

I send you all the love I have in the world, from the stars and beyond.

For I do truly love you.

David."

The Room was silent. Each member of the family was in tears. Satutu was crushed by his news, if only he had shared his burden, she might have been able to help more, but then she did not want her secrets told too.

Big Joe's thoughts were practical. How do they lodge an appeal to get their father's guilty verdict reversed? He wondered.

For Sunetta the issues were far more complex, for she certainly understood him keeping his secret, for she had secrets too, but the only thing she could hear was her brain shouting: "I'm carrying my cousin's baby. For Christ sake, will it be alright? Will it be alright? she wondered repeatedly. She knew of the possible mental health problems of children born to cousins and her pulse raced uncontrollably as she absorbed the news.

Before Creedon had stood up to read her father's Will, Sunetta's thoughts had been entirely on another matter. After the initial shock had waned it was on this other matter that Sunetta decided she had to concentrate, as there would not be a better moment.

Sunetta went upstairs to her bedroom, sat at her desk and took out from the top draw her old diaries and, as she turned the pages, she studied them carefully. On a plain piece of paper she started to write down a series of dates. She checked through her diaries once again just to make sure that she had included every occasion on her list. She knew there were times missing but for her immediate purposes the dates she had listed would do.

Downstairs, with the list firmly folded in four quarters, she wandered around unobtrusively getting closer to the white lawyer.

"Mr. Creedon, I wonder if I might have a private word with you before you leave?" she asked.

"Yes, of course."

A few minutes later they both moved away from the rest of the family into the hall.

"Is Mr. Harrison still a partner in your firm?" asked Sunetta.

"Mr Peter Harrison or his son John?" asked Creedon.

"John."

"Yes, he's doing very well. He became an equity partner this year, when his father retired."

"Is that good?"

"Yes, it's a promotion. Why do you ask?"

"It's just that…" Sunetta stopped and walked into her father's study. Creedon followed as she expected.

"It's just that we had an affair for many months after I came back from the UK, after university." Sunetta steeled herself for the next bit. It had to be well delivered if she was to have the effect she wanted. "On the last occasion he raped me, and I became pregnant. It was the reason I went back to the UK … to have an abortion." Sunetta knew the rape part was untrue but she decided to embellish her story to add to the gravitas of the charge.

"I am so sorry, said Creedon I'd no ..."

"I'm not expecting you to believe me," interrupted Sunetta. "I am sure Mr. Harrison will deny the charge." Sunetta deliberately used his surname as it sounded far more official like that.

"Here is a list of the dates when Mr Harrison and I met and the names of the hotels. If you check your records you will find that your firm billed my father not only for the time that Mr Harrison was ... er, ... entertaining me, but also for the costs of the room. My father has been charged by your firm for...." Sunetta paused as she tried to find the right words ... "for services for which he had given no explicit instructions."

Creedon took the paper and slowly looked at the list. It was long, eighteen to twenty entries. He looked up into Sunetta's eyes. His poker face was in play.

"And?" he said, prompting a response.

"It is illegal to charge someone for work not done, is it not?" said Sunetta knowing she was playing her trump card.

"Mrs Bussell, it is illegal for you and Mr Harrison to have.., as you claim...., slept together."

"Mr Creedon, I can live with the scandal. I will simply go back to England and continue my life. I would suggest that your firm would not be as fortunate."

"What do you want done about this?" asked Creedon, knowing that, even if what Sunetta was saying was half true, he had a problem. What added to his concern was that, from the tone of the lady in front of him, he knew it was a problem which wasn't going to go away.

"I think Mr Harrison should be sacked, ... shall we say by 12 noon tomorrow; sacked not resigned, so that when you write to clients to say he's left, you will make it clear that it was as a result of a breach of trust."

"A breach of trust?" enquired Creedon.

"Yes," said Sunetta emphatically. "A breach of trust, because that is exactly what it was."

Creedon looked into Sunetta's eyes. The game of poker was over. There was no doubt that the steel of David Daunier, rarely used, had been inherited by his daughter.

"No doubt what you say is true, but to be fair to Mr Harrison I will need to check the facts in the morning."

"Of course."

"And if I do as you say, will we keep New Found Estate as a client?"

Sunetta looked at him bemused. She thought it a very selfish and self-centred question, but then that was just as John Harrison had been. "That is up to my mother and brother, but if this conversation remains confidential. I will raise no objection," she replied.

They stared at each other a little longer, each weighing up the other. Creedon could see that Sunetta was set on revenge and if he didn't act, and quickly, then the situation was going to get much worse.

"I think we should get back," Sunetta said, and with that she turned and was gone. There was no more she wanted to say or convey.

Three days later Satutu received in the post a substantial cheque made payable to the New Found Estate. The covering letter from Creedon said no more than he had been checking his records and, as a result of an unfortunate error, Mr Daunier had been incorrectly charged for time and expenses. This money was being reimbursed with interest and a sincere apology. In a small paragraph at the end of the letter, reference was made to a Mr John Harrison no longer being a partner in the firm. There was no reference to a breach of trust.

Sunetta looked at the letter from Foure Chetty and Steyn, which her mother had left with the cheque on the kitchen table. Her immediate reaction was one of disappointment as she hadn't got everything she wanted. Much later, when she came to consider her alternatives, she realised she hadn't any. Creedon had already worked that out. It was, she realised, why he was the senior partner in one of Cape Town's leading law firms.

Sunetta picked up the cheque. She absent-mindedly studied it, while her thoughts were on how she felt. She wasn't sure. There was a sense of being pleased. What she wanted to happen had happened, but there was also a hollowness in her victory which she didn't like. Perhaps, she concluded, as she put down the cheque, revenge is not that sweet, whether served hot or cold. What her father had said about revenge, after Little Joe had been killed, was true: "When seeking revenge, dig two graves, not just one."

It took Sunetta some time to realise why she was feeling so empty. In her imagination she could see her daughter running around the kitchen. As she did so the same overwhelming yearning to have a baby swept through her body. Her thoughts turned to Henry for she loved him so much that sometimes it truly hurt. She wanted him here with her now, and she wanted his baby safely born.

Chapter 107

London October 1976

HENRY HEARD FROM Harriet almost immediately after David Daunier had died. He offered to fly down to Cape Town and be at her side for the funeral, but she rejected the idea while, at the same time, secretly wishing he would ignore her and come all the same.

Henry thought hard about ignoring her instructions not to go there to support her, but in the end, he decided that their relationship was too complicated, and it would be best if he stayed away. He sent a wreath and two very kind and carefully worded letters of sympathy to Satutu and Harriet, sending the latter all his love.

It was in the evening, the day after David's funeral, that Henry received an express courier package from South Africa. It was from Foure Chetty and Steyn. In it was a letter from Creedon telling Henry he was a joint executor of David's Estate and revealing that David Daunier was, in fact, his great-uncle Penrose Dovington. Henry's reaction was the same as Harriet's, complete shock and bewilderment. How in God's name had he come to be sleeping with his cousin?

Creedon enclosed a copy of David's letter to Satutu which had been read immediately after David's funeral. Henry read it carefully. He knew exactly where the David Daunier's defence papers were stored as, one day, Juliette had made him promise that they would be safely looked after for a further one hundred years.

Creedon also enclosed a private letter from David to Henry. Like the original letter to Satutu, the letter from David to Henry was also double enveloped.

Strictly Private and Confidential

Dear Henry

I am sure you will have heard that I am your great-uncle. Your grandmother Juliette was my sister. I hope the news is not too much of a shock.

I am only able to write this letter as a result of the bravery of your Grandmother Juliette and Grandfather Étienne. I am immensely proud of them, and grateful too.

At the end of the Great War, I was subjected to a show trial and sentenced to death. Before I could be shot, I was badly injured. I was sprung from hospital by Juliette and Étienne and convalesced at de Gressier. It was there that I wrote the defence against the charges laid against me which I was unable to present at my Court Marshal.

Now I am gone, and the British government can do no worse to me, I have a feeling my children may want to seek a posthumous appeal. In the vaults of The Cellars at Château de Gressier you will find all my papers and the case for my defence. I wonder whether you would be so kind as to find those papers and share them with Satutu, Big Joe and Sunetta. I know they would much appreciate any assistance you can give them.

I need to explain why I have asked you to be an Executor. South Africa is in troubled times. Its future is uncertain, laid to waste by the distrust brought about by the colour of a person's skin, made worse by the unjust and unfair treatment by the whites of the blacks for far too many years. It is all madness.

It is in the spirit of bipartisanism and colour agnosticism that I have appointed one black and one white lawyer to look after my affairs. They are the best in Cape Town. You may trust their judgement on matters of law. However, they know nothing of running a vineyard or a winery. This is your expertise. You should not need to involve yourself in the day to day running of New Found Estate for Satutu, Joe and Sunetta will be able to do that. However, they might need your support. I simply ask that you help as best you are able, should they one day need it.

There is one final wish. In the churchyard at Welborough Green is the grave of a young woman called Drew Stubman. Please forgive a foolish old man if, in the strictest of confidence, he tells you that she was his first true love. Her photograph is on my desk. I look at it every day and wonder what might have been. It is there to remind me that the future is uncertain. We would probably have been married if things had been different. Unfortunately, she was killed in the war and, because of my difficulties with the British Government, I have never been able to visit her grave. I have never forgotten her and have always felt guilty at not being able to pay my respects in person.

Would you be so kind as to go to Welborough Green churchyard and make sure her grave is properly tended. It needs to be so. Please place some flowers on her grave from me. I know 1918 is a very long time ago, but those that die young never grow old.

Would you be so kind as to talk to the vicar and see what an appropriate memorial to her might be. Is her grave properly marked? I fear not, in which case I would like it so. Might I buy a bench seat to go in the graveyard for people to sit and be with their loved ones? Or is there a window in need of some stained glass which could commemorate both her and all those who died in both wars? I have made provision in my will for the costs of any of this.

I ask this of you because, seeing in the newspapers the photographs of Sophie and you, and the love you show for her in your eyes, you will know exactly what to do.

With my sincere thanks.

David Daunier
né Penrose Dovingdon

As Henry put down his great uncle's letter, so it was, six thousand miles away, that Sunetta was also putting down a letter. She had been through all the letters her family had received when Little Joe was killed. Amongst them she found the letter she had been looking for. It was from Hank Bellanger just as Henry said he had written. Her eyes focused on the last few words. *'I send you my prayers and love,'* he wrote. In the quiet of her bedroom Sunetta held Henry's letter to her chest and burst into tears, for she realised she was needed here by her mother at New Found Estate. Sunetta knew she would never be able to return to London to live and work with Henry. Once again, her heart felt as though it was being broken in two.

Chapter 108

London October 1976

THE MAN DIDN'T notice John Chabani watch him leave the van, which he had parked outside Found House, and descend the outside steps to the basement door. The man knocked gently and when it opened, he handed over a £10 note to a woman who, in turn, handed over a large purple plastic disposable bag. Neither of them was aware that their actions were being recorded on newly installed CCTV cameras.

The man climbed the stairs, opened the back door of his van and threw in the plastic bag. He returned to the driver's seat where he looked for the key which he thought he had left in the ignition. The man was looking around, searching his pockets when he heard the rear door of his van open. John was taking out the purple plastic bag.

"What the fuck," shouted the man, leaping from his van ready to take on any challenger.

"This is mine," said John calmly, waiving the bag in the air.

"Like the fuck it is," said the man. "I've just paid for it."

"To someone who had no right to sell it," said John. "D'ya wanna debate it with the police 'cause I am ready, just say."

The man leaned forward, and John stepped back keeping the plastic bag out of his reach.

"I just need information, that's all I need," said John, "and you'll get your keys back."

"You've got my fucking keys," said the man ready to take on John, who prepared himself for the attack, just as the man was having second thoughts. While the driver might win, he knew he was going to suffer a lot of damage in the process.

"Wha'dya wanna know? asked the man.

"Who are you working for? Who gets the bag?" asked John.

"It's only fucking paper," said the man.

"Pretty damn important paper if you're prepared to pay £10 a day for it. If you're in doubt, it's all recorded on CCTV."

The man paused as he thought through his options. He realised he had few. He wasn't being paid enough to take this kind of grief.

"The photocopies are of those papers left on the top of the boss's desk; they go straight to Tolts."

"The private investigators?"

"Yes, the rest I have to go through. Mainly its thrown away scrap paper or discarded photocopies, but I have to summarise them in a report," said the man.

"Who gets your report?"

"Tolts."

"Who are Tolts working for? asked John.

"I don't know."

"Who do you think?" asked John, waiving the man's keys over a drain cover.

"My guess is Haverings."

"What, the merchant bank, why?"

"Because they've used Tolts before."

John handed the man his keys.

"And the bag?" asked the man, pointing to the purple plastic sack.

"I think not, don't you," said John. "I think you'd better tell Tolts what's happened."

The man nodded.

"Don't come back, will ya," said John, "otherwise, next time, I'll phone the police."

The man smiled a knowing smile, and John watched as he drove away.

John made his first port of call the photocopier on the ground floor. The counter had increased by 574 since he'd been the last person to leave the night before. It was time to talk to the cleaner.

Henry and Ainsworth sat quietly, feeling badly chastened, as John reported orally on a complete lack of security throughout Found House.

"We have nothing of value," pleaded Henry, "apart from some equipment."

"You clearly do," said John testily. "At least with sufficient value that they're prepared to pay your cleaner a lot of money to get it."

"So Tictac's been spying on us, but why?" asked Henry, who was more perplexed than angry at the invasion of his privacy.

"'Cause he's going to get a huge finder's fee should Clydesdale buy us," explained Ainsworth.

"It's a huge gamble. What if we don't sell," said Henry.

"Look," said Ainsworth, "the City trades on information. Most of it is useless, but every now and again one small nugget makes it all worthwhile. It's a tiny part of the costs of them doing business."

"What about the other places?" asked John.

Henry and Ainsworth looked at each other non-plused. Their meeting was suspended to allow John to call the General Managers at Maison Rabôut and the Vaults. He quickly established that both had suffered huge increases in the use of photocopier paper over the last few months. An hour later and following an examination of the video recordings at the Folkestone warehouse and the Paris shop, it was clear that they were being spied on too.

There was agreement that everyone would be briefed on what had happened and security would be increased. Immediately there would be instituted a clean desk policy, shredders by each desk, the locks would be changed, and the photocopiers would have access codes on them. The security guards at the Vaults and all the cleaners would be changed. John was given an additional job. He would now be in charge of security. It was a job he would relish.

Chapter 109

South Africa October 1976

THE DRIVE FROM the airport through the mountains and fields, particularly in the early morning autumn sunlight, to New Found Estate is always a delight. Henry now wished he had made the journey immediately after he had heard of David's death, but then he didn't know he was going to be appointed an Executor.

Throughout the flight from London, Henry's thoughts had been wide ranging. He tried to watch an in-flight film but there was nothing which took his fancy. He drifted in and out of consciousness with the same repeating thoughts. How to get Sophie well again, his children and their happiness. His decision to explore selling his companies and, if he did so, he wondered whether he would be letting his employees down, and, of course, there was Harriet.

Henry felt a certain frisson as he turned off the road and onto the drive of New Found Estate. As he stopped his car close to the front door of the immaculately presented house, Henry wondered what he was going to say. He had the same feelings of anxiety of finding the right words which everyone has when meeting a grieving widow for the first time.

No sooner had Henry got out of the car than Satutu was at his side. She was in the same uniform she had worn when they first met. Tight white jeans, white shirt, white denim jacket and, of course, her trademark white crocheted bonnet. The afro haircut, which she had adopted after Little Joe had been killed, was gone, but the red shoes she wore in his memory were still on her feet.

Henry and Satutu shook hands. He said some clumsy words of sorrow as he kissed her on both cheeks. She smiled the most cautious of smiles. Henry thought how little she had changed. She was ageless when they first met, she was ageless when they last met, and she was ageless now. Her skin remained perfect, the whites of her eyes were clear and bright and her hair still soft and wild, like the mane on a lion.

Satutu was thinking the opposite about Henry. She was concerned by how much he had aged. His athletic body at the time of their first business meeting had become thicker set and overweight. Although aged 34 he was looking distinctly middle-aged. His hair was thinner and beginning to recede. He had the air of a man with the burden of the world on his shoulders.

No sooner had Satutu and Henry said their hellos, than Sunetta came bounding through the front door and into their greeting. She wanted to leap into Henry's arms but instead, suddenly aware of her mother's presence, she restrained herself, offering just her hand. As Henry kissed her on both cheeks, she felt his warm breath against her ears and her knees weakened just a fraction. Once again, Henry expressed his condolences, this time to Sunetta but, in her excitement of seeing him, she did not hear his words.

Before he had died David and Satutu had built three identical gîtes style bungalows on the land where their stables and paddocks once stood. They were built in the hope that, if they had somewhere of their own to stay, it would encourage Big Joe and Sunetta to visit them more often. The third chalet, each told the other, was for their guests but secretly both David and Satutu knew they were building it for Little Joe, even though he would never see it. When parents identify themselves as having three children then things will always get thought of in threes, even when one of them is no longer around.

"Let me show you to your bungalow, where you're sleeping," volunteered Sunetta.

"Come and join me as soon as you've settled in," said Satutu. "There'll be coffee, and later lunch, around the kitchen table."

"This one's Big Joe's," said Sunetta as they walked past the first gîte. "This one's mine," she continued as they walked past the second, "and this one will be yours."

Henry lugged his suitcase up the steps on to the veranda where he paused and looked around. Wherever he was in the world he found there was something truly magnificent about seeing a vineyard wake up after its winter's sleep.

The gîte was open plan with two large bedrooms at the rear, but it was devoid of character or any personal touch. It could've been any hotel suite anywhere in the world.

"Which bedroom?" asked Sunetta pointing ahead. "Both are identical, the same size."

Henry wandered aimlessly into one. It had a huge sliding patio door at the far end with more magnificent views across the vineyard and up into the mountains beyond. He threw his case aimlessly on to the settee which was in the room and started to open the lid.

"If there's one thing I need before anything else it's a shower," said Henry. "Only then will I feel human again."

Sunetta started to feel uncomfortable. Perhaps it was because they were now meeting for the first time as cousins. Perhaps it's because they were at her parents' house. Whatever it was, the physicality of their relationship, particularly now they were alone, seemed to have changed.

Sunetta withdrew to the sitting room where she wandered around aimlessly, feeling both confused and rejected. She listened as his electric razor ground against his beard. She then heard the water of the shower. It was a noise which was too much to resist. With the same mindless impulse which had driven her throughout her life, Sunetta got up, went into Henry's bedroom, stepped out of her clothes and into the bathroom. The shower cubicle was filled with water and steam. Sunetta opened the door just slightly and squeezed in. There she stood embarrassed by her actions.

"Hello cousin," said Henry, as he turned to take Sunetta into his arms. The shampoo from his hair fell uncomfortably into his eyes. Nevertheless, he instantly held her as tight as tight could be, and with it, her heart sang. She was so in love with this man she didn't want him to let go, ever.

Sunetta's demands on Henry were such that it was nearly lunch time when they entered the kitchen of New Found House for coffee.

He was physically and mentally exhausted. If the truth were to be told he just wanted to sleep; the sleep of the contented and satisfied. Sunetta's feelings were very different. She felt alive, invigorated, as though she had successfully danced the first act of a six-act dance, with the rest of the show to look forward to.

The atmosphere at lunch was light and cordial. Henry was surprised to find the servants sitting around the kitchen table eating with them. He didn't know it was the way David had organised his household from the moment Satutu had first joined him.

Henry apologised to Satutu for having been thrust into her personal affairs. Satutu, for her part, had come to accept it; sometimes thinking that it might be for the best. As he talked, Satutu could not help but notice the similarities between David and Henry. Now knowing, perhaps she was looking for them, but they were there to be seen. There was something about Henry's mannerisms, the softness with which he spoke, the care he took to choose his words but underneath she could see the same determination which made David so strong at times of adversity. Above all, it was David and Henry's form of conversation which Satutu thought was so similar. Unlike most men, David and Henry rarely said, I think, I did, I like when in the company of others. Instead, they would ask: What do you think? What do you want? What do you like? and in a way which showed a genuine interest in the answer.

Satutu noticed, almost immediately, how quickly her daughter had changed now she was in Henry's company. It was clear to those that had seen them work together that Sunetta had become Henry's third arm and second head. She had an intuition as to what he wanted, sometimes long before he knew it himself. They had a symbiosis which, as the two sat close to each other at the table, became as obvious to Satutu as it had been to every one of their work colleagues. Sunetta no longer appeared to worry about herself. She worried only about him, willingly, almost yearningly, wanting to please him. However, it was the way in which Henry sought Sunetta's consent, almost identical to the way that David had sought Satutu's, which set Satutu's mind racing.

As the sun fell from the sky, Big Joe came in from the fields to join them. Although it was chilly, evening supper was served on the veranda where Henry directed most of the conversation around Big Joe's work, which he found enviously fascinating.

As the two men chattered, Henry learnt that Big Joe's materials sciences research programme, at Imperial College, was at the forefront of the digital computing revolution. His work centred on developing better quality materials for use in microprocessors to get them smaller, whilst increasing their capacity and speed, at the same time minimising the amount of heat they produced. Henry was riveted, happy to sit at the feet of an expert and learn.

To the joy of Satutu and Sunetta, Henry asked Big Joe question after question, forcing him to make the complex seem simple, for until that moment they had no idea what he did. The fact that Henry was genuinely impressed with what Big Joe was doing, and the enthusiasm with which he spoke of his work, added to Satutu and Sunetta's pride in their son and brother.

"Within 10 years we will all be carrying mobile phones around in our pockets," Big Joe confidently predicted.

When challenged by Sunetta at the absurdity of his prediction, Big Joe repeated Moore's Law: "Every year since their invention, the number of microprocessors on an integrated circuit board has doubled and the cost has halved. From what we are seeing at Imperial there is no reason why this cannot continue for the foreseeable future," he explained. "But that's not why we're going to have mobile phones. We've just seen the development of the first digital-to-analogue converter and vice versa. I promise you. The impact of that will be huge."

But this conversation hid a secret. Big Joe had received a job offer from Intel in California. He had been about to accept it with enthusiasm not least because, for the first time, he was being offered a mouth-watering salary. But now, after his father's death, he knew he had to think about helping to run the farm, or at least accept that California was too far away. Whereas, if he was needed, London to South Africa was only an overnights journey.

After supper the four of them walked the estate. Unknown to any of them, it had been a tradition copied from de Gressier and Henry's grandparents. The cloudless skies and the brilliance of the moon and the galaxy of stars lit up their journey. They first walked to the tree where David and Little Joe were buried. They tallied there awhile no one saying very much. Then Satutu, linking arms with Sunetta, set off on the same walk she had done with David from the day they returned from their honeymoon. Big Joe and Henry followed behind.

"If you want him, you're going to have to take him," said Satutu, when they were some way in front of the two men.

"What?" asked Sunetta surprised, while knowing exactly what her mother was saying.

"If you want Henry, you're going to have to take him," said Satutu, repeating herself. "It's what I had to do with your father. He wouldn't come to me, so I had to go to him."

"Why won't they ask?" said Sunetta, remembering that, as soon as he had arrived, she had done exactly as her mother had suggested.

"The English are extremely complicated," said Satutu. "They have their own set of self-imposed rules. They're sensitive to black-white, master-servant, man-child, junior-senior, man-woman ... a whole host of relationship things which makes little sense to me, but it makes it complicated for them."

"What made you... ?" asked Sunetta, knowing she didn't have to finish her sentence.

"George Washington, it was he who gave me permission. Immediately I knew a black woman was sharing the bed of the President of the United States, well that gave me the freedom to ..."

"What about us being cousins?" asked Sunetta.

"You're not pure first cousins. His mother is your first cousin. He's your first cousin once removed. In any case, a lot of first cousins marry. The bible says they can," replied Satutu firmly.

"He's married. He has children," said Sunetta.

"I know, she's in hospital and she's not going to come out, is she? I've read the papers."

"Then you'll know he won't marry me," said Sunetta, in a whisper not wanting to be heard by the men behind. He won't divorce her. He's not that kind of man."

"If he was that kind of man, I wouldn't want him for you. As I say child," continued Satutu, "if you want, you take, as no one is going to give you permission."

They both walked on, not looking at their surroundings but at the gravel and dust under their feet.

"If there's a baby one day then I'm sure he'll look after you. He's a good man. In any case, your home is here."

Sunetta stopped walking and looked straight into her mother's eyes to make sure she understood what she was being told. Then, without a word being spoken between them, she knew exactly what her mother was thinking. She wanted a grandchild to secure the succession of New Found Estate. This wasn't George Washington giving permission. This was Satutu.

"He's a good man," repeated Satutu. "Everything will be alright, I am sure of it."

After their walk, Satutu returned by herself to New Found House while Big Joe, Sunetta and Henry walked on to their respective bungalows. No sooner had Big Joe shut the front door to his chalet, than Sunetta had left her bungalow and was naked in Henry's bed

"Contraception?" said Henry, as Sunetta moved on to him.

"Bit late to think about that," she teased. "Smarties," she replied.

"Smarties?" asked Henry confused.

"The pill," she lied.

Henry smiled, not realising that every morning and evening, until he caught his plane home, Sunetta would have him in training for the Sex Olympics. There was no debate. Henry was going to be the father of her child, and he was going to have to perform to make it happen.

Chapter 110

London December 1976

BETWEEN OCTOBER AND December Henry travelled extensively between London, Hertford, Paris, Bordeaux and Bamberg making his life frantic as the autumn through to Christmas was one of the key times for his business. It was a time for the Matterers Lunches when the important wine investors got entertained and made their purchases. The supermarkets wanted the wine they had ordered into their warehouses ready for Christmas and the New Year buying spree, and the vineyards were busy with their wine making.

Even though each of his businesses had their own bosses, more than capable of running them without him, Henry felt he had to make time for each of them, if doing nothing more than encouraging them in the decisions they were taking. All this meant Henry only gave occasional thought and very little time to the sale of his business; a process which Ainsworth was running very efficiently. The only time Henry interfered was when Clydesdale International's accountants decided, for reasons which he found unfathomable, that they should study the books of accounts of de Gressier and Rabôut vineyards. Fearing their request was simply there to satisfy Toucher or Tracts' curiosity, it was something Henry stopped immediately, reaffirming that those businesses were definitively not for sale.

For weeks on end Henry's offices seemed to have been occupied by strangers, as papers arrived by courier from accountants and lawyers, sometimes over two or three inches thick. On the advice of Ainsworth, he didn't read them. "They're only drafts," he was told. "We'll take you through them in a meeting when we are close to the end. So on the corner of his desk sat a pile of untouched papers getting higher and higher, until Ainsworth thought the deal was nearing completion and it was time it had some of Henry's input.

Henry and Ainsworth arrived separately at the offices of Cranster Solicitors to go through the papers to sell Henry's businesses. It was first thing in the morning when they gathered. Henry had just got off the plane from Cape Town. He had been dealing with David's Estate during the day and satisfying Sunetta at night. He was exhausted.

Cranster Solicitors were chosen by Ainsworth because their partner, Stephen Challenge, had outgunned his lawyer in the last transaction he had worked upon. As befitting Cransters, Challenge was young, articulate, engaging and very clever. He was ranked by his peers as one of the top merger and acquisition lawyers in London. Challenge was accompanied by two assistants, one a qualified lawyer and the other still in training, both of whom were equally as bright. They had learnt to live without weekends and on just five hours sleep a night, such were the demands of their job.

Henry was presented with a pile of papers nearly four inches thick. With Challenge acting as the 'master of ceremonies' they ploughed quickly through the money section dealing with how much Henry and Sophie were getting in repayment of their loans, how much Sophie and Henry were getting for the shares in the companies being sold and how much Ainsworth and each of the employees, including Harriet Bussell, Robert Raboût, and John Chabani, were receiving as loyalty bonuses.

Henry had insisted that the same formula be used for working out his employees' bonuses as he had learned that David Daunier had used to calculate the gifts to his employees on his death. It was one which recognised seniority by salary and length of service by time. When Henry saw how much money his colleagues would be getting from the transaction his guilt at selling his business was slightly assuaged. Some would be able to pay off their mortgages, others would be able to buy a new family car and Ainsworth would never have to work again.

Next on the agenda came a long conversation on warranties. "It's the way the purchaser finds everything out about the business their buying," said Challenge. "If you warrant something and it's untrue and the buyer suffers a loss then they will sue you for the losses."

Seems reasonable thought Henry.

"The way we mitigate against you facing a warranty claim is that we write a disclosure letter in which we tell them everything about the business, including all the bad bits," said Challenge. "If they still buy in the knowledge of the things you've disclosed then they can't sue you for those things."

The look on Henry's face told Challenge that he wasn't sure he understood what he was being told, so Challenge gave an example.

"Let us say you unfairly sacked someone," said Challenge.

"But we haven't," interjected Henry defensively.

"But let us say you had. If we've disclosed that you've sacked that person, and it later transpires the company has to pay that employee compensation for their wrongful dismissal then you are not liable. It must be paid by the buyer without any claim against you. If you hadn't disclosed it, then the compensation could be reclaimed from you."

Again, Henry thought all this sensible.

He was then told about indemnities and the buyers absolute right to get their money back if something happened against which he had given an indemnity. By way of an example, Challenge said that: "if after Clydesdale International had bought the company, it was found to have a big tax liability which related to the time Henry owned it, then Henry would have to pay that tax. Henry had no problem with this. Again, he thought it was fair.

For the next two hours all those in the meeting read and discussed each of the clauses. The discussion went on ad nauseum. They turned page after page dealing with laws and regulations which Henry had never heard of, let alone knew whether or not he had complied with them.

"Didn't we have their accountants in our office for weeks on end studying our business?" asked Henry when they were about two thirds of the way through the documents.

"Yes," said Ainsworth, "but we still haven't seen their draft report."

"We've insisted on seeing it," added Challenge, "but they've not yet released it. I've told them you won't sign until we've had time to read it."

"What else have we told them about the business," asked Henry.

"We've put everything about it in what's called a data room. We have copied every single contract, license, agreement, the accounts, bank statements et cetera. These are in about twenty-five, maybe thirty folders. Their lawyers have had access to them and have been going through them for days."

"Is there a maximum amount I'm liable for under the warranties and indemnities," asked Henry.

"Yes, were getting to that. We've managed to limit those liabilities to the total amount of money you are getting," said Challenge, knowing that he had negotiated the industry standard.

"But that includes the money the company's borrowed from Sophie and me, and from my mother, doesn't it?" protested Henry.

"It's because Clydesdale consider those loans to be part of the capital of the business."

"Well I don't," retorted Henry sharply. "I consider them to be like ordinary bank borrowings."

Ainsworth and Challenge decided to say nothing.

"So I could sell my business and at the end of this not have my company and be hugely in debt because the amount I'm liable for is more than the amount I'm getting."

"Because?" asked Ainsworth looking at Henry confused.

"Because, of the money I'm not getting. I'm giving over £5 million away to you and the others. Surely, you should be giving these warranty things too?"

It was a point which Challenge had raised with Ainsworth many times, and he would have mentioned it to Henry, except he was already on it.

"What do they know about the counterfeit wine?" asked Henry, not waiting for an answer.

"Nothing," said Ainsworth. "It doesn't concern them."

"What counterfeit wine?" asked Challenge, very quickly.

Henry told the story, occasionally interrupted by Ainsworth who had the detail at his fingertips.

"The liabilities are not ours," said Ainsworth confidently." It's a problem that has long gone. In fact, the only true liability is with the son, Maurice and he's inside."

"It goes to the heart of the goodwill that they are buying," argued Challenge.

"It doesn't," said Henry. It goes to the goodwill of Château Rabôut which they are not buying.

Ainsworth and Challenge took up arguing the point for some fifteen minutes. Henry kept out of the debate. Instead, as they were talking, he continued to skim read and turn the pages of the documents in front of him. Just as they were coming to the end of their discussion, Henry closed the papers he had been reading and assiduously marking up. He stacked them neatly, one on top of the other.

"Stephen," said Henry quietly. "Thank you for your hard work, and you too Vincent, but I can't sign these. I am sorry but I won't sell on these terms." He pointed to his pile of papers, which he had now wrapped with a large elastic band.

There was a stunned silence in the room. No one knew what to say.

"I can see how much effort has gone into this, but I'm not signing this contract." Henry continued: "Stephen, you need to send me your bill for all your work. It will be paid."

Challenge and Ainsworth looked aghast as Henry stood up. Just as his grandmother had done before, he was leaving irrespective of what others might think.

"What's wrong with the terms?" exclaimed Ainsworth, in frustration, as he followed Henry to the edge of the meeting room door.

"The warranties and indemnities," said Henry calmly.

"But we said we'd give them. It's in the document you signed with Dick Toucher," protested Ainsworth.

"Reasonable, as advised by my lawyers," said Henry, referring to the precise wording in the non-binding heads of terms agreement.

"All these are reasonable," protested Ainsworth, looking to Challenge for support.

"I am sorry they are not! For a start I don't understand half of them," said Henry.

There was an impasse.

"I will warrant I own the shares. I will give an indemnity that we've paid all the taxes we should have paid, but that's it. They can have the disclosure letter. They can have all the information in all the files you've prepared. They can even keep their accountants report without us seeing it." Henry had spoken very calmly, but now his voice rose: "But warranties, indemnities, no, and as for this idea that some of my money goes into an escrow account to protect them, well no to that as well!"

Challenge now set about proving why he was often described in the legal press as 'the London corporate lawyer to watch.' Very calmly he regrouped and noted his client's instructions, making sure he understood not only Henry's objections but the sentiment behind each of them.

"You have to remember that Haverings have been stealing our information for at least three months, probably six months, if not longer. They know everything there is to know about us, believe me."

"What, Haverings Bank?" asked Challenge.

Henry and Ainsworth nodded in unison.

"But they're the corporate finance advisers to Clydesdale International on this transaction," said Challenge, with surprise in his voice."

"Precisely," said Ainsworth, who outlined to Challenge what they knew of the intelligence activities of Tolts. Challenge may have been wise, even street wise, but it was the first time in his career he had come across industrial espionage of this kind. He started to feel distinctly uncomfortable as to his firm's security arrangements. Had Tolts been spying on their papers too, he wondered.

Henry moved past Ainsworth to shake Challenge by the hand. "Please send me your bill. It will be paid," he repeated. "Now, if you will excuse me, I must phone Dick Toucher to tell him the deal is off.

No doubt you'll want to finish off here," he said to Ainsworth, before he walked through the already half opened door.

Henry walked down the stairs and out into the winter chill. London's dirty air seemed better in his lungs than the stifling dry heat of the boardroom he had just left. He stood still on the pavement for just a moment. He felt a huge sense of relief. Since he'd signed the heads of terms with Toucher, he had felt like a traitor, a Judas Iscariot to his employees and his customers. Perhaps he could redeem himself.

Chapter 111

London December 1976

BACK AT HIS office, Henry phoned Toucher. He slowly and carefully explained why he wouldn't be selling his company on the terms set out in the draft contract negotiated between their two lawyers. "I agreed that I would sell on the basis of reasonable warranties. What I was being asked for was unreasonable, not least because I didn't understand half of them," he said.

"You know, don't you, that Haverings Merchant Bank have had private detectives investigating my companies for six months, even to the extent of going through our dustbins," reported Henry. "They know more about my business than I do, and I'm sure you now know everything they know. Otherwise why would you have engaged them."

"What, Tictac?" asked Toucher, confused. It was true that Tracts had been providing 'Insight Reports' on Henry's businesses which had been very useful, but he had no idea where the information had come from.

"What do you want, more money?" asked Toucher instantly thinking that he was being blackmailed, because of Tracts' nefarious activities.

"No," said Henry frustrated. "The money's not the issue. What I don't want to do is warrant my shoe size."

"Shoe size? repeated Toucher confused.

"You know what I mean," said Henry defensively.

"Let me find out what's been going on and I'll call you back," said Toucher anxiously. He was keen to find out what the hell had happened because he had already been telling his mates in the City of London about the deal and, most importantly, his company's share price was rising nicely on the back of it.

"I'm leaving now for the day," said Henry. "I'm going home to collect my children from school. I'll be back in the office on Monday. We can speak then if you like."

"Fucking, fucking lawyers," shouted Toucher as he slammed down the phone. He couldn't believe the conversation he'd just had. How could a man casually walk away from a £40 million cheque just so he could collect his children from school?

At the same time as Henry was on the phone to Toucher telling him the deal was off, Challenge was on the phone to his counterparty, the solicitor acting for Clydesdale International. The man was as round as he was tall. He was notorious for his chain smoking and the absent-minded way he allowed his cigarette ash to fall down his portly waistcoat and around the papers he was working on. As one of the senior partners he no longer did the heavy lifting, getting his current work through a brilliant reputation, and the contacts he had built up over the years. But now he was out of date. It meant that technically and, in speed of thought, Challenge easily outshone him.

Challenge explained what had happened. The two men agreed that Henry was being unreasonable.

"He genuinely can't be complaining on those grounds," said Toucher's lawyer. These warranties have been used thousands of times."

"Tens of thousands of times," replied Challenge.

"It must be because he's changed his mind," said Toucher's lawyer. "This is just an excuse."

"We don't think so," said Challenge. "I'm here with Vincent Ainsworth. We were in the meeting with Henry together. He'll confirm it all started very positively, as though he was ready to sell and then, as he went through the detail, he just turned against it."

"Do you think the deal can be brought back into play?" asked Toucher's lawyer.

"Yes, if you don't want any warranties other than Henry owns the shares, but you do get all the tax indemnities," said Challenge. "Oh, and by the way, he doesn't want to see your accountants' report, if that helps."

I'm not sure my client will be able to agree to that," said Toucher's lawyer. "If they do then we'll have to write a professional caution letter which the board won't like. That, in itself, is likely to kill the deal."

Challenge could only agree.

"It was a very angry Toucher who first phoned his director of strategy and then his solicitor. His conversation was almost identical with both. "What the fucks been going on?" he yelled.

His lawyer explained his understanding of what had happened.

"I don't give a flying fuck about any fucking warranties and indemnities," he yelled. "If you fuckers don't know what you're buying by now then I don't fucking need you! For fuck's sake fix it!" he screamed. "This guy's a fucking flake," he continued. "He can fucking forget about joining my fucking board. For Christ's sake, get the fucking deal done. Next fucking Friday. Exchange and completion on the same day and then everyone out of his office and into our place no later than 1st January. Do you understand. I want this deal done!"

Toucher's next phone call was to Sir Patrick Tracks. "You fucking c***," was his opening explosive remark. You can fucking forget about any fucking fee in respect of Found Vintners," he yelled. "Why the fuck did you get anybody to go through their rubbish. He's just pulled out of the bloody transaction because of your fucking private dicks. If you're thinking about billing me then go fuck yourself!" He slammed down the phone.

Chapter 112

London and Bamberg December 1976 - January 1977

AS HENRY HAD worked out from the start, Dick Toucher was a man who got his own way. He didn't phone Henry back. Instead, he screamed and yelled at everyone responsible for the transaction from his side to make sure it got done. So, it was just ten days later, and with just three days to go before the Christmas break, when Henry put his signature to a contract which was exactly fifteen pages thick. Once all the London Stock Exchange formalities were completed by mid-late January, Henry expected £30 million would arrive into his bank account. This was after all his loans, including those from Sophie and his mother, had been paid off, and the deal he made with Ainsworth and his staff had been honoured.

It was when Henry read the newspaper reports on the acquisition of his business that he learnt the real reason why Toucher had put such pressure to get the transaction done. On the back of the announcement to the Stock Exchange, Toucher had sold a tranche of his shareholding for over £3 million thanks to Tracts and Haverings Bank. Toucher had just got divorced and he needed the money to pay off his ex-wife. Havering Bank was going to get paid its fee in full: 3% for creating the deal, 3% for arranging the finance and 2½% for placing Toucher's shares; nearly £2.5m in all. Perhaps a little industrial espionage had, once again, paid off, thought Henry.

Henry didn't go back to his office after he'd signed the sale contract. He didn't know how to face any of his staff. He was too embarrassed to attend the staff parties in both London and Paris; an event he had never missed in the past. Henry hoped that the money they would all get paid would allow them not to think too badly of him.

Henry only said goodbye to two people, Ainsworth and John.

Ainsworth's loyalty was transferred from Henry to Toucher immediately the ink was dry on the contract. Toucher's plan had been to immediately sack the "crooked gay accountant" but when he learnt what it was going to cost to break Ainsworth's contract, he had a harder look at the man to find out who he really was. There was no question that Henry had been the entrepreneur who had founded and driven the growth of Found Vintners, but it was Ainsworth who was the professional manager. He bought discipline and order to the business. He was the natural successor to Henry for whom, Toucher had made it very clear, there would be no further role.

When Henry and Ainsworth met up to say good-bye and good luck on the day after the contract was signed, Ainsworth's focus was on getting everyone and everything out of Found House and into Clydesdale's London Offices so that Found House could be handed back to Henry.

By midnight on 31st December the offices in Found House were as empty as the day Henry first walked through the front door after he had inherited it from his grandfather.

John knew he was going to be made redundant immediately the sale had gone through. Henry had offered him the chance to come with him as his chauffeur, but he'd had enough of driving. He wanted to settle down. He had moved into Sophie's flat with Imra, her daughter and mother. There was something about their pasts which had attracted them together. For the first time in her life Imra felt protected, and not threatened, by a man. Under his protection Imra had put on a little weight, and her face had filled out, smoothing out the sharp angles, making her even more attractive.

In the quiet of Sophie's flat, and with no friends in London to disturb her, Imra had written her life story in record time. It had become a Christmas bestseller and, on the back of that, she had been invited to become a columnist for the London Evening News starting in the New Year. Her modelling days were not over but there would be no more catwalks and no international assignments.

John had decided he was going to open a sandwich bar in Marylebone, using his redundancy pay out and the money he got from the sale of Henry's business as the deposit. Above all, John wanted his relationship with Imra to work and for this he knew she had to be the centre of his attention.

Henry spent Christmas at his mother's with Andrew and Peter. He knew he should have been able to relax as he had nothing to do but look after and play with his children, but he felt a huge void not knowing what he should be doing next. For years, his every waking moment had been filled by an ever-expanding jobs' list. Now he found it horribly unsettling that there was nothing he needed to do urgently.

After Christmas, Henry took Andrew and Peter to Bamberg to see Sophie. They stayed with Walter and Inga who were now very elderly and, although they loved having their grandchildren, they found the energy and chaos of two boisterous boys hard to deal with.

Just like Henry, Walter had spent a large part of the previous year selling all his businesses too. He had held on as long as he could but, with no obvious successor, and without the energy he used to be able to provide, he knew his businesses were all drifting. In the back of his mind was the need to make sure that Sophie was provided for, not knowing that, with the sale of his businesses, Henry had secured Sophie's care until the end of her days.

Sophie did not recognise Henry or her children when they turned up to give her their Christmas presents. Her children were growing and no longer looked the way she might have remembered.

Henry was delighted to see Sophie looking as beautiful and as elegant as ever. She was dressed, as she was dressed every day, in a smartly tailored trouser suit and, as was her wont, she walked nearly all day long; around and around the grounds if the weather allowed her to go outside, or up and down the corridor if it was bad. She now had only two emotions: no emotion at all or, if scared, a frighteningly overpowering anger. It was why she had the same routine, never changing, day in day out.

It was immediately obvious that the care Sophie was getting was outstandingly good, and for that, Henry was overwhelmingly grateful. The thought of her suffering or being badly treated was not one he could bear. The thing which pleased him more than anything was that she was being given no drugs, apart from the occasional antibiotic. The nursing philosophy was about keeping the environment calm. A place where patients would not only feel safe but one where they were physically stretched each day. It meant encouraging exercise and activity so that oxygen fed their brains so that, at night time, they could sleep without sleeping pills.

Mental and memory exercises took place regularly throughout the day in the hope that, like a muscle, the more it was used the stronger it would become. The big difference with other nursing homes was that no one was elderly. All the patients were in their late twenties to early forties, all destined to grow old together. Some became companions walking, swimming or watching television, but none became friends. To become friends required a mental capacity which most of them no longer had.

As the children, ignored by their mother, played at her feet, Henry told Sophie what had been happening in his life. The sale of the business, the news of Imra and John, but none of it was familiar to her anymore and, once it was told, it was forgotten, but somehow he felt better telling her what he had been doing on their behalf.

In the end Henry just sat calmly by Sophie's side holding her hand. Her delicious, delicate, exquisite hand; a hand with warmth and softness and when, for the first time, she squeezed his hand in a sign of recognition, tears streamed from his eyes for a past that was, and a future which would never be.

Chapter 113

New Found Estate, South Africa March 1977

HOW DO YOU tell a woman it is unlikely that she will become pregnant, especially a woman who is yearning for a child? You tell the news as gently as you can, knowing that half the words you are speaking will not be heard.

Each time Henry flew back to London, Sunetta was convinced she was pregnant, but it was not to be. She checked her diary carefully for her dates, time and time again, but these only confirmed to her that nature should have done its work. She had become pregnant so easily last time and, as she had these thoughts it dawned on her ..., had her abortion stopped her having more children?

Now Sunetta was hearing the news. She was one of the unlucky ones, one in one thousand. The lining of her uterus had naturally thickened as a result of the abortion, but this should not have stopped her conceiving. However, part of her womb had been damaged with a form of scar tissue. It explained why she had such bad stomach cramps after the operation. This meant that the chances of a fertilised egg embedding itself in her uterus wall were significantly reduced. It wasn't that Sunetta couldn't get pregnant. It was just less likely.

As part of breaking the news, Sunetta's doctor talked for a long time about the psychology of getting pregnant after an abortion. "Some women need to give themselves permission to get pregnant again," she said assuredly. "It is why so many women, who think they can't have children, find they get pregnant soon after they've adopted," she explained.

Sunetta misheard all the words of her doctor. More difficult became impossible. Take a bit longer she heard as never. With each of these words Sunetta became crushed. She had assumed that one day she would have her own children. Now she was learning that it wouldn't happen and the effect on her was devastating. What was the purpose of her life? What had she to look forward to? All she saw ahead was a timeless void of loneliness.

She hurt so much. She wanted Henry by her side, not as a lover but, as her best friend to comfort her and he wasn't there.

Chapter 114

Welborough Green, England April 1977

HENRY CAUGHT THE train from Victoria Station to Billingshurst assuming, incorrectly, that there would be a taxi waiting at the station to take him on to Welborough Green. From a phone box, he called for a cab and then waited in the spring sunshine on the station platform studying its Victorian architecture, noting that little had changed in the last hundred years.

The drive through the countryside was quite delightful. Being midweek and a light workday, the driver was prepared to milk the journey to its fullest extent which meant travelling as slowly as possible. Henry didn't mind as, with his window wide open, he was enjoying the views of the countryside as they drove towards the South Downs. The trees and hedgerows were coming into bud after a long hard winter.

Welborough Green possessed a beautiful English village church, built in 960AD and then added on to over many years. Churches like this gave Henry a feeling of permanence; that however bad things were, the enduring spirit of man and his relationship with God would survive.

The church was locked when Henry tried to enter. It was just coming up to lunch time. He hated it when churches were locked during the day. They were places of sanctuary. They should never be locked, except at night, he thought crossly.

Henry went in search of the vicar only to find he was not there. With a declining flock, he now had to serve several parish churches, as well as a widely dispersed number of parishioners. Instead, Henry found the Churchwarden who, when Henry explained why he had come, proved most helpful. He produced a large piece of paper on which was plotted every grave in the churchyard.

With paper in hand the Churchwarden set off at a pace and Henry followed. Very quickly, they identified the spot where Drew was buried between her mother and father. They had no gravestone, but that was common along their burial row, and the next and the next.

"You want to put up a headstone to mark her grave?" asked the Churchwarden, in a disapproving tone.

"Yes," answered Henry, not thinking this could possibly be controversial.

"You'll be changing history," he said, "and it wouldn't suit."

"But no one knows they're here," argued Henry.

"God knows," said the Churchwarden, certain that was enough of an answer.

The look on Henry's face said that it was not.

"After the First World War there wasn't any money, but most importantly there weren't the men around to carve headstones. Those with that skill were working flat out on war memorials. What you see here is our social history. Why do you want to change it?" asked the Churchwarden.

Henry could see his argument. More importantly, one new headstone, or even three, in that spot would be inappropriate.

"This is Drew's aunt. She died from tetanus," said the Churchwarden, pointing to a space five or six yards away from Drew. "She had no next of kin, so all her money went to charity, including this church. We got a tidy sum which was needed because the tower was falling down and in such a bad state that the bells could no longer be rung. Its thanks, in a large part to her, that our bells are now ringing."

Henry found it all rather depressing. The same people who loved you and you loved, who came each week to put flowers on the graves, were now dead too.

"There is something you could do," said the Churchwarden. "Some churches have a solid wooden board on which are screwed small brass plaques which have the name of every person buried and their dates engraved on it."

Henry didn't like the idea of a memorial roll, as though listing past captains of some golf or rowing club. It was when the Churchwarden added that the brass plates were placed on the wooden board in the same manner as the graves were laid out in the churchyard that the idea had appeal.

"Could the board be dedicated to Drew's memory?" asked Henry.

"I can't see why not," replied the Churchwarden.

"Do you know where everyone is buried?"

"Yes, we do, I believe as far back as 980 A.D, when the church was first consecrated. However, we'd do what every other church has done when they start one of these."

"What's that?" asked Henry.

"We'd start with the latest; you know, those that died over the last couple of hundred years. We can do that without any research. To go back further will take a little more effort."

"Where will this board go?" asked Henry.

"We'd need to discuss that with the vicar. Some of 'em are hung in the church porch while others are erected outside like notices for people to read."

Henry liked the idea, and the two men swapped names and contact details. After they had said goodbye, with Henry promising to write, he went outside and sat on one of the memorial benches placed around the churchyard.

In the peace of West Sussex, Henry could well understand why Drew was buried here. It was a place you wanted to be. It felt like home.

Henry thought about his own burial. I'm one quarter French and one quarter English, and I've been brought up here in England. Perhaps I should go and lie alongside the Colonel, he thought. It was only then did he appreciate he had been struggling with a lifelong problem. His mind, his logic, his character lay in England, but his heart, his soul, his true being, lay in au pays de Château de Gressier. He knew his destiny. His final resting place. It would be the church of Latoire Village, in the line of the Guégan family.

Chapter 115

Paris April 1977

HENRY SPENT THE first few weeks of his unemployment clearing out Found House. The emotional things of Sophie's - her jewellery, her photographs, her mementoes, the pictures and antiques she had chosen, he carefully packed up and sent them to de Gressier for safe keeping. A few items of her clothing, the classic timeless quality pieces he sent to her in Bamberg as he thought she might wear them, and the ball gowns went to a charity shop. The things Andrew and Peter wanted had already made their way to Victoria's house in Hertford.

Henry ruthlessly went through his own possessions, again sending to de Gressier only those things which he wanted to keep. Then he called in a house clearance firm to take everything away. Not a cup, saucer or spoon was left behind. He then organised for the place to be painted from top to bottom and, once the new carpets were fitted, he shut the front door. He had no plans for Found House. He just knew he would never be coming back there to live.

The highlight of March was an invitation from Robert and Pascale Rabôut to join them for dinner. At long last, Robert's divorce had come through and they had been able to get married. Further, Robert's share from the sale of Henry's business was enough to give him back some of the financial security he had lost as a result of his son's counterfeiting activities. Maurice was now in an open prison and his release date was coming into sight.

The dinner, Henry was told, was simply for Robert and Pascale to say thank you. It was therefore a totally surprised Henry, who, when he casually walked into the Paris restaurant, found everyone standing up and clapping him. It was full of the staff of the businesses which had been sold. Rather than feeling let down or betrayed, as Henry had feared, they were there to thank him. The only person not in the room was Harriet. With her share of the sales proceeds, she could easily have afforded to come, but she was finding it hard to accept that she was unlikely to have a family of her own, and the thought of people talking happy families was more than she could bear.

Ainsworth made a very correct speech. Robert made an amusing, light hearted speech. Both were well prepared. The man who caused everyone to cry from laughing was John Chabani. Completely unplanned and unscripted, he stood up and deliberately broke the chauffeur's bond of secrecy, as Imra looked on aghast. He swapped between English and French, mimicking Henry's mannerisms and voice, as he told of faux pas after faux pas. There was a lot of healing that night for Henry, and a lot of other people in that room too.

Unable to sleep, Henry walked the streets of Paris in the early hours of the morning. He had missed both Sophie and Harriet from being at his side at the dinner. For different reasons they deserved to be there, and their absence made him feel isolated and very alone.

Henry often wondered what Sophie would say of Harriet if she knew of their relationship. He knew she would be furious but, if she was capable, would she understand. He wasn't even sure if Sophie would have liked Harriet because their temperaments were so very different. He had often wondered if the reason he got on so well with them both was because their characteristics sat either side of his personality fulcrum. Nevertheless, during a rare moment of self-awareness, Henry had already concluded that he felt weaker and less assured by their absences.

As he walked the washed pavements by the side of the River Seine, Henry worried about why it was that, at the dinner, Sophie would have sat by his side as an equal partner, but he could not, for some inexplicable reason, grant Harriet the same status. She had been an outstanding assistant, an excellent bedfellow but she was not his consort. A good friend yes, a lifelong friend yes, an intimate friend yes, a soulmate yes, but she had one missing ingredient, the ingredient of equality and he knew she couldn't bring this into their relationship however hard she tried.

Henry examined his consciousness to see if he was being racially prejudice against Harriet. He was genuinely worried that this might have been the case. He was certain that their inequality didn't come from colour, for he loved the colour, the texture, the smoothness of her skin. He was certain it wasn't cultural, for her upbringing was as European as his own. It wasn't a class or money issue for they both came from families with money. It was just he wasn't as proud of Harriet as he had always been proud of Sophie. He found that a terrible thing to say, so he started to look for excuses.

With his head down and watching only his feet pace out in front of him, Henry considered the two women's physical beauty. Was one estimably more beautiful than the other, he wondered. Unquestionably, Sophie was the more photogenic, but that was just a fraction of the whole question. Henry thought about the subject of beauty deeply, but he found it an impossible question to answer. In any case, he concluded, it was irrelevant.

As he walked under the Eiffel Tower feeling chilly and, on his way, back to his hotel, he found the reason he was looking for. He was certain the issue was one of nurture and not nature. Apartheid South Africa, and an authoritarian father, had made Harriet see herself as a second-class citizen. It was never going to change, even if she lived for one hundred years. In any relationship she would always place herself as second, as the underdog, and then fight to have her views heard. Without true equality, it was a relationship which, Henry concluded, had no long-term future. It had to end. Not least, because he had to be here in Europe. Harriet had to be there in South Africa. It was impossible for it to go on.

Chapter 116

Latoire Village March 1977

DOMINIQUE HILAIRE DIED at the age of 84 after a short illness.

Pierre Hilaire, her son, cut a forlorn and lonely figure as his mother's coffin was lowered deep into the ground in the cemetery at the side of Latoire Church. As Juliette had promised, Dominique's final resting place was in the grave of her second husband, Henri Hilaire. As befits a woman of the Resistance, her coffin had been draped in the Tricolore of France, but now that national emblem was neatly folded, held under Pierre's arm and pressed heavily into his side.

Dominique's funeral was well attended, not only by those who knew and loved her, but by representatives of the many organisations in which she had been involved. The traditional black book of condolences was full of effusive praise. The Lormont Orchestra, which Dominique had conducted for years, played La Marseillaise as her coffin left the church. There was not a Frenchman or woman who didn't stand a little taller, whose chest wasn't a little broader and whose heart didn't beat a little faster at the sound of the French national anthem.

The wake was held at Maison Presson which was now Pierre's family home. Victoria found it most unsettling as she walked into its garden, as she could remember every small detail about the last time she was there. It was the day her stepfather had been executed for murdering her father. Her mother had instructed all her workers to come up from the de Gressier fields and carry everything out of the house to be burned. So huge was the fire that it attracted the attention of fire brigades from all around.

Although the house had been extended and improved, such that it now looked very different, Victoria could not bring herself to go inside. She knew of its horrors long ago, and along with those directly affected, she would never, could never, forget. Instead, she stayed outside, the March chill digging deeper and deeper into her bones as she sought shelter from the wind.

"Would you like to walk with me?" said Pierre to Victoria, as the wake was beginning to come to an end. "I want to go back to the cemetery to make sure the gravediggers have done their job. You know, make sure she's snuggled up for the night."

Victoria found the invitation strange for the two did not know each other well.

"Shall I ask Henry?" she enquired.

"We won't be long," said Pierre, immediately sensing her hesitancy.

Victoria said nothing as she knew the distance was not a short one and was certain there were others he should invite, and not just her.

"Come," he instructed. "It's too cold to stand around."

They walked side by side in silence, Victoria not knowing what to say, while Pierre's mind was in turmoil. He was bursting with one question he was desperate, but too frightened to ask.

As they walked past the entrance to Château de Gressier, Pierre was able to find his voice: "Henry's done well, hasn't he?"

"Yes, I think so. He was fortunate. His great-grandfather gave him a good start, but he took what he was given and worked hard to make it better. So yes, I think he can be proud of what he has achieved."

"But without Sophie he seems a bit lost."

"Indeed, and particularly now he doesn't have his wine-trading business ... he's found that a little disorientating."

"He needs to find something soon because his depression is not serving him well. It is obvious he's unhappy as he keeps starting new projects, mostly unimportant ones, just to keep himself busy. The trouble is that it causes a huge distraction to the routine jobs we must do every day. The thing is - Henry's knowledge of winemaking is probably one of the best in the world. Even the Université de Bordeaux says so. He's loved and admired here, but he's got to find his old self soon 'cause otherwise ... well things will start to go wrong."

Victoria said nothing for she was shocked to find that others were thinking about Henry in the same less than flattering light as she was.

Pierre and Victoria paused at the memorial stone which marked the place where Étienne, Victoria's father, had been murdered.

"I don't know if you knew, but your father gave my mother a necklace. I thought you might like it," said Pierre, choosing to do something now which he had intended to do at their gravesides. He searched deep into his anorak pockets to find an old, yellow, tarnished jewellery case which he handed over. Victoria opened the lid, and in the evening half-light, she looked down on a double string of glistening pearls, joined by a platinum and diamond clasp, and resting on padded silk.

"I remember these," she said, looking deeply into Pierre's eyes. Your mother wore them at my father's funeral. I admired them then. Thank you. They're lovely."

"You remember what my mother wore?" asked Pierre astonished. "It was years ago."

They started to walk on again.

"Yes, forty-seven years, but I remember that day better than yesterday."

"Do you remember what my mother was wearing on her fingers?"

Victoria turned and looked at Pierre and wondered why he was testing her.

"Yes. She was wearing her engagement and wedding rings."

It wasn't her engagement ring. It was the ring your father gave her."

"Really?" she exclaimed. "The large cut diamond with smaller diamonds clustered all around to make it oval shaped? It was exquisite!"

"You remember it that well?"

"Yes. Are you saying that was a gift from my father?"

"Yes. Her engagement ring from Georges, her first husband, was a rather nice solitaire. In the evening, after Étienne's funeral, she took Georges' and your father's rings and sewed them onto an emerald silk cushion she had stitched, one on top of the other, with their jewels side by side."

"How do you know this?"

"She told me when she made me promise to make sure she was buried with them."

"Oh, how sweet."

"She's buried wearing Henri's engagement and wedding rings, and in the other hand she's holding the cushion with Georges' and Étienne's rings on them. You don't mind?" he asked.

"No, of course not. I think it's lovely. Very romantic," she paused. "Is the wedding ring Georges gave her buried with her too?"

"No. Dominique had it altered and polished. I gave it to my wife when we got married," said Pierre proudly, before noticing Victoria's frown. "You're probably suspicious, thinking the ring may be unlucky, given Georges and Dominique weren't married very long."

Victoria said nothing for that's exactly what she was thinking.

The two walked along in silence, turned left at the T-junction and in the lowering sun started to walk down the hill towards the church. The trees were slowly coming into bud.

"I am surprised your mother wanted Dominique buried here given how close she now lies to Étienne," said Pierre, as they walked through the church gates. "You know they had a bit of a thing?"

"Given the quality of that ring it must have been more than a bit of a thing. I know it went on for years, but I'm not surprised," replied Victoria.

"Why?"

"You don't know this, but it's in the de Gressier diaries. I can show you. My mother and Stephen had a bit of a thing too, during the war. She may have thought that if your mother's body came here then Stephen's might come too."

"They had an affair? You're joking?"

"I am not. There was something very special between those two. Everyone thought I would marry Stephen. Even I thought so, but you only had to be with Mummy and him for a moment to know. I think it made me quite jealous at the time."

"Did my mother know?"

"Yes, she found out many years later, at Juliette's funeral, when she read part of the de Gressier diaries my mother had been keeping. She wrote that you had to have been there, to have lived during those war years and the intensity of it all, to be able to understand. Just as your mother was leaving, she deliberately came to find me to tell me that she had lived through that time too, and therefore understood. It seemed such a poignant moment that I recorded it in the de Gressier diaries which I had just started keeping."

Pierre suddenly thought that this was his chance. It was the question he had been waiting for years to ask. It was the prime reason for their walk.

"Is Henry Stephen's son?" he asked crisply.

Victoria stopped walking. "No!" she said emphatically, before pacing away.

"It's just there's a rumour around the village that in England you are known as Mrs Bellanger," said Pierre, as he rushed to catch up.

Victoria said nothing.

"So Henry's not a relative? I'm not a half-uncle or something? It's what people in the village are saying."

"Henry is not Stephen's son!" said Victoria sharply. "I find it best to ignore all the rumours around here for they are inevitably wrong. It was once said that Étienne was Stephen's father. People thought we might have been brother and sister. They gave it as the reason why we didn't marry."

"Are you? Were you brother and sister?"

"Who knows? Who cares?" said Victoria dismissively. "Forget the rumours. They're meaningless."

Pierre's question created an immediate and obvious tension between the two of them. It lasted until they arrived at the mound of earth now lying on top of Dominique's coffin.

"Are you going to move Stephen here, to be next to his mother?" she asked. "There's a place for him right there." At that, Victoria pointed to his memorial stone engraved with the words: 'Hero of France.' "He'd be next to me and my brother."

"I thought about it. I thought about it hard, but I don't think so. For a little while I thought I might bury her in the Saint Clothilde Cemetery near Bruges on the outskirts of Bordeaux. It's where Stephen's buried. But since I'm coming into this cemetery when my turn comes, I thought it best she's in here too."

"Do you know Stephen's been dead for 36 years? I can't believe it. Where has that time gone?"

"I don't know ... It just seemed wrong to disturb him after so long."

Victoria nodded her agreement.

"But the main reason I've decided to leave him there is that he is lying alongside two others who were shot by the Germans on the same day in the same reprisal killings at Camp de Souge. Somehow it seemed to make it less French if there were just two of them and not three. Our flag, the Tricolore has three colours, we speak of Liberté, Égalité, Fraternité, three words, and even Alexander Dumas had three musketeers."

"But there were four of them!" protested Victoria.

"And there are four here now: Étienne and Juliette. Dominique and Henri," retorted Pierre, with a smile on his face. "They were all remarkable people whose lives, for some inexplicable reason, became intertwined. Maybe it's because they shared a common trait. They each had a kindness, an empathy, that's found deep in the soul of de Gressier.

Chapter 117

Château de Gressier Easter 1977

VICTORIA HAD TRAVELLED to France with Andrew and Peter for Dominique's funeral which had taken place at the start of their two-week school holiday. She was determined that de Gressier be inculcated into their lives, as it had been for Henry and herself. They all lived in the Cellars, as the Cottage wing, albeit set aside for Victoria's use, had been mothballed.

Andrew and Peter were constantly entertained as they were put to work by the estate farm hands. Far too quickly, it was time for the two boys to return to Hertford and the term time regime Victoria had established for them at her home. Henry and she both knew the two boys were better for the security it gave them. It was a happy family which left de Gressier for Bordeaux station, and there was fun and laughter, as Henry waived good-bye to his children as the train for Paris pulled away. They would only be apart a few days.

Early that evening, and in his boredom, Henry wandered the Cellars and then the Cottage, mindlessly touring every room. Both wings had the same desolate, chilly feeling. They had the air of a mausoleum. Without the noise of his children, Château de Gressier felt deserted. The little things which moved, as people used them every day, made the house come alive. They were now stationery. He noticed how the grandfather clocks in the halls, at either end of the Cellars and the Cottage, had stopped, and with it, each house had lost its heartbeat. It was as though the Soul of de Gressier was slowly dying.

Henry climbed the stairs to the Gallery where he looked out first to the front, across the lawn, past the vines to the trees beyond.

He crossed to the back of the room to look out through the back windows, over the vineyards flowing down to the river, into the fields and then the sky beyond. He had heard his grandmother talk of La Bête Blanche and, now he had the money, he wondered if he should rebuild it, but he didn't know what for. Henry watched as the sun set causing long shadows to be thrown around the ground.

As he stood looking out, a sense of loneliness overwhelmed Henry. It was this time of evening when Sophie and he would have walked the grounds, talk of the day they'd had, what they would do tomorrow and their plans ahead. But he knew his loneliness was far more than missing his wife and children. It was a return to something much deeper, ingrained into his long and distant past. It was the loneliness of being a single child, the loneliness of boarding school, the loneliness of university, the loneliness of being a salesman on the road; but above all it was the loneliness which comes from being a single parent with two boys to bring up.

Henry's eyes moistened and his stomach tightened in self-pity. He accepted the simplicity of being alone. He only had himself to please. He acknowledged that there was a complexity in being married as you had to think about the other, but thinking about Sophie, and her needs and wants, had never been a burden for him. In fact, it was something which made him happy and feel good. Nature had made it that way for both of them from their very first meeting, but now Sophie was spiritually unable to accept his gifts with the joy that she had in the past. It meant he was alone from her, and, the more he thought about it, he found his heart was physically hurting.

Henry moved to his great-great grandfather's desk and sat down. At the side was a pile of papers. On the top was the Completion Statement showing the amount of money which had been paid into his bank account from the sale of his businesses. It told him he would never have to work or worry about money again. Except, at that moment, this benefit was no comfort as with the sale came the loss of his life's purpose. He was grieving for its going. He would have given all the money he had ever received to have Sophie back. There was, he thought, no purpose to every day without her. She had given him the reason to live.

As he sat down, Henry saw a green velvet jewellery case in the middle of the desk. He instantly knew what it was. He had seen it before at his mother's house in Hertford. It was resting on an envelope with the word Henry written neatly on the front. He opened the case and took out the gold pocket watch. He ran his thumb over the engraving of the Dovingdon family crest and the word Victoria. Henry studied the brilliant diamonds at each hour on the watch face as his thumb passed backwards and forwards over the glass front. He would swear that, in the whole world, only Sophie's skin was smoother, softer and gentler to touch, and then he remembered the softness of Harriet's skin and wondered. Luckily, Henry's melancholic torpor and his mental conflict of which woman had the smoothest skin, was broken by the tip of his finger feeling a sharp edge from the watch's winding mechanism.

Henry opened the envelope and read the letter from his mother. In anger, he discarded it on to the desk. The contents had agitated him. Now feeling restless, Henry got up and started to pace up and down the Gallery. Taking both the watch and his mother's note he went downstairs and wandered aimlessly until he came to the Cellar's library. There he took out Juliette's most recent diary, the one she had been working on when she died. He went to sit in her chair. It had been re-upholstered since then, but it was his grandmother's chair all the same.

Henry was surprised to find that there were eight or ten pages written by Sophie in her neat hand, but even those were a couple of years ago. The next entries were pages and pages written by his mother. They comprised an outpouring of hurt, written to correct, or at least give a different view of, what Juliette had written about Victoria's exodus from France in the middle of the war.

Realising that there was a lot more history to be written, and he needed to write it, Henry took the latest de Gressier diary, Victoria's gold and diamond watch and the note from his mother and moved to his grandmother's writing table. He opened the centre drawer looking for paper and pen. There, placed at the side, were several pages of paper folded neatly in to a square, held together by two incredibly old paper clips. It was obvious that these pages had been opened and closed many times. Henry had never seen them before. In fact, he couldn't ever remember opening the drawer.

Henry unfolded the pages and started to read. He was absorbed from the very first line. It was a typed copy of Henri Hilaire's letter, read out to the congregation at his funeral service, after he had committed suicide. Henry read it three of four times fascinated by its history and philosophy. Was this another of the reasons the Guégan family had a debt to Pierre Hilaire? he wondered.

Henry didn't go to bed that night. He stayed in the library moving restlessly from chair to chair as he read the last hundred years of the de Gressier diaries. Some pages he skipped, others he found totally absorbing and read them several times. It allowed him to understand the complexity of the relationship between his mother and grandmother. He also understood in greater detail the family's debt to Pierre. There was no question that it was Pierre's mother, Dominique, who, had not only suffered at his family's hand, but had bravely helped secure its future. He now fully understood Juliette, Victoria and his debt. It would be one he would be delighted to honour until the end of Pierre's days.

The sun was rising when Henry went to bed exhausted. It was high in the sky when he woke. He knew his task for that day, and the next few days, had changed. He would bring the diaries up to date, for only he could close the knowledge circle of Penrose Dovingdon, alias David Daunier, tell of the Rabôut Estate saga and everything else that had happened.

It was early evening when Henry freed himself from Estate work and settled down at his desk in the Gallery to update the diary. He opened the note from his mother. He did not know how, or where, his diary writing would begin. However, despite it being, in part, hurtful, he knew it should end with her letter. He could see in his mother's words both honesty and love. As had been instilled in him, honesty was the key ingredient of any diary, for without it they were useless. Just the scribblings of the vain. His mother's letter would, Henry decided, be included as the last page to be bound in to the finished work and sent to the bookbinders. He was certain that this particular diary should end with this letter and today. It was, after all, the end of an era.

Henry re-read his mother's flowery writing.

Château de Gressier
Latoire Village

Sunday 10th April 1977

Darling Henry,

Today is Easter Sunday. A day which is remembered for the resurrection of Jesus and, although I know you have no Christian beliefs, it is an important day because it symbolises renewal. It is about forgetting the past and starting afresh. It is no coincidence that Easter always takes place in Spring which, of the four seasons, is about new life and starting again. It is a time to look forward and it is about that which I now write.

Throughout your life you have been praised for your enthusiasm. There is no one admired more for their determination to pursue their chosen course of action. We have all envied your ability to persevere when others would have given up long before; but now you seem to have given up too.

It was extraordinary how you used to devour this extraordinary gift called life, parcelled out in 24-hour units, with alacrity and passion; but for the last three months you have been behaving in a manner which does not become you.

I believe life has treated you exceptionally well. It has given you little reason to complain. You have been exceedingly fortunate. You have a good body and good mind and, with de Gressier, Louis and Rabôut, you have been blessed with a job and an income which gives you freedom and purpose.

Moreover, and most importantly, you have been able to share your life, albeit for a short period, with a remarkable woman. In this time, you have known true, deep, spiritual love. It is an experience of outstanding joy and unbelievable agony, which most people will neither know nor understand.

You must accept Sophie will never come back to you in the manner of her past. I understand the comfort which can be derived from being deeply depressed. It is a mood which in the most part draws attention and brings sympathy. But it is also self-centred, as those who are depressed suck energy from all those around them. It is what you are doing. It is selfish and not becoming. More importantly, this is not you. By your nature you are an energy generator.

Your children need you to be your old self. I need you to be your old self. Above all, Sophie would expect you to remain positive and upbeat for your family. It is why I urge you to pick yourself up again and seek to find the joie de vivre which, for so long, has been the hall mark of your character.

At present, you appear to have chosen to ride the helter skelter of life downwards and into a state of despair and deep depression. It is time you turned around and started the upward climb. As a child you sought to walk up the downward slide. Your memory will tell you the journey is hard. You have to stop for many breaks, but the one thing you can be assured of when you are at the top; the view is so much better from there than at the bottom. It is a climb which you must now take, not least because it is worth it.

I have left on your desk the gold pocket watch which Bear gave me when I was born. I think it now belongs here with you at de Gressier rather than with me in Hertford. Please keep it safe. It is so very precious.

Just as we must accept Sophie's situation, I think we have to accept that your father is probably dead. Thirty-five years is long enough to wait for someone to re-appear.

I now bitterly regret giving my brother's watch away. I honestly thought your father would bring it back to me once the war was over, but it has not been. The only thing I have of my brother's is his pillowcase. It still lies beside me every night, but it is thin and worn and will not last forever.

I desperately want Victor's watch to come home and sit alongside mine. They are a pair, just as Victor and I will always be a pair. Victor's watch has to be found. I am sure it is out there somewhere because it is far too precious to have been thrown away.

If we find Victor's watch, we might find out what happened to your father.

Please, Henry, will you start looking for Victor's watch for me. Put your talents, your energy, and your fortitude in bringing my brother's watch back home.

With love and affection
Mummy.

Henry looked at Victoria's watch carefully. Without its twin, it reflected his sense of loneliness. At that moment, he recognised the desolation he was feeling at the loss of Sophie was the same as his mother would have felt at the loss of her twin brother. How had she lived with such pain all her life. He could not contemplate it.

Suddenly the outside lights of Château de Gressier automatically switched themselves on as they had done almost every day since the end of the war. It was like the lodestar telling all those in the valley that all was right with the world, that it was safe to come home. Its beam broadcast what the house and the Guégan family stood for, and that was hope. A hope that, from today's efforts, tomorrow will have been made just that little bit better.

The lights coming on was just the prompt Henry needed as he remembered their significance. Yes damnit, he thought, he was going to climb that helter skelter his mother wrote of. He was going to find out what had happened to his father, find Victor's watch and bring it home to his mother. It was the very least he could do for her.

Thank you for reading The Soul of de Gressier. I do hope you enjoyed it.
If you liked this book, it would be helpful if you would post a positive review on Amazon at www.amazon.com

If you would like to know more about the life of Henry Guégan né Bellanger and his sons then this is told in the next book,
The Watches of de Gressier.

If you would like to know when the next book in the de Gressier series will be published, then please follow us on social media at:

Facebook Page: @DeGressier
Twitter: @deGressier
Website: www.degressier.com

About the Author

Charles Bunker was an international corporate financier and entrepreneurial businessman before retiring to become an essayist, pamphlet writer and author. He uses his experiences in business and politics, his interest in history and international affairs, and his observation of people as the bedrock of his writing. Widely travelled, Charles is the proprietor of the famous Orchard Tea Rooms in Grantchester renowned for its connection with Rupert Brooke, Virginia Woolf, E.M Forster and many other literary, philosophical and scientific talents over the last 120 years.

Printed in Great Britain
by Amazon